# Absolutely Wonderful

CHERYL HOLT

NEW YORK TIMES BESTSELLING AUTHOR

**Absolutely Wonderful**



Cover Design: Dar Albert, Wicked Smart Designs, www.wickedsmartdesigns.com
Paperback and Digital format: Dayna Linton, Day Agency, www.dayagency.com

ISBN: 979-8-88895-081-4 (Paperback)
ISBN: 979-8-88895-082-1 (Digital Book)

Library of Congress Pending

First Edition: 2023

10 9 8 7 6 5 4 3 2 1

Printed in the USA

# Praise for *New York Times* Bestselling Author
# CHERYL HOLT

"Best storyteller of the year . . ."

*Romantic Times Magazine*

"Cheryl Holt is magnificent . . ."

*Reader to Reader Reviews*

"Cheryl Holt is on my 'favorite authors' list. I can't wait to see what she'll write next."

*The Reading Café*

"A master writer . . ."

*Fresh Fiction*

***Here's what readers are saying*** . . .

"OMG! I just started reading this series yesterday. It was hard for me to close my Kindle and go to bed. So, so good!"

*Artemis*

"Cheryl Holt has packed in so much action that the reader is constantly spellbound. So many characters, so vividly portrayed! Rogues, unfaithfulness, loyalty, and delightful dialogue. You will love this book!"

*Gladys*

"It was fabulous! I laughed, I cried, I got angry, and I smiled. I read the whole book without stopping."

*Robin*

"Action, drama, and intrigue. I read it in one afternoon. I couldn't put it down!"

*Gina*

"You just can't wait to turn the page to see what happens next. Outstanding!"

*Margaret*

"This book is such an emotional roller-coaster. I cried and laughed and cheered. It was so good!"

*Colleen*

# BOOKS BY CHERYL HOLT

**LINKED HISTORICAL ROMANCE SERIES**

***RUINED!!***
ABSOLUTELY PERFECT
ABSOLUTELY WONDERFUL
ABSOLUTELY MINE

**BAYWICK**
HAPPILY EVER AFTER
LOVE EVER AFTER
MERRILY EVER AFTER

**CADS**
CAD'S WISH
CAD'S PICK
CAD'S CHOICE

**LOST GIRLS**
SOMEONE TO LOVE
SOMEONE TO CHERISH
SOMEONE TO WED

**ALWAYS**
ALWAYS
ALWAYS YOURS
ALWAYS MINE

**JILTED BRIDES**
JILTED BY A CAD
JILTED BY A SCOUNDREL
JILTED BY A ROGUE

**FOREVER**
FOREVER YOURS
FOREVER MINE
FOREVER AFTER
FOREVER

**BABY CALEB DUET**
ONLY YOU
ONLY MINE

**LOST LORDS OF RADCLIFFE**
HEART'S DELIGHT
HEART'S DESIRE
HEART'S DEMAND
SCOUNDREL
HEART'S DEBT

**RELUCTANT BRIDES**
WICKED
WANTON
WONDERFUL

**LORD TRENT**
LOVE'S PROMISE
LOVE'S PRICE
LOVE'S PERIL

**SPINSTER'S CURE**
PROMISE OF PLEASURE
TASTE OF TEMPTATION
DREAMS OF DESIRE

**EROTIC HISTORICAL ROMANCES**
LOVE LESSONS
TOTAL SURRENDER
ABSOLUTE PLEASURE
COMPLETE ABANDON
MORE THAN SEDUCTION
DEEPER THAN DESIRE
FURTHER THAN PASSION
TOO HOT TO HANDLE

**EROTIC HISTORICAL ROMANCES (cont)**
TOO TEMPTING TO TOUCH
TOO WICKED TO WED
SECRET FANTASY
FORBIDDEN FANTASY
DOUBLE FANTASY

**HISTORICAL ROMANCES**
SWEET SURRENDER
NICHOLAS (republished as MY SCOUNDREL)
MY ONLY LOVE
MY TRUE LOVE
THE WAY OF THE HEART

**CONTEMPORARY ROMANCES**
MOUNTAIN DREAMS
SEDUCE ME
KISS ME
LOVE ME

**NOVELLAS**
MEG'S SECRET ADMIRER
KNIGHT OF SEDUCTION
SEDUCING THE GROOM

**OTHER NOVELS**
A SUMMER WEDDING AT CROSS CREEK INN
MUD CREEK
THE WEDDING
SLEEPING WITH THE DEVIL

**NONFICTION**
LITTLE MIRACLES

# Absolutely Wonderful

# Prologue

Katherine Hastings sat at the desk in her office. The door was closed, but it didn't completely block out the noises drifting down from the upper floors.

She was the manager of *Mrs. Pettigrew's Private Home for Young Ladies,* which was a sly and fancy name for it being an unwed mother's home. At the current moment, there were three guests laboring to give birth and the babies weren't in any hurry to arrive. The stress had put everyone on edge.

The prior month had been extremely hectic. It was April and scoundrels had been very active the previous summer. The facility was located near the seaside town of Baywick, with the much larger and more glamorous town of Brighton just up the coast.

London dandies frequently toured the area. The wastrels would enjoy a holiday, then head back to the city, and they never worried about the calamities they left behind. Some days, it seemed that Katherine couldn't throw a rock without hitting a ruined maiden.

It was scandalous to have a child out of wedlock. The Church deemed it a sin. Society viewed it as a moral failing. And it was against the law. Fortunately, their local authorities weren't overzealous. They didn't arrest girls who found themselves in the family way. They were allowed to hide with Katherine, and her dedicated staff of servants and midwives helped them through their ordeals.

The door opened and she glanced up, expecting it to be a housemaid with a report about the conditions upstairs, but when she realized who it was, her jaw dropped in surprise.

"Margaret Adair!" she said. "What are you doing in Baywick? When you departed in January, I was convinced I'd never see you again."

"Are you busy? May I come in?"

"Yes, of course." Katherine waved to the chair across from the desk, watching as her friend staggered over and eased down.

She and Margaret were the same age of twenty-five, and for twelve months, Margaret had resided in Baywick. She'd worked as a companion to an elderly cousin, but the woman had died and her house was for sale. Margaret, who was an orphan and spinster, had been forced to move away to live with other relatives.

She was very beautiful, with chestnut hair and big green eyes that flashed with merriment when she smiled. They shared similar opinions, that life was absurd and it was exhausting to be a female in a world dominated by men. Their personalities had melded perfectly, and in a short period, they'd forged a tight bond.

Katherine had once been seduced by a cad and she'd birthed a bastard child. She wasn't circumspect about the debacle and she used herself as a model for how to thrive after tragedy. Margaret hadn't ever been seduced, but as an adolescent, she'd been caught in a compromising situation that had destroyed her reputation, so she'd become the black sheep of her family.

Their experiences meant they were wary of the opposite sex, and thus, it had cemented their relationship.

After Margaret had fled Baywick, Katherine hadn't heard from her. She'd penned several notes to inquire about Margaret's journey, but she'd received no reply. Apparently, she should have been more adamant about establishing contact.

Margaret appeared haggard and fatigued, as if she'd suffered a recent disaster. She'd lost weight, and she was very pale, as if she'd been ill. The cheery sparkle in her eyes had faded away.

"I wrote you numerous letters," Katherine said, "but you never wrote back."

"I'm sorry. I was overwhelmed by events and I didn't have the energy to correspond."

"My goodness. You look as if you've been sick. What happened?"

"I'm mortified to tell you what occurred."

Katherine was no fool. She ran a home for unwed mothers and she'd been an unwed mother herself. She studied Margaret, then sighed with resignation. She reached into a drawer and pulled out a kerchief. She was employed at a job where women wept constantly and she had a whole drawer crammed with kerchiefs.

She handed it over and Margaret grabbed it and dabbed at her tears. "I need your help," she said. "I didn't know where else to turn."

"Was it a man?" Katherine asked. "Are you in trouble?"

For an eternity, Margaret stared down at her lap, then she murmured, "Yes, I'm in trouble."

Katherine sighed again. She never ceased to be amazed at how readily a libertine could wear down a female's defenses. Margaret was intelligent and shrewd, and she understood how duplicitous a rogue could be, how cunning and persistent in obtaining what he craved. Yet a handsome roué was so hard to resist.

Mrs. Pettigrew, the facility's patron, was determined to erase some of the stigma and shame that came with illicit childbirth. All of the burdens fell on the woman, and the philanderers typically skipped away with no penalty.

Katherine had a vicar who provided spiritual counseling and a lawyer who provided legal assistance to collect damages. Those were the endings Katherine liked best: when scoundrels had to cough up money to pay for their transgressions.

"Would you like to stay with us?" Katherine asked.

"I was hoping you'd offer," Margaret said. "If you'd refused me, I can't imagine where I would have gone."

"I'll ring for a maid and we'll settle you in a bedroom. Then we'll have some tea and you can fill me in on the gory details."

"I'm too wretched to confess my stupidity."

Katherine clucked her tongue with offense. "Don't fret about it. Where charming cads are concerned, we females are always stupid. It's a problem with our gender."

"I assumed I was smarter than this," Margaret miserably stated.

"Given the right circumstances, none of us are smart enough to behave as we ought. Does the oaf in question realize what's transpired? Have you spoken to him?"

"It would be pointless for him to be apprised."

"That can't be true. I could have my lawyer track him down. Would you like that?"

"He's marrying my cousin. She's a great heiress and he'd never relinquish her dowry for me. There's no reason for a lawyer to intervene."

"I will hate him forever then," Katherine said. "And if he'd pick a fortune over you, he's an idiot, so what good is he anyway?"

# Chapter 1

*Four months earlier…*

MARGARET ADAIR SAT ON the sofa by the fire. It was a cold January afternoon, but the parlor was small, so the flames warmed the room to a balmy temperature. She didn't need to wrap up in a shawl.

She was snuggled in the gardener's cottage behind the manor. The property was located a mile or two outside the village of Baywick, so she could walk to it if she needed company, but she was completely alone. She was trying to read a novel, but she couldn't focus on the plot. She kept gazing out the window, cataloging the scenery so she'd never forget.

With it being the dead of winter, the colors were grey and bleak, the trees having shed their leaves, the grass withered and eager for spring to return. Her elderly cousin had owned the estate, but she was deceased, so it was for sale. Margaret wondered who would own it when the seasons changed.

Would they care about the garden? Would they hire competent servants to tend it? Or would they simply let it go to seed?

Off in the distance, beyond the dunes, she could see the ocean. For once, it was fairly calm, the tide not stirring huge waves to crash on the shore. The sky was a brilliant blue, the water too, the sun very bright.

It was so beautiful, and she thought about bundling up and trekking out to the beach, but she couldn't muster the vigor required for a brisk stroll.

In another four days, she'd proceed to the coaching inn, board the public coach, and travel to London. Her sojourn on the coast would end. The depressing prospect left her terribly despondent. She had such big dreams and plans, but she was never able to bring any of them to fruition.

Suddenly, she was surprised by a knock on the door. It was so quiet, and the noise so peculiar that, at first, she wasn't sure she'd actually heard it. When it sounded again, she stood and went over to answer.

The staff had been dismissed the prior week so she was the final straggler. She was off the main road, in a meadow nestled between two headlands. The spot wasn't exactly visible to a passerby, and most of her acquaintances figured she'd already departed, so she had no idea who it might be.

She peeked out to find a very attractive man standing on the stoop. He was tall and brawny, his hair an unusual golden-blond, worn longer than was proper and tied with a ribbon. His eyes were a deep sapphire shade that drew her in and made it hard to look away.

Ordinarily, she didn't like handsome men. They were spoiled, entitled, and disreputable. He didn't emit any tendencies as a fiend though, so she warned herself to stop being so judgmental.

He was dressed for the icy weather in a heavy wool coat, woolen trousers, and fur-lined boots on his feet. He had a jaunty red scarf curled around his neck, as if he was a bandit or highwayman. He had an earring in his ear too, and she suspected he would have many interesting tales to tell.

He was probably thirty or so, and she was twenty-five, so he was a bit older than she was. But it was obvious his years had been a tad more gripping than hers. He had furrows on his cheeks, as if he toiled away in the wind. His hands were clasped behind his back, his posture braced, as if he was on a ship and struggling against the roll of the waves.

She supposed he'd once been a sailor. Maybe he still was a sailor.

"May I help you?" she asked.

"I hope so. I was riding by and I noticed the For Sale placard on the gate. I'm visiting in Baywick and it's a stunning area. I was wishing I lived here, and then, I saw the sign. I'm a superstitious fellow and it seemed like an omen I shouldn't ignore. Is there anyone who could speak to me about the property?"

"I can furnish quite a lot of information. The owner recently died and I'm the sole resident still on the premises. She had no heir to whom she could bequeath it and her lawyers are handing the transaction."

Her explanation was simple, and as she offered it, her expression was carefully blank. The reality was that she'd thought the estate would be hers when her cousin perished. The deceitful witch had repeatedly promised Margaret that it would be a reward for her loyal efforts, but where her relatives were concerned, she'd learned early on not to trust them.

Her father had been a gentleman, and her mother—depending on the fabrications being shared—had either been a sweet and pretty vicar's daughter or a dissolute actress who'd lured him to his doom. She'd loved them both, but they'd passed away when she was very young, and she'd been at her family's mercy ever since.

She'd been so keen to have a home of her own, to finally belong somewhere, that she'd naively believed the house would be hers, that the bequest would occur. She'd forgotten how her Adair kin reveled in treachery and duplicity. Disappointment was her constant companion.

She was an optimist though and she refused to buckle under this current bout of bad luck. She'd journey to London, would enthusiastically jump into her new situation, and she was certain matters would improve. That was likely deranged thinking, but it would be too discouraging to admit defeat.

"The manor is boarded up," he said, "but I knocked anyway. No one answered, but smoke was puffing out of your chimney, so I decided to pester you."

"I'm loafing the afternoon away so you're not pestering me. What is it you need?"

"Do you have a key to the main house? Could you show it to me?"

Her initial impulse was to deny that she had a key and that she had no authority to tromp about, but she tried to never be unpleasant or disobliging. With how disagreeable her cousins could be, she worked diligently to be a different sort of person entirely.

"I'd be happy to show it to you," she said. "Come in and warm yourself by the fire while I grab my cloak and boots."

She motioned him in and shut the door, then she went into the bedroom to retrieve her things. When she returned, he was leafing through the novel she'd been reading. He was a cocky oaf and, at being caught snooping, he was unabashed.

"Are you a fan of adventure novels?" he asked. "I wouldn't have pegged you for a female who would like stories about pirates."

"I'm not all that interested in them, but Sebastian Bramwell was here in December. At the theater? I met him." Bramwell was the hero in the narrative, but also a real-life earl and buccaneer whose feats of derring-do had been featured in several books.

"You met him?" he asked. "I'd like to talk to him myself, but I haven't had the chance. I imagine he and I might have a lot in common."

"He was very nice." She sounded ridiculously awestruck and her cheeks heated with embarrassment. She forced it away and asked, "Are you ready?"

She fetched the key and started out. He followed her, and though he kept his distance, he exuded a masculine aura that overwhelmed her feminine senses. He radiated a vigor and energy that were so powerful they were almost stifling.

"Would you like to go in the front or the back?" she asked, as they strolled down the path that skirted the manor.

"Let's use the front. That way, I'll get the full effect."

"It's a wonderful house and I'm sure you'll be charmed. Next I know, I'll hear that you've bought it and moved in."

"I'd be thrilled to be by the ocean."

"Are you a seafaring man?"

He snorted. "Why would you think so?"

"How about from your posture and your obvious affection for the area?"

"I was a sailor—for fifteen years. I've recently retired, so I'm landlocked, and I don't like it."

"I've been told that sailors never completely retire, that their first and only love is the sea, and they have trouble adjusting after they quit."

"I'm finding that statement to be very true." Then he asked, "What's your name? May I inquire?"

"It's Miss Adair. Margaret Adair." He didn't supply his own in response so she said, "And you are…?"

He hesitated, as if it was a secret he couldn't share. After significant debate, he said, "Captain Crawford." He frowned and added, "I shouldn't call myself *Captain,* should I? Now that I'm basically a gentleman farmer, I don't believe I'm allowed to continue claiming a grander title."

"Well, I will confess that Captain Crawford has a much more important ring to it than Farmer Crawford."

He laughed. "You know precisely how to stroke my massive ego. I will spend the whole afternoon in your company, so you can shower me with attention and make me feel better about my choices."

He smiled down at her, and for a bizarre moment, they were frozen in place, as if he were a sorcerer who'd bewitched her. The wind stopped blowing, the birds ceased cawing in the sky. There was the eeriest perception in the air that the universe was marking their encounter, anxious for her to mark it too.

She shook off the uncanny impression and asked, "Why did you retire? May I satisfy my curiosity? Or am I being too nosy?"

"You're not being nosy and I'm a very vain fellow. I like to talk about myself."

She chuckled. "I could have deduced that about you."

"The sailing life is hard and I'm growing older."

"How old are you? A hundred?"

"I'm twenty-nine, but I was weary so I came home."

"But you're not happy about it," she said.

"No, not at all."

"Is your wife glad to have you back? Or have you been driving her mad?"

He gave a mock shudder. "I don't have a wife and I'm in no hurry to be shackled. I'm still very much a bachelor."

They rounded the building and arrived at the front door. They paused for a minute so he could study the façade. It was a grand residence, three stories high, constructed from a cream-colored stone mined from a local quarry. Normally, the large windows would have gleamed in the bright sunshine, but they'd been boarded over. At least the lower ones were boarded. The upper floors hadn't been covered.

"Are you the caretaker?" he asked.

"No, there isn't one. The lawyers didn't want to waste the money, and Baywick has become so popular with Londoners. They expect to sell it quickly."

"Why are you roaming about then?"

"I won't be much longer. The property was my cousin's. She was very ill and I stayed with her as her condition declined."

"With her being deceased," he said, "what are your plans? Or am *I* being too nosy?"

"I'm going to London to live with some other of my family. There's always someone to welcome me."

"Are you the poor relative?" It was a cheeky query, but there was a twinkle in his eye, so she didn't feel insulted.

"Yes, I'm the poor relative, and I can firmly declare that every single comment you've ever heard about the humble position is absolutely correct."

He chuckled too. "I shall pity you forever."

She'd clarified more than she should have. Her parents had died four months apart, when she was seven. She'd been shuffled among her various kin ever since. She was lucky they provided shelter, but they were a rich and snobbish bunch who begrudged every penny they'd ever expended on her behalf.

Even though she was family, she had to work like a dog, for no compensation. If there had ever been a female upon whom Cinderella was based, it was Margaret Adair. She didn't need to air her dirty laundry for Captain Crawford though, so she changed the subject.

"What is your opinion of the house so far?" she asked him. "From the outside, it looks magnificent, doesn't it?"

"Yes, it does. What's it called? The sign at the gate said Beachhead."

"Yes, that's it: Beachhead Cottage."

"How long did you tend your failing cousin?"

"A little over a year."

He scowled. "You frittered away a whole year on a death watch? You're definitely a patient and devoted soul."

"Or maybe just a foolish and unfortunate one."

She didn't confide that Beachhead Cottage had been her father's when she was a girl. It had been their summer residence, built before Baywick was even a town. After she'd been orphaned, she'd never wondered what had happened to it. She'd been apprised that her father had died in debt, that his assets had been sold to satisfy creditors, so she'd been fifteen when she'd learned that a relative still owned it.

It was a bone of contention she occasionally gnawed on with all of them. She didn't know how it had remained in the family, but she figured it had been stolen from her somehow. She'd never been able to pry out any admissions, but as her father's only child, shouldn't she have inherited it?

Her ailing cousin had offered to bequeath the property to Margaret, but the promise hadn't been kept. She'd been tricked out of it yet again, which was typical conduct from people she viewed as thieves.

She should have hired a lawyer to help her unravel the scheme that had yanked it away from her in the first place, but she didn't have the funds, so she didn't dare rock any boats. Her kin were crafty villains who, if she angered them, would kick her out on the road. She had no doubt about it, so she had to put up with their nonsense.

"Shall we go in?" she asked. "The temperature will be chilly, and the rooms will be dark, but we can light a lamp."

"Yes, please let me snoop. I haven't even crossed the threshold and it already seems as if it should belong to me. It's that kind of house, where you instantly feel at home."

"I'm glad you noticed." She sighed with regret. "I wish I didn't have to leave."

"I can certainly understand your reluctance. Don't you hate being a female? It means you have so few choices."

She grinned. "Why, Captain Crawford, that was such an astute assessment and you are a man. I am stunned that you have such a perceptive grasp of feminine issues."

"It's a blessing to be born a male. If times are dire, and we're stuck in bad circumstances, we can pick up and flee. Women have to hunker down and muddle forward."

"It makes us tougher and stronger than men."

"Ha! I am trying to impress you so I won't reply to that absurd comment."

She opened the door, and they walked into the foyer, then she stood off to the side so he could examine the entryway. It was imposing, with marble floors, high ceilings, and a splendid staircase.

"It's icy in here," he said and he shivered. "Are you freezing?"

"Yes, but I'll survive."

He clasped her arm and guided her through the downstairs parlors. Because of the frigid temperature, they snuggled closer together than they ought to have, but neither of them was inclined to step away.

He was a curious, observant fellow and he noted every detail. He peppered her with questions, and as she answered them, she could have been a proud parent. They chatted extensively, but when they were silent, it wasn't awkward in the least. A comfortable companionship had quickly developed and she might have known him forever.

It had been an eternity since she'd strolled with a handsome bachelor. The prior occasion had been at age seventeen, when she'd been cajoled to mischief by a dashing scoundrel. She'd been caught in a compromising situation with him and her battered reputation had never recovered.

She'd been living with cousins in a village near Dover, and a regiment of soldiers had been stationed in the area. All the unwed maidens in the neighborhood had been thrilled, and with so many young men needing to be entertained, it had been a summer of suppers and balls. She'd attended most of them.

One rogue, a fiend named Charlie Moneypenny, had fancied her. She'd begun to foolishly suppose he was interested in a more permanent connection, but his intentions hadn't been honorable.

She and three other girls had been lured to a private party at a country house. The secret invitation had made them assume they were special, that they'd been singled out, and they'd accepted without hesitation.

Once they'd arrived, Sergeant Moneypenny and his chums had been drunk and surly, and in hindsight, she suspected an awful incident had been planned. Disaster had been averted when the house's owner had returned unexpectedly.

He'd ended the furtive fête and had escorted the four of them home, where he'd bluntly tattled about what he'd witnessed. They'd been disgraced and humiliated, but Margaret had been particularly shamed. She'd been branded a trollop and sent to reside with yet another branch of the family.

Ever after, wherever she traveled, her youthful indiscretion traveled with her, and her judgmental relatives never let her forget her one, ridiculous lapse. It was a method for them to feel superior. She comprehended that it was, but it didn't mean she liked it. Their condescension was infuriating.

She worked valiantly to prove that she had no wicked qualities, and she struggled to demonstrate that they were wrong about her. None of them noticed though, so it was wasted effort.

With all that heavy baggage weighing her down, it was lovely to share a covert interval with Captain Crawford, and she realized she was walking ever more slowly. She wanted to drag out the moment and he wasn't in much of a hurry either. They talked and explored, until they ran out of reasons to continue. Gradually, they wound up back in the driveway and she spun the key in the lock.

He reflected and pondered, then he said, "Does the furniture come with it? Do you know?"

"Yes, everything is included."

"It would be easy to move in."

"Yes, but you should be aware that the servants have been released. Baywick is a small town, but it's gotten very popular. It's winter, but they've found positions already. You might have trouble hiring staff."

"Other than that problem," he said, "I think I'd be happy to own it. I'll contact the lawyers and discuss a purchase."

"I'm delighted to hear it and I hope you'll be able to arrange it. As I traipse off to London, I'll imagine you here. I've been praying the place would sell to someone who would cherish it."

They meandered to the gardener's cottage, and much too quickly, they were at her door. They were facing each other, and they were studying features, cataloguing memories.

"You seem so familiar to me," he said. "Have we met before, but I don't recall?"

"No, we've never met. I'd definitely remember you." She couldn't bear for him to depart and she brazenly said, "You must be freezing. Will you join me for a cup of hot tea?"

"I wish I could, but I'm staying with friends, and I've vanished for hours. They'll be worrying about where I am."

"Why vanish? Were you bored? This is a beautiful spot, but it can be quiet."

"It's very quiet and I require constant entertainment. The weather has kept me trapped inside and I desperately needed some fresh air. It's why I rode by."

She yearned to ask where his lodging was located, who his friends were, but she figured—if he'd felt like apprising her—he would have.

"Thank you for showing me around," he said. "I had a marvelous afternoon."

"I did too. Perhaps I should take up a new line of employment and become a tour guide."

At the comment, he chuckled, and that peculiar sensation swirled again, as if the universe was marking the encounter and she should too. Had they been destined to cross paths? Had Fate organized it? So what? They had no future together.

"I don't like you being out here all by yourself," he said.

"I'm fine and the neighborhood is very safe."

"Any type of miscreant might accost you."

"*You* accosted me and I lived to tell the tale."

"Yes, and I am the biggest miscreant of all so you were lucky." He smirked and asked, "When are you leaving for London?"

"On Tuesday." It was Friday so it was four days away.

"Have a good trip."

"I will," she told him, "and please buy this property. I want to think of you in it after I'm gone."

"I probably will buy it."

He smiled and she smiled too. They were perched on the edge of sentiments that oughtn't to be voiced aloud. She thought he might suggest they socialize before she left. *She* nearly suggested it, but the man had to seize the initiative, and he didn't grab hold.

"I shouldn't delay you any further," he said, nodding to the door. "I've wasted enough of your time."

"I didn't mind."

Without another word, he spun on his heel and marched off. In the blink of an eye, he disappeared around the corner of the manor. She dawdled, expecting him to return to have that cup of tea after all, but shortly, she heard his horse trotting away. She scoffed—with regret, with amusement, with disappointment—then she went into the cottage.

The fire was out, the temperature frigid. She stacked some kindling and stirred it to life, then she sat in her chair and waited for the room to warm.

Eventually, she removed her cloak and boots, and she tarried, realizing that she was more alone than she'd ever been. His dashing presence forced her to recognize, despite how she pretended, that her existence was tedious and untenable, and she wished he hadn't knocked.

Maybe it was a benefit that she was headed to London. Maybe it would work out for the best. She doubted that was true, but she would make it true. If it killed her, she would find a better situation for herself, one that was more stable and steady.

She picked up her adventure novel and tried, yet again, to read about the pirate, Sebastian Bramwell, but after meeting Captain Crawford, she especially couldn't focus. It dawned on her that she hadn't learned a single detail about him. She hadn't asked about his people, or where he was from, or how long he'd been retired.

Like a smitten schoolgirl, she'd been too agog to pry out any information.

Well, she had a vivid imagination and she'd invent a history for him. She'd create a story where *she* was included and where she was front and center in a happy ending.

# Chapter

# 2

Michael Crawford, the previously celebrated and decorated naval hero Captain Crawford, who'd been Earl of Sutton since he was eighteen, surveyed the paltry rural dance pavilion and hoped he wouldn't be required to tarry for long.

Baywick, for it being a small coastal village, was trying to attract a wealthy clientele. There was actually a gambling club and his friends had already gone there. He should have been with them, but his half-brother, Caleb, had begged him to stop by the dance first.

Caleb hated to gamble, and he hated for Michael to gamble, and he worked hard to rein in Michael's worst excesses. He was never very successful, but he never gave up. He didn't engage in wicked conduct himself, so he served as Michael's moral compass, and Michael had to admit it was a thankless task.

The town held public dances on Saturday nights, with civic leaders attempting to provide activities for visitors who would otherwise be bored on quiet weekends. The winter evenings were especially tedious and he couldn't wait to return to the city.

He was a great snob who reveled in his elevated position and he was fussy about his amusements. In his view, a rustic fête didn't qualify as entertainment.

He didn't like to loaf in the country. He was a Londoner through and through and he thrived on merriment and vice. His bad habits were legendary.

His parents had been stern, unhappy Puritans, who'd wasted their lives reading the Bible and complaining about how wicked the world had grown to be. When they hadn't been sermonizing, or patting themselves on the back for being pious and perfect, they'd exhausted themselves by nagging at him for being an awful son.

According to them, he'd been wild and incorrigible, a corrupt and dissolute soul who was headed straight to Hell. Yet when he reflected on that early period, he couldn't see that he'd been overly depraved or disobedient. He'd merely been rambunctious and curious and he'd involved himself in a boy's typical mischief. To have heard their ranting, he'd sounded like Lucifer reincarnated.

By the time he was seven, they'd shipped him off to a strict military academy, and they'd rarely allowed him to come home after that. Not that he'd minded. He'd rapidly assimilated to that structured life, and he hadn't missed his parents or wished they'd been closer.

He'd joined the navy at fourteen and his mother had died the following year. He'd been sailing on the other side of the globe so he hadn't been able to attend her funeral. His father had died when he was eighteen and he'd had to skip that funeral too.

His superiors had sent him to England on furlough though, so the estate lawyers could finish up the transfer of title. He'd become earl, but it hadn't been a designation he'd craved, so he'd been in no rush to claim it. He'd spent another decade in the navy before he'd resigned his commission, and he didn't regret a single minute of his exotic adventures.

His thirtieth birthday was approaching in June so he had to shape up and put his house in order. His father hadn't believed Michael would ever settle down, so the pious goat had deposited a huge chunk of the family's money in a trust fund. Michael wouldn't receive it unless he was wed when he turned thirty.

He frequently stewed over the situation, and he often thought about thumbing his nose at his father, letting the fortune be lost, but if he didn't buckle down and shackle himself, it would be donated to the Church instead.

With how gleefully his parents had embraced their brutal religiosity, and with how they'd been such flaming hypocrites, Michael couldn't permit it to occur. Plus, he couldn't imagine forsaking such a large windfall. To obtain it, he had to marry, which was a conclusion every man of his station had to accept sooner or later.

It wouldn't kill him to be a husband so he had to hurry and pick a bride. He couldn't keep delaying. His sister, Hester, was his matchmaker, and she'd planned several parties where various young ladies would stay with them at Sutton. He simply had to choose the one he liked best, and the matter would be resolved quickly and easily.

His problem was that he loved being a bachelor, loved carrying on with trollops and tarts. Faithfulness and monogamy held no appeal whatsoever, and while he'd never tamp down his dreadful tendencies to please his wife, he was certain he'd have to behave a bit better after he was a husband. He was gnashing his teeth over the entire, distasteful idea.

The room was packed and it was an interesting mix of locals and visitors. A trio of musicians was belting out one cheery tune after the next and couples were promenading down the floor. There was a second room, where a buffet was arranged, and there were tables to sit, eat, and chat. It was packed too.

The whole gathering was cozy and agreeable and—if he could have been charmed by ordinary circumstances—he'd have been delighted to participate.

As usual, there were more women than men. Caleb liked to flirt and mingle, so he'd already danced three sets, as Michael lurked in the corner and scowled like a grump. The wallflowers peeked at him, hoping he'd begin selecting partners too, but he remained blind to their beseeching glances.

He could be such an ass. He couldn't deny it and he'd much rather be drinking and wagering at the gambling club. Apparently, a gaggle of gorgeous whores had been brought over from Brighton, and he couldn't wait to carouse with some naughty doxies.

The song ended and the audience clapped for a job well done. Then the fiddler announced a break and the crowd headed to the buffet. Caleb sauntered over and he was grinning. He was handsome and polite and the girls were drooling over him.

He was twenty, so Michael was a decade older, but it was clear they were brothers. The Crawford family was a bunch of runts, who were plain and unremarkable, with dull brown hair and eyes, but he and Caleb were so different from their relatives that the stork might have dropped them at the wrong location.

They had similar facial features, the same blond hair and blue eyes, but Michael was taller, over six feet in height, and Caleb was a few inches shorter. Michael was brawny across the shoulders, a solid wall of bone and muscle, honed from seafaring and war battles that had left him tough and lean.

Caleb was smaller, thinner, slight in his frame. He'd sailed with Michael for ten years, initially serving as his cabin boy, then his aide, but he'd never been a warrior. He was too kind to fight and he'd never met a man he didn't like. Michael, on the other hand, was a seasoned veteran, a brawler, a winner. He had a uniform covered with medals to prove it.

"You didn't join in once," Caleb said, as he grabbed Michael's glass of punch and downed it in a slow swallow. "You've disappointed the ladies and you're glowering like such a grouch. If looks could kill, every person in the room would be dead."

"Are we finished?" Michael asked. "May we leave for the gambling club?"

"I can't go yet. I've promised to step out with three more partners."

"I could depart without you," Michael said.

"And miss out on all this fun? Can't you at least try to enjoy yourself? Baywick has become such a popular destination; there are people in London who would cut off their right arms to be here."

"If this is what excites people in London, it's obvious they've been misled as to what this place is really like. If it grew any more tedious, I'd fall asleep."

"Do you ever stop complaining?"

"No. Never."

Caleb wasn't actually chastising him. They'd been glued at the hip for ages and his brother understood him better than anyone. It was merely the reality of their situation that Caleb was sunny and amiable, while Michael was aloof and jaded. Neither of them was inclined to change.

Caleb was the prime example of his parents' hypocrisy. Their father had regularly railed about sin and damnation, but he'd engaged in a salacious affair with a secret mistress, and Caleb had been the result.

His mother had died during the birthing, then Michael's father had shuffled him off to be reared by a tenant farmer. The man had been ordered to raise Caleb, but he'd later sworn to Michael that he hadn't known Caleb was the Earl's son. The stupid oaf had been paid an annual stipend to defray costs so it was hard to believe he'd been truthful.

The greedy fiend had never used any of the money on Caleb. Caleb had been beaten, starved, and worked nearly to death.

Until Michael had inherited at eighteen, he'd had no idea that he had a half-brother. He'd learned about him from an accountant when he'd questioned the expenditure for Caleb's upkeep. With Michael having only one sibling, that being his unlikable, bitter sister Hester, he'd immediately rescued Caleb and had whisked him away from Sutton for an entire decade.

They were more tightly bonded than any two brothers could ever be. But they were back in England now and they were adjusting.

Caleb wasn't keen to tarry at Sutton House because Hester resided there and she was horrid to him. She thought it was an outrage that Michael had welcomed Caleb into the family. The despicable tenant farmer was still at the estate too, so it was awkward all around.

Michael was about to wed and bring a wife into the picture, and he wasn't sure how he and Caleb would weather it. The prior day, at Beachhead Cottage, he'd considered buying it for Caleb, so he could have a home of his own, one that was far from Sutton, but it would mean they'd be separated and he simply couldn't fathom that conclusion.

He was more bored by the minute, and he might have abandoned Caleb to his paltry fun, but as he spun toward the buffet, he was delighted to discover that Margaret Adair had arrived. She was with another woman and they appeared to be acquainted with everyone. They were strolling about, saying hello, and he studied her without her realizing he was.

She was very beautiful, but in a fresh way that was different from the slatterns who tantalized him in London.

He was stuck in a world where most every girl was blond and blue-eyed, so her chestnut hair and green eyes set her apart. She was also smart and amusing, was kind and interesting. She was a damsel in distress too, living on her relatives' charity and pretending her plight wasn't precarious.

He didn't envision himself as a fellow who would be enticed by a female who needed help. Generally, he was selfish and self-centered, but her woeful predicament had him anxious to jump in and be her savior. Wasn't that a bizarre notion?

She exuded a strange aura that had left him eager to wallow in her presence, to spew promises of assistance and support. He was a flagrant liar though, so he'd never have followed through on any vow.

At Beachhead, she'd thoroughly charmed him, but when she'd invited him to have a cup of tea, he'd fled in a quick hurry. He'd been afraid that he'd be ensnared in her web of problems. But here she was and he viewed it as a sign. Just what sort of sign it would turn out to be was debatable.

When he'd been a sailor, he'd been ruled by superstition and omens, and he didn't suppose he should disregard the chance encounter. What might come of it?

She finally noticed him and she smiled and walked over. As she neared, there was an electricity in the air, as if their proximity was igniting sparks. He was genuinely glad to have bumped into her, and the prospect of tarrying at the dance suddenly seemed like a grand plan.

"Captain Crawford!" she said. "How nice to find you enjoying our trifling attempt at entertainment. I doubted we'd ever see each other again."

"I doubted it too."

They were grinning like fools, but Caleb was glaring. If Michael introduced himself as Captain Crawford, rather than Lord Sutton, it was because he was flirting when he shouldn't be. Caleb was aware that, if Miss Adair assumed he was Captain Crawford, Michael was engaged in mischief he shouldn't be pursuing.

Caleb wouldn't spill the beans and announce his true identity, but Michael would get an earful later on.

"This is my brother, Mr. Caleb Crawford," Michael said to her. "He insisted I be sociable and he dragged me in against my will. He won't let me leave either. Caleb, this is Miss Margaret Adair."

Caleb had very pretty manners and he bowed over her hand. "It's lovely to meet you, Miss Adair. How do you know Captain Crawford?"

He put special emphasis on the word *Captain*, but Miss Adair didn't note it.

"I live out at Beachhead Cottage. It's just outside the village and it's for sale. He was riding by and he stopped and brazenly requested a tour."

"Really? He didn't tell me." There was never an innocent motive to any act Michael performed and Caleb peered at him and asked, "Are you thinking of owning property in the area?"

Michael shrugged. "I might. I've been feeling so landlocked and it's right on the water. I could sit in the rear parlor and gaze out at the waves crashing on the shore."

She asked, "Have you spoken to the estate lawyers?"

"Not yet, but I will," he fibbed.

There wasn't a reason to purchase it. Initially, he'd thought of giving it to Caleb, but his brother never liked him to be generous, and Michael didn't actually want it for himself. He hated loafing in the country and he rarely went to Sutton because of it. He shouldn't compound his idiocy by buying a rural abode he didn't need and wouldn't cherish.

Miss Adair's companion approached. She was another fetching maiden, about Miss Adair's age, but she was a more typical British blond.

Miss Adair pulled her into their small circle and said, "Katherine, this is Captain Crawford and his brother, Caleb Crawford. They're visiting from..." She cut off, then asked, "Where are you from, Captain? I just realized I have no idea."

"London," he replied, so Caleb couldn't confess that it was Sutton House, which was one of England's great manors.

And he did reside in London. Mostly. He liked the vices available in the city. Plus, Hester managed Sutton for him, but she was an unpleasant person to be around. He couldn't stand to dawdle with her, so he stayed away for lengthy periods.

"This is my good friend, Miss Katherine Hastings," Miss Adair said. "She and I are having a final night together before I depart on Tuesday."

The four of them chatted for a few minutes, and Caleb was such an amiable oaf that he drew out all sorts of information Michael could never have obtained on his own. Miss Adair explained more about caring for her dying cousin and her pending move. Miss Hastings shockingly admitted that she ran a home for unwed mothers. At mentioning her job, she was very blunt about it and exhibited no discomfort over the peculiar revelation.

He'd never talked to a female who held such an odd position, and he'd have liked to probe for details, but the musicians were finished with their break. The fiddler struck a chord, the sound calling the participants back onto the floor.

Caleb and Miss Hastings both had partners arranged so they flitted off to step into the line. Michael was left with Miss Adair.

"Are you a dancer, Captain?" she asked.

"Not usually, but with our crossing paths again, it appears we're bound to socialize. Shall we join in?"

"I'd like that very much."

They wedged themselves into the group of boisterous couples and it had been ages since he'd danced. Whenever the opportunity arose, he was always too busy drinking or gambling. Luckily, he was nimble and athletic so he wouldn't trip over any feet.

The song started, and as they marched and twirled, he had so much fun that they continued through the next three sets, only quitting when they were hot and sweaty. With such a mob packed into the two rooms, and the stoves burning, the air was thick and stale. Baywick had a promenade that fronted the bay, and the weather was cold, but calm and dry for a change. He was eager to cool his heated face.

"It's so stuffy in here," he said. "Would you go outside with me? Or is that a risqué suggestion? We're not in London, so are the rules a tad more relaxed? Can you accompany me? Or should we have Miss Hastings tag along?"

"I'm twenty-five and I've been making my own decisions for most of my life. I'm certain I can accompany you and the world will keep spinning on its axis."

He smirked. "You're not terrified to be alone with me?"

"We've already been alone, remember? Out at Beachhead? You didn't frighten me once."

"Maybe I was tamping down my dangerous tendencies and they're about to burst out."

"I doubt it. I'm an excellent judge of character. You seem quite harmless to me."

He could have disabused her of her mistaken impression, but he didn't. He liked having her assume he was normal and common. He might have been an actor playing a part in a theatrical comedy.

They had to have an usher find their outer garments, then they had to locate Caleb and Miss Hastings to apprise them of their stroll.

Eventually, they were able to wander out into the dark night. They didn't have The Promenade all to themselves though. Many other revelers had had the same idea.

Lamps were lit and hanging from poles and benches were strategically placed so people could pause to rest. He guided her away from the crowd, the sounds of frivolity swiftly fading. The sole noises were their breathing, their footsteps, and the waves crashing over the jetty out on the edge of the bay.

The tide and churning water called to him, reminding him that he loved the ocean, that he missed the ocean. Why wasn't he out on a ship and sailing away?

She was nestled to his side and she fit there perfectly. For reasons he wouldn't try to clarify, he felt marvelous in her presence, and he was so glad to be with her.

He shouldn't have been glad though. He was sending a thousand erroneous signals that she would completely misconstrue, but he ignored his folly and proceeded, despite the warning bells that were clanging in his head.

It was a crisp evening, and he was walking, arm in arm, with a pretty girl who thought he was wonderful. Life rarely got any better than that.

"How long are you staying in Baywick?" she inquired after a bit.

"I'm trapped until next weekend."

She laughed. "The town's founders would be so despondent to have you describe yourself as being *trapped.* They've worked so hard to make it an interesting spot for visitors."

"I apologize for being persnickety. This is a magnificent area and I really am having a pleasant holiday."

"What brought you here?" she asked. "It's the middle of winter so it's not exactly a premium time to be traveling."

"I was over in Brighton, gambling. Then my friends discovered there was a gambling hall in Baywick too, so we came over."

"You're a gambler? Shame on you." She tsked with offense. "Are you addicted, as some fools seem to be? Or do you simply wager for sport? If you're addicted, lie and tell me it's only for fun."

"It's not so much that I like to gamble. It's that I enjoy the camaraderie and commotion of the gaming rooms. I'm partial to the alcoholic beverages and the trollops too."

"Are you a scoundrel, Captain?"

"Yes. My reputation is atrocious. I'm renowned for my bad habits and I never behave myself."

"Well, so far in our short acquaintance, you've appeared to be a very decent fellow. You haven't provided me with a single hint that you're a wastrel."

"I'm hiding my worst inclinations from you. Am I succeeding?"

"Definitely. If I ever discuss you later on, I'll insist you were boring and ordinary, and there wasn't a whiff of scandal about you."

They passed an empty bench. He led her over to it and they snuggled down. It was chilly, a breeze blowing, and she shivered. He draped an arm over her shoulders and pulled her close. They'd just met, so it was an astonishingly personal embrace that ignored all of Society's restrictions about flirtation, but he wasn't about to shift away. She didn't put any space between them either.

"What will you do with yourself in London?" he asked. "You've already stirred my sympathies by confessing you're the poor relative. What is your plan?"

"I have a cousin who is husband-hunting. She constantly attends parties and suppers as she frantically searches for Prince Charming. Her mother is usually her chaperone, but she broke her foot, so she's housebound. They requested I help out until she's betrothed."

"Will the experience be awful for you? Or are you looking forward to it?"

"I'm looking forward to it very much. I had a very quiet sojourn in Baywick, but in London, I'll get to strut about at fancy events and hobnob with toplofty people. It will be a nice change."

He nearly asked the name of her cousin, nearly pried into her family's history and circumstances, but he managed to bite down any queries. He had no desire to become immersed in her world. He didn't dare hear about her kin or learn where she'd be located.

He was oddly fascinated by her, and he was suffering from the rather alarming perception that—should he know where she'd be living—he might begin to show up there. Which would be a disaster. Once they departed Baywick, it was his specific intent that he would never see her again.

For a moment though, he silently pondered, recollecting the bridal candidates—a group of heiresses and debutantes—Hester had culled for him from the newspaper gossip pages. Before sending out invitations to Sutton, she'd let him review the guest lists, and he recalled that one of the girls had a surname of Adair.

Was that right? Or was he misremembering? What if Miss Adair waltzed into Sutton as her cousin's chaperone? Would that be amusing or horrible? The prospect was too implausible to calculate so he shoved it out of his mind.

"What will *you* do in London?" she asked. "It sounds as if you'll gamble and generally be a nuisance to all who come in contact with you."

"You've perfectly summed up my dreary hours. These days, I'm a hopeless scapegrace."

"Were you always a degenerate or is this a new proclivity?"

"It's new. I spent most of two decades in the navy and I was occupied with valuable tasks. I served the Crown to the best of my ability."

"Have you a uniform covered with medals?"

"Yes, and I'm quite brave and notorious."

She smiled with delight. "That doesn't surprise me."

"It's just since I've been home that I've lost my way. When I don't have a ship to command or orders to carry out, I can't figure out how to stay busy in a responsible manner. I grow bored and I wind up engaging in nefarious deeds."

It was such a stunning admission that he'd shocked himself. He never talked about his emotions and he wasn't prone to wallowing in self-pity. He was a tough, courageous warrior who barged through life like a bull in a china shop. He never rued or regretted. He never fretted or second-guessed.

Why lament? It was pointless.

She was staring at him so kindly, her pretty green eyes twinkling in the lamp light, and he was embarrassed to have put her in a position where she had to extend sympathy. She looked shrewd and wise, as if she understood him better than anyone ever had, and he couldn't bear to realize he wasn't a mystery to her.

He leaned over and rested his forehead on hers, their breath mingling, their hearts beating in the same slow rhythm.

"I'm a mess, Miss Adair," he whispered.

"No, you're not," she whispered in reply. "Not really. You're simply adjusting to your circumstances."

"I'm completely adrift and I hate it."

"How long have you been retired?"

"Seven months? Eight?"

"Could you go back to the navy? Would you like that? Would you be more content?"

"I couldn't go back. I have too many responsibilities in England. I can't keep shucking them off."

"Things will gradually improve," she said. "I'm sure of it."

"Are you an eternal optimist?"

"Of course I am. Considering my low condition, if I didn't remain optimistic, I can't imagine how I'd drag myself out of bed in the morning."

"You make me happy," he blurted out like a sentimental dunce. "I'm glad we met."

"So am I."

Their burgeoning infatuation thrilled him, and like the fool he could definitely be, he dipped in and kissed her. It was a quick brush of his lips to her own, but with her sitting so near and being so sweet, he couldn't resist.

In the history of kisses, it wasn't all that passionate, and she was dear enough to let him proceed, even if it was for a short minute. He drew away, and she was smiling serenely, looking shrewd and wise again, as if she'd learned his secrets and he couldn't hide them from her.

He'd deemed the embrace to have been very pleasant, but he couldn't have predicted how she'd viewed it. When she finally spoke, he chuckled at her comment.

"We should probably return to the dance at The Pavilion," was all she had to say.

"Why? There's no hurry."

"I'm freezing and we shouldn't dawdle on this dark bench and misbehave. It might be a bit more than I should allow."

"I'm not sorry."

She chuckled too. "I'm sure you're not and it's occurred to me that I'm out of my depth with you. I have a very tender heart and I'm leaving on Tuesday. If I'm too involved with you, I'll start to yearn for endings I can never have."

He liked that she was so blunt. With him concealing his true identity from her, he was being quite awful. He shouldn't have been so furtive, but once he slithered out of Baywick, he was anxious for her to have fond memories of him.

"We can head back," he said, "but you have to snuggle by my side."

"I wasn't joking when I complained that I'm freezing. I will stand so close that you'll wish you hadn't offered."

He stood and he lifted her to her feet. Then she surprised him by raising up on tiptoe and delivering a kiss of her own. She'd shocked him so his reflexes were too slow. He tried to grab hold, so it would last a tad longer, but she was smarter than he was, and she hastily stepped away.

"I had to do that," she said. "One kiss from you wasn't enough and I needed one more to sustain me. Now, I'm ready to return."

She took his arm and they sauntered off. They were silent, pensive, even though he could have voiced a thousand remarks. He wanted to unburden himself over so many issues: about his strict, cruel parents, how their caustic attitudes had shaped him so he'd become an immoral wretch merely to prove he was different from them.

He wanted to tell her about the rumors around his neighborhood, how people claimed that his mother couldn't get her spouse's seed to catch in her womb, so she'd lain with the estate's horse trainer. Due to the fact that Michael didn't resemble any of his relatives, but that he was the spitting image of the horse trainer, it seemed as if the gossips might be correct.

The horse trainer had left Sutton before Michael was born. He'd suddenly and magically received an unexpected inheritance that had permitted him to buy his own farm. The conclusion had simply stirred the pot of innuendo.

He wanted to explain about his father's hypocrisy in siring Caleb, about Caleb's hidden, abusive boyhood. He wanted to tell her about his sister, Hester, how she worked hard to be just like their parents, how exhausting she was, how sad he was about it.

Most of all, he wanted to tell her how he had to be married by his birthday in June. He wanted to tell her that he'd be a terrible husband, that any girl he chose would be miserable forever. He was certain she'd understand and commiserate, but he never shared his problems with others and he wasn't about to begin with her.

Much too quickly, they were at The Pavilion. The party was still in progress, the festivities lively. Caleb was out on the floor, Miss Hastings too.

Miss Adair led him through the crowd to the front entry, where an usher was keeping track of coats and boots. She assumed they were staying to join in the merriment, but he had no intention of tarrying. She knew the usher and was chatting with him, handing over her outer garments.

If Michael dawdled, he'd grow even more besotted, which was dangerous and senseless, so while she was distracted, he snuck away and went into the dancing room. He motioned to Caleb that he was off to the gambling club, then he crept out the other door so he wouldn't have to talk to her again.

It was incredibly rude behavior, but he was strangely worried that he didn't have the power to yank himself away from her. He'd taken more liberties with her than he should have dared so, like a thief in the night, he slipped out into the cold once more. He didn't glance back either.

He was afraid she'd be searching for him and he'd see her in a window. If he did, he suspected—like a magnet to metal—he'd rush to be with her. But he refused to continue acting so stupidly.

It was time to revel with his disgusting friends. It was time to flirt and consort with a few slatterns too. That would be a much more productive way to spend the remainder of his evening so he increased his pace and hurried on.

# Chapter 3

MARGARET WAS SITTING IN the parlor in the gardener's cottage behind the manor. It was late, dark, and quiet. She was alone on the property, and she imagined a different woman, a more timid woman, might have been unnerved by the solitude. It didn't bother her in the least.

Since she was seven, she'd lived with her relatives. She'd be offered shelter in exchange for chores such as supervising children or serving as a companion to someone who needed assistance. She'd stay with a family for a few months or a year, then they'd grow weary of feeding her and they'd shuffle her off to yet another home.

Normally, she'd have her own bedchamber, but occasionally, she'd be stuck up in the attic with the servants. Other times, she shared with the nanny or governess. The prior two weeks, after the manor had been shuttered and the staff let go, she'd moved into the cottage. She was delighted to have her own space, with no one to boss her or complain over how she was carrying on.

She was dressed for bed, wearing a heavy nightgown and robe, woolen socks on her feet, a thick shawl draped over her shoulders. Her chestnut hair was down and brushed out, and her head was covered with a mobcap to hold in the warmth on such a cold night.

She'd reveled at the dance, so she should have been exhausted and snuggled under the blankets, but she couldn't calm down enough to rest. There was a cheery fire burning in the grate, and she was staring at the flames, replaying the entire evening in her mind. She and Katherine had attended together, and Margaret had viewed it as a goodbye party to mark her departure.

She would miss Katherine after she left, and they'd promised to correspond, but from bitter experience, she was aware that it was difficult to keep in touch. In the beginning, they'd write frequently, then they'd write less and less, until they didn't write at all. Katherine would become another lost friend from her past.

The event would have been perfect except that Captain Crawford had wedged himself into the middle of it, and the romantic interlude had her unsettled and annoyed.

His absurd entry into her staid existence had stirred the cravings she constantly tamped down. It was merely a fact of her personality that she was never satisfied with her circumstances. She yearned to be rich and marvelous, to have a cadre of famous acquaintances, so she'd be the envy of everyone she met.

She yearned to have a grand life as a hostess in London, to have her opinions coveted, her ideas heeded, her patronage courted. Most of all, she yearned to fall in love with Captain Crawford and have him as her handsome, dashing husband.

She was a female who hungered for much more than she'd been given, but she had to vigorously suppress her desires. The Captain's flirting had ignited her worst impulses, then he'd snuck away without a word. She'd handed her cloak and hat to the usher at the door, then she'd turned around to find he'd vanished.

She hadn't even searched for him in the crowd. Where he was concerned, she had a heightened sense about him, and she'd recognized immediately that he'd fled. Yet she was driving herself mad with asking why he had.

For some reason, he'd simply had enough of her company, and the only way it could have concluded more humiliatingly was if he'd walked away on the dance floor, while people were watching.

She was sipping a whiskey and she'd emptied the glass. It was a secret vice she savored, but typically couldn't indulge. She resided with her stingy kin and they would never like to see her helping herself to their liquor. Plus, they relentlessly scrutinized her in order to have her low morals confirmed, and she'd have been accused of being a drunkard on top of her other failings.

Women weren't supposed to drink hard spirits, but it was a stupid edict she ignored. Whenever she had the chance, she treated herself. As she'd locked up the manor for the lawyers, she'd stolen several whiskey bottles from the liquor trays. She'd stuff them in her luggage and bring them to her cousin's house in London.

That's how pathetic her life had grown to be: She stole liquor and furtively imbibed when she was hidden away in dark parlors.

She was debating whether to refill her glass, when there was a noise outside. She heard a horse's hooves crunching on the gravel, and she suffered a momentary spurt of panic, but she quickly shoved it away.

Baywick was very safe, so she doubted a miscreant would be sniffing about and looking for trouble. If a burglar was lurking, assuming the property abandoned, he'd note the smoke rising from her chimney, the glow of the lamp over on the table.

If those hints didn't scare him away, she had a pistol in the desk. The old gardener had shot varmints with it. He'd shown her how to load it and she wouldn't hesitate to use it to chase off an idiot.

The hooves crunched again, the saddle leather creaking as someone dismounted and boots hit the ground. She tiptoed over and peeked out the curtain. On realizing who'd arrived, she was surprised, but she wasn't surprised too.

She went to the door and pulled it open. "Captain Crawford! It's after two! What are you thinking?"

At being scolded, he was unabashed. "I didn't say goodbye to you at the dance. I've felt awful about it ever since."

"I will agree that it was horrid conduct on your part, but that doesn't mean you can bluster in in the middle of the night to apologize."

"May I come in? It's freezing out here and I'm in desperate need of some feminine tending."

The comment sounded extremely risqué. "What sort of feminine tending? In light of what a libertine I deem you to be, I'm sure—whatever you require—it's not an act I would deign to supply."

He stepped nearer and she was astonished to discover that his eye was black and blue. He had a cut on his forehead, the kind that wasn't deep, but that bled copiously. He had a scarf pressed to it to staunch the flow. Apparently, he'd been in a fight, but why he'd seek her out afterward was a genuine mystery.

"I'd really like to sit down," he said. "May I?"

Alarm bells chimed. It would be the height of folly to consent. So far in their fleeting liaison, he'd been very polite, but he was a stranger. She was by herself, in an isolated cottage. If she admitted him, and he became aggressive, she wouldn't be able to fend him off. On the other hand, she was thrilled to see him.

What could it hurt to let him in? Who would ever know?

"Stay right there for a minute." She marched to the fireplace and grabbed the poker. Then she brandished it at him. "You may come in, and I'll nurse your injuries and listen to your tale of woe about how they were inflicted. But I will keep this poker close by. If you so much as look at me the wrong way, I will beat you to a pulp. Are you still interested in tarrying?"

"If we tussled, do you suppose you could win?"

"Yes, because I'm more determined than you. And I'm sober."

A strong odor of alcohol wafted off his person, and she suspected, after he'd slunk away from The Pavilion, he'd engaged in an evening of drunken revelry that had ended in fisticuffs. She didn't feel sorry for him in the slightest.

"My dear Miss Adair," he said, "I promise to be on my very best behavior."

"I'm afraid you'll have to prove that I can trust you."

She waved him in and he staggered across the threshold and directly to a chair. He eased down, groaning miserably, and as he rubbed a palm on his ribs, she noticed that his knuckles were cut and swollen.

She tsked with offense. "Brawling, Captain Crawford? How old are you? Ten?"

"I was protecting a woman's reputation after she was insulted by a pompous cretin. She was a trollop, but she shouldn't have to be denigrated for it."

"That's why you were sparring? Can a doxy possess a reputation worth defending?"

He scowled, as if it was a trick question. "Should I have ignored him when he was being so obnoxious?"

"Yes. It's what sane men do, so I'm worried about your mental state. Are you deranged?"

"It's been claimed that I am."

"Wonderful. I've allowed a lunatic to wander in."

"I'll try to control myself."

"Thank you. I would appreciate it."

She puttered around him, like a wife with an intoxicated husband. She removed his coat and hat, and she tugged off his boots so he could warm his toes by the fire. She stirred the flames so they burned more hotly and heated the room to a better temperature. She filled her whiskey glass and gave it to him, leaving him to sip it, as she poured water in a bowl to wash him up.

She began with the wound on his head, applying pressure, as he grumbled and swatted her away.

"Be quiet," she said. "You trotted out here to have me tend you so you can't complain about any of my cures. If you're too much of a nuisance, I'll kick you out the door."

"After I travelled quite a distance merely to pester you, you wouldn't be that cruel."

"You'd be amazed by how grouchy I can be at two in the morning, so don't push your luck with me."

"I always push my luck," he said, "and I always get my way."

"I'm sure that's true. I'm sure you're a veritable pain in the rear to everyone who's ever had to put up with you."

"I might be renowned as a bit of a troublemaker."

"That news is not surprising."

She dabbed the blood off his face, then dipped his knuckles in the bowl of water, letting the cool liquid take out some of the sting. His cravat was covered with blood droplets, and she untied it and attempted to wash out the stains, but it was a lost cause. The beautiful lace was ruined.

She'd been over by the work table, fussing with the cravat, and she brought it back and stuck it out so he could assess the damage.

"You've destroyed a perfectly good item of clothing," she said, but he simply shrugged.

"I have plenty of others. Or I'll buy another one."

"It must be nice to be so rich that you can be flippant about your wardrobe."

"I am rich and I like it."

"How could you be rich? Was the navy a lucrative career? How could you have earned a fortune? Did you pillage, rampage, and enjoy the spoils of war?"

"Basically, yes."

She stared into his mesmerizing blue eyes, and she was positive she could detect a thousand falsehoods buried there. "I don't believe you."

"Would I lie?"

"Yes, absolutely."

He snorted with amusement, then he pulled her onto his lap. Suddenly, her bottom was nestled to his muscular thigh, and she tried to jump up and escape, but she didn't try very hard. He rested a hand on her waist, and just that effortlessly, he kept her right where she was.

He kissed her, both of them sighing with pleasure as he drew away.

"I'm sorry I left the dance," he told her.

"You should be sorry. It was very rude."

"I regretted it all night."

"I'm delighted to hear it."

"I was so surly over it that my companions accused me of being a grump."

"Is that why you were really fighting? You were in a bad mood?"

"Yes. I was enraged by that dunce, but I don't even remember his precise remark. I hit him and it's your fault."

"*My* fault? How could that be? I wasn't there and I barely know you."

"I've already explained why," he said. "I was horrid to you and I was wretched because of it."

"So you started a brawl? Your brain certainly works in mysterious ways."

"Weren't you listening? *I* didn't start it. The other fellow was the instigator. He was being belligerent, and I warned him to be silent, but he didn't stop."

"So you started a brawl," she repeated.

He frowned, as if she'd confused him. "Well, yes. His friends and mine joined in the fray and we made quite a spectacle of ourselves."

"Where did this humiliating event occur?"

"At the gambling club. I was such a whirling dervish that it took six burly footmen to wrestle me out the door. I can't recollect when I was last tossed out of a saloon. If I wasn't so miserable, I'd probably think it was funny."

"I'm not about to offer you any sympathy."

"You should. I rode here specifically to have you commiserate."

"I would never condone fighting and you're deranged if you imagine I would."

He lifted the glass of whiskey and downed the remainder of the contents. Then he smacked it on the table and reached for the bottle to refill it. She shoved it away so he couldn't continue to imbibe.

"Are you a heavy drinker, Captain? From the liquor I can smell, it seems as if you might be."

"On occasion, I have been known to drink to excess."

"You're a fighter and a drinker. Have you any other ridiculous habits you'd like to disclose?"

"Those are the least shocking of my many vices. If I provided you with a full list, I'd have to talk until dawn."

"You're not tarrying until dawn," she said. "In fact, you should leave now."

His frown deepened. "I'm not in any condition to go."

"You haven't noticed, but *I* am dressed for bed, and it's outrageous for you to barge in. How am I to assess your bizarre conduct? I can understand why you'd be distressed after your scuffle, but I can't fathom why you'd assume I should be the one to furnish you with solace. Can you clarify your reasoning for me?"

"You make me happy. I feel better when I'm with you."

It had been on the tip of her tongue to scold him furiously, but the comment was very sweet, and the compliment charmed her. It stroked her battered ego and she was eager to be the woman he desperately required.

"Don't suppose you can flatter me and instantly be forgiven," she said.

"I would never suppose that. You're a tough virago."

He tugged off her mobcap to uncover her chestnut hair, and he studied her features, his expression tender and affectionate.

"You're so pretty," he said. "Why aren't you married? Why don't you have a husband who adores you and a dozen babies pulling at your skirt?"

"No one ever asked to wed me and I don't have a dowry. I could never have attracted a suitable candidate."

"Men are idiots," he said.

"I can't argue the point."

"Did you ever have a serious beau?"

"I thought so once, when I was seventeen. He was a soldier and I believed I was madly in love."

"What happened to him? Why didn't he propose?"

"He was a scoundrel. He might have uttered a proposal, but it would have been completely opposite from what I was expecting."

His jaw dropped with surprise. "He ruined you?"

"He ruined my reputation. He lured me into a risqué incident, but we were caught, and I was rescued before a despicable act could occur. My family has castigated me for my folly ever since. It's exhausting."

"Are you a fallen woman?"

"Not a fallen one. I just tripped a bit when I was a girl."

"I'm glad to hear that no libertine has ever enticed you. I would hate to think of you fancying anyone but me. Promise me you'll never be tempted in the future."

His tone was fervid and insistent and she chuckled. "You are very intoxicated, Captain Crawford."

"I know and my head is spinning. Could I lie down on your bed?"

"No! And how dare you request it. We need to sober you up so you can ride to Baywick. Could you find the route? Or will you get lost, and I'll learn tomorrow that you tumbled off your horse and froze in a ditch?"

"I'm fairly sure the animal can haul me to my lodging without any of my dubious assistance."

"Shall I make a pot of tea? Would you drink any of it?"

"No. Are you positive I can't lie down?"

"I'm positive."

He pressed his forehead to her nape. For a minute or two, he nestled there, his warm breath sending goosebumps down her arms.

"You're kind," he murmured. "These days, I rarely meet people who are kind."

"If that's even remotely true, maybe you should socialize with different acquaintances."

"Maybe I should."

He straightened and kissed her again. She kissed him back with enormous enthusiasm. She shouldn't have been so eager, but how could it hurt? It seemed as if they were trapped in an odd bubble and the outside world couldn't intrude. If they misbehaved, who was there to complain?

They leapt into the fray, and they carried on for such a lengthy interval that the fire burned out and the room grew icy. Yet they continued. It began innocently enough, but it swiftly became quite impassioned. By the end, they were clawing and scrapping, as if they were shipwreck survivors trying to keep from drowning.

Eventually, they were shivering so violently that they had to stop. They stared in a bewildered manner, as if they couldn't deduce what had spurred them to such negligence. Then they started to giggle, like naughty children engaged in mischief.

"I kissed you so long that I've sobered up," he said.

"I'm delighted to have provided a valuable service to your grand self, but it's probably time for you to leave."

"I still don't want to go."

"I don't want you to go either, but one of us has to come to our senses. It might as well be me."

They stared more poignantly, a hundred unvoiced declarations swirling, then he said, "I feel as if I've always known you. We're so compatible, but you're not my type in even the slightest way."

She sputtered with feigned offense. "Was that a compliment? I couldn't tell."

His cheeks heated with chagrin. "I'm notorious for reveling with slatterns. Since you're not a doxy, I can't imagine what's driving me."

"I'm a very nice person, so how could you resist?"

"How could I indeed?"

They paused, and while it was bizarre, the prospect of a betrothal was suddenly hovering. The notion of marriage had crossed both their minds. The perception was so powerful, it might have been a tangible object she could have reached out and touched.

When an ardent couple dallied as they just had, it was the only accepted conclusion. They were strangers, but they were so intimately attached. Why not bind themselves? They might wind up being happy forever.

Like the obtuse oaf he was, he instantly dashed her flight of fancy.

"I doubt we'll ever see each other again," he said.

"I doubt it too."

"I'll always be glad we met."

"I'll be glad too," she said. "At least I assume I'll be glad. You brag about your vices and depravities, so if I subsequently learn hideous details about you, I'll be incensed."

"Ha! You're leaving Baywick on Tuesday, and until then, you're tucked away at this isolated estate. You'll have no opportunity to discover anything too embarrassing."

"I will hope that remains true."

"I insist you have fond memories of our brief amour."

"Was it an amour?" she asked. "Is that what we're calling it?"

"Oh, yes. I don't kiss just anybody."

She smirked. "I'm certain that's a bald-faced lie. Aren't you the fellow who just brawled to defend a tart's reputation? I'm betting you kiss every female who glances in your direction."

"You'll never get me to admit it."

She slid off his lap and he didn't prevent her. Apparently, they were finished for the night. She fussed around him again, helping him to pull on his boots, to don his coat and hat.

She showed him his ruined cravat. "I'm keeping this as a souvenir so I'll always recollect what a wretch you are."

"That's a pathetic memento." He had a ring on his pinkie finger, a gold band with a stone that—if it was genuine—had to be a small diamond. To her great consternation, he plucked it off and offered it to her. "Take this instead."

"You're not giving me jewelry. Absolutely not."

"I want you to have it."

"It would be a totally inappropriate gift." She wedged it onto his finger, then waved the cravat at him. "This stained lace is enough for me and it's a more accurate token of who you really are."

"You are an unusual vixen, Miss Adair."

"I will confess to being unusual, but I'm not a vixen."

"You could be—if the right rogue enticed you."

"The *right* rogue isn't you though, so you need to depart. Will you?"

He hugged her tight and she hugged him back. To her astonishment, she had tears in her eyes, as if she couldn't bear to part from him, and she would be brokenhearted once they separated.

He drew away and said, "Don't you dare fall in love in the future."

"I won't. I promise."

"Be careful in London. Be safe."

"I will tell you the same: Be careful. Be safe."

"I'll miss you."

"I'll miss you too."

With that, he strolled out. She couldn't guess how long they'd misbehaved, but there was a hint of dawn on the eastern horizon. She watched him chat with his poor horse. The animal had been very patient and had to be freezing, but it appeared to have forgiven the Captain for making him wait through the chilly hours.

The Captain mounted, saluted her, then trotted away.

He wasn't keen on goodbyes and he'd said plenty inside the cottage. Still though, she'd foolishly expected him to glance back, to call out a farewell. But he vanished into the trees, and she dawdled in the frigid air until the sound of his horse's hooves faded away.

She went into the parlor and the room was very empty without him in it. He'd burst into her life like a blazing comet, and she was thrilled that he'd enlivened her last days in Baywick. She'd remember him fondly and smile over the fact that—however briefly—she'd charmed a scoundrel. It was a secret she'd carry deep in her heart.

She was finally exhausted and she staggered off to bed. She yawned and snuggled under the quilts, and she thought she might toss and turn, that she might replay every moment of the delicious encounter in her mind, but she dozed off immediately. She didn't dream of him at all.

# Chapter 4

"It's about time you arrived. I was so afraid you'd be late."

Hester Crawford glared at her brother, Michael, wishing she could shame him with a glower, but he was a dedicated libertine who couldn't be brought to heel. Their parents had tried to control him. His school masters and navy commanders had tried, but he was an incorrigible wretch who thought he was smarter and better than everyone else.

He was handsome, dashing, and exuberant, and he marched through the world like an arrogant king. She, on the other hand, was meek and quiet, was subservient and dutiful, as was appropriate for an aging spinster. She was devout and modest, was moral and decent. She strictly obeyed the men the Good Lord had placed above her and she never rocked a boat or caused a scene.

Any person studying them together wouldn't have guessed they were siblings. There was naught about them that was similar. He was possessed of such striking looks that neighbors often whispered about how he couldn't possibly be a Crawford, that their mother must have had an affair. Their prior horse master, whom he resembled exactly, had been named as the culprit who'd sired him.

She was the typical Crawford: short, plain, ordinary, with very average brown hair and eyes. All of their relatives shared those same features. Michael, with his golden-blond hair and mesmerizing blue eyes, was the one who was completely different.

He was muscular and fit from his hard labor in the navy, while she'd grown very thin and could be described as emaciated. She was all jagged edges, her bones sticking out, as if spite and disappointment were eating her away on the inside. She'd never had the chance to marry and she was wasting away from her unending resentment.

She'd fallen madly in love once, with an actor in a traveling troupe who'd spent several weeks in the area. He'd been blond and gorgeous, flamboyant and exotic, and she'd been desperately anxious to be his wife. Her father had refused to allow the match though, and her dearest beau had fled in the middle of the night, never to return for her. At being abandoned by him, she'd been so bereft that she'd expected to pass away from despair.

A girl's parents picked her husband, and eventually, she'd forced herself to accept her father's edict, but it had left her bitterly unhappy and she'd never married. But a female wasn't supposed to remain single. What benefit was a spinster?

The debacle had altered her forever. Her eyes were dull and her brown hair had faded so it was mostly grey. Her face was lined with wrinkles from suffering decades of crushed hopes. She was only six years older than her attractive, exciting brother, but she was decrepit enough to be his grandmother.

"I told you I'd be here for the party," he said in answer to her comment. "Why would you have fretted?"

"You never keep your promises. Why would I have assumed you were being truthful?"

"I have to wed, Hester, and I have to wed in a hurry. You've found some viable contenders for me to consider so this distasteful process will be easy for me. If you've invited anyone suitable, I'll be able to select a bride with very little effort. Of course I'd show up to socialize. I want to finish this as much as you do."

He flashed a smile that made him look young and innocent, as if he could have been a cherub painted on a church ceiling. But she was aware of the corrupt heart that beat in his chest. His soul was blackened by vice and excess, and when he perished, he was going straight to Hell.

"Who is our first visitor?" he asked. "I've forgotten her name."

She sighed with exasperation. "This is important. Would you pay attention? I've repeated her personal information a dozen times so you're deliberately trying my patience."

"If she's tedious, and she doesn't tickle my fancy, why would I remember any detail about her?"

It was the sort of flippant remark he enjoyed spewing, and he knew it would aggravate her, so she hid her annoyance. "It's Miss Annette Adair. She's a great heiress and rumored to be very beautiful. As you have a shallow preference for a pretty face, I'm sure that news will thrill you. She's the premier candidate to appear on the Marriage Market in ages."

"Didn't you tell me she's twenty and she's been husband-hunting for three years already? If she's as splendid as people are claiming, why hasn't she been snatched up?"

"I believe she's fussy. She's so rich that she doesn't have to rush her decision. She can delay until she meets the precise fellow she's dying to have."

"What's your prediction, Hester? Will it be me?"

Hester snorted with disgust. "No. You're too obnoxious and she'll notice immediately that you're a scapegrace who has repulsive habits. I'm told she's seeking a malleable spouse who will dote on her constantly."

"That's probably not me."

"Exactly my point."

They were seated at the dining table in the breakfast parlor at Sutton House. Michael was eating and Hester was watching him. He'd reached the estate very late the prior evening and he'd slept the morning away. At two o'clock in the afternoon, he'd strutted down and demanded a plate of bacon and eggs.

The servants had jumped to accommodate him, but Hester was irked by his selfish conduct. He only thought of himself, and because of it, they were always at odds.

Sutton was the Earl's main residence, but Michael was never present. He hated the country and he never had a positive word to share about their parents. It shocked her to hear him denigrate them, to blithely ignore the Lord's Commandment to 'honor thy father and mother'.

As opposed to him, she'd never left home. She hadn't even gone away to boarding school, but had been taught by governesses in the nursery up on the third floor. Her sole wild escapade had been her furtive amour with the actor. After he'd broken her heart, after her father had pitched in to destroy her, she'd been too devastated to have a satisfying life.

Michael had inherited at eighteen, when she'd been twenty-four, and he'd been happy to stay in the navy, to let her run the manor her own way, but that era was ending. She was his older sibling, so it was her job to help him choose a bride, but she was in no hurry to bring his marriage to fruition.

Once he was wed, his wife would be mistress of Sutton House. She would make the rules and supervise the servants. Where would that leave Hester? She couldn't abide the notion of a stranger moving in and implementing procedures. The whole idea had her breathless with panic.

What if her sister-in-law didn't like her? What if she insisted Michael kick her out? Would he? If so, where would Hester go?

The situation was alarming and her nerves were on a frayed edge. Michael needed to wed, but she didn't want him to wed. It was a fatiguing conundrum that vexed her beyond her limit.

"When Miss Adair arrives," she said, "will you please be on your best behavior?"

"I'm always on my best behavior."

"Don't compound your sins by lying to me."

He smirked with amusement. "Will you be on *your* best behavior? Will you be cordial and welcoming for a change? You're frequently grouchy, but currently, you seem worse than usual. What's wrong?"

"The entire prospect of finding you a bride is very stressful for me."

"You don't have to do it. I specifically remember telling you that you didn't have to bother. You swore you were delighted to assist me."

"Yes, but the pressure is enormous. What if the girls are all horrid? What if you don't like any of them? Or what if you like one of them, but she turns out to be awful? What if you marry her, then you grow to loathe her? If you wind up in a doomed union, it will be my fault."

"The final decision is mine so how could it be your fault?"

"If it becomes a debacle, I'll be blamed. I'm always blamed."

"That might have been correct when Father and Mother were still with us, but when have I ever blamed you for anything? Name one occasion where I castigated you."

While she ceaselessly berated him, the truth was that he was very kind to her. No matter how she acted, or how vociferously she railed, he never railed back. She spent so many hours mentally reprimanding him that she forgot how he really treated her. He was such an indolent, apathetic wastrel that he was never distressed over any issue. He couldn't be stirred to outrage or fury. If catastrophe arose, he barely noticed.

She figured it came from his commanding navy ships. He was a brave, decorated warrior who'd survived many dangerous battles.

Nothing disturbed him and his typical lack of concern was so aggravating. He never fretted and she fretted incessantly.

The differences in their temperaments were a thorn in her side, and she felt as if he'd received all the stellar traits from their bloodline, and she'd received the piety and naught else.

"Your brother is with you," she caustically said, when she shouldn't have mentioned it. Caleb was a sore subject for them and they couldn't talk about him in a rational manner.

Michael was instantly on the defensive. "By *brother,* I assume you mean Caleb—who happens to be your brother too. You have to stop pretending he has no connection to us. You complain as if he's a stray mutt that wandered in the door when we weren't looking."

"Well, that's how I view him."

He gnawed on his cheek, biting down the curt comments he was yearning to hurl. "It's such a beautiful day, Hester. Don't annoy me with this nonsense. It's my first afternoon at home in months. Can't we avoid bickering over pointless topics?"

"I begged you not to bring him along. For the next several weeks, you're meeting various bridal candidates. They're from toplofty families so it's insulting for us to force them to endure his company. If word spreads in London that you have a bastard sibling strutting about, some of the mothers might refuse the invitations I've extended."

He tsked, as if she was a great trial. "Caleb is as welcome here as you are," he said, "and if a girl visits me, and she's a snob who can't understand my affection for him, then it will prove she's not the right wife for me."

"You always claim his presence isn't scandalous."

"It's not scandalous. Not to me anyway. Father was a monstrous hypocrite who bloviated about sin and damnation, but in the end, he was just as lust-filled as any other man. It's not Caleb's problem that Father couldn't keep his trousers buttoned."

She hated it when he uttered lewd remarks and her cheeks heated. "If people ask me about him, what am I to tell them? How will I explain his relationship to us?"

"It doesn't matter to me how you explain his relationship to you. As to me, he's my cherished little brother, who served as my cabin boy when he was younger, then my aide when he was older. I trust him with my life and he possesses all of my affection. How about that? Does that about cover it?"

"I couldn't describe him that way. I'd die of shame."

He tsked again. "I feel sorry for you, Hester. I wish you wouldn't be so judgmental. When you are, you sound exactly like Father, and I can't fathom why you'd ever want me to compare you to him."

He'd finished his meal, and he tossed down his napkin, stood, and sauntered out.

"Where are you going?" she asked. "We should discuss your socializing with Miss Adair. We should assess the activities I have planned for you."

He shivered with feigned horror, then halted and glanced back. "I won't engage in any activities. I'll speak to her a few times, then I'll apprise you of my opinion."

"She's scheduled to stay with us for two weeks."

"If she's dreadful, why would we have her tarry? I can't imagine that a fussy heiress, one who's searching for a husband who will dote on her, will capture my fancy at all. I'm betting it will be over quickly and we'll swiftly move on to the next girl."

He continued on, and she remained in her seat, ignoring the repugnant statement he'd voiced about Miss Adair. A footman was lurking in the corner and he'd heard the exchange. Shortly, he'd be down in the kitchen and the staff would be gossiping about it.

She dawdled so it wouldn't seem as if she was running out of the room. After a sufficient interval had passed, she left too, strolling slowly, as if she didn't have a care in the world.

If she was lucky, he'd pick Miss Adair and the whole charade would conclude rapidly. Or he might not like any of the girls she'd invited. The entire Spring Season might be consumed with him trying to decide—then not deciding. If that was the direction they were headed, how would she bear it?

Initially, when he'd asked her to scrounge up some candidates, she'd been proud and thrilled. Now though, it was simply exhausting and impossible. She was anxious and ill, and she rushed up the stairs to her bedchamber, desperate to hide and calm down.

Michael was easily bored at Sutton and he spent his hours out-of-doors, hunting, riding, or pursuing other manly interests, such as drinking himself silly at the tavern in the village. When she returned to the lower floors later on, he would likely be out of the house, and he'd have taken his bastard brother with him. She could only hope.

"I CAN'T BELIEVE I'M allowing you to traipse off alone."

Annette Adair scoffed with exasperation at her mother, Ambrosia.

"I won't be alone," Annette said. "Cousin Margaret will be with me. I'll be fine."

"I'm having a talk with Margaret before you depart. I have to clarify what I expect from her."

"Margaret doesn't need a lecture from you."

"You're aware of her sordid history."

Annette liked Margaret very much. She always had and she rolled her eyes in irritation. "She was seventeen when she flirted with those soldiers. They were sophisticated and very corrupt. You can't blame her for not recognizing the danger they posed. Besides, nothing happened!"

"So she says," her mother muttered.

"She was merely caught at a party she shouldn't have attended. A naïve girl is fodder for an unscrupulous rogue, and it's a mystery to me why you persist with persecuting her."

"After a female's base tendencies are revealed, it's important to make note of them. If they're let loose, they're rarely tamped down. A woman's life can spiral out of control very fast."

Annette snickered with amusement. "Normally, I think you're a very modern person, with modern attitudes and ideas, but then you spew an absurd remark like that, and it's obvious you're stuck in the prior century."

"A female just has her reputation as an asset. If it's squandered, she has no value."

"If you're so worried about her being my chaperone, why have her accompany me?"

"Who else could have done it? In addition, she's family so we don't have to pay her. That's always a benefit."

"You're being incredibly surly this morning and I figure it's because you're feeling poorly."

They were in her mother's bedchamber, and Ambrosia was snuggled against the headboard of her bed, her broken leg propped up by pillows. The splints and bandages detracted from her typical chic appearance. She hated to ever be viewed as less than glamorous.

The previous few months had been very stressful, and Annette suspected the strain had contributed to her mother's deteriorated state. Annette had been briefly betrothed to Nathaniel St. James, Lord Grenville, but it had collapsed in disaster. Ambrosia had been preoccupied over the fiasco so she hadn't been as focused as usual.

She'd slipped on the ice while climbing out of a carriage. The injury had been painful and incapacitating, but according to their physician, it was healing quickly and she'd soon be able to hobble about with a cane.

The news hadn't mollified her though, for she couldn't bear to be observed walking with a cane. She was forty, but she looked twenty-five, and she flaunted the notion that people thought she was much younger than she actually was. She intended to live forever and couldn't imagine growing old.

Annette was twenty, and they socialized together, being more like sisters than mother and daughter. They were rich, statuesque goddesses, with striking blond hair and stunning blue eyes. When they sauntered into a room, spectators gaped in awe, but Ambrosia's accident meant that many of their plans had been scuttled.

Most especially, it was preventing Ambrosia from making the trip to Sutton House. Annette would be introduced to Lord Sutton, with matrimony a possibility, and Margaret was escorting her instead. The Earl had finally retired from the navy, and he was home and preparing to select a bride. He wanted a hasty wedding and insisted on holding the ceremony before his birthday in June.

Annette was the first girl his sister, Hester, had arranged to stay with them, and it indicated she was the premier candidate. And she was; she wasn't being vain about it. It was simply a fact that she was wealthy, elegant, and beautiful, and at the moment, she had no competition on the Marriage Market.

No doubt Lord Sutton assumed *he* was scrutinizing her to discover whether she'd be suitable, but she would be assessing him just as avidly.

If she didn't like him, she didn't care what his opinion might be. She was the one who would have to tolerate his quirks and habits and she was very fussy. As she'd learned in her betrothal debacle with Lord Grenville, the road to the altar was very bumpy, and she wouldn't be tricked, shamed, or disrespected. She'd latch onto a spouse who would meet her lofty standards or she'd keep searching.

Her mother asked, "How will you explain your severed engagement to Lord Grenville? What about the legal claim we've filed for breach of promise? Lord Sutton will inquire about it and you must supply a satisfactory response."

"I'll tell him the truth: that Grenville was a lunatic who didn't deserve me. Everyone in the kingdom realizes he's insane. We gave him every chance to prove he should be my husband, but he failed every test we administered. For pity's sake, he wed his governess rather than me! If that doesn't demonstrate how deranged he was, I don't know what would."

Ambrosia clucked her tongue. "You have to be more subtle about it. Lord Grenville may be a renowned madman, but the aristocracy is a tight-knit club. They erect high walls and guard each other's backs. Lord Sutton is probably acquainted with Lord Grenville. They were probably chums at boarding school when they were boys. Even if they're not friends, he won't like to hear you denigrating a member of his exalted class."

Grenville had been a decorated soldier who'd been captured by Spanish mercenaries. He'd been a prisoner, in dire circumstances, and once he was ransomed, he'd returned to England in a desperate condition. The ordeal had wrecked his health and rattled his wits, so in agreeing to a betrothal, Annette had been taking a huge gamble, but her mother had convinced her it would be worth it in the end to be his countess.

He was a handsome devil, and he could be very charming when he tried, but during their abbreviated courtship, he'd repeatedly exhibited unhinged traits. She could have overlooked his eccentricities and faults, but he'd been in love with his governess. He'd refused to part from her, so Annette had cried off, then Ambrosia had sued him for wasting their time.

She and her mother were still coping with the aftermath, and while they struggled valiantly to pretend they'd been unaffected by the split, there was rampant speculation over what might be wrong with Annette, over why Grenville hadn't liked her. In any matrimonial mishap, the woman was always blamed, and the gossip was infuriating and exhausting.

"After what I endured with Grenville," Annette said, "I'm not in the mood to play games with a second nobleman. If Lord Sutton doesn't like my answers about Grenville, or on any other topic, he doesn't have to choose me. I'm not about to beg."

Ambrosia sighed. "You're twenty, Annette. If you're not careful, you'll wind up a spinster. Your reputation has already been dented because of Grenville's nonsense. You can't afford to immerse yourself in another quagmire. The rumors from your previous engagement haven't waned yet. Just imagine how frustrating the stories would be if Sutton tossed you over too."

"Don't rewrite my history with Grenville. He didn't toss me over! I walked away—due to his continually acting like a lunatic."

"People believe you're responsible," Ambrosia said. "It's the way the world works. You're aware of that fact."

"I'm very rich, Mother, and as you've always counselled, money smooths over many problems."

"It can't restore tarnished character."

"I'll keep that in mind."

Annette couldn't force herself to worry about her mother's warnings with regard to Lord Sutton. Ambrosia was being a particular grouch, and again, Annette chalked it up to her being injured. She had the constitution of a war horse, and she viewed herself as being too tough and resilient to be laid low by a paltry broken bone.

Annette's elderly father had earned his fortune as a sugar importer and she was his only child. Ambrosia had married him when she was very young and he'd had the good grace to die shortly afterward. He'd bequeathed everything to his widow and daughter and they used it to great effect.

They resided in ostentatious mansions. They wore clothes designed by the finest dressmakers in Paris. They draped themselves in expensive jewels, crafted by the eminent goldsmiths in Venice. Each step they took out in public was plotted to elicit a spectacular result, but she often felt as if she was an actress in a stage farce.

It was fatiguing to have to constantly be so magnificent, to have crowds staring, to never conduct herself in an ordinary fashion. Once she was wed, once she'd snagged the man of her dreams, she'd carry on more normally. She wouldn't have to be quite so grand and imperious.

"You're leaving tomorrow morning," Ambrosia said, "and you'll be at Sutton tomorrow night. You must write to me every evening to describe your daily interactions with the Earl. I'll reply immediately with advice about managing him."

Ambrosia loved house parties, and Annette understood that her mother couldn't bear to miss out on the fun. She said, when she didn't mean it, "I will send so many letters that you'll grow weary of reading them all."

Ambrosia always had Annette's marital candidates thoroughly investigated. She'd had Lord Sutton investigated too, but the invitation to Sutton House had arrived so swiftly that they hadn't obtained the full report she typically demanded. There were large holes in the information they should have gleaned.

"Don't forget what we learned about Lord Sutton," Ambrosia said. "He's aloof, abrupt, and detached. He doesn't like frivolous events or silly ninnies. Don't suggest any ridiculous outings and don't be silly around him. Spend every minute cajoling him so he assumes you have opinions and attitudes that are similar to his."

"His preferred hobbies are gambling and trollops." Facetiously, Annette asked, "How should I persuade him that we have similar likes and dislikes? Should I gamble with him? Should I be loose with my favors?"

"Don't be smart with me!" Ambrosia chided. "It makes me keen to scold you and I'm not sufficiently spry to engage in a bout of castigation."

Aristocratic men were raised to be cretins. From the moment they popped out of the womb, they were fawned over and told they were special. They believed it and caroused however they pleased. They wagered to excess. They consorted with dubious friends and involved themselves in reckless situations.

Most exasperatingly, they kept mistresses and reveled with slatterns. If a woman was insane enough to wed one of them, she had to turn a blind eye and ignore every moral lapse. Ambrosia had trained Annette to be a countess so she grasped what would be expected of her: She would have to tolerate her husband's infidelities and scandals.

She was trying to convince herself that she could be a meek wife, but deep down, she truly didn't suppose she was that accommodating.

"I'm running out of energy to continue our conversation," Ambrosia said. "Would you have Margaret attend me? I need to speak to her, then I'll have a nap."

"I'll find her and send her to you, but don't badger her about her past or about our trip to Sutton. I couldn't bear to depart on our journey, with her thinking I don't want her to come—or that you're certain she can't behave herself."

"I won't badger her."

"Famous last words," Annette mumbled.

"I simply wish I was escorting you myself. I hate that I'm not and I'm peevish because of it."

"I know."

"I've never met Lord Sutton," Ambrosia pointed out, "and I'd desperately like to take his measure. I should be there to evaluate his demeanor."

"I promise it will play out swimmingly so stop your fretting. You're not hale enough to worry about me."

"You're my only child. I can't help but worry."

Annette patted her mother's shoulder and left to locate Margaret. She and Ambrosia were closer than any mother and daughter had ever been, but on occasion, Ambrosia could be a suffocating parent. Annette was a tad gleeful to be traveling to Sutton without Ambrosia tagging along to watch her every move.

Margaret would be a much more obliging chaperone and they would have a marvelous visit. If romance flared, or if mischief occurred, Margaret would never tattle and Ambrosia didn't necessarily have to be apprised.

---

"You'll write to me every evening after the socializing winds down."

"I will."

Margaret smiled at Ambrosia, feeling sorry that she was injured, but also feeling very merry that the accident had opened such an amazing door—for Margaret!

It had been an eternity since she'd gone to a house party and she couldn't wait. She loved the country, loved fancy manors, loved gorgeous rooms and expensive décor. She loved being pampered by competent servants and she planned to pretend she was a princess on holiday.

"You'll provide me with every detail about Annette's day," Ambrosia said. "I'll be especially interested in her exchanges with the Earl. I'm curious about his sister too. She picked the contenders he's interviewing so she must have extra sway with him. Annette has to charm her. I can't risk that Annette might lose out on this opportunity merely because the spinster sister doesn't like her."

"Annette will be wonderful, Cousin," Margaret told her, "and I'm sad that you're in such a dither. You've raised her for this moment and she won't let you down."

"Are your clothes ready? Have the maids finished the alterations?"

"Yes, my clothes are ready. I will be so magnificently attired that people will assume *I* am the bridal candidate, rather than Annette."

Margaret was being flippant, and she'd intended the comment to be funny, but Ambrosia wasn't amused. Her gaze narrowed and she said, "While you're at Sutton, don't be putting on airs. A few new gowns can't better your circumstances."

"I apologize. I shouldn't have joked."

Margaret survived on her relatives' charity, and she was often supplied with pin money for essentials, but she had to work for the funds she received. She had an acceptable wardrobe, but the items were mostly conservative garments, with long sleeves and high collars, sewn in dull shades of grey and brown. Most times, anyone observing her would presume she was a governess.

Annette had whole rooms filled with her castoffs, and with Margaret heading to Sutton House, which was a mansion celebrated for its grandeur, Ambrosia hadn't been eager for her to show up looking like a pauper. She'd had Annette grab some gowns she didn't like or didn't want, and the maids had been in a stitching frenzy, reshaping them so they fit Margaret who was shorter and thinner.

Margaret would arrive at Sutton, appearing rich and settled. It was a sweet gesture, but at the same juncture, she was gnashing her teeth over Ambrosia's imperious manner. The stark differences between her situation and Annette's simply underscored that the world was a very unfair place.

She could have refused her cousin's rejects, could have marched into Sutton like a beleaguered nanny, but she hadn't refused. She wasn't sure what that capitulation indicated about her character, but she suspected she could be bought off with a pretty dress.

She'd known Ambrosia since she was little, but despite Ambrosia's excess wealth and her owning several large homes, she'd never offered to have Margaret live with her. And though Margaret had always liked Annette very much, Ambrosia had never allowed a genuine friendship to develop.

Whenever she'd attended various gatherings with her kin, Ambrosia would watch Annette like a hawk and whisk her away if she and Margaret grew too fond. For many years, Margaret had enjoyed a secret fantasy that she and Annette were twins who'd been separated at birth, that an evil fairy had separated them. In Margaret's very vivid imagination, the evil fairy had resembled Ambrosia exactly.

Ambrosia interrupted Margaret's pathetic reverie. "Annette has been apprised of Lord Sutton's preferences and aversions. Please study their encounters and be certain she's cozying up to him correctly. Keep focused on the Earl's sister too. Lady Hester? Don't permit Annette to ignore or aggravate her."

Margaret swallowed down a sigh of exasperation. "Annette will be fine and she'll handle this visit perfectly. You shouldn't fret over it so much. Your condition is so reduced and it can't be healthy for you."

"As I informed Annette, I don't mean to be surly, but the consequences are very important to our family. With how her prior betrothal collapsed, we can't have problems arise."

"If problems arise," Margaret loyally stated, "it will be the Earl's fault. Annette would never stir any trouble." Margaret paused, then added when she probably shouldn't have, "Annette tells me that Lord Sutton's name is Michael Crawford. I was recently introduced to a Michael Crawford, when I was in Baywick. You don't suppose it's the same fellow, do you?"

At the discovery, Margaret had been rattled, but Crawford was a common surname. What were the chances that the Earl had been slumming in Baywick? Would he have been playing a trick on lower mortals by hiding who he was?

Aristocrats engaged in that sort of juvenile antic. If she walked into Sutton House, and he was standing there, she would die of shame.

"In Baywick," Ambrosia asked, "was he presented as Sutton?"

"No. He'd been in the navy so everyone called him Captain Crawford. Even his brother referred to him as Captain."

"What did he look like?"

"Tall, blond, brawny, dashing. He was quite fascinating."

Ambrosia scowled. "I haven't met him, but I've met others of his kin. They're short, dark-haired, and plain in their features so it wouldn't have been him. Plus, a nobleman loves to have people bow down so he would never have concealed his identity. And as far as I'm aware, he doesn't have a brother."

"If Lord Sutton is short and plain," Margaret said a tad too impishly, "would you still like Annette to marry him?"

"She's marrying his title. Not him. His attractiveness—or lack of it—is irrelevant."

Margaret nearly choked on her scoff of derision. She'd been tantalized by two rogues in her life—Sergeant Moneypenny and Captain Crawford—and she thought handsomeness was paramount in assessing a beau. What sane maiden would willingly pick a short, plain suitor?

Annette was tall for a woman. What if Lord Sutton was shorter than she was? Wouldn't that be awkward?

Ambrosia was fading, clearly needing a nap, and Margaret was hoping to be dismissed. But Ambrosia wasn't finished with her, and when she spoke again, Margaret couldn't tamp down a wince.

"As to you," Ambrosia said, "and how you'll conduct yourself at Sutton, I'm sorry, but I have to offer a few comments."

Margaret bristled. "I wish you wouldn't."

"I realize you would like us to forget your adolescent scandal."

"I don't understand why all of you constantly harp about it."

"You proved yourself to be naïve and gullible. You also proved that, given the right circumstances, you'll exhibit loose morals. You don't make wise choices."

Margaret bit her tongue so hard that she was surprised she didn't draw blood. She yearned to utter a scornful reply, but when she and Annette were leaving in the morning, she wouldn't voice any remark that might cause Ambrosia to change her mind about Margaret escorting Annette.

"I was a girl when it happened," she said as steadily as she could manage, "and I'm almost a decade older. I learned my lesson, and since that humiliating evening, I haven't once disgraced myself."

"Let's keep it that way. A house party is a veritable den of intrigue and amour. They're often compared to sea voyages, where strangers flirt briefly and behave in a fashion they wouldn't normally countenance. I have no doubt the Earl will have several exciting guests in attendance. They will be London scoundrels who spend their leisure time seducing trollops."

"A scoundrel couldn't entice me if he paid me a thousand pounds."

"Virtuous females suppose that to be the case, but a libertine can be so alluring. It's a problem with our gender that we can't resist a roué. You must swear you'll carry on appropriately. You can't participate in a single deed or conversation that would bring disrepute to me or Annette."

Margaret considered grabbing the pompous woman and shaking her for being so infuriating, but she responded as calmly as she was able. "I won't embarrass you. I swear it."

Ambrosia studied her dubiously, as if Margaret was not only a renowned tart, but a renowned liar too. Ultimately, she nodded with satisfaction, as if her stern lecture had drummed out Margaret's awful proclivities.

"When you're done at Sutton," Ambrosia said, "if you've performed up to my high standards, I'll find you another situation. It will be a spot that's fun and worthwhile, as a reward for your stellar assistance."

"I appreciate it and I won't disappoint you."

"That's good to know. You're excused."

Like an arrogant queen, Ambrosia gestured toward the door. Margaret flashed a fake smile, then slipped into the hall. She hovered silently so her temper could cool.

Ambrosia wasn't even an Adair. She'd married into the family, but she flaunted herself as if she were the supreme ruler of it. Her husband had left her very rich, and she presumed her wealth made her superior and important, but she'd started at a level in the world that was much lower than Margaret's. Fate and luck had lifted her up and it was galling for Margaret to be demeaned and scolded.

How dare Ambrosia nag at her! How dare she assume Margaret would act improperly!

Well, Margaret was heading to a posh, fabulous country party, and Ambrosia was trapped in her bed, with her leg bound in splints. For all of Ambrosia's affluence and pretension, she only had Annette in her life. Margaret was alone too, but she was going to revel for two whole weeks, and she wouldn't permit Ambrosia's cruel words to bother her in the slightest.

She spun away and hurried to her bedchamber, eager to check her traveling trunks to be sure the maids hadn't forgotten to pack any of her pretty gowns.

She hoped Lord Sutton's home was filled with London dandies, that they thought she was gorgeous and glamorous. If Ambrosia ever complained about it, Margaret would tell her to mind her own business. Then she'd waltz off with her new friends and be ecstatic forever.

Her dreams never came true, but she didn't stop wishing. There was a peculiar energy in the air, and she was feeling that any wild ending might be possible. Lord Sutton's event could change everything. Why couldn't she expect it would?

Why not?

# Chapter 5

THE COACH SLOWED, THEIR driver maneuvering the turn onto the Sutton estate. Margaret tugged on the curtain and peeked out as they passed under the sign that indicated they'd arrived.

There was a ton of snow on the ground, the air cold and blustery, so it was a horrid time to be traveling. Only the heartiest souls were out and about, but Lord Sutton wanted to marry quickly, so girls who were interested in applying for the position of wife/countess had to bundle up, brave the elements, and pretend they hadn't frozen on the way to his home.

In the summer, the area would be lush and verdant, but at the moment, it was miles of grey and brown. The weather would lock them inside for the duration of their stay, so they'd fill the hours with playing cards, reading by the fire, and having quiet conversations.

Margaret didn't require excessive activity in order to enjoy herself, so for her, the placid entertainments would be fine. She didn't suppose Annette would like them though. Her cousin was used to socializing in London so she was accustomed to livelier events. She liked being the center of attention too, and when she would be surrounded by only a small group of Lord Sutton's friends and relatives, it wouldn't provide her with much of a stage upon which to flaunt herself.

They'd journeyed to Sutton in Ambrosia's fanciest vehicle, and it was being pulled by six matching white horses that had ribbons braided in their tails and manes. There were four outriders on the corners, dressed in the Adair red livery. With a huge crest on the door, it would appear as if royalty was approaching, but then, Ambrosia always liked to make a showy entrance.

She was determined that the Crawford family, but especially Lord Sutton, be agog over her obvious wealth.

"It looks like we're here," she said to Annette.

"Praise be. The blankets have kept me plenty warm, but I'm starting to feel the chill."

"Are you nervous?" Margaret asked. "Are you excited? Or are you completely apathetic?"

"I'm not nervous or excited. I'd just like to get my marriage arranged once and for all. This husband-hunting has been exhausting."

"I can't fault you for your delays. It would be a disaster to wind up shackled to the wrong fellow."

Annette sputtered with amusement. "True, and I can't forget how lucky I was that Lord Grenville slithered off my hook to wed his governess. What if he and I had tied the knot, but he'd persisted with his affair? Can you imagine the shame I'd have had to endure?"

Her failed betrothal still had tongues wagging in High Society. People couldn't stop tittering about it. If Margaret hadn't liked Annette quite so much, she might have found the stories to be humorous, but she was fond of her cousin, and she hated that Annette's name was being maligned.

"Your mother told me that Lord Sutton is short, plain, and ordinary," Margaret said. "Weren't you hoping for a spouse who is handsome and dashing? After your lengthy nuptial search, wouldn't you rather glom onto a suitor who makes your pulse race?"

"Lord Grenville was very handsome, which I liked, but he was also a deranged lunatic who treated me hideously. It taught me that I shouldn't focus on physical characteristics and I've lowered my standards."

Margaret chuckled. "What standard is guiding you now?"

"I want a man who is kind and devoted, who will esteem and admire me. I won't have a gambler or philanderer. I won't have a husband who consorts with trollops, where I am constantly humiliated. I need someone better than that."

Margaret had never known of a nobleman who didn't revel with tarts, who didn't carry on in disgusting ways, so Annette was being incredibly naïve, but she didn't mention it.

"What if Lord Sutton is awful? What then?" Margaret asked.

"Then I'll continue searching. When you consider the size of my dowry, I ought to be able to find the perfect candidate, and I'm too much of an optimist to settle for less than I deserve."

It was the type of comment Ambrosia might have voiced, as if Annette was slowly turning into her mother, and Margaret was depressed to witness it. Deep down, Annette had a sweet disposition, but Ambrosia ruled her with an iron thumb. With each passing year, they were more similar.

"Ambrosia's maids were gossiping about Lord Sutton," Margaret said. "They claim he's a gambler and womanizer. Have you heard that too?"

"Yes, I heard it. Mother had him investigated and his base traits were thoroughly documented. There are never very many aristocrats available for matrimony so she forced me to accept his invitation anyway."

"We haven't even met him yet," Margaret pointed out, "but he's already been described as possessing numerous qualities you abhor. Are we walking into a trap? Will this be a futile visit?"

"Probably," Annette admitted, "but may I share a secret with you?"

"Yes, of course. You're aware of how circumspect I can be."

"I expect to have fun at this party, whether I like the Earl or not." Annette flashed a wicked grin. "I'm so glad you accompanied me instead of Mother. On occasion, she can be very fatiguing, and I will confess to being aggravated with her over the entire debacle with Lord Grenville."

Margaret was stunned that Annette would utter a negative criticism of Ambrosia. "Why are you aggravated? What did she do?"

"She pushed me relentlessly to ignore his faults. Even when it became clear he was a wretch and a liar, she kept insisting he'd improve if we were patient. He simply grew worse, and now, she pretends she's blameless for how it collapsed. The weight of the scandal landed on me, but she acts as if she was an innocent bystander."

"My goodness, Annette. I can't believe you confided all of that."

Annette shrugged. "Who else would I tell? You're a true friend and I trust you. You won't blab my complaints to the world."

"Your opinion about your mother has definitely changed."

"I try to be obedient and dutiful, but she can really be annoying. She's not here and you are. Let's make a pact to engage in every bit of amusement we can manage to garner for ourselves."

"I will agree to that, just so our conduct never devolves into genuine mischief. I can't misbehave myself and I can't allow you to misbehave either."

"I not talking about *mis*behavior," Annette said. "I'm talking about having the freedom to breathe without Ambrosia sucking all the air out of the room."

Margaret likely should have offered a cautionary statement, but she was forestalled by the coach rattling to a halt. She peeked out again and discovered that they'd reached the manor.

It was a magnificent house, four stories high, with a center section and two wings that went on forever. The older portion must have once been a castle for there were turrets and what might have been a drawbridge.

The winter days were short so the sun was setting in the west. The sky was painted in shades of orange and lavender, the waning rays reflecting off the hundreds of windows, so the building appeared to glow. In the distance, there were barns, stables, orchards, parkland, and cottages for the upper-level servants.

The property was immaculately groomed for maximum effect. The careful tending verified the longevity of the Crawford family, their lengthy connection to the loftiest echelons of the British aristocracy, and it underscored the prize Annette would secure for herself if Lord Sutton picked her to be his countess.

Outside the vehicle, their outriders were busy lowering the step. Annette had brought an enormous amount of luggage—enough for a decade, they'd joked before their departure—and it was being unloaded.

A large cadre of servants had flooded out to stand at attention. There was a skinny, elderly woman in the middle, and from her plain gown and weary countenance, Margaret figured she was the house-keeper. There wasn't a single male who might have been the Earl.

Surely, he would be present to greet Annette. Wouldn't he be?

Annette was thinking the same and she asked, "Is Lord Sutton there? What's he look like?"

"I don't see anyone who might be him. There are many servants, with the housekeeper seeming to have assumed the role of official welcomer."

Night was falling so the temperature was rapidly dropping. The servants weren't bundled for the weather and they were starting to shiver.

"People are freezing," Margaret said. "We should hurry and debark so they don't turn into ice sickles."

Annette frowned. "I can't get out until Lord Sutton is there."

"He's probably waiting for you in the foyer."

The door was yanked open and an outrider stuck in his hand to help them down.

"I'm not ready!" Annette hissed to Margaret, an unusual fit of nerves sweeping over her.

"You'll be fine," Margaret insisted. "I'll climb out first. How does that sound?"

"Thank you. I just need an extra minute to muster my courage." She leaned nearer and whispered, "And if Lord Sutton is horrid, don't you dare leave me alone with him."

Margaret snickered caustically. "I won't abandon you. I swear."

The outrider guided Margaret down, then Annette emerged too. For a moment, they dawdled, wrapped in their expensive fur hats and cloaks. The servants assessed them, trying to decide which one was the bridal candidate and which the companion. Margaret placed a palm on Annette's back and urged her forward.

She took the hint and marched over, heading directly for the woman Margaret had supposed was the housekeeper. On closer inspection though, she wasn't as old as she'd initially appeared. Her face was lined, and her brown hair mostly grey, but she had to be in her thirties.

She smiled a thin, cool smile, then said, "Hello, Miss Adair. I am Lady Hester Crawford. I am Lord Sutton's sister. We're so glad you've come."

"Hello, Lady Hester. I am delighted to meet you." Annette glanced at Margaret and said, "This is my cousin, Miss Margaret Adair. We're thrilled to have the chance to visit."

Margaret sensed Annette's surprise at laying eyes on Hester Crawford. She was suffering her own bit of shock. With Lady Hester playing matchmaker for her brother, they'd expected a beautiful, glamorous sibling. Not this scrawny, petite, obviously miserable female. She seemed unhappy and unpleasant, as if she'd been beaten down by circumstances. Margaret hoped her brother wasn't possessed of her same dour bearing.

Lady Hester pointed out some of the more important servants, then she gestured to the front doors. There was still no sign of Lord Sutton.

"Shall we go in?" Lady Hester said.

"Yes, let's do," Annette responded.

"You must be chilled to the bone from your trip so we have fires burning in your bedchambers. The flames will warm you on the outside, and we have mulled ale to warm you on the inside."

"You're very kind," Annette told her.

The group walked in, with Lady Hester and Annette leading the way. Margaret was behind them, then the butler, housekeeper, footmen, and maids. In the foyer, they shucked off their fur cloaks and hats, as the footmen hauled in their luggage. Lord Sutton still wasn't introduced to them.

In the chaos, it was easy for Margaret to murmur to a housemaid, "Will we be meeting Lord Sutton this afternoon?"

The girl's cheeks flushed with embarrassment, and she peered about to ensure no one was listening. Then she murmured too. "He's been out. Riding? We heard he'll be here this evening, but that doesn't always turn out to be true."

Lady Hester was talking to Annette, explaining, "Supper will be served at nine, with beverages and socializing at eight. I've assigned maids for both of you. If you need anything, if you have questions or requests, let them know. They'll show you up to your rooms and I'll see you at eight."

As they were escorted up the stairs, Margaret whispered to Annette, "Lord Sutton isn't on the premises."

Annette raised a brow. "What would you imagine that indicates?"

"I wouldn't try to guess. He's been out riding, but he's supposed to be back soon."

Annette scoffed and facetiously muttered, "Aren't I special that I can drag him home?"

It was a bad beginning and Margaret suspected it would go downhill very fast.

---

MICHAEL WAS HEADED TOWARD the drawing room where their guests were waiting for him. Along with Annette Adair, he'd forced Hester to invite a dozen people from London. They were a motley collection of his dubious acquaintances, as well as his current paramour, Rowena Smithwaite.

Hester had been loathe to include them, but he hadn't been inclined to tarry at Sutton without them being around to enliven the festivities. He'd demanded, and she'd folded, but she was incensed about it. If Caleb bothered to eat with them, and he normally wouldn't, there would be seventeen in all. In Michael's view, that was about twelve too many.

He was in a foul mood and in no condition to fraternize, but he was working hard to control his temper and adjust his attitude. Hester had been in a nervous frenzy over Miss Adair's arrival, but Michael hadn't worried about it until the time had neared for the bloody girl to roll up the driveway.

In most instances, he pictured himself as being very brave, but apparently, in the matter of picking a bride, he was a complete coward. The more he'd pondered the situation, the more terrified he'd become. Ultimately, he'd saddled a horse and had snuck away. He'd galloped down rural lanes for hours, stopping occasionally at taverns to have a whiskey and warm himself by the fire.

Darkness and the frigid weather had pushed him home, and he'd perfectly planned his absence so he'd missed Miss Adair's grand entrance. Hester had already accosted him over his inexcusable conduct and her nagging had been exasperating. He wasn't ten and he didn't appreciate being scolded.

He realized he'd been discourteous, so he and Miss Adair had gotten off on the wrong foot, but he wasn't concerned about her tender sensibilities. If she was a trembling ninny who could be distressed over such a minor slight, she wasn't the correct candidate to be his wife.

He approached the door, and the butler was hovering, watching for him. The old fellow liked to wallow in the pomp of the moment. Michael winked at him and he stepped in and announced, "Ladies and gentlemen, may I present Captain Michael Crawford, our most-revered Lord Sutton?"

Everyone froze, then his friends—who never saw much of his haughty demeanor in town—laughed and clapped. But it was in a sarcastic way, meant to apprise him that they didn't deem him to be all that marvelous.

He gamboled in town with villains and trollops, and he carried on despicably so he'd seem like one of the crowd. Yet with his being anxious to intimidate Miss Adair, he was flaunting his status and wealth. He was dressed in formal attire, a black velvet suit, soft white shirt, a cravat sewn from the finest Belgian lace.

His blond hair was tied with a black ribbon and slicked down with a fragrant pomade. He'd finished off his ensemble by retrieving a stash of jewels from the vault. His fingers, cravat, and cuffs sported an array of gems that were probably worth more than the budgets of several small countries combined.

Miss Adair and her mother were up-jumped nobodies, with new money, and they paraded themselves through High Society like royalty. They were eager for him to believe *he* was lucky they were considering him, but he was very rich too, and he was descended from a lengthy line of aristocrats who'd ruled England for centuries. He'd gone overboard in displaying his own splendor and magnificence.

He strolled into the room and Hester was waiting for him. She took his arm and escorted him over to a female who had to be Miss Adair. His first impression was that she was stunning. She was blond and voluptuous, and she exuded a willowy languor that a man couldn't help but notice. He was a randy dog and he immediately calculated how difficult it would be to seduce her.

He should have been ashamed of himself for thinking it, but he'd never learned to mind his manners.

His second impression was that, if this was the type of girl Hester had found for him to evaluate, then she'd done a bang-up job and they were on the right track.

"Michael," Hester said, "this is our special guest, Miss Annette Adair. Miss Adair, this is my brother, Lord Sutton."

Miss Adair studied him scathingly, her pique evident. Eventually, she gave a snotty nod and claimed, "I'm delighted to finally cross paths with you."

She put extra emphasis on the word *finally,* informing him that he was a rude beast. He flashed a winning smile, the one that made fetching maidens melt in their slippers. "I apologize for being away when you arrived. I was riding and it was such a lovely afternoon that I couldn't force myself to stop."

He offered the comment politely enough, but he wanted to be sure she recognized that he'd deliberately stayed away, that *he* had selected the time when they'd be introduced. It was a petty vanity, but then, he was a renowned narcissist who suffered from many trivial conceits.

Off to the side, a woman gasped with astonishment, then a champagne glass fell to the floor and shattered with a loud crash. People whipped around to find out who had dropped it. The crowd parted, and there was Margaret Adair, gaping at him as if he might be a ghost.

When he'd stumbled on her in Baywick, he'd wondered if she might be related to Annette Adair, but he'd refrained from inquiring because he'd refused to pry out any details about her. Now, she was standing before him, like an unexpected gift. She'd appeared, as if by magic, and the party had just grown a bit more interesting.

He smirked, relishing how he'd surprised her, how he'd tricked her, how he'd astounded her. "Hello, Margaret. Fancy meeting you here."

"*You* are Lord Sutton?" she asked, sounding aghast.

"In the flesh." He chuckled, as if his true identity was all a big joke.

She didn't think it was funny though. She spun to her cousin and said, "Would you excuse me, Annette? I'm not feeling well." Then to Hester, "I must beg your pardon, but I won't be able to join you for the meal."

Hester was confused, Annette too, and Annette said to Margaret, "Do you know each other?"

"No!" Margaret firmly stated, as Michael boasted, "Margaret and I are old, old friends."

Margaret huffed with outrage and told her cousin, "He and I are not friends. We're not anything."

She dashed out, frantically shoving onlookers as she raced off. They watched her leave, the peculiar exit like a scene in a theatrical play. Once her footsteps had faded down the hall, the group began to chatter about what they'd witnessed.

Miss Adair was about to question him over the odd incident, Hester too, but they were prevented by the butler ringing the gong and declaring, "Supper is served! If you'll follow me?"

Like ants marching through the grass, they moved into their appropriate places. He was at the front, and normally, Miss Adair would have been farther back, but as Hester had mentioned, she was their honored guest. He would be at the head of the table, and she would be in the next most prominent seat, as his nearest companion, so they could become acquainted.

It had already dawned on him that the meal would be a slow torture. She was very pretty, but she was easily offended, so she'd never be amused by his antics. He was adept at being irritating, but usually after he'd behaved like a buffoon, he could charm an irked female into forgiving him.

Hester had previously apprised him that Miss Adair was snooty, proud, and very set on herself. She wouldn't be inclined to ignore his flaws and it would be difficult for him to muster the energy to put a smile on her face. He was snooty and proud too, and he didn't suppose he should have to placate any woman. Particularly not one who was hoping to be his countess.

He led them into the ostentatious dining room and he sat down and motioned for the wine to be poured. But all the while, he was staring at the rear door, wishing Margaret would calm down and return. If she had, she'd have been located at the other end of the table, so he couldn't have talked to her, but he would have savored the opportunity to glance down and see her.

After they'd separated in Baywick, he'd pushed her out of his mind, but it occurred to him that he might have enjoyed their flirtation much more than he should have. He might have missed her much more than he'd understood.

She would tarry in his home for two weeks, and as he'd noticed in Baywick, he couldn't stay away from her. The universe was demanding they remain cordial and Fate had brought her to his side again. There had to be a reason for it and he was excited to have the chance to discover what it was.

He couldn't wait to get started.

# Chapter 6

Margaret had been pacing in her bedroom for hours and her anger and alarm were both on a sharp edge. She was frantically debating what her next steps should be. There was no question that she needed to flee Sutton House. Immediately. She couldn't tarry and watch Lord Sutton court Annette.

She'd packed her bags, then had unpacked them. Then she'd packed them again and had unpacked them. She written a dozen rather hysterical letters to Ambrosia, informing her that she couldn't stay at Sutton, then she'd torn them up and had thrown them in the fire.

There wasn't a single excuse she could supply to Ambrosia that would sound plausible. Her kin already viewed her as naïve, flighty, and loose, and if she tried to quit—on the first day of her temporary post—she'd be labeled as irresponsible and unreliable too.

The door opened and she whipped around, suspecting it would be Annette, finally coming to check on her, but her fingers were crossed too that it wouldn't be her cousin.

Margaret had to explain her prior liaison with Michael Crawford, but she couldn't imagine confessing it. How could she ever clarify the affection that had swirled between them in Baywick? How could she remain at Sutton and be a distraction during Annette's marital maneuvering?

But her visitor wasn't Annette.

"Get out of here! Right now!" she fumed at Lord Sutton.

He was a vain wretch so of course he didn't heed her. He shut the door with a determined click, and he had the audacity to lock it, then stick the key in his pocket.

"I'm sorry I didn't sneak up earlier," he said, "but with me being the host, I couldn't escape."

"Are you insane? You can't be in my room!"

"I've arrived, and I'm not leaving, so your complaint is moot."

"Give me that key!"

"No."

He sauntered over to her, and there was an exciting charge in the air, almost as if their proximity was igniting sparks. In the short period she'd been in London, she'd forgotten how thrilling it was to wallow in his presence. He approached until they were toe to toe, and he smiled down at her, looking decadent and wonderful. Her anatomy, down to the smallest pore, rippled with pleasure.

"Were you surprised to stumble on me?" he asked. "Have I astonished you?"

"When you were flirting with me in Baywick, were you aware that Annette was my cousin? Did you ingratiate yourself as some sort of sick game? Are you hoping to humiliate me? To shame me? What?"

"I didn't know you and Annette were related."

She scoffed with disgust. "I don't believe you."

"I had been apprised that I would meet with a bridal candidate named Annette Adair, and when I learned your surname, I briefly pondered whether you might be connected to her. Ultimately, I decided it was too far-fetched. I mean, what are the odds?"

"You're such a liar and this isn't funny. I'm devastated by this turn of events."

"No, you're not." He snorted like the arrogant ass he could definitely be. "You're ecstatic to have crossed paths with me again."

"You are so full of yourself."

"You could be right about that. Have you missed me?"

"If I have, I wouldn't stroke your massive ego by admitting it."

Without any warning, he dipped down and kissed her. For a fleeting instant, she sighed with delight and kissed him back, but her common sense quickly kicked in and she lurched away.

"Ah!" she shrieked. "What are you thinking?"

"I'm *thinking* I've missed you very much. You're too proud to admit it, but I'm not. I'm so glad you're here."

"I'm in your home, *Lord* Sutton, because Annette is contemplating marriage to you. In case you didn't realize it, she's eager to become your countess."

"I can't deny that it would be a grand elevation for her," he pompously stated.

"Yes, it would be, but you and I had a previous dalliance!"

"Yes, so?"

"I have to tell her about us, then I have to head to London."

He gaped at her as if she were a madwoman who was speaking in tongues. "Why would you have to tell her and why would you flit back to town?"

"Since you're her possible fiancé, I can't be her chaperone. It's highly inappropriate."

"Inappropriate for who?"

"For Annette and for me."

He appeared bewildered by her vehemence, and she supposed he was so accustomed to reveling in vice and iniquity that he rarely focused on the more detailed aspects of social interaction.

"You being ridiculous," he said, "and I'm not listening to you."

"How am I being ridiculous? You and I are intimately attached, yet you're considering a betrothal to my cousin. You seem to presume it would be humorous to have me dawdle and watch you court her. Have you any idea how much that would hurt me?"

"It would hurt you? Really?" He chuckled, as if the prospect amused him.

"Yes, you aggravating dunce. It would kill me."

To her great horror, tears flooded her eyes, and on observing them, his expression softened.

"Don't be sad," he murmured and he pulled her into his arms.

She should have yanked away, but she didn't. There had been so few occasions in the past when anyone had extended sympathy, and she was like a winter flower needing his affection like spring sunshine. If he felt like extending comfort, she didn't have the strength to resist.

"I don't have anything that's truly mine," she babbled like the pathetic ninny she was. "I don't have any money. I don't have a husband or home. I have no power to control my fate. Since my parents died when I was seven, I've had to grovel to my relatives for every tiny boon and they are stingy and greedy. My existence is an unending slog of placating cruel dolts I don't like or respect."

"You don't like or respect Annette?" he asked.

"I love Annette," she loyally insisted. "Out of all my kin, she's the only one who's ever treated me kindly, but I don't want to share you with her. I want to keep you for my very own."

"You sound as if you'd like to be my wife instead of her. You know that's not possible."

"It's not that. I recognize that I'm not an aristocrat's daughter or an heiress, so I could never bring any item of value to the nuptial negotiating table. It's that our flirtation in Baywick was very special to me. You're a private secret that made me happy, and now, it can't belong just to me anymore."

"I'm not that marvelous," he said. "I'm not worth suffering any woe."

"I agree. You're rude, temperamental, and abrasive. You have no manners and you don't care how others view you."

"Those are some of my least offensive traits. Trust me. I'm a thousand times more appalling than you could ever imagine."

"Exactly, but Annette is determined to be a countess so she won't mind. She'll probably wind up wed to you, so where will that leave me? Can you answer that question?"

"No, except to firmly declare that you're not departing for London. If you try, I swear I'll chase after you and drag you back."

She tsked miserably. "I'm sure you would."

"You have to tarry at Sutton so you can entertain me."

"Have you the slightest clue of how dreadful that would be? How, precisely, would I entertain you? Would I walk behind you and Annette when you stroll in the garden? Later on, would I be required to gush over how perfect you look together?"

"Do you think she and I would suit?"

"Ooh, be silent! Please! Have mercy on me!"

She shoved him away and staggered over to the dresser. After she'd fled the drawing room, a housemaid had delivered a supper tray and it was still sitting there with the food unconsumed. She'd been too agitated to eat. A decanter of wine had been included, and she poured a glass and swallowed a huge gulp, desperate to quell the shaking of her hands.

He studied her every move, as if she were a peculiar creature in the forest he'd chanced upon by accident.

"I'm serious, Margaret," he said. "What is your opinion about my marrying your cousin? Take yourself out of the equation and tell me if she and I would be compatible."

"She'd be the ideal bride for you," she caustically spat. "She's gorgeous, sweet, and educated. She would be an asset to your family and she's so beautiful that your friends would drool with envy over your managing to snag her."

At her recitation of Annette's stellar qualities, she couldn't have predicted what his response might be, but the one he chose made her laugh—but with despair.

"I don't really have any friends," he said.

"Then who are those people fawning over you downstairs?"

"They're sycophants and hangers-on. They're gamblers, wastrels, and slatterns who enjoy being able to boast having a connection to me."

"That is a very sorry statement about the condition of your life."

"Isn't it though?"

He grinned as if they were conspirators, then he sidled over to her. He grabbed her wine, downed the contents, then put the glass on the tray.

"I'm tired of talking about your cousin," he said.

"I'm not particularly thrilled to discuss her with you either."

"We won't debate the fact that I could wed her. We'll focus on *you* and how delighted I am to have stumbled on you again."

"Weren't you listening? I'm *not* delighted and we could be speaking in different languages."

"I grasp what's vexing you. You're dismayed that you can't be the girl I'm seeking. You hate that your cousin fills the role exactly, but you never could."

"Well…yes."

"You're depressed that you and I are incredibly besotted, but it's your cousin who will get to have me as her husband."

"Right again."

"So we'll ignore those issues and deem them to be irrelevant."

"How can we? You're an experienced libertine who likely has a paramour lurking around every corner, but I'm just a spinster and poor relative. I have a very tender heart and I can't let you break it."

"I won't break it. I swear," he said.

"You shouldn't tell lies. You might be struck by lightning and I'm standing so close to you that I'd be struck too."

Apparently, she wasn't being sufficiently amenable. She wasn't accepting his falsehoods and fictions and he was a bit irked. "How would you rather proceed?" he asked. "Shall we avoid each other? Shall we act as if we're strangers? Shall we pretend we're not smitten?"

"What other solution is there?"

"You're being absolutely absurd and you've exhausted me with your complaints."

With that, he kissed her again, their bodies crushed tight from chests to toes. She shouldn't have allowed the embrace, but she was overcome by affection and desire for him and she couldn't build any walls to deflect his enormous charm.

When they were together, an eerie perception swirled, as if they were meant for one another. Fate seemed to be pushing them into a collision, but to what end?

There could be no viable conclusion for her. He was a dedicated scoundrel who could carry on in any negligent fashion that tickled his fancy, but she didn't dare succumb to his sly seduction. Only ruin could result, yet when he was holding her, when he was kissing her, it was so difficult to remember the moral code that was supposed to guide her and restrict her options.

There might have been an angel and a devil perched on her shoulders. The angel was warning her to behave herself, but the devil was urging her to forget every lesson she'd been taught about right and wrong. The devil's voice was much louder than the angel's, and she was terrified she'd heed his destructive advice.

On that quiet night in Baywick, when Michael had knocked on her cottage door and had needed his wounds tended, she'd convinced herself that she could flirt with him without consequence. She'd convinced herself that no one would be hurt by it, but with Annette in the picture, that was no longer true.

Annette would be hurt by any dalliance. Ambrosia would be hurt by it. His sister, Hester, would be hurt. And Margaret would be thoroughly and completely destroyed. Yet still—*still!*—she didn't desist.

The interval began innocently enough, but it grew to be passionate and even a tad desperate. She comprehended that she was being ensnared in his web of deceit and scandalous conduct, but she didn't care.

They continued forever, until the fire was out and the lamp started sputtering. The house was silent, as guests had slunk off to their beds. She and Michael might have been the last two people in the world. They were locked away and it was clear their wonderful, dangerous fascination had been reignited.

No doubt it would collapse into a huge morass and she'd fall into a deep hole from which she'd never be able to extricate herself. But he was just so amazing and he was kissing her as if he'd never wanted to do anything else. How could she regret what they'd commenced?

Finally, he drew away, but he didn't release her. He kept her cradled to his chest, as if she was precious and rare.

"Promise me you won't sneak back to London when I'm not looking," he said.

"I should leave," she grudgingly mumbled.

"But you won't."

"No, I probably won't."

"There's a magical spell wrapping around us," he said.

"It's not magic. You're simply a very skilled libertine and I don't have the strength to resist you."

"Why would you resist me?"

"Must you consider Annette as a bridal candidate? If you betroth yourself to her, it will kill me."

"I can't decide what I think about any of this."

"I realize how selfish you can be, and that it would be a massive leap for you to worry about someone other than yourself, but could you try to view this from my perspective?"

He didn't reply to her plea, but said, "You've sworn to remain at Sutton with your cousin and you're serious, aren't you? You're not a liar like me? You've given me your word and you mean it."

"Yes, I mean it," but she wasn't sure she was sincere.

She specifically noticed that she'd begged him not to proceed with Annette, but he'd conveniently neglected to respond. If he began to court Annette, Margaret wouldn't tarry to watch it unfold, and she'd break any vow she'd offered. He couldn't force her to dawdle and cheer him on.

He hugged her tight, then he eased away and went to the door. He spun the key, then he paused to stare over at her.

They shared a poignant visual moment, where any comment might have been uttered, but as she'd previously learned about him, he didn't like goodbyes. He nodded, then tiptoed into the hall. He didn't peek out first to check that the coast was clear. He simply blustered out.

It was normal behavior for a man like him. If he was discovered departing from her room, no ramifications would flow in his direction. They would all sweep her away, but she wasn't sorry she'd participated in the torrid encounter.

As his footsteps faded, she was already speculating over how soon he could visit her again. And it never occurred to her that she should lock her door to keep him out.

---

MICHAEL REACHED THE LANDING on the main staircase, and he halted, feeling as if he was at a crossroads. He could head down to the lower parlors in case any of his friends were still reveling. He could drink and gamble until dawn.

Or he could head up to the next floor, to the master suite, and crawl into bed. He could sleep, then rise at a reasonable hour and bump into Margaret a bit earlier. The prospect of perhaps having breakfast with her appeared to settle it.

She was distressed to be at Sutton when he was contemplating marriage to her cousin, but he wasn't concerned about the issue. He was adept at compartmentalizing the various segments of his life. Her presence was irrelevant to the situation with Annette Adair. He would wed Annette—or he wouldn't. His evident affection for Margaret would have no bearing on his choice.

He floated through London, carousing, wreaking havoc, and enjoying himself. He never attached moral tests to his conduct and he didn't waste energy fretting over his failings.

Still though, would it be cruel to marry her cousin? Would it be wrong? Would it matter to anyone but Margaret? She was mostly a stranger to him. If she was the only one who'd be devastated, did he care?

Fleetingly, he tried to imagine himself as Annette's husband, but constantly running into Margaret. How could they ever attend the same family gatherings? How could they show up at Sunday dinners or holiday suppers? It was madness to suppose that sort of quagmire could be maneuvered with any finesse.

He climbed up to his suite, and he slipped inside, but he wasn't tired. Margaret had fueled his lust, and he wished she was a tad looser so she could have supplied what he truly needed. Then again, if she'd been a trollop, he wouldn't have liked her quite so much.

The fire in the sitting room had burned out, but there was a candle lit in the bedchamber, and he could see a woman stretched out on his bed. She was wearing a skimpy corset and frilly drawers, the kind that drove him wild.

He walked over and leaned against the doorframe, as his paramour, Rowena Smithwaite, gestured for him to join her. She was a voluptuous, gorgeous, debauched tart, with lush auburn hair and big green eyes, and she also just happened to be the most wicked slattern he'd ever met.

No profcssional whore could match her dissolute proclivities, and she was never ashamed about any act she perpetrated on a mattress.

She'd wed young, to an elderly fool, and he'd died shortly after, so at age twenty-five, she was a wealthy widow. Her status imbued her with a freedom and independence that she wholeheartedly embraced. She loved his same vices so they were perfect partners.

He suspected she harbored a secret desire to be his bride. She'd never hinted that she'd like a permanent bond, but he understood women and how they assessed amorous entanglements. Whenever he discussed his nuptial search with her, she'd snicker and disparage the girls who were coming to Sutton.

He'd been waiting for her to suggest that he should abandon his quest and pick her instead. In a different world, he might have been amenable, but she was rumored to have fornicated with most of the men in his social circle. He liked how they wallowed in iniquity together, but apparently, he had a few standards and he wouldn't dip below them for her.

He hadn't invited her to sneak in, so he was irked that she'd dared, but he was delighted too. His trifling with Margaret had left him randy as a bull and he could definitely use some feminine treatment by a vixen who knew how to please him.

"I missed you when you vanished from the party," she said.

He shrugged. "I was busy."

"I hope you don't mind that I crept in." Her voice was sexy and sultry and his cock stirred with anticipation.

"I don't mind this once," he told her, "but it shouldn't become a habit. In the future, if I want you here, I'll ask you."

"I predict I'll be a frequent visitor." She thrust out her curvaceous breasts. "Where have you been? Were you with someone besides me? Should I be insanely jealous?"

Her tone was flippant and teasing, but underneath the query, he detected significant irritation. She was starting to feel possessive, but he never permitted any paramour to dig her claws in too deep.

"What if I was with someone else?" he inquired, merely to annoy her. "I don't believe it would be your place to complain about it."

"I can tantalize you better than any rural maiden. Why bother with an inexperienced ninny when you can have me?"

"Why indeed?" he murmured.

She slithered to her feet, and with a flick of her wrist, her lingerie was somehow unhooked and it dropped to the floor. She posed for him, in all her naked glory, then she sashayed over and snuggled her shapely body to his. Of course he couldn't resist. He lifted her, carried her over to the bed, and tossed her onto it. He followed her down and fell onto her like a rapacious beast.

He kissed her for a bit, and when he came up for air, she said, "Have you been tumbling a housemaid? Is there one who is your favorite? Does she welcome you home with special tending? Just admit it. I shouldn't have to stew over the possibility."

"If I have a favorite, would it aggravate you?"

"Absolutely." She stared him down, expecting him to confess who it had been. He didn't speak up and she asked, "Is she prettier than me? And you should be careful how you answer that question."

"You're much, much prettier," he fibbed.

For some reason, he thought Margaret was the most stunning female he'd ever fancied. He regularly consorted with great beauties, so it made no sense, but he was thoroughly enamored. When he compared her to any other woman, she won hands down. He wasn't stupid enough to explain it to Rowena though.

He drew onto his haunches and tugged off his shirt. Rowena watched, her gaze avaricious and appreciative, and when he nestled down again, she said, "That's more like it. You're mine for the evening, and when you're with me, don't you dare ponder your innocent little housemaid."

"I wouldn't dream of it."

"Your comment is music to my ears. Now lie back and let's have some fun."

She rolled them so she was on top, and he was on the bottom, and he relaxed, content to have her lead the way.

# Chapter 7

Annette was standing at a rear door, wrapped from head to toe in a plush fur cloak, fur hat, and boots. She was planning to take a stroll in the bleak, dreary garden, but one of her mittens was missing. She must have dropped it on the stairs.

It was a chilly winter morning, the temperature freezing, and there was snow on the ground, but a few paths had been swept. It was insane to venture out, but she felt as if she was suffocating. If she didn't get some fresh air, she couldn't imagine how she'd survive the impending hours of intense socializing in which she was expected to participate.

She'd spent the previous evening with Lord Sutton and his friends. They were a collection of obnoxious dandies with whom she had naught in common. There was a young widow in the group too, Rowena Smithwaite, and she was snooty, pretentious, and very beautiful. She'd stared down her nose at Annette, as if she were a queen who didn't have to be courteous.

At the moment, Annette was richer and more celebrated than most any female strutting about in the kingdom, so Mrs. Smithwaite's condescension had been extremely exasperating. Whenever the conceited shrew had thought Annette wasn't looking, she'd glare imperiously, then whisper to her male chums. They'd smirk and snicker, and Annette was convinced she was being insulted and they were having a laugh at her expense.

In addition, Mrs. Smithwaite appeared to have a very fond relationship with Lord Sutton. She'd loafed by his side and had cooed over his jokes and remarks. Annette had been left with the distinct impression that Mrs. Smithwaite was no better than she had to be, but also that she was romantically involved with the Earl.

Was that likely? Was he such a debauched wretch that he would bring his paramour into his home? Would he allow her to saunter about when he was entertaining a bridal candidate?

The whole notion was too upsetting to contemplate, so she was struggling to not contemplate it. But she couldn't ignore her fear that Mrs. Smithwaite had a special place in the Earl's affections. After what Annette had suffered during her failed engagement to Lord Grenville, where he'd been obsessed with his governess, she couldn't abide the possibility that she might be facing the very same dilemma with Lord Sutton.

Her mother had paid for a quick and superficial investigation of him, but if Ambrosia had learned of an illicit amour, she hadn't mentioned it. Then again, Ambrosia was determined that Annette marry into the aristocracy. It had been the driving force of her mother's life. If Ambrosia had received news of a passionate liaison, but had kept it from Annette, it wouldn't be a surprise.

She'd like to ask someone about Mrs. Smithwaite, but who could she approach?

She wouldn't gossip with the servants. Nor could she pester his sister. Hester Crawford had lurked on the edges of the party, never joining in the merriment, never chatting or trying to fit in. She was one of the most tedious people Annette had ever encountered.

Why would she possess any risqué information about her brother? By her own admission, she'd deliberately sequestered herself in the country. She never went to town and had no connections there. She wouldn't be in a position to hear rumors on any topic.

Margaret might have noticed the Earl's mischief, but she'd fled before supper had been served. She hadn't returned either, and Annette had yearned to dash upstairs and ask her what was wrong, but she'd been the guest of honor and hadn't been able to sneak away.

Margaret hadn't come down to breakfast, and Annette was wondering if she'd hide for the remainder of their visit. The prior night, when Lord Sutton had finally been introduced to them, Margaret had had an odd exchange with him. It had seemed as if she and the Earl might have an earlier acquaintance, one of which Annette was unaware.

Annette had inquired of Lord Sutton as to how he knew Margaret, but he'd claimed that—when he'd boasted about Margaret being a friend—he'd been jesting. Annette was certain he'd been lying.

Suddenly, a footman rounded the corner, and he marched down the hall toward her. He was a very bold fellow, and he showed no signs of deference at stumbling on her in the isolated spot. In fact, he acted as if she were invisible.

He was about her own age of twenty, and he was very handsome, blond and blue-eyed, with features that melded in just the right way. He was attired like a farm laborer, perhaps one of the boys from the stables, and he was heavily bundled in winter outerwear.

"You there," she haughtily said to garner his attention so he didn't run her down, "I require your assistance."

She was in a foul mood, and she shouldn't have spoken to him so rudely, but she'd been raised at an elevated level, where underlings were trained to be submissive and obsequious. Sutton House was very grand, and she demanded perfection from the staff that was supposed to constantly pamper her.

He halted and frowned. “Were you talking to me?”

“Yes. I’m going to walk in the garden.”

“You shouldn’t; it’s very cold. You’ll freeze to death.”

“Thank you for that wise piece of advice,” she sarcastically said, “but I don’t need a weather report from a servant. I’ve dropped my mitten and I’d like you to retrieve it for me.”

“I’m busy,” the cocky oaf stunned her by replying. “I’m sorry, but you’ll have to retrieve it yourself.”

“You’re busy? That’s your answer? I’m sure Lady Hester would like to be informed of how insolent you’ve been to me. Shall we find her and apprise her of what you just said?”

She was being snobbish in a manner she never was, but it was distressing to be trapped in a marital interview, as if she was on stage every minute and having to play the part of the ideal female. She was still annoyed that Lord Sutton had been away from the house when she’d arrived. During supper, and the socializing afterwards, he’d been a tad more polite, but he was an uncouth boor and she didn’t like him very much.

It was only her first full day in residence. What if the sojourn never improved? How long would she tarry, while she grew to like him less and less?

The footman yanked her focus back to him. At her warning about tattling to Lady Hester, he chuckled snidely. “Yes, by all means, protest about me to Hester. Then let me know what sort of response you receive. I’ll be on pins and needles, waiting to hear.”

“I’ll get you in trouble with her. Don’t you care?”

“Not really. She’s never liked me so you couldn’t do much damage.”

“Honestly! What kind of attitude is that?”

"I believe it's called a *bad* attitude, but then, a lengthy stay at Sutton always has that effect on me."

He circled by her and continued on to the door, as if he'd had enough of her badgering. It was an enraging realization. People loved her. She was pretty and marvelous, brimming with positive traits and no negative ones. Everyone agreed about it so she was absolutely flabbergasted by his disrespect.

She stamped her foot like a spoiled toddler. "I beg your pardon! I haven't excused you!"

He drew up short, whipped around, then stomped back, not stopping until they were toe to toe. She was so astonished by his audacity that she didn't push him away. She was alone in a deserted area, and he was a stranger, but she sensed no menace. She wasn't scared of him, but she couldn't deduce how to gain control of the situation.

He wasn't physically large so he didn't tower over her like Lord Sutton. She was quite tall herself for a woman so, as he studied her, she was able to look him in the eye. It was obvious he wasn't impressed by her, and again, she was bewildered by his lack of regard.

"I beg *your* pardon, Your Majesty," he facetiously said. "I didn't understand that I required your permission to depart from my own home."

She scowled, being puzzled by the comment. "You are a servant and you're not serving me. I need my mitten!"

It was a silly command, but since she'd arrived in the blasted mansion, nothing had gone as she'd planned. If she couldn't make a footman obey, if she couldn't dress appropriately for a winter stroll, what else might happen?

"What's your name?" he asked.

"I am Miss Annette Adair."

"Ah, the blushing bride-to-be."

"You are being entirely too obnoxious. Please step back."

"I won't oblige you, for you see, *I* am Caleb Crawford."

She gaped with confusion. "So? You're a Crawford? Are you related to the family somehow? Should I grovel at your feet?"

"Michael is my brother."

"Michael who? Do you mean Lord Sutton?"

"Yes, that would be him, Princess, so I have more right than you to be in this hallway."

"Lord Sutton doesn't have a brother. My mother would have told me."

"Either she was misinformed or she presumed my presence would be too scandalous for you to tolerate."

Annette would admit that she wasn't the smartest girl in England so she didn't grasp what he was telling her. "Why would your presence be scandalous?"

"I'm certain you'll figure it out eventually. You could gossip about me with the housemaids, but then, you're so posh, it's probably beneath you to converse with them. Can you even see them from your toplofty perch?"

She huffed out a shocked breath. "Are you accusing me of being a snob?"

"Yes, and I can't abide your juvenile antics. Fetch your own damn mitten. I have chores to complete."

He stormed out the door and slammed it as he went. She tiptoed over and peeked out a window to watch him disappear. She dawdled for a bit, letting her temper cool, letting her chagrin fade.

Numerous details became clear: He wasn't a footman. He was the Earl's brother, and apparently, his existence was a fact her mother hadn't bothered to share. He had to be a natural-born son, so there was a bastard prancing about on the premises, and she was expected to put up with him.

He was very handsome though, very forceful and direct. He didn't like her and thought she was prone to juvenile antics. He hadn't been afraid to say so.

A wave of embarrassment washed over her. She supposed, before too many more hours had passed, they'd be officially introduced. The encounter would be awkward and humiliating, and she'd have to devise a method to smooth over the hard feelings that had been generated during their initial meeting.

What if he complained about her to his brother? What if Lord Sutton rejected her because of it. What then? Her mother would kill her for ruining her chance. Ambrosia would literally kill her!

Annette was swamped once again by the overwhelming sense that the visit was doomed. She felt as if the universe was shouting at her, pointing out that she wasn't destined to wed Lord Sutton. Or was she being too melodramatic? Was she being too emotional so it was making her assess the situation incorrectly?

She didn't think so.

"Fetch your own damn mitten!" she muttered in a mocking voice.

She whirled away and stomped down the hall, finding it around the first corner. She tugged it on, returned to the door, and stepped outside.

The frigid air hit her lungs like a battering ram, and she inhaled, desperate to shuck off the perception that she'd been suffocating in the house. She plodded into the garden and trekked down one of the swept paths, but it was slippery and slow-going. She had to move carefully, each stride likely to bring disaster.

Why had she decided to take a walk anyway? She should have simply lounged by a hot fire and waited for Lord Sutton to bluster up and irritate her too. At least that way, she'd have been warm when she was being insulted.

---

CALEB WAS IN THE barn, talking to the men about a fence that had fallen. Several head of cattle had roamed onto a neighbor's estate. The fellow was elderly and grumpy, and he'd sent a messenger to Sutton to demand they corral the animals and repair any damage.

Caleb was helping to load a wagon with supplies, then he'd ride off with the group to complete the task. It wasn't his job, and he didn't need to bother over it, but he liked to work with his hands and exert himself with physical labor.

He was an earl's brother, but he was also very ordinary, and he liked to mingle with other common men. It kept his mind centered and his attitudc humble. He would hate to ever begin putting on airs and forgetting who he was deep down.

In England, where bloodlines controlled a person's rank, he'd started out at a very low spot. His first decade of life had been particularly grueling, but after Michael had rescued him from dire circumstances, he'd thrived magnificently.

He'd been fostered out to a tenant farmer who'd been a violent, illiterate drunkard. The old earl, Caleb's father, had arranged for Caleb to be hidden away, his parentage never mentioned, but people had suspected the truth. He'd been taunted over his being the Earl's by-blow, and because of it, he'd grown a very thick skin. There wasn't much that ever upset him.

He'd been a quiet, watchful boy who'd secretly dreamed that he was a lost prince. When Michael had trotted up to save him—on a white stallion, no less!—the moment had played out like a scene from a fairytale.

He loved his brother, and he would always be grateful to him, but he and Michael were nothing alike. They were possessed of the same stubbornness and pride, but Michael would never pitch in to fix a fence. He'd never roll up his sleeves and engage in manual labor. Caleb assisted with those sorts of chores because he was kind, but also because he wasn't grand and imperious like Michael. He wouldn't stray too far from his modest roots.

He was trying to focus on the broken fence, trying to join in the banter, but to his great disgust, he was thinking about Annette Adair. He repeatedly glanced out the barn door, hoping he'd see her in the garden. He'd told the foolish ninny that she should stay in the manor, but she'd ignored him. She seemed to be precisely the type of bungling female who would fall into a snowbank and not be able to climb out.

Over the next few months, Michael would interview many young ladies whom Hester had invited to Sutton House, but Hester was a fusspot and she never went to London. She had no friends there and wasn't privy to the gossip or news, so Caleb had been concerned about Michael's asking her to be his matchmaker. Yet to his surprise, Hester's initial attempt had been a whopping success.

Miss Adair was very beautiful. But *not* to his surprise, she was annoying, pretentious, and very rude. She was a rich heiress though, so what had he expected? It was the reason men agreed women shouldn't have their own money. It had them assuming they were more important than they really were.

He was mortified by how their encounter had unfolded. Sooner or later, they'd be officially introduced, and with how they'd traded barbed comments, it would be awkward and embarrassing. He never liked others to have a bad opinion of him so he supposed he ought to find her and apologize for being an ass.

He hadn't meant to be so snippy with her, but the minute she'd bumped into him, she'd automatically presumed he was a servant. He'd been dressed for toiling away out in the weather, so it was an understandable mistake, but he was an earl's son and an earl's brother. He couldn't deny that he had a huge chip on his shoulder. When he was denigrated or maligned, he didn't always react politely.

She appeared to be an ideal girl to be Michael's bride and Caleb shouldn't scuttle the chance for his brother. He didn't want Miss Adair to reject Michael, simply because Caleb had behaved like a cretin.

He decided to track her down, and he offered a false excuse to the other men, claiming he had to retrieve an item from his bedchamber, that he'd catch up with them out in the pasture. Then he left the barn and headed to the garden. He stood on the edge, searching for her, and he was dismayed to discover that she'd crossed all the way over to the park where the snow was much deeper.

She was trudging through a drift to get back to the swept path. Her foot skidded on a patch of ice, and she was hurled into a somersault that was a feat an acrobat might have performed in a circus.

She yelped with astonishment, then hit the ground with a thud. She didn't move, but laid motionless, gazing up at the bright blue sky. The whole scene might have been hilarious, but for a terrifying instant, he was afraid she'd knocked herself unconscious.

He sprinted over to her, slipping and sliding as he maneuvered in her direction. As he reached her, she'd sat up and was dusting snow off her fur cloak.

"My goodness, Miss Adair!" he said as he rushed up. "You gave me the fright of my life! Are you all right?"

"I think I am."

She wiggled her arms and feet, as if checking for broken bones, but she wasn't injured. Her fur hat had fallen off, and her curly blond hair had tumbled down, so she looked endearingly rumpled and unkempt.

She groaned and he said, "You landed so hard. I hope you haven't cracked your skull open."

"My skull is fine, but I bet I'll have a fierce headache today."

He lifted her up, and he should have released her immediately, but he was worried about her balance, so he kept his grip very tight. It was improper to touch her, but he couldn't exactly state that he was in a hurry for the interval to end.

Once she was in a better condition, he bent down to pick up her hat, and he tugged it on for her and straightened it himself. Suddenly, an odd sensation festered. Time seemed to stand still. The breeze ceased to blow and no birds were flying.

They were staring fondly, neither of them able to pull away. He was overwhelmed by the peculiar realization that he could grow smitten very fast and that Michael didn't deserve her.

"I warned you not to take a walk," he said, smiling.

"I have a bad habit of refusing to listen to bossy men."

"And I can be very bossy."

"I noticed that about you," she said.

"My brother, Michael, is incredibly bossy too, so I try to never act like him, but I don't always manage it."

"I'm sorry for how I spoke to you in the house."

"You're forgiven," he said, "and I'm sorry for being so short-tempered with you. I possess many aggravating Crawford qualities. I work to bury them, but occasionally, they poke out when I'm not paying attention."

"I wasn't aware that Lord Sutton had a brother."

"The family doesn't usually boast about me. He and I had the same father, but my mother was a London doxy."

"Is she still alive?"

"No, she died birthing me. I was fostered out to a tenant farmer, and when I was ten, Michael whisked me off to sea. I traveled with him for a decade, and I served as his cabin boy, then his aide. How could you not have been apprised? Didn't your mother have us investigated? Didn't she unearth the skeletons in our closet?"

"If she did, she didn't share the more shocking tidbits with me."

"Are you disturbed that I am on the premises?"

"No. I'm just debating how I should view you."

"Must you treat me differently than anyone else? Must there be special guidelines?"

"I can be quite a snob," she admitted, "so I'm required to be offended by your audacity."

He snorted with amusement. "I've already figured that out about you."

"I'm also supposed to be aloof and rude when I bump into you."

"And I imagine *I* am supposed to be meek and humble."

"Yes, and let's not forget that I desperately needed my mitten and you wouldn't find it for me."

"You poor, inept child. Did you find it yourself?"

"Yes, but you thrust a great chore on my shoulders."

"Are you finished strolling?" he asked. "Have you had enough fresh air for one morning?"

"I believe I have. I'm about to march inside and demand the servants pamper me. What would you guess? Will they be more accommodating than you?"

"Everyone in the manor is more accommodating than me. Except maybe my awful brother."

At the petty denigration, she smirked. "Shouldn't you be extolling his virtues? If I'm to be convinced to join your family, shouldn't you be praising him to the rafters?"

"Where his marital search is concerned, I'm minding my own business."

She studied him, obviously struggling over a difficult issue, then she rattled him by inquiring, "Would I be happy as your brother's wife? What is your opinion?"

His initial impulse was to be completely frank and suggest she race back to London as fast as she could, but he wouldn't interfere in Michael's quest to pick a bride.

"Am I the person you should ask?" he said. "I'm probably not."

"Who but you might tell me the truth? I won't gossip with the servants and I wouldn't dare bother Lady Hester."

"She might be candid about him. She likes to rant about his faults."

"Has he many faults? From my brief acquaintance with him, I'm predicting he does."

"He has too many failings to count," Caleb blurted out when he should have shut his mouth.

"I was afraid that might be the case."

Caleb shook off his momentary spurt of veracity and said, "Ignore me. I love my brother. He's a grand fellow and you'd be lucky to have him as your husband."

She assessed him, then scoffed with disgust. "You are the worst liar."

She spun away and started for the manor. She walked slowly, and she was limping slightly, as if she'd gotten banged up during her fall.

"Shall I escort you, Miss Adair?" he called. "I can hold your arm so you don't slip again."

She halted and glanced back. "I don't need any help, but thank you for offering."

They were frozen in place and he was suddenly tongue-tied as a green boy with his first girl. A thousand important comments swirled between them, but he couldn't speak any of them aloud so he settled for inanities.

"I apologize again," he said, "for being so irritable when I stumbled on you in the house."

"Don't worry about it. You've turned out to be much nicer than I expected."

"I am very nice, much nicer than my brother."

"That, Mr. Crawford, is a very low bar."

He couldn't bear for her to go and he tried to prolong the conversation. "There are neighbors coming tonight after supper. Hester has arranged musicians and dancing. If I ask you to dance, will you?"

She grinned impishly. "Will you deign to show up for the event? So far, you've been noticeably absent."

"If you agree to dance with me, I'll make it a point to be there."

"I will let it be a surprise."

She continued on and he tagged after her, keeping his distance, but watching her until she was safely inside. He hovered like a spurned suitor, figuring she'd wave or maybe voice a poignant farewell, but she was a genuine snob. She hadn't been joking about it, and apparently, she'd supplied all the attention she'd felt like furnishing.

After she disappeared, he dawdled for several minutes, reviewing the encounter and being disturbed by how she'd fascinated him. It seemed as if he'd been flirting with her. Had he been?

She'd journeyed to Sutton so Michael could evaluate her with an eye toward marriage. Caleb should butt out of that situation, but evidently, he had other ideas with regard to her.

She and Michael were likely perfect for each other. They were gorgeous human beings who were rich, entitled, and conceited. But he was suffering from the strongest impression that he should steal her away from his brother—if he could.

The notion was dangerous and disloyal, but he couldn't stop pondering the prospect. It meant that the next two weeks would be much more exciting than he'd imagined. He couldn't wait to discover how it would ultimately unfold.

# Chapter 8

Margaret was walking down a deserted hall, headed for the women's retiring room. Hester Crawford, for all her timid habits, had thrown quite a fun party. Supper had been delicious, then neighbors had been invited for dancing and cards after the meal.

There were plenty of men in attendance, and she would have joined in the dancing, but her combs had come loose. She had to repair her hair or her whole chignon might fall down her back.

Michael hadn't been present at the supper table and there had been no comment about his absence. Hester and Caleb Crawford had both been there, and since they'd acted as if naught was amiss, everyone else had had to act nonchalant too.

He'd finally arrived, briefly, after the dancing had started. He'd pop in occasionally, then pop out almost immediately. She supposed the men had a separate salon where they were gambling and drinking to excess.

During his odd, infrequent appearances, he hadn't approached her, hadn't tried to talk to her, and she couldn't decide if she was happy to have been ignored or not. In some ways, they were closer than two people could ever be, but in other ways, they were strangers.

If they had chatted, with the large crowd watching, they wouldn't have been able to mask their fondness, so it was best for him to avoid her. Wasn't it?

She'd spent the day in her bedchamber, hiding and fretting. Michael was very sly about luring her into mischief, and she had to save herself before she engaged in behavior that was indecent and extremely regrettable. Her problem was that she didn't want to be saved from him.

Throughout her hours of private obsessing, she'd expected Annette to barge in and inquire as to why she was being such a hermit, but thankfully, Annette had been content to leave her alone. Margaret was struggling to deduce the appropriate path with regard to Annette. Should she tattle about her flirtation with Michael? Or should she remain silent? Again, she couldn't decide.

She was passing a dark parlor, when she heard a female chuckle in a sultry manner that indicated an amorous rendezvous was in progress. Margaret ordered herself to hurry on by, but at the last second, curiosity won out and she peeked in.

The ardent couple probably assumed themselves to be concealed by the shadows, but they were over by the window, the winter moon shining in and reflecting off the snow, so she could clearly observe them. To her great astonishment, it was Michael and he was kissing the insolent widow, Rowena Smithwaite. From how comfortable they were in each other's arms, it was obvious this wasn't their first kiss either.

Margaret was so shocked that she nearly collapsed to the floor in a stunned heap. She staggered away, lurching blindly, until she found the retiring room and stumbled inside. She felt as if she'd been pummeled with a club, and her heart was pounding so furiously she was surprised it didn't burst out of her chest.

Was he having an affair with Mrs. Smithwaite? Was she a London doxy with whom he regularly dallied? Was he so debauched that he'd bring her to Sutton when he was interviewing a bridal candidate?

There was a pitcher of water and a bowl on a dresser, and Margaret dipped a cloth and patted it over her heated face. The incident reminded her that she didn't really know much about him. They seemed so intimately connected, but her perception of their liaison had been a charade.

Was he attached to Mrs. Smithwaite in particular? Or was he sneaking off with all the women at the party? Was that the reason he kept vanishing?

She'd never been so humiliated. She'd persuaded herself that he sought her company because he thought she was special and unique, but evidently, he trifled with any female who sauntered by. She was such a dunce! She was such a fool!

She'd been picturing herself as Cinderella, and he was her dashing Prince Charming, but if she'd learned one thing in her life, it was that her dreams never came true. It was pointless to wish and yearn. She'd let her guard down and she was paying the price.

The door opened and she glanced around to find that Annette had caught up with her.

"There you are!" her cousin said. "I've been searching for you all day. I even stopped by your bedchamber this afternoon, but the door was locked. I knocked and knocked, but you didn't answer."

Margaret feigned innocence. "You knocked? I must have been napping."

Annette didn't notice the lie. She was in high spirits, her eyes merry, her cheeks flushed. She'd been dancing constantly, but mostly with Caleb Crawford. They'd painted a pretty portrait. They were both lithe, blond, and gorgeous, and their bodies had fit together perfectly as they'd moved through the steps.

Margaret hadn't had the energy to butt in and counsel caution, but this was an issue any competent chaperone would address. They weren't in London, so the rules for socializing were more relaxed, but it wasn't proper for Annette to dote on Mr. Crawford. It certainly wasn't proper for her to partner with him over and over, not when she was supposed to be focused on his brother.

Then again, Lord Sutton hadn't danced with anyone, and besides, he was down the hall and kissing Mrs. Smithwaite. Even if Annette had tried to garner his attention, how could she have?

The retiring room provided chairs for loafing, wine for sipping, and a mirror for primping. Annette went to the mirror to check her hair and gown, while Margaret lurked behind her, feeling that Michael had betrayed her with Mrs. Smithwaite. It was an idiotic impression though. She had no claims on him, and they weren't officially bound, but it seemed as if he was cheating on her.

Annette must have noted her pallor, for she frowned and spun around. "You've been markedly absent from the festivities. Now, I locate you in this deserted parlor and you look as if you're about to faint. What's wrong? You're not sick, are you?"

"It's not that."

"Good, because I'd be a terrible nurse so you'd be on your own."

The comment should have been amusing, but Margaret didn't laugh. She gestured to the chairs and said, "Could we talk for a minute?"

Annette tsked with exasperation. "Honestly, Margaret, what is vexing you? You're miserable as an undertaker at a funeral."

"I have to tell you something."

"Does it involve Lord Sutton?" Annette asked.

"Yes."

"Then are you sure you should proceed? Should I hear gossip about him?"

"You have to hear about this. I've been debating whether to apprise you or not, but I can't keep it a secret."

"Well, that sounds rather ominous." Annette sat down, and Margaret trudged over and sat too, then Annette said, "Let me have it and don't worry about my tender emotional state. Don't hold back any details—as Mother likes to do to me."

Without pause or preamble, Margaret said, "I know Lord Sutton."

Annette cocked her head. "You *know* him…how? Please don't admit it's in the Biblical sense or you might give me an apoplexy."

"No, it's not that illicit. Once I realized who he was, I should have spoken up immediately. I met him in Baywick, shortly before I departed for London."

"From how oddly you reacted when we were first introduced to him, I suspected there was more to this story than had been revealed. Why was he in Baywick?"

"He was gambling and carousing with some of his odious acquaintances. He was simply Captain Crawford and we enjoyed a bit of a flirtation."

"How much of a one?"

"I've kissed him several times, and…" Margaret cut off her sentence and moaned with mortification. "Ooh, this is so difficult."

"Just spit it out," Annette calmly urged.

"All right, all right." Margaret inhaled a deep breath, then she said, "Last night, he was with me in my bedroom."

"Margaret!" Annette swallowed down a squeal of astonishment.

"Nothing happened! He merely kissed me some more. Actually, we carried on for a lengthy interval."

For an eternity, Annette was quiet, mulling the news, then she said, "I asked him about you. I figured you were friends, but the ridiculous oaf lied and insisted you weren't, that his greeting had been a crude joke meant to rattle you."

Margaret scoffed with disgust. "Typical male."

"Are you in love with him?"

"No! Absolutely not. When we're alone, he seems so fond of me. He can be very charming and I haven't been able to resist him."

"He doesn't have any honorable intentions toward you."

"Of course he doesn't. I'm not stupid."

"I'm not being condescending about it. I'm simply pointing out that you have to watch yourself around him."

"You don't have to tell me that and I'm so sorry about this. I wasn't aware that I was interfering in your nuptial plans. In Baywick, he never told me who he was."

"That's another strike against him that proves he has bad motives."

"I'm so embarrassed," Margaret said. "Should I return to London? Would you like me to?"

Annette snorted with derision. "No, you shouldn't return. If you left, I'd have to accompany you, and I refuse to leave early. I'm having a grand holiday, despite the fact that Lord Sutton is an ass. We're staying for the entire two weeks, but you need to be more careful. You definitely need to lock your door!"

"I feel awful about this. Are you certain you're not angry with me?"

"Why would I be angry? He's a pompous fiend, and if he ever lowered himself to propose, I doubt I'd accept."

"You've only just met him though. You can't have formed such a negative opinion already. You have to be patient and not rush to judgment."

"He reminds me too much of Lord Grenville. He doesn't have the grueling ordeal in his past that Grenville had, so he's not mad. He's simply rude and selfish and I won't shackle myself to such a domineering prig. Besides, I like his brother much better."

"Your attitude indicates that I have to warn *you* to be careful," Margaret said. "You can't be toying with Caleb Crawford. You've been so blatant in your choice of dance partners that people are noticing your heightened attention."

Annette snickered with offense. "I would have been socializing with his brother, but the obnoxious dolt has barely deigned to show himself in the ballroom."

"You'll never guess what he's been doing instead."

"What? And may I confess that I won't be surprised by whatever tale you share? I think he's capable of any hideous conduct."

"At the moment, he's off in a dark parlor and kissing Mrs. Smithwaite."

"No!" Annette bristled with outrage. "I was wondering about her relationship with him. They're too cozy for words. Might she be his mistress? Would he have brought her here while I am in his home?"

"It's possible she's his paramour. He's a dedicated philanderer and he has a particular penchant for doxies."

"How did you discover that little tidbit?"

"In Baywick, he was in a fight. He brawled over an insult to a whore."

"He is such a menace," Annette fumed. "Why are prominent men so repulsive?"

"They're told from birth that they're remarkable so they grow up assuming they can act however they please."

"Are you devastated by his consorting with Mrs. Smithwaite?"

"I'm temporarily devastated," Margaret said, "but I'll get over it. I had convinced myself that he was besotted with me so it was a shock to stumble on him."

"He doesn't deserve you," Annette loyally stated, "and if he'd spend the evening with her, rather than you, then he's an idiot."

"I'll keep telling myself the very same."

Annette stood and tugged Margaret to her feet. She startled Margaret by grabbing her and hugging her tight. They weren't an affectionate family so it was a strange, but comforting gesture.

"You can't fret about him," Annette said as she drew away. "Let's return to the party and we'll have so much fun with the other gentlemen that you won't contemplate him for a single minute."

"That's a marvelous idea."

"And your bedroom door will be locked from now on. Yes?"

"Yes," Margaret agreed.

Annette hugged her again, then she said, "I'm so glad you confided in me about him. It's supplied me with a reason to reject him if he proposes. He won't propose though; I'm sure of it."

"Every aristocrat has to wed sooner or later."

"The other guests have been gossiping about him. He's not keen to marry, and he's not really concerned over *who* he picks, but Time is passing so he's being pushed into it. I won't have a husband who isn't madly in love with me. He can inflict himself on some other unsuspecting maiden. I'd be delighted with that conclusion."

Annette linked their arms and marched them out. Quickly, they were in the ballroom and immersed in the crowd. It ended any opportunity to discuss Annette's decision to snub Michael. It also dumped Margaret into the middle of the merriment so she had to paste a smile on her face and pretend she wasn't stunned and heartbroken.

Was she heartbroken? Would she permit Michael Crawford to crush her? No.

When one of his London chums blustered up and asked her to dance, she nodded and followed him out onto the floor.

As Annette had counselled, she wouldn't ponder Lord Sutton a single minute.

Hester had been down in the kitchen, checking on the food trays for the buffet. The servants were very busy so there was no footman available to haul any of them upstairs. She lifted one and headed up to the dining room with it.

Some women of her station might have scoffed at her meager attempt to pitch in, but she wasn't too grand to behave like a normal person when circumstances required it. The world wouldn't stop spinning.

She wasn't paying attention and she rounded a corner and bumped directly into Caleb. The tray wobbled and she nearly dropped it. He leapt to steady it, so for an instant, he was touching her. She lurched away, intent on putting space between them, but they were wedged in a narrow hall so she couldn't maneuver by him.

He was always unfailingly polite to her and he said, "Hester, I'm so sorry! I didn't hear you approaching."

"It's quite all right." She yanked out of his grasp and would have continued on, but he was blocking her route.

"Why are you fussing with this?" he asked. "Aren't there any footmen to help?"

"They're occupied with various tasks and I can't have our guests supposing we're misers who have run out of food."

"You needn't bother with this. I'll take it up for you."

"I can manage!"

They engaged in a brief tug-of-war, which he won. He wasn't a particularly large man, but he brimmed with Michael's stubbornness.

She was the one to relent and let go. "Fine. If you insist, you may have it."

"Are there more trays in the kitchen?" When she nodded, he said, "I'll fetch those too. Don't worry about them."

She should have been grateful, should have offered a courteous comment, but she could never figure out how to behave toward him. Even now, when they were sequestered together, she couldn't look at him.

She couldn't bear to be in his presence, and her gaze was focused over his shoulder, so she wouldn't have to stare at his handsome face or blue eyes. Every detail infuriated her and she was vividly reminded of how much she'd had to surrender in her life.

It was the height of outrage for Michael to have shoved him into her path when she didn't want him there. His connection to them, the shocking facts surrounding his birth, were a terrible humiliation. She struggled repeatedly to explain to Michael that Caleb shouldn't be welcomed, but Michael never listened to her. Caleb was allowed to prance about as if there was no scandal dragging along after him.

She spent her days praying, repenting, and mentally flogging herself for not being a good daughter, for not being a good person. Her sins were huge and unforgivable, and despite how fervidly she sought to atone, she couldn't pardon her father for his role in ruining them.

She could only become a better Christian than he'd been. She had to be more pious, more devout, and perhaps she'd eventually wipe away some of the tarnish he'd visited on them with his unbending attitudes and obstinate posturing.

Her father had always thought he knew best, and he'd ground her and her mother down until they'd been forced to obey his every command. Caleb had been the result, but where was the benefit in having a bastard roaming the halls? It made them appear foolish and oblivious to proper morals.

Caleb was waiting patiently for her to depart, and if her rude disregard distressed him, he never furnished the slightest hint of it. In her dealings with him, she came away from every encounter feeling that he was decent and kind, while she was bitter and exhausting.

He was happier than she was. He was obviously much more content.

"You head out," he told her. "I'll be right behind you with the tray. Then I'll bring up the rest."

"Thank you."

Her jaw was clenched so tight that she was surprised she didn't crack a tooth. She whipped away and hurried off, anxious to escape his abhorrent company and to ignore the awful memories he constantly stirred.

Rowena Smithwaite loafed on the edge of the dancing, and she was studying the other women. She was usually the richest, most beautiful female in any room she entered, but Annette Adair was giving her a run for her money, and she didn't like having any competition.

Michael had been her paramour for several months, and from the moment they'd been introduced, it had been apparent they were destined to be together. They enjoyed the same hobbies and vices, and he was a randy dog who was wild in the bedchamber.

Although she pretended to be virtuous out in public, the sorry truth was that she was a wicked vixen with the soul of a harlot. She loathed how women were restricted in their choices and options, and she believed that Society put entirely too much emphasis on a female's reputation. Men didn't have to fret over such ridiculous standards, and she refused to be bound by rules she didn't wish to follow.

With her fortune providing protection from most consequences, she could engage in any corrupt deed that tickled her fancy.

She was watching Miss Adair and wondering why she was openly flirting with Michael's brother. Rowena was thrilled to have Annette prefer Caleb Crawford. It would distract her from Michael's courtship, and if she ultimately landed herself in a jam with Caleb, it would skuttle any chance she might have had to become Michael's bride.

In Rowena's opinion, it was hilarious that Michael was hunting for a wife. She was especially amused that he'd had his dour, spinster sister play matchmaker. Hester had walked the typical nuptial road by inviting heiresses and debutantes to meet him, but such naïve ninnies would drive him mad.

Rowena had hated being married herself, and when her elderly husband had died shortly after her wedding, she'd been relieved to be free of her shackles. She'd convinced herself that she'd never wed again—she was having too much fun being a widow—but Michael had altered her view of matrimony.

She would love to be a countess. She'd definitely be very good at it.

She was intrigued by the fact that he'd brought her to Sutton House with their other friends. He liked to have regular sexual congress, and it was the main reason he'd insisted she be added to the guest list, but it also showed that he was growing overly fond, that he couldn't stand to be parted from her for even a few days.

Her ploy was to tarry on the fringes of his marital search. She would denigrate the candidates, would slyly urge him to find fault with all of them, and after he was weary of the chase, she would point out that *she* would be the perfect wife for him. She had no doubt that he'd concur.

A footman strolled by and she grabbed a glass of wine off his tray. She spun away to sample it, and as she did, she glanced down a deserted hall that led away from the ballroom. At the far end, in the shadows, Michael was involved in a heated argument with Miss Adair's cousin, Margaret Adair.

Rowena wasn't aware that they were acquainted so the discovery was a tad disturbing. Might they be amorously attached? Was that likely?

Michael had her backed up against the wall, his torso touching hers, holding her in place, and it wasn't a polite spat. Their eyes were flashing daggers, their proximity practically causing sparks to ignite. Rowena had never observed such blatant passion, and Michael had certainly never gazed at *her* in such a hot, ardent fashion.

He uttered a stupid remark, and Miss Adair shoved him away and stomped off, disappearing further into the shadows. Michael loitered for a minute, nearly raced after her, then thought better of it. He took a deep breath to calm his raging temper, then he sauntered toward the ballroom as if nothing peculiar had just transpired.

Lest he notice her spying on him, she slipped into the crowd, her own temper on a slow boil.

Of all the problems she'd expected to encounter at Sutton, the possibility that he might be infatuated with a nobody like Margaret Adair had never occurred to her. Whatever was festering between them, it couldn't be allowed to continue.

Rowena had to stop it, but how could she? She didn't dare intervene herself so she'd have to push someone else to resolve the situation. Who could she tell? Who would be most incensed by the burgeoning dalliance? Who could rid her of Margaret Adair in the quickest, quietest way? Annette Adair? Her mother, Ambrosia? Hester Crawford?

On the spur of the moment, Rowena couldn't decide, but Margaret Adair's petty romance couldn't be tolerated. Shortly, she'd vanish as if she'd never been there at all.

"Out of sight, out of mind," she mumbled to herself.

Once she was gone, Michael wouldn't think about her again. He was casual in his affairs and he was easily bored by any paramour. A common female like Margaret Adair could never interest him for long.

Rowena would make sure of it.

# Chapter 9

MICHAEL WAS STROLLING TO the huge parlor where people were dancing. They didn't have an official ballroom, but it was big enough to hold a very large gathering.

He hadn't danced yet. Whenever he visited Sutton and they hosted events, Hester invited many of the local girls. They yearned for him to fraternize with them and they gazed at him with cow eyes. He couldn't abide their fawning and he avoided them like the plague.

The footmen had arranged a men's gambling den at the rear of the house and he'd spent the bulk of his evening in it. He preferred the company of men to women, but he'd grow bored, so he'd head out to the main salons for a few minutes. He'd grow bored there too, and he couldn't settle in any one location.

He wouldn't admit that his purpose in observing the dancers was so he'd have an opportunity to furtively spy on Margaret. She didn't realize how keenly he was assessing her and she'd be wondering why he was ignoring her. The pathetic fact was that he was completely focused on her, to the point where he was scaring himself.

He'd had to tamp down the urge to bluster up and lead her out onto the floor. He hadn't dared because he couldn't have hidden his intense fondness. He didn't like suffering from such virulent swings of affection, and he couldn't figure out how to free himself from his enticement. She might have been a sorceress who'd cast a magic spell to keep him infatuated.

With her on the premises, the energy seemed to have been skewed, and he was bewildered and off-balance. Annette Adair's presence wasn't helping either. She drove home the reality that he was about to marry, and it added to his perception that matters had floated far off course and he had no idea how to correct his route.

He'd been so overwhelmed that he'd allowed Rowena to drag him into an empty parlor for a quick tryst. She'd worked hard to persuade him to sneak up to his bedroom, but he'd retained enough of his wits that he'd declined the lewd suggestion.

The prior night, she'd barged into his suite, and he didn't want her to feel comfortable there. He definitely didn't want her to make it a habit. He'd warned her not to repeat her folly, but she was precisely the type of brazen tart who would disregard his edict.

He rounded a corner, and to his great delight, Margaret was walking toward him. He was concealed in the shadows so she hadn't seen him lurking and studying her. She was so pretty and he never had his fill of looking at her. His heart flip-flopped in his chest, as if it didn't fit under his ribs just right.

"Hello, Margaret," he softly murmured, not eager to startle her.

She blanched with surprise, then said, "Why are you skulking in this dark hall? Why don't you simply march into the ballroom like a normal person?"

Her tone was a tad snippy and he stepped to her and said, "Where are you going? I was planning to ask you to dance."

"You were not. Don't be such a nuisance and you still haven't told me why you're behaving so oddly. Would it kill you to socialize with your guests?"

"I don't like any of them."

"Then why invite them to Sutton?"

"I constantly ponder that dilemma. My sister demanded we carry out my nuptial search in the usual way, which means holding unending events that exhaust me. According to Hester, we must proceed in the accepted fashion, but if it had been left up to me, I'd have stayed in London with my dubious acquaintances."

"Yes, getting married is such an onerous chore, isn't it?"

Apparently, she was in a snit about something and he deemed her churlishness to be out of character. In his opinion, she was the most steady, unflappable female he'd ever met.

"What's wrong?" he asked. "Why are you upset?"

"I'm not upset. I'm tired and I'm heading to bed."

"But it's only eleven o'clock. Let's return to the party."

"No, thank you."

He was an expert at flirtation, at illicit amour, and he understood women much better than a bachelor ought. She was just as fond of him as he was of her so he was stunned by her refusal.

She skirted by him, but he hadn't expected such a swift departure, so she was able to flit off before he rushed over to block her exit. He leaned in, his body pinning her to the wall. It was outrageous conduct, with a high risk of discovery, but he didn't move away from her.

His anatomy was on fire, his torso—down to the tiniest pore—celebrating the chance to be so close to her.

"What are you doing?" she hissed. "You're being obnoxious. Stop it!"

"No."

"I'm too irked to fuss with you and I'm going to bed."

"May I join you there?" he cockily inquired, as if she were a strumpet, and it occurred to him that he might have had too much to drink.

She gasped with offense. "If I wasn't afraid we'd be observed, I would slap you silly for uttering such an insulting remark."

"I was joking," he insisted.

"No, you weren't. Is this why you keep pestering me? Are you assuming I'm loose with my favors? Or if you're not assuming that, are you so convinced of your own magnificence that you figure I'll be thrilled to ruin myself for you? Is that why you're inflicting yourself on me? Are you viewing me as easy prey? Are you predicting I'll be so bowled over that I won't be able to resist you?"

"What are you talking about? You're furious with me, but I haven't spoken to you all night. I can't have committed a sin that would have driven you into such an incensed state." Ire flashed in her eyes and he hastily added, "And for the record, I don't think you're loose with your favors. I think you're wonderful."

Out of the blue, she said, "Is Rowena Smithwaite your mistress?"

"Who told you that?" he asked, his expression carefully blank.

"It doesn't matter who told me so answer my question. Is she your mistress?"

He scoffed, as if the allegation was preposterous. "No. Why would I bring a paramour into my home? My sister is here; you and your cousin are here. I would never behave so shamelessly."

His cheeks were flaming with embarrassment so he was glad they were in the dark spot where his strident reaction was mostly concealed. Who had tattled about him? Who was gossiping? Had his London chums been babbling? Or had Rowena been boasting when she shouldn't have?

He had such revolting acquaintances, and he immersed himself in lewd circumstances, so he often forgot his manners when he was trapped in a more respectable situation.

She snorted with disgust. "I don't believe you."

"Why would I lie about her?"

"Why would you lie?" She bristled with what could only be described as apoplectic wrath. "It's dawned on me, Lord Sutton, that you are a despicable fiend, and there's no one who can force you to cease your nonsense. Do you have any regard for others? Do you ever worry about anybody but yourself? It's very likely that you have wallowed in iniquity for such a lengthy period that you don't even realize when you're being an ass."

He could have tendered any response, but he absurdly chose, "Don't call me Lord Sutton. Call me Michael."

"We're not on familiar terms and I have no desire to pretend we are."

He always hated to have his requests refused and his temper flared. "We're very close. Don't you dare claim we aren't."

"Not only are you quite dreadful, I'm beginning to suspect you're a bit insane too."

She shoved him very hard and stomped away. Like a spurned suitor, he hovered, struggling to deduce what had just happened. Yes, he was slightly inebriated, but she ought to be willing to overlook his reduced condition.

He was annoyed by her flippant disdain, and his first and very powerful instinct was to run after her and give her a piece of his mind. Women loved him and were anxious to attach themselves in any fashion he would allow. Except for Hester, they never sassed him or chastised him for his awful antics.

He was such a pompous beast that he truly felt his status rendered him immune from criticism. Margaret supposed she could cross any line and he'd permit her to be impertinent. She'd heard rumors about him and Rowena and it had sent her into a baffling frenzy he didn't comprehend.

Was she jealous? Did she think he was cheating on her? If so, it was a deranged attitude to have. They were two strangers who enjoyed a very potent attraction. If she'd been a tart, they'd have already proceeded to salacious conduct. Instead, they could merely share a few delicious kisses when they were tucked away out of sight.

If Rowena was his paramour, why would Margaret imagine it was any of her business? It was madness for her to presume, because of their infatuation, that he had a duty to carry on in certain ways.

Obviously, he'd angered her and he was too intoxicated to have a serious conversation about any topic. If he raced after her, he had no doubt he'd simply dig a deeper hole for himself. He'd say things he didn't mean and he'd distress her even further.

He started for the dancing salon, being determined to ignore her and her fit of pique. He'd track her down in the morning, when he was sober. He'd be merry and charming and she'd forgive him. She was a kind person and she wasn't the sort to fume and stew over trifles.

He would dance with her cousin, then with Rowena—just to prove he could. He might even squire some of the neighbor girls out onto the floor, and he'd relish every minute of his duplicitous socializing.

He really could be an ass. Margaret had been correct about that, but for reasons he couldn't explain, he yearned for her to view him as grand and marvelous, a gallant knight who strove to do good deeds. The problem for him was that he didn't have any gallant tendencies, and he wasn't interested in being anyone's hero.

He was a cad and a bounder, but he liked that she saw a different side of him. It was a false side that didn't comport with reality, but he was happy to have her fascinated.

He marched down the hall and he hadn't taken ten steps when he whipped around and marched in the other direction. She was furious with him and he felt terrible to have upset her. He couldn't bear to have the night end with them quarreling. She couldn't want that either, could she?

He'd never chased after a woman in his life, but evidently, he was about to begin with her. He dashed after her, hot on her heels, and eager to accost her before she reached her bedroom and locked herself in.

In light of his mood, he thought he might kick in the door in order to speak with her. She'd pushed him out onto that type of bizarre ledge, and now that she had him dangling in such a precarious spot, it was her responsibility to talk him down to safety.

MARGARET WAS IN HER dressing room, seated at the dressing table and yanking the combs from her hair. After chatting with Annette, she'd agreed to return to the party, but her heart hadn't been in it. At the first opportunity, she'd slipped away and headed for her bedchamber.

Fate was conspiring against her though and she'd immediately bumped into Lord Sutton. He'd been inebriated and obnoxious and she hadn't had the patience to tolerate him.

He'd had plenty of practice at flirtation and she was so pathetically lonely that it was very easy for him to overwhelm her. He was also an accomplished liar and fraud, and he assumed he was very enigmatic, but she could read him like a book.

He'd denied being involved with Mrs. Smithwaite, but he was so ridiculously transparent. Could he actually believe he could fib to her and she wouldn't notice?

She tossed the last comb on the table, her hair falling down her back in a chestnut wave. She attempted to drag a brush through it, but she was too aggravated to bother. She decided to don her nightgown and retire. A maid had been assigned to assist her, but the girl was busy with chores, so Margaret hadn't asked her to come upstairs.

She was used to managing without a servant and she didn't dare grow accustomed to it. Once Annette's visit concluded, either with Lord Sutton proposing or Annette spurning him, Margaret's role as her chaperone would be over. She'd be shuffled off to live with other relatives and she couldn't guess what situation would be supplied. She definitely wouldn't have a personal maid.

She stood to fetch her nightgown out of the wardrobe, when a strange noise caught her attention. When she'd rushed into the suite, she'd spun the key in the lock, but someone was fiddling with it. She tiptoed over and peeked into the bedroom, already deducing who was about to arrive. The door swung open, and as Lord Sutton slunk in, she could only sigh with irritation.

"I had my door locked for a reason," she said. "It was to keep you out. You tried the knob, and found your entry barred, so why would you automatically suppose you should bluster in anyway?"

"My home, my castle," he arrogantly stated. He wiggled a key in her direction, then stuck it in his pocket. "In case you didn't realize it, these keys work on every door, and I grabbed this one from the room across the hall. It's impossible to prevent a miscreant from sneaking in."

She'd known that of course, but a sane man—which he certainly wasn't—wouldn't have strolled in despite being unwelcome.

"To normal people, a lock means *stay out,*" she said.

"Yes, well, I considered kicking it in, but I didn't imagine you'd like me to be overheard causing a ruckus. Besides, it would have been idiotic to ruin a perfectly good door."

"You always have an excuse to justify your despicable actions. Why is that?"

"I'm an earl and my position makes me superior to everyone else. It warps a fellow's perception of his place in the world."

"I don't require a lecture on your philosophy of life," she said. "I'm weary and about to climb into bed so you need to leave."

"I'm sorry I was awful downstairs. Occasionally, I can behave like a fool."

"I won't argue the point."

He looked very contrite, and with his claiming to be sorry, some of the wind went out of her sails. She'd expected him to be pompous and annoying, but if he was truly remorseful, how was she to deal with his confession?

She wasn't ever angry or bitter, and she never harbored grudges, but her attitude was very dour, and at the moment, she didn't have the energy to spar with him. She had no doubt—given the chance—he'd quickly spew comments that would irk her beyond her limit.

He sauntered toward her and she might have been a rabbit with the hawk circling up above. It seemed that her destiny was approaching, that trouble was approaching, that joy was approaching. She was frozen in her spot, held rapt by the affection in his eyes.

She should have run away, but there was no rear exit. There were just the two rooms, the bedroom and dressing room, so there was nowhere to hide.

He pulled her into his arms and hugged her tight, their bodies pressed together all the way down. She should have shoved him away, and she would have, but he forestalled her by resting his forehead at her nape. His warm breath flowed over her shoulder, and he stroked his palms up and down her back, cradling her as if she was precious and rare.

"I hate that I distressed you," he said.

"No, you don't," she churlishly replied. "I think you love aggravating people. I think you revel in it."

"Most times I do, but I'm tamping down my nonsense for you. I'm so fond of you and I can't bear to imagine that I've squandered your esteem. Am I forgiven? Please tell me I am."

It was a pretty speech, and she should have ignored his entreaty, but when he was oozing regret, it was so hard to maintain any fury. She would be at Sutton House for a handful of days, then she'd never see him again. Why quarrel? Why chastise and bicker?

He'd offered no promises to her and they weren't officially bound. If he dallied with a doxy like Rowena Smithwaite, what was it to Margaret? His sins and foibles weren't any of her business and she had no right to castigate him.

If she remained grumpy, she would wreck a large portion of her visit to his home. She'd never met anyone like him and she had to view their acquaintance as an adventure. It would be such a waste to spend her brief holiday fuming and complaining.

He would never alter his sordid habits and she could never mold him into a more decent man. It would be futile to try. He was who he was: a handsome, rich, corrupt rogue. She could avoid him and be miserable or she could put up with him and be miserable. After they parted forever, she'd have much happier memories if she put up with him.

"You drink too much," she muttered, even as she scolded herself for being a total milksop.

"I know."

"When you're foxed, you grow insufferable."

"I know that too."

"You have foul vices and you consort with low associates who aren't really your friends."

"Why would any sane person be my friend? I'm an undependable wretch. Respectable gentlemen can't abide my sloth and belligerence, and they won't tolerate my whims or quirks. I only manage to attract other wastrels."

"Truer words were never spoken," she said.

He straightened and smiled down at her. His gaze was so dear that she was absolutely floored by it. How was she to deflect it? Why would she want to deflect it?

There was no finer thing in the world than to have Michael Crawford's undivided attention.

"Why are you in such a bad mood?" he asked. "You've never been short with me before. What did I do? I can't figure it out."

She should have provided a fake reason, but she wasn't about to pretend with him. If he was involved with Mrs. Smithwaite, the facts should be out in the open. She refused to listen to gossip and cringe over rumors.

"I saw you kissing Mrs. Smithwaite," she bluntly stated. He was about to deny what she'd witnessed so she hurried to add, "I saw you with my own two eyes so don't claim it didn't happen."

He smirked. "Are you jealous?"

"I'm not sure what I am."

"I'm on expert on these matters and I'm declaring that you're jealous."

She scoffed with exasperation. "I have no hold on your affection so I shouldn't be concerned about any mischief you perpetrate. You owe me no fidelity, but it seems as if we're connected somehow. Does that make sense?"

"It makes complete sense."

"So I'm struggling to determine where I stand with you. If you sneak off with a trollop, it's irrelevant to me, so why am I feeling as if you've deliberately wounded me?"

"We enjoy a peculiar bond," he said, "and I would never intentionally hurt you."

"You might hurt me unintentionally though. Is that what you're admitting?"

"I have a reputation as an unreliable libertine."

The remark wasn't very encouraging and she asked, "Is Mrs. Smithwaite a tart?"

"Most definitely."

"Is she your constant companion in London?"

"That's an accurate assessment."

She scowled ferociously. "And you brought her here? To your sister's home? While you're entertaining a bridal candidate? What is wrong with you?"

His cheeks heated, so evidently, he was capable of some shame. He shrugged and said, "I'm not a saint and I never have been. You can talk to my sister about my failings and she'll have plenty to confide on the topic. She insists I'm going to Hell."

"Don't brag about it!"

He chuckled. "I won't mind if I end up there. I'll like the people there much more than I'd like to be trapped with the pious souls who will float up in the other direction."

She tsked with annoyance. "You are horrid."

"Maybe, but roués are much more fun than moralistic fellows. It's why maidens always fall for scoundrels."

"Is Mrs. Smithwaite your mistress? Everyone has noticed that you have an unusual relationship with her so don't lie to me. I'll know if you are."

He hemmed and hawed, then said, "I don't have a mistress, but she and I frequently revel when we shouldn't."

"I won't even ask what that means. You've painted a picture that's too salacious to consider."

"Have I mentioned I'm not a saint?"

She glared up at him, wishing she could remain angry, but her ire was slowly drifting away. He was so unrepentant, almost proud of his base disposition and bad decisions. How was she to evaluate such a dodgy character? Why would he work so diligently to be maligned and disrespected? She didn't understand him at all.

"If I begged you to send Mrs. Smithwaite back to London," she said, "would you oblige me?"

"I probably wouldn't, but only because I would hate to stir a huge brouhaha by demanding she depart. I don't believe she's staying the whole two weeks so she'll be gone soon."

"Then could you at least promise you won't loaf in dark parlors with her? Could you rein in that much of your lewd conduct? If I have to walk down another deserted hall and stumble on you with her, I might be ill."

He grinned a devil's grin. "You are jealous. I think I like it."

"I can't bear for you to be so foolish. Couldn't you ignore her—just for a few days? I'd like to have that much of a positive effect on you. I'd like to imagine you might try to make me happy."

He pondered the notion, as if he'd never previously expended energy on anyone else. He was such a rude oaf; perhaps he hadn't. How fond was he? Would he grant her this one small favor?

Ultimately, he said, "It would amuse me to make you happy. How hard will it be?"

"Well, if you swear you'll avoid Mrs. Smithwaite, I would be ecstatic. You'd be able to please me by barely exerting any effort."

"I am very lazy so I like the prospect of not having to exert myself."

"And *I* am easily placated so you'd succeed quickly."

"Will you be putty in my hands?"

"Very likely, yes."

They stared for a lengthy interval, a thousand poignant comments swirling between them. He was on the verge of uttering remarks that shouldn't be voiced aloud. She couldn't predict what they might be, but she was terribly afraid they'd be false vows that she would take to heart. She'd wind up yearning for things that could never be.

He dipped in and kissed her, and for a moment, she participated, then she mustered a bit of fortitude and pushed him away.

"Ew! You were just kissing Mrs. Smithwaite!" she said.

"That was over an hour ago."

"In my opinion, that is a very recent activity. You don't get to kiss her one minute, then kiss me the next. While I am in residence, you have to choose your amorous antics. I'm fine with you picking Mrs. Smithwaite over me. I'm *not* fine with you expecting you can misbehave with both of us."

It was a shockingly ribald edict and he was humored by her vehemence. "I'll have to contemplate the situation," he said. "I'll have to decide which one of you tantalizes me the most."

She might have thought he was being obnoxious, but there was a naughty gleam in his eye that indicated he was teasing.

"Would you go away?" she asked. "You had started to seem like a normal human being, and I was starting to forgive you for being such a despicable ass. Don't crush my pardoning mood by being an idiot again."

"Will you come back to the party and dance with me?"

"No. I'm climbing into bed and you're leaving."

She went over to the door, but he still had the key, so she couldn't shoo him out. He stood across the room, smirking, but not budging.

He was showing her that he'd depart when he was ready, but not because she'd insisted.

Finally, he sauntered over to her, and like a silly debutante, her pulse fluttered as he neared. He reached around her, stuck the key in the lock, and turned it. She knew he loathed goodbyes, so she figured he'd slip out without another word, but at the last second, he leaned in and trapped her against the wall.

He studied her, then said, "I pick *you.* I'd like to make you happy."

"Do you suppose you can?"

"I guess we'll just have to see."

He opened the door and vanished, and he didn't peek out first to be certain the hall was empty. He simply blustered out, as if he were the king of the castle. Which he was.

It occurred to her that her knees were weak, as if he'd left her faint and wobbly. She staggered over to the bed and plopped down on the mattress. She hovered there, replaying the entire encounter in her head. She was marching down a very reckless road with him. Where would it lead? Where would it end?

Nowhere good; she was sure of that.

She should have gotten up and locked the door, but what would be the point? She couldn't keep him out, and truth be told, she didn't want to keep him out. She wanted him to visit whenever he liked.

My, my, but wasn't she in trouble?

# Chapter 10

"Why are you bundled up? Where are you off to?"

Caleb glared at Michael and said, "I'm going on a sleighride."

"By yourself?"

"What a ridiculous question. Why would a man go alone?"

"I have no idea," Michael said. "Why would he do it alone or with someone else? It's freezing outside."

"Annette and Margaret Adair are feeling housebound. I mentioned they might like to tour the old Viking ruins, then maybe we could swing by the church grounds to look at the ancient graves in the cemetery. There was a fresh snow last night, so I suggested a sleighride, and they accepted."

"I repeat: It's freezing. You'll turn them into blocks of ice."

"I'll try my best to keep them warm."

Caleb pulled a flask from his coat and waggled it at Michael. Michael frowned and said, "You'll ply them with liquor?"

"It's hot chocolate, you dunce. Don't be an idiot."

Michael was grouchy. His head was pounding and his spirits were very low. He'd just eaten a late breakfast, but it hadn't settled his stomach or his mood. He desperately needed to get a grip on his nocturnal reveling and excessive imbibing. Ever since he'd retired from the navy, he'd been engaged in a never-ending bout of parties and gambling. He hated to wake up with a hangover, but he couldn't find a reason to cut back or behave better.

He'd dawdled in the dining room, hoping to bump into Margaret, but she hadn't strolled by, and it wasn't as if he could ask about her. Their furtive relationship was terribly inappropriate and he didn't dare draw attention to it.

Now, he was being apprised that his brother was taking her on a sleighride. The news was much more irksome than it should have been. He viewed Margaret as his very own, but Caleb was charming and polite, and he possessed none of Michael's bad traits. He was precisely the sort of oaf she would fancy and Michael didn't like the prospect one bit.

Michael had stumbled on Caleb in the foyer as he was preparing to depart on his outing. Caleb had several thick quilts stacked in the corner, as well as a basket that probably contained a hearty picnic. The sight was cozy and quaint, and it hinted at an afternoon of pleasure, the likes of which Michael had never participated in himself.

If he'd been a normal person, he might have been jealous to picture Caleb escorting Margaret on such an ordinary jaunt. He might have wished *he* had arranged the excursion, but he could never have escorted her anywhere.

The sleigh was parked in the driveway, the horse harnessed and impatiently waiting for the humans to arrive. Caleb and a footman carried out the supplies, and as the door was opened and shut, a wave of frigid air flooded in.

Michael shivered. He was suffering from the worst urge to dissuade Caleb from proceeding, but he couldn't figure out how. His brother was too eager.

As Caleb walked back in, he stomped snow off his boots, and Michael said, "You're mad to traipse about in this weather. I can't believe you convinced the two ladies to accompany you. You'll likely deliver them home with pneumonia."

"I promise to return them in perfect condition. Stop nagging."

"I'm not nagging," Michael insisted. "I'm just pointing out the obvious."

"No, you're nagging. You're envious because I'll spend hours, snuggled with two beautiful girls in the sleigh. What will you be doing?" He pretended to ponder, then said, "I bet you'll be drinking by three and wagering by four."

"I'm very busy today," Michael lied, "so I won't be loafing."

"Right. I will make note of it: Michael is very busy today." Caleb scoffed with derision. "Can't you at least try to get your act together? Your sloth and vices are so embarrassing. Our guests are trapped inside and able to track your every move. It's difficult to ignore the fact that you're falling apart."

"When I need a lecture from you on my conduct, I'll let you know."

Margaret and her cousin chose that moment to march down the stairs. They were a gorgeous duo, bundled up in fur cloaks and hats, woolen mittens on their hands. They were very merry, chattering like magpies, and he and Caleb smiled up at them like a pair of lucky suitors.

"Are you ready?" Caleb asked them as they reached the foyer.

"We're ready!" they replied in unison.

"I have blankets and a picnic," Caleb told them. "Shall we go?"

They hadn't noticed Michael so he butted into the amiable scene. "Are you ladies certain you've thought this through? It's so cold that I'm afraid you won't enjoy the trip very much."

Even to his own ears, he sounded like a fussy old goat, and he was stunned to be such a grump. They spun toward him and Margaret said, "Lord Sutton! How nice to see you out of bed before three."

At the cheeky comment, he grumbled, "Very funny."

"I think we're dressed for the icy temperature," Margaret said, "so you needn't fret. I'm sure your brother will take very good care of us."

"Yes, I'm sure I will," Caleb brusquely concurred, almost as if he was taunting Michael.

Out of the blue, Margaret asked, "Would you like to join us? There's room for him, isn't there, Mr. Crawford?"

The invitation surprised all of them, and for an instant, Time seemed to stand still. Michael could have grabbed a coat. He could have sent a footman running up to fetch his winter boots. He could have frittered away the afternoon at an amusing pursuit.

The three of them were staring at him as if he were a strange bird that had just flown out of the forest. Annette Adair and Caleb were especially vexed by Margaret's suggestion, and he received the distinct impression that they didn't want him to come. Nor did he want that. He wanted Margaret to stay in the manor with him, and he wanted Caleb to stay far away from her.

"I'm too lazy to tag along," he said and they sighed with relief.

"Then you'll miss out on a grand adventure," Margaret told him. "Your brother claims there are wondrous vistas to behold in the neighborhood."

Michael snorted. "This is Sutton, Miss Margaret, so he might have been exaggerating."

"We'll tell you all about it when we're back," she said.

"I predict you'll be frozen solid"—he sounded like a curmudgeon again—"so I will keep a hot fire burning to welcome you."

"I'll be looking forward to it."

Caleb was tired of Michael delaying them. He extended his arms and they each clasped one. He ushered them out the door, and Michael was anxious to follow them out, to watch them depart, but he managed to restrain himself. Instead, he meandered over to a window and peeked out the curtain, spying on them as Caleb helped Margaret in, then Annette. He seated himself between them and he made a great show of covering them with the quilts.

The driver cracked the whip and the horse trotted off. As the vehicle glided away, they whooped with glee and laughed like naughty children. Before he could drop the curtain and sidle away, Margaret glanced over and saw him. She winked, as if they shared a secret, then they were gone.

A profound silence descended and the house was very empty and quiet without them in it. It dawned on him that he should have accompanied them. Why hadn't he?

Well, for one, he wasn't the sort of fellow who went on sleighrides. He also hated to be cold and didn't strut about in chilly weather unless it was absolutely necessary. Finally, he wasn't about to sit on the sidelines as Caleb flirted with Margaret.

He realized that Annette hadn't spoken a word to him, not even a hello, so he was definitely neglecting her. Was he inclined to repair that situation? With her being Margaret's cousin, could he seriously consider her as a marital candidate? He doubted it, but in his current muddled state, he could never pick a viable path.

He whirled away from the window as Rowena flounced out of a parlor.

"Who was leaving?" she asked.

"My brother took the Adair cousins on a sleighride." He felt compelled to explain why he was loitering. "We haven't had the sleigh out of the barn in ages, and I was checking to be certain it was still in a useable condition."

Rowena smirked. "Those Adair cousins are such a frivolous nuisance, and it's a mystery to me why your brother would agree to escort them. Why would anyone in their right mind tarry outside on a day like this?"

"It was my question exactly."

She sauntered over and nestled herself to him. "There's a card game starting in the gambling room. Shall we join in?"

For once, the notion of wasting hours at cards held no appeal. He didn't particularly want to dawdle with her either. He wanted to have left with Caleb and Margaret so he could keep an eye on them. Caleb wouldn't become infatuated, would he? Margaret wouldn't be charmed, would she?

He walked off with Rowena, but he'd already recognized that he wouldn't bet much money during the wagering. Margaret was front and center in his musings so he wouldn't be able to concentrate on any topic but her.

MICHAEL WAS LOAFING BY himself, hiding in a rear parlor. He was seated on a sofa and sipping on a glass of wine. The sun had set and he was staring out at the shadows on the snow. The sight stirred his wanderlust and he wondered why he'd allowed himself to be trapped in England.

He ought to be sailing south, standing at the helm of a ship and guiding it through the waves. His body yearned for that life with a hunger that was tangible. It had him debating the purchase of Beachhead Cottage in Baywick. If he lived by the water, he might be happier, but as with so many issues, he couldn't forge ahead.

He was at loose ends and nothing seemed worthwhile. Plus, matters were changing—or about to change—and he was positive he wouldn't like the conclusions that were about to arrive. Caleb would likely move away from Sutton so they'd be parted. Michael had to marry so he'd be bringing a bride into the house. Hester wouldn't like it so he'd have to arrange different lodging for her.

All of it vexed him so he couldn't focus on the Baywick property. He figured he'd decide to buy it, but he'd proceed too slowly, and he'd learn that a quicker, smarter man had snatched it up.

The manor was quiet, the servants in the kitchen and having tea prior to the hectic push to put supper on the table. The guests were up in their rooms, primping and dressing for the evening's socializing. He had to get going too, but he couldn't force himself upstairs.

He was feeling nauseatingly sentimental in a manner he never was. His lengthy bout of gambling with his London friends had left a bitter taste in his mouth. His years in the navy had been busy and dynamic, and he'd been occupied with important chores that had been vital to the nation. Now, the days trudged by at a torturous pace, and he couldn't deduce how to fill them with meaningful activities.

He wound up drinking and carousing with dubious sycophants. Didn't he have more to offer the world than that? Shouldn't he find more productive ways to carry on?

He was thinking he should contact the navy, perhaps seek an administrative post that would provide him with significant tasks that needed completing. Or perhaps he could meet with the Prime Minister and request a government appointment.

The problem was that he'd been reveling so outrageously that no sane official would hire him for any job. He was generally viewed as a wild, destructive womanizer who was spiraling out of control. When he hit bottom, no reputable person wanted to be hovering too close. They might be buried in the rubble.

Footsteps echoed out in the hall and he hoped it wasn't Hester coming to nag. He was hoping too, or not hoping, that it was Margaret. He couldn't determine if he'd like to be sequestered with her in the isolated parlor or not. It was too risky.

A housemaid had mentioned that the sleighride was over and the participants back in one piece. Michael hadn't bumped into any of them yet. and he couldn't bear to hear Margaret babbling about his marvelous little brother.

If she started to be sweet on Caleb, Michael suspected he would send Caleb to London to the apartment he owned there. If a romance was festering, he couldn't watch it unfold.

To his surprise, it wasn't Hester or Margaret. Annette Adair peeked in and they both froze. They'd chatted several times, at the dining table or wherever, but every encounter had been awkward. He hadn't realized that nuptial plotting would be so difficult. Each conversation was stilted and tricky, and he was constantly worried that he'd utter an idiotic comment that would be misconstrued.

Miss Adair was laboring under the same onerous burden. She appeared to regret stumbling on him, but it was impossible for her to vanish with any aplomb.

"Oh! Pardon me, Lord Sutton," she said. "I was searching for your brother to thank him for our excursion. I'm sorry to interrupt."

"Hello, Miss Adair. May I call you Annette? Would that be all right?"

"Yes, that would be fine. And may I call you Michael?"

He wasn't really keen to be so familiar with her, but with his making the initial overture, he couldn't refuse. "Yes, of course. You may use Michael. Or Captain. Or Sutton. I answer to any of them."

She snickered. "I will try them all to discover which one suits you."

"I haven't seen Caleb anywhere. I'm hiding and having a glass of wine. Would you like to join me?"

A wince flashed across her face, indicating she'd rather flit out and avoid him, but she'd been raised properly and had very pretty manners, so she mostly concealed her aversion to the idea.

"I would love to join you," she said. "You have a fire roaring and I still haven't warmed up from the sleighride. It will be a relief to tarry in a spot where the temperature is balmy."

He stood and gestured to the chair nearest the hearth. There was no footman to tend them so he went to the liquor tray in the corner and poured her a glass of her own. He handed it to her, then sat down, even as he prayed they could muddle through the next few minutes without it becoming too excruciating.

She was in no hurry to begin any discussion so he asked, "Other than your almost freezing to death, how was your adventure?"

"It was informative and the countryside is very beautiful. Your brother claimed that the oldest section of your church was constructed four hundred years ago. I didn't believe him until I read some of the dates on the tombstones in the cemetery."

"We Suttons have been in the area forever and we're a devout bunch. Well, everyone but *me* has been devout. The church was the first building my ancestors erected."

"You're not devout? Are you a heathen then?"

"I guess I am. Does that news distress you? If I admit that I never attend services on Sunday, will you faint from shock?"

"It would take quite a bit more than that to have me swooning. Why have you given up on religion? Is it a recent decision or were you always opposed?"

He wasn't in any mood to clarify the situation for her, but he blandly stated, "My parents were incredibly strict and pious, and they drummed out any affection I might have possessed for moral proclivities."

"What a stunning confession. Is your sister like you or is she more like your parents?"

"With regard to religion? She's definitely like my parents and she's certain I'm going straight to Hell. It vexes her."

She chuckled. "Has Lady Hester always resided at Sutton House?"

"Yes, always. She never even left for boarding school."

He understood that it was a sly query about his plans for Hester. If he brought a bride home, he couldn't have Hester lurking in the background. No wife would want her hovering and nitpicking. He hadn't figured out what he'd do with her after he was wed, but it would have to be a drastic solution.

He wasn't about to debate the issue with Annette though. Since she was a bridal candidate, she had a vested interest in how the matter resolved, but they weren't sufficiently acquainted that he would review his options with her.

It occurred to him that he could review them with Margaret. He was able to talk to her about anything, and briefly, he wondered what it signified. Was Margaret more his type of female? Did he have a type he preferred? He'd presumed he liked all kinds.

A silence ensued that was very uncomfortable. They sipped their wine and struggled to determine what the next topic should be. Eventually, she said, "May I ask you a question?"

"You can ask and I'll answer if I can."

"When I initially arrived at Sutton, you snubbed me by being out of the house. You were aware that I was coming, yet you fled the premises. Why would you?"

He'd been very rude to her, but he was too pompous to admit it. "Did you deem it a snub? I assumed it was me being my usual lackadaisical self and trotting in too late to greet you."

"Are you lackadaisical?"

"Unfortunately, yes."

She snorted with amusement. "I was finally introduced to you that evening, and it was clear you knew my cousin, Margaret, but you pretended you didn't. I asked you if you'd met her previously, but you lied about it. Can you explain yourself?"

His cheeks heated with chagrin. He hated to be interrogated and he was never eager to provide justifications for his actions. "May I mention the word *marriage* in your presence?" he asked. "It's the reason you're at Sutton, but we're supposed to carry on as if it's merely a friendly visit."

"You can mention marriage and you can voice any remark about it you like. If you slip up and seem to tender some sort of vow, I won't hold you to it."

"Marvelous. Here goes: I crossed paths with your cousin when she was in Baywick. We didn't realize we were connected through you, and when she strolled into my front parlor, I was startled. You're at Sutton on a nuptial trip so I didn't imagine I should immediately announce that she and I were cordial in the past. She surprised me and I didn't handle the encounter very well."

"How would you describe your bond with her now?" she asked.

The query sounded innocent enough, and it appeared she was shrewder than he'd given her credit for being. Had Margaret confided in her? Had Margaret divulged the amour that had flared?

If she had, she shouldn't have been frank about it, and he wasn't about to confirm the truth. He simply said, "I like her very much and

I feel sorry for her. It has to be hard to stagger along as a poor relative. The predicament hasn't ground her down though. I find her to be amiable and cheerful."

"I feel sorry for her too. My kin take advantage of her, and we mistreat her so hideously that it's almost become a family joke."

"Are you included in that group? Do you take advantage of her?"

At the allegation, she laughed. "Absolutely. Margaret has to put up with me in every instance and I'm very spoiled. She's probably the only woman in the kingdom with the patience and temerity to tolerate me on a regular basis."

He had no desire to chat about Margaret so he changed the subject. "May I ask *you* a question?"

"Of course you can, but my mother constantly accuses me of being too candid. I hope none of my replies offend you."

"I was in the navy for fifteen years. It's rare that I'm offended by any comment."

"That's good to know. Ask your question. Let's see what response you can drag out of me."

"Tell me about your failed betrothal to Lord Grenville."

"Aah, my mother warned me that you'd inquire."

"The rumors about you in London are nasty, but then, the woman is always blamed in any romantic fiasco, so I don't necessarily believe them."

"I'm delighted to hear it," she said.

"It's being bandied that you were flighty and disagreeable, so he tossed you over, but I'm a decent judge of character and you appear rather normal to me."

"Thank you for declining to jump on the bandwagon with my detractors. It was a very frustrating period and I bore up as best I could. May I be blunt about what occurred?"

"I would like you to be."

"Were you ever informed about Lord Grenville's ordeal in Spain? He was a soldier in the army and he was captured by bandits and held for ransom."

"Yes, I'm extremely familiar with the details."

In fact, he'd captained the ship that had whisked Grenville to England once he'd been freed. The unlucky devil had been starved nearly to death and had been half out of his mind from being tortured. It was a miracle he'd survived, but apparently, he was recovering nicely.

If he'd been a bit addled, or if he'd had trouble fitting in, no one should have been surprised. Michael didn't point it out though. He stared her down, anxious to have her reveal her version of events. It would help to clarify the type of person she was deep down.

"His tragedy had scrambled his wits," she said, "so he was scattered in his thinking and actions. I understood his confusion and how difficult it was for him to carry on in an ordinary way. I could have overlooked his foibles and faults, but it was the *other* problem that wrecked it for me."

Michael frowned. "What problem?"

"He was madly in love with a servant. He had a bastard son and he'd hired her to be the boy's governess. My mother and I begged him to send her away, but he refused."

"Some of this sad tale is swirling in town."

"The gossip about it has been horrendous."

"You've weathered it well," he said.

"Not that well. I've kept my mouth shut about it, and I haven't defended myself, but my silence has fanned the flames of the scandal. People filled in the blanks with the worst stories and I'm hoping it will die down soon."

"It was wise to be silent. You couldn't have won any arguments."

"It was my opinion exactly."

"In the end, he wed the woman, didn't he?"

"Yes, he wed her."

"Perhaps it was a love match after all. What do you suppose?"

"I won't share my thoughts on the subject," she said, and a hint of rage flashed in her eyes. Obviously, the debacle had been a humiliating embarrassment.

He'd have been content to cease their discussion of the topic. She'd verified what he'd presumed to be the truth, but she was compelled to add, "I recognize that men are allowed to have affairs and to dabble with mistresses. I've been taught that, once I'm a wife, I'll have to ignore my husband's illicit conduct, but I couldn't have begun my life with Grenville when he was obsessed with someone else. I might have been able to tolerate it in the future, after the novelty of our union had faded, but right at the start, I viewed it as very unconscionable behavior."

The declaration was a shot across his bow. She was apprising him of what she'd permit—and what she wouldn't—in a marriage. He was a scoundrel who'd never found a reason to practice monogamy, so her attitude should have removed her from his nuptial deliberations, but her feelings weren't unusual.

Any wife would be opposed to her spouse's philandering, and he was impressed that she'd been brave enough to voice her reservations.

She'd remain on his list of matrimonial contenders, but he was desperately keen to solve the problem of Margaret being her cousin. He couldn't deduce how to mention the dilemma though, and he was forestalled as she downed the last of her wine and stood. Clearly, she intended to flee so he couldn't raise a more thorny issue.

"I'm sorry," she said, "but I'm running late and it takes me forever to dress for supper."

"If you bump into my brother, tell him where I'm hiding. Tell him to find me. I have to talk to him."

"I will tell him and thank you for inviting me to chat. It's been very instructive."

She sashayed out, and as the air settled with her departure, he was left to wonder if she meant *instructive* in a good way or bad.

He was assessing her as a possible bride, but she was assessing him too. The man decided whether to propose or not, but rumor had it that she'd already rejected dozens of offers. She was very fussy and not inclined to lower her standards.

Wouldn't it be hilarious if he proposed, only to have snooty, rich Annette Adair claim she wasn't interested? It would serve him right for being such a pompous, unlikeable ass.

He didn't have much of a clue as to what she was seeking in a spouse, other than the fact that she was using her fortune to buy herself a title. Hester had told him that she wanted a doting husband, which he would never be, so why waste energy on her?

Margaret was wedged between them, her presence like a huge boulder that was blocking any valid evaluation of her cousin. How could he contemplate Annette when Margaret was taking up so much space?

He ought to simply send Annette back to London. He could have Hester politely inform her mother that he'd determined they wouldn't suit, but if he sent Annette home, Margaret would leave with her. He wasn't finished flirting with Margaret so Annette had to stay—so Margaret would stay.

And who could guess? Maybe he'd tire of Margaret and shackling himself to Annette would begin to seem like a grand idea. Maybe Margaret would cease to be an impediment.

"Annette Adair, Countess of Sutton." He spoke the words to the quiet room, as if testing how they sounded.

It occurred to him that he ought to visit Lord Grenville to pry out his perspective on the failed engagement. He also needed to meet Annette's mother who, if there ever was a marriage, would become his mother-in-law. She'd broken her leg, and her injury had prevented his being introduced to her, and he deemed her absence to be incredibly convenient.

Might Ambrosia Adair be trying to avoid him?

He'd be wed to Annette Adair, not Ambrosia, but Annette had commenced several of her sentences with anecdotes about her mother who appeared to run her life. Of all the situations he couldn't bear to experience, it was the notion of having an interfering mother-in-law. By the very nature of the relationship, it was a dicey proposition, and he wouldn't bring a domineering harpy into the family.

He chugged down the rest of his wine, then tamped down the fire in the hearth. He'd been thinking of skipping supper, but he was anxious to watch Margaret with Caleb. If a romance was flaring, he had to nip it in the bud.

What if Caleb grew overly fond? What if he fell in love with Margaret? What if he ultimately decided to wed her?

The questions had Michael so disturbed that he felt dizzy. He marched out and headed for his bedchamber to change his clothes. He'd arrive in the parlor prior to the other guests, and he'd keep a stern eye on the festivities to ensure no mischief was transpiring.

Margaret could never be his bride, but still, he viewed her as belonging to him. If Caleb was about to butt into that liaison, Michael had to be certain he butted out!

---

"I STUMBLED ON HIM by accident," Annette said to Margaret, referring to her conversation with Lord Sutton, "and I would have tiptoed away, but I couldn't figure out how."

Margaret grinned. "Was the encounter horrid?"

"Not really," Annette replied. "He insisted I join him for a glass of wine so I couldn't escape. In the beginning, it was awkward, but by the end, we managed to have a pleasant chat. He asked if he could call me Annette."

Margaret snickered. "Did you tell him he could?"

"He's so arrogant. How could I have refused?"

"Has he offered you the same courtesy? Are the two of you on a first-name basis?"

"Yes, we're the best of chums. He told me I may call him Michael, Captain, or Sutton, whichever I prefer."

They were in Annette's bedroom suite, engaged in some final primping before they went to supper. They'd spent the afternoon out of the house on their sleighride. The temperature had been frigidly uncomfortable, but Margaret and Caleb had been wonderful company, so it had been a perfect day.

"When you get Lord Sutton off alone," Margaret said, "and away from his fawning audience, he can be very charming."

"He wasn't quite as irksome as usual so that was a relief." Annette smirked impishly and said, "I asked him about you."

"You didn't! What did he say?"

"He admitted that you have a previous acquaintance so he's stopped denying that he knows you."

Margaret snorted with disgust. "That was big of him."

"He feels very sorry that you're a poor relative."

"Shoot me now," Margaret muttered.

"I confessed that our entire family treats you atrociously and that I'm the worst of all at abusing you."

"If you denigrate yourself to him, you'll be throwing a huge wrench in your mother's marital plans."

"I can't imagine being wed to him. I've always thought I was eager to snag a nobleman, but I've been socializing with Mr. Crawford, and it's occurred to me that I might be happy with a different sort of man."

Margaret scoffed. "An *ordinary* sort of man? Is that what you're claiming?"

"A less prominent fellow wouldn't be so abrasive or egotistical. He might love me and dote on me. An ass like Lord Sutton could never lower himself."

"I agree that he can be terribly pompous, but trust me, you'd never be content with a commoner, especially one with no prospects like Mr. Crawford. Don't delude yourself. You're too spoiled and you like your ostentatious pleasures too much."

"I've been so swept up in Mother's scheme to marry me to an aristocrat that I've never considered anyone without a title."

Margaret had been leaned over the dressing table and studying herself in the mirror. At hearing Annette's comment, she straightened and frowned.

"Caleb Crawford has been flirting with you when he shouldn't have. I've watched you with him and you're much too fond. You're encouraging him when you shouldn't be."

"I'm just being cordial," Annette lied. "There's no harm in it."

"Annette!" Margaret's tone was scolding. "This is Margaret you're talking to. You can't fool me. You're besotted and you're sending the wrong signals. It's cruel to tease him."

"I'm not teasing him. He's very sweet and he would be so good for me. He'd tamp down my more exhausting impulses and shape me into a better person."

Margaret clucked her tongue like a fussy nanny. "People don't change, Annette. You are who you are: a rich, pampered princess who's bound to wed very high. Mr. Crawford could never be your husband. Your mother would never allow it."

"If she met him, she might like him."

Margaret tsked with derision. "That has to be the most idiotic remark you've ever uttered in my presence. Your mother would loathe him."

Annette sighed with regret, but with exasperation too. "I don't want what Mother wants. I assumed I did, but Lord Sutton has underscored for me how misguided I've been in my nuptial plotting. I've listened to Mother when I should have been asking questions and forming my own opinions. She's run roughshod over me."

"She's your mother and she's focused on what's best for you. If you suggested a match with a nobody like Mr. Crawford, she'd immediately declare him a duplicitous cad who's after your money. In light of you being an heiress, you have to constantly be concerned about that possibility."

"Mr. Crawford isn't a fortune-hunter."

"I realize he's not, but other wastrels might be, and your mother would never permit you to shackle yourself to someone she'd view as a conniver. If you tried to thwart her, she wouldn't hand over your dowry, so you'd have to live in poverty and squalor."

"I could survive with less."

Margaret scoffed again. "No, you couldn't. Don't be ridiculous. Early on, it might seem romantic, but you'd quickly grow weary of barely getting by and having to practice thrift. Then where would you be? It's what *my* life is like and I can guarantee you wouldn't like it."

"I'd have a spouse who loved me. Why couldn't that be enough?"

"A woman in your position never marries for love, Annette. You know that and you're scaring me. I'm worried about your affection for Mr. Crawford. Should we return to London? Should we announce that you and Lord Sutton wouldn't suit and that we're leaving?"

Annette's heart constricted in her chest. Panic assailed her and she struggled to steady her breathing. Margaret was correct that she was too fond of Caleb, but their petty amour was the only exciting thing that had happened to her in ages. She couldn't part from him yet and she was determined to continue their illicit liaison.

Who was it hurting? Why shouldn't she experience a bit of joy before Ambrosia fettered her to an arrogant fiend like Lord Sutton? If that was her ending, Annette truly thought she might die from despondency.

She trusted Margaret, but she figured her cousin was writing to Ambrosia every night. She doubted Margaret would deliberately tattle about her infatuation, but Annette couldn't risk that her mother might learn of it. It would either bring Ambrosia winging to Sutton to set matters aright. Or it would result in Ambrosia ordering her home. Both conclusions were too untenable to contemplate.

She forced a smile and said, "I'm sorry if I'm distressing you. I just hate all these matrimonial machinations. I've been working to pick a husband for three years and my nerves are on a sharp edge. I'm spewing nonsense so you should ignore me."

Margaret smiled too. "Consider yourself ignored."

"Are you ready? Shall we go down?"

"I am ready," Margaret said, "and I insist that we be the most gorgeous, enticing women in the room. Let's make every other female green with envy. Especially Mrs. Smithwaite."

"I like the sound of that."

They grabbed their fans off the bed, linked arms, and swept out together.

# Chapter 11

Margaret was in her bedroom, in the dressing room, when the door from the hall opened and shut. Whoever had entered was sneaking in, being very furtive about it, and she didn't have to ponder to deduce who it would be.

The evening's festivities were over and they'd been very pleasant. No outside guests had been invited from the neighborhood, so it had just been Michael and his family, along with the entourage he'd brought from London. Everyone had been on their best behavior.

Supper had been delicious, the food excellent, the conversation stimulating. Afterward, people had engaged in ordinary activities. Some had played cards. Some had read by the fire. Some had sung duets in the music salon. For once, Michael had been present through the whole affair and it had heightened her enjoyment.

He hadn't joined in any of the games or singing, but he'd smiled, told stories, and chatted. He'd lorded himself over the event like a fond uncle and he'd tried to fit in and be part of the group.

It was probably wishful thinking, but she felt that he'd been studying her all night. She'd kept an eye on him too, while diligently concealing her heightened interest. Mainly, she'd been curious as to how he'd interact with Mrs. Smithwaite. To her great delight, her prior discussion with him about the gorgeous widow seemed to have had an effect.

He'd been cordial to her, but he'd exhibited no extra fondness. Margaret thought Mrs. Smithwaite had been irked by his cool reserve, but that might simply have been her imagination painting a picture she was eager to see.

At his arriving in her bedchamber, unwanted and unwelcome, she sighed with aggravation, but with a bit of excitement too, then she walked out to greet him. He'd spun the key in the lock, to prevent an interloper from entering after him. There was a wine tray on the dresser and he went over and poured himself a glass.

"I suppose it would be pointless to scold you," she said.

"Yes, it would be so you can save your breath."

"Apparently, your clandestine visits are to become a habit. Have I sent a signal so you assume I'm fine with such recklessness?"

"It was torture for me to spend so many hours with you down in the lower parlors. I had to pretend we're barely acquainted."

"We are barely acquainted."

"I watched you constantly. Did you notice?"

"I noticed, but I'm certain I'm the only one. Thank you for not being overly blatant."

"How many more days will you and your cousin be at Sutton? Nine? Ten? What will we do when you leave for London?"

"What will we *do*? You sound as if we've established some type of enduring bond."

"Haven't we?"

It was a dangerous question she didn't dare contemplate. In the world where they resided, there was no road they could travel together. A man like him could never be friends with a woman like her, so a casual attachment was impossible. She wasn't a doxy, so she couldn't revel with him in the demimonde where he thrived. And he was about to marry a debutante or an heiress and she possessed neither designation.

He downed his wine, then put the glass on the tray. He sauntered over to her and she was frozen in place, like a mouse caught in a trap. He was a fascinating rogue and she was so stupidly infatuated.

She was still attired in the gown she'd worn down to supper, but she'd removed her jewelry, as well as the combs from her chignon, so her hair was hanging down in a curly wave. He slid an arm around her waist, pulled her close, and kissed her. She kissed him back and it was a decadent embrace that continued for an eternity.

His caresses ignited sparks of desire she'd never be able to quell later on. The agitation being produced was so enticing that she was frightening herself. She understood that he had no honorable intentions toward her, but he was very cunning in coaxing her to accept that their amour was perfectly permissible.

She yearned to make him happy, to surrender whatever would please him, and she was worried she'd eventually participate in conduct that was hazardous and wrong.

"I want to keep you by my side forever," he said, as he broke off the kiss to nibble at her nape.

For a fleeting moment, she was stunned into presuming he was about to propose, but she shook off the absurd notion. Where he was concerned, she couldn't wallow in fantasy.

"You're not serious," she said.

"Yes, I am. Would you be my mistress? What would you think of that?"

"No, I wouldn't be your mistress and you insult me by suggesting it."

She eased away from him and went to the dresser to pour her own glass of wine. She'd already had plenty down at the party, but his lewd proposition had rattled her nerves and she needed to calm down.

He sidled over and stepped in so their bodies were crushed tight from chests to toes.

"Doesn't it feel as if Fate has dragged you into my path?" he asked. "I assume I'm finished with you, then you reappear, as if by magic."

"There's no magic involved. We met in Baywick, and we met at Sutton, but I'll depart very soon and you'll forget about me."

"I won't forget. I'm convinced of it. Tell me the truth. Can you bear to have our liaison conclude so abruptly? Can you flit off to London and never see me again?"

"That has to be our ending. I'm a poor relative, remember? My life is very small and I can't grab hold of what I crave. I've had to learn to settle for less."

"I could lodge you in a posh apartment. You'd have servants, a beautiful wardrobe, and a carriage. I'd furnish you with an allowance. I could change everything. I could make your small world very grand—if you'd just agree."

"How long would this splendid utopia last?"

"It would last for as long as we were content with one another."

"As long as *you* were content, you mean. Once you grew bored with me and kicked me out, where would I go? My family would never take me back."

"Maybe I'd never grow bored," he ludicrously said.

She snorted with exasperation. "You are such a liar."

When he was standing next to her, it was hard to concentrate. She tried to ease away again, but he wasn't about to release her. They were near the bed, and before she realized his scheme, he lifted her, whirled around, and tumbled them onto the mattress. It was a perilous spot for her to be, and she would have scooted away, but he stretched out atop her so she was stuck beneath him.

If he'd been a genuine scoundrel, she'd have been afraid of what was about to happen, but she sensed no menace. He was smiling down at her, his eyes alight with mischief, as if he'd played a humorous trick.

"Isn't this more comfortable?" he said.

"No! Are you insane? Let me up."

"Sorry, but I can't. I'm delighted to remain right where I am."

"Michael Crawford!" she fumed in her strictest schoolteacher voice. "You're scaring me."

"I am not. Don't be ridiculous."

"You don't scare me, but I'm terrified of what sins you might commit."

"I would never hurt you. Haven't I previously sworn I wouldn't?"

"Yes, but I didn't believe you then and I don't believe you now. Are you hoping to ravage me? Is that your plan?"

He scoffed with derision. "I've never forced myself on a woman. If I ever bothered to press the issue with you, I can guarantee you'd be totally amenable."

"Ooh, you are such an arrogant beast."

"I definitely am. I can't deny it."

He slipped off of her and onto his side. She was freed from his weight pushing her down, so she should have mustered her moral indignation and slithered off the bed, but to her great disgust, she was in no hurry to escape.

She rolled toward him so they were nose to nose, their breath mingling, as they catalogued features and silently wondered where they were headed.

He was the first one to speak again. "I can't abide the prospect of you returning to London. How am I supposed to part from you?"

"I can't abide the prospect either," she said, "but after I vanish, you'll barely notice my absence. I'm sure of it."

"You're so wrong. It's why I asked you to be my mistress. I wasn't insulting you; I'm trying to devise a method for us to stay together. Won't you ponder my request? I hate that you automatically refused."

"I didn't have to ponder. I'm not a trollop and I would never sell myself for a few baubles. You have the attention span of a toddler and you're like any other cad. You relish the chase, the hunt, but after you catch your prey, you lose interest very fast."

He frowned, then muttered, "You could be correct."

"If I relented, and you had your way with me once or twice, you'd move on to some other naïve, gullible girl. Then where would I be?"

"You're not naïve or gullible. I'd like to keep you with me, but I can't figure out how to manage it."

"You could marry me." At her brazen comment, he looked so astonished that she giggled with merriment. "You are so amusing."

"I can't wed you," he said.

"You *could* if you were sincere in your affection, but we both know you're not. It's one of those rules of the universe that a nobleman never weds *down.* I'm so far below you that I'm surprised you can see me and I can't fathom why you persist with our flirtation."

He shifted onto his back to stare at the ceiling, and he drew her to him, so she was draped over his chest. Her ear was directly over his heart, so she was mesmerized by its steady beating, and she thought it was the best moment of her life. If she'd died that very instant, she'd have been ecstatic when she flew up to Heaven.

After a lengthy pause, he said, "I don't want to get married. Not to anyone."

"Every earl has to bite the bullet sooner or later. Your trip to the altar has finally arrived."

He snorted at that. "I have to accomplish it by my birthday in June."

"Why then?"

"I'm about to be thirty, and my father arranged his estate so a huge pile of our money was placed in a trust account. He deemed me to be incorrigible, and he was concerned that I'd never settle down and behave more responsibly. He tucked the funds away so I couldn't squander them in my twenties, and if I don't shackle myself by my birthday, it will go to the Church."

"I'm betting you're a heathen so that would be a horrific ending for you."

"You have no idea," he told her. "My parents were extremely religious so they were cruel and judgmental. In their opinion, I could never do anything right. Yet when I reflect on my childhood, I wasn't all that bad. I was simply rambunctious and spirited, but they couldn't handle me. It created such a wedge between us."

"I'm sorry to hear it."

"My younger years were quite unbearable so I don't have a pious bone in my body. I rarely visit Sutton, merely because it stirs so many exhausting memories."

She was stunned by his frank admission and she was astounded that he'd confessed it. It made her feel closer to him than ever. It made her feel as if she knew him better than anyone ever had.

"Wait a minute," she said and she popped up on an elbow. "Isn't Caleb your father's natural-born son? If he was so devout, how was Caleb sired?"

"Have I neglected to mention that my father was an incredible hypocrite?"

"It sounds as if he was."

"Rumors abound too that he wasn't really my father, and it's why he detested me so much. There has always been gossip in the neighborhood about my mother, that she couldn't get a babe to catch in her womb and that she seduced a groom so her husband could have an heir."

Her jaw dropped. "Honestly, Michael! Don't you spew that terrible tale ever again. Don't even talk about it to me in the future. I'm flattered to have you confide in me, but it's too salacious to repeat."

He shrugged. "We have many skeletons in our closet, and if you stay at Sutton long enough, you'll stumble on the servants tittering about us."

"I wouldn't listen to them! And you shouldn't either! It's your mother they're disparaging."

"I never had much of a relationship with her. She was even more vehement about my conduct than my father. I've shared some of our sordid history so you'd understand why I have such ambivalent feelings about Sutton. I'm supposed to wed and start my nursery, so I can secure my line, but no one believes it's *my* line to protect. I don't care about my obligation to the title, but I'm expected to carry on as my station demands."

"You're trapped by your birthday approaching, and it's a sort of cudgel imposed by your father to keep you on the straight and narrow. Is that it?"

"Yes, and I never like being ordered about. He's manipulating me from the grave and it galls me to give him any satisfaction."

She bristled with annoyance. "It doesn't matter what type of stories have swirled. You're an aristocrat through and through. You possess every awful trait a nobleman is required to exhibit. You're arrogant, domineering, cocky, and impossible. If we pulled out a knife and sliced open one of your veins, blue blood would flow out."

"Do you really think so?"

"I know so. Don't be such an idiot."

He snickered and eased her down again. He was quiet for awhile, then he said, "I'll marry so I can receive my money, but I'll never be happy about it."

"Then I'll always fret about the candidate you wind up picking, and you're being such a grump tonight. Can't you simply be grateful for the many boons you have? In my view, you're very lucky."

"Even if I have to choose a bride I don't want?"

"Even then."

"Will I like being a husband?" he asked.

"No. You enjoy being a bachelor too much."

"Will I be any good at it?"

She laughed with glee. "No, you definitely won't be any good at it."

"I hope you're wrong. I constantly ponder the poor girl who may be fettered to me. How will she weather the debacle?"

"I'm certain you never set foot in a church," she said, "but I attend services every Sunday. I won't pray for you. You're beyond redemption, but I will pray for your wife—that she's not too despondent over the years."

She could sense him smiling and she was curious as to what thoughts were rocking him. He was probably picturing himself as a miserable husband with an even more miserable wife. She'd pity him, except for the fact that he was rich and privileged. He was so spoiled and it was irritating to have him whine about any issue.

"When we're back in London," he said, "could I call on you occasionally?"

She lay very still, trying to envision how that scenario might unfold, but she couldn't imagine it. He couldn't stop by. Not ever. Society's rules were so strict. If he strolled in, maybe to take her on a carriage ride or to the theater, it would have to be because he was courting her with an eye toward marriage, but he'd been very clear that she could never be his bride.

Plus, she doubted he was sincere in tendering the request to visit. She was positive they'd part the following week and he'd never contemplate her again. On her end, she was so besotted that, if she believed he'd show up someday, she'd spend the rest of her life staring out the window and anxiously watching for him to trot up the street.

She wouldn't count on him, wouldn't deliberately create a situation where she'd yearn and pine away. She wouldn't write a different, false future for them.

"You couldn't call on me," she said and she sounded very glum. "It's an insane idea."

"It might be insane, but I'm an earl and I can act however I please."

"You can, but *I* can't. Besides, once Annette and I leave Sutton, I won't be in London, so you couldn't visit me even if I'd agreed you could."

He froze, as if she'd shocked him, then he asked, "You won't reside with Annette and her mother?"

"No. Her mother doesn't like me and she'll shuffle me off to other relatives. She already told me so."

"Where will you be?"

"I don't know, but my kin will figure it out. They won't let me starve in a ditch."

"Annette claims they abuse you."

She tamped down a wince. "They can be awful, but their disdain and mistreatment have toughened me up and I've grown a very thick skin."

"I wish you'd consent to be my mistress. I could vastly improve your circumstances."

"And I wish you'd quit mentioning it. It hurts my feelings that you have such a low opinion of my character."

"I don't have a low opinion. I think you're wonderful."

At the compliment, she sighed with contentment. "It's lovely to have you stroke my ego."

"You have an ego?" he asked. "I thought only men had them."

"Women have them too, and mine is enormous, larger than yours, I'm sure."

"That's not possible. I have the biggest ego of any oaf in the kingdom." He was silent for a minute, then he said, "Do you like my brother?"

"Yes. He's very nice—and he's very fond of you. He talks about you in such glowing terms and his obvious affection makes me like him very much."

"But do you fancy him?"

She popped up on an elbow again and she was scowling. "In a romantic fashion? Absolutely not."

"If he declared himself infatuated, would you welcome his attentions?"

She sputtered with hilarity. "Are you jealous of your brother? Even if you're not, lie to me and pretend that you are. The memory will delight me for ages."

His cheeks heated. "Caleb is marvelous in all the ways that I'm not. If he ever started to dote on you, you wouldn't be able to resist."

"I'd resist," she firmly stated. "I'm absurdly smitten with you and it has me realizing that I'm partial to rogues. Your brother could never tempt me and I would never tempt him. He's sweet on Annette. Haven't you noticed?"

He frowned. "You can't be serious. Isn't she considering marriage to *me*?"

"Supposedly, yes, but if you're beginning to assume you might propose to her, you ought to hurry up or he might jump in line ahead of you."

"Caleb can't abide rich, spoiled girls. He'd never be interested in her."

"If you say so."

"I say so," he staunchly insisted, "and I am always right."

She chortled merrily. "You are so full of yourself."

"Yes, I am and it's why you should listen to me. I'm frustrated that you won't let me make your life better. You refuse to be my mistress and it's an idiotic decision."

"I'm not a doxy, and even if I accepted your lewd offer, by the time you could move me into an apartment, you'd be wed. I'd never be the *other* woman in your marriage. I would never betray your wife. You're being ridiculous so please cease your badgering."

"If I pester you relentlessly, I might change your mind."

"You could never change it."

"You might be surprised by how persistent I can be."

"No, I wouldn't. When a notion lodges in your deranged male brain, you're like a dog at a bone. You can't stop obsessing, but you have to ignore this idea. It pains me to have you blather on about it and I'm sad that I can't be the paramour you need."

She suspected he'd reply with a poignant comment about how much he cherished her, but he said, "I'm exhausted. I should sneak out before I doze off."

"If you fell asleep, I'd have to murder you, and I'd rather you didn't drive me to homicide."

He slid away from her and stood next to the bed, while she dawdled on the mattress, like a courtesan with her lover. His gaze was troubled, as if a thousand difficult ruminations plagued him, but he didn't voice any of them aloud.

Eventually, he leaned down, his palms on either side of her, and he kissed her so tenderly that it brought tears to her eyes.

"I'll see you in the morning," he said.

She pressed her luck. "Shall we have breakfast together?"

"At eleven?"

"At nine, you sluggard. Don't you dare disappoint me."

"I've been disappointing people all my life, but for you, I will try to come up to snuff."

"Nine o'clock it is. Don't be late."

He smirked and walked out. Once again, he didn't peek into the hall prior to exiting. He simply sauntered off.

She blew out a heavy breath and relaxed on the pillows. The room was incredibly empty without him in it, and she was worried about how she'd survive the loss of him after she departed. He was like a blazing comet, streaking across her personal sky and lighting up her world with joy and excitement.

Perhaps she should have agreed to be his mistress. Why not? Her existence was so tedious and untenable. What did she possess that was of any value? Why not leap into a grand affair?

The instant the crazed thought popped into her head, she shoved it away. Michael Crawford was a dashing, amazing scoundrel, but for an ordinary female like her, he would be a very bad bet.

She stepped to the floor and went to the dressing room to don her nightgown and climb into bed. The fire had died down, so the temperature was very chilly, and she rushed about, then scampered under the blankets.

The moon was up, reflecting off the snow, and painting the walls in pretty shades of silver. She stared out at the stars, thinking of him, thinking of how happy he made her, thinking of how destroyed she'd be after she left.

She sent a prayer winging in his direction, wanting him to know she was contemplating him. He likely wouldn't sense her message, but she'd pretend he'd sensed it. She'd pretend he'd contemplate her in return and he'd be glad forever that they'd met.

# Chapter 12

Rowena was tiptoeing up the stairs to her bedroom. She'd been in the gambling salon, playing cards and hoping Michael would return. He hadn't, which was frustrating. It was very late, and when the last of the stragglers had declared themselves done for the evening, she'd had to call it a night too.

He'd left early, claiming he was headed to bed, but she was certain he'd snuck off to visit his paramour. She was frantically trying to deduce who it might be, and she figured it was a fetching housemaid who tended him whenever he was home. She refused to believe it might be Margaret Adair, with whom he'd been arguing in that dark hallway.

Rowena was anxious to get him back to London where she'd have him all to herself and wouldn't have to share. The ladies in town were aware that she was greedy and vindictive and they stayed away from him, rather than incur her wrath.

She'd reached the landing when a door opened farther down. It was Margaret Adair's room and she halted, watching and curious as to who would emerge. When Michael strutted out, she was astonished, but she wasn't astonished too.

She was being pummeled with questions, but with disturbing scenarios too. Her determined goal was to keep him from marrying anyone so he'd eventually recognize that *she* was the best choice to be his wife. But Annette Adair had been invited to meet him, and Annette was the girl he was supposed to be considering as a bride.

Clearly, he was having an affair with her cousin, so what was Rowena's opinion about it? Should she have an opinion? Her moral compass hadn't worked for years, or maybe it had never functioned properly, but there were many disconcerting aspects to what he was perpetrating.

She should probably ignore the entire debacle, but she understood Society's rules. The person who broke them was cast out to become a pariah. Michael was an earl and a male, so he would never suffer any consequences, but what about Margaret Adair? She enjoyed no protections.

He was philandering with a spinster in his sister's home. It was the type of juicy scandal that would rock London for months. It was the height of folly, the lowest kind of dishonorable conduct he could perform.

What was he thinking? Well, he wasn't thinking; that was the problem. He was an unscrupulous libertine and lust controlled his actions. He wouldn't like to be observed creeping out, so her initial instinct was to fade into the shadows, but she'd never been a coward. She wanted him to know she'd seen him.

He spun toward her, and for a lengthy interval, he stared, his mind racing as he dithered over how to handle the awkward moment. Currently, she was his favorite doxy, and in the world of scoundrels and tarts where they thrived, they'd promised no fidelity.

A man of his station could revel however he pleased, and she wasn't allowed to fret over it, but they were a devoted couple—as much as people were in their circle. She felt entitled to be exasperated. She also felt an obligation to point out the danger he was fomenting.

He wouldn't like to hear it, but she couldn't be silent. If nothing else, he was her friend and she would hate to stand idly by while he carried on like a fool.

Ultimately, he grinned and smirked, as if they had a secret, then he winked and walked off in the other direction. He tromped up the rear stairs to the master suite on the next floor. She was rooted to her spot, mulling the situation, mulling her role, her place, then she traipsed after him. No doubt she was making a grave error, but she had to talk to him.

She approached his door, and she knocked once, then slipped inside without waiting to be summoned. He was in the sitting room, over by the hearth. He'd shed his coat and cravat and had poured himself a glass of liquor. He was sipping on it and he studied her over the rim.

"Did you need something?" he casually asked.

She could have uttered a coquettish remark, could have pretended she'd chased after him for carnal purposes, but they were beyond dissembling.

Without preamble, she said, "Margaret Adair, Michael? Really? Have you thought this through? I mean, what will happen to her if you're caught? Isn't she a poor relative who's supported by her family? You're putting her in terrible jeopardy."

He debated several replies, then said, "You and I are cordial, but you shouldn't presume it furnishes you with some authority to comment on my behavior."

"I realize that fact, and normally, I wouldn't butt in, but you're stirring a boiling pot of trouble. I must mention that you are prone to outrageous carousing. It appears to me that you've wandered out onto a very steep ledge, and I should coax you down off of it."

"Do you imagine you can?"

"I hope so."

She moved toward him, figuring she'd pour herself a whiskey, that they'd hash out the dilemma, then crawl into bed. But before she'd taken two steps, he held out a palm, indicating she should stop.

"The other night," he said, "you visited me without an invitation. At the time, I didn't raise a fuss, but I specifically told you not to barge in in the future unless I requested you join me."

"I haven't forgotten, but this is an unusual circumstance so I decided to ignore your edict." She smiled, assuming he'd shrug off her brazen entry, but apparently, she'd crossed a line he couldn't forgive.

"I recognize the issue you'd like to address," he said, "but we're not discussing it, and I'm astounded by your audacity. You and I are not officially bound so you have no right to caution or scold me."

"I wouldn't dare scold you, but a few words of advice are in order."

"If I want ethical advice, I'll locate my brother. He guides me in my choices; you don't. You are simply my paramour and I dally with you when it is convenient. Just now, it's not convenient."

"You don't have to be so surly."

"You've begun to misconstrue your position in my life. We gamble, frolic, and occasionally fornicate, but that is the extent of our dealings."

"Quit being such an ass! I'm merely struggling to convince you to logically assess your conduct with Miss Adair. What if your affair is exposed? What will become of her? Or what if it's not exposed and you wind up married to Annette Adair? How could you wed her after you've seduced her cousin? That's a very low bar—even for a rogue like you."

She smiled again, to lighten her reprimand, but he was too grouchy to listen. "I frequently immerse myself in wicked predicaments, but that's my own business. It's none of yours."

"It certainly seems as if you need to be lectured so you'll come to your senses."

"I never let anyone lecture me. You're aware of that and you don't get to start."

"Would you climb down off your high-horse for a minute?"

"No." He set down his glass and he went over to the door and yanked it open. He shooed with his fingers, as if she were a mutt being kicked out. "Goodnight, Rowena."

A muscle ticked in her cheek. She yearned to march over and shake him for being such an idiot, but she'd been dismissed. Why had she believed she could chastise him? He was correct that she'd misconstrued her role. She was positive she'd grown to be important to him, but his view of their relationship was the complete opposite of hers.

She was no shrinking violet though and she stomped over to him and said, "Think about Miss Adair, would you? Think about the trouble you could cause for her. You're a notorious lecher, but you're not generally cruel. You can't want to destroy her."

His response floored her. "I shouldn't have brought you to Sutton so you'll have to head home in the morning."

"What? No! You can't throw me out simply because you're in a bad mood."

"My mood is fine."

"I refuse to leave," she said like a spoiled brat.

He sighed as if she was a great trial. "The maids will be in at seven to pack your bags and I'll have my coachmen prepared to depart at eight. Please don't be a nuisance about this. If you're not ready, or if you delay, I'll carry you out in your nightclothes. You can wail and create a scene, but I'll carry you out anyway."

"You're being a callous beast. You have ice in your veins!"

"Yes, I've always been told that I do."

"I was just trying to help," she fumed. "You're thinking with your cock so you aren't rationally evaluating this situation."

"No. You're jealous and you feel you hold such an elevated spot by my side that you can interfere in one of my amours. You can't, and I'm stunned that you assume I'd put up with it." He gestured into the hall and repeated, "Goodnight, Rowena. I appreciate you traveling to Sutton with me, but your sojourn will have to be cut short."

"Bastard," she spat. "Will I see you once you're back in town?"

"Why wouldn't you see me?" His expression was innocent as a saint.

She circled by him and stepped out of the room. "If you stir a scandal with her, don't say I didn't warn you."

"Trust me. I will never say that."

He shut the door with a determined click, and cretin that he was, he spun the key in the lock so she couldn't bluster back in and argue a bit more.

She was seething, wondering what had possessed her to admonish him. He was the most pompous, most egotistical male she'd ever met, but she'd had too much to drink and alcohol goaded her into making awful choices.

They were lovers and companions who enjoyed the same vices and dubious acquaintances. She'd begun to believe—quite wrongly, it seemed—that she'd earned a special place in his heart. To her enormous regret, she'd forgotten that he had no heart so she couldn't have earned a place in it.

She hovered, anxious to knock and quarrel, to hurl curses and call him obscene names, but he'd laugh at any outburst. She stormed off, and fleetingly, she considered speaking to Margaret Adair. The woman was a naïve fool who would never have previously crossed paths with a wretch like Michael Crawford.

She'd deem his fondness to be sincere, and she was probably hearing wedding bells, but they would never chime for her. Should Rowena point out Michael's lewd intentions? Should she apprise her of what Michael was truly like?

At the notion, she scoffed with derision. She was concerned about Michael and the possibility of him landing himself in a jam. She *wasn't* concerned about Miss Adair or the problems that might arise due to her illicit fling. Margaret Adair could have him—with Rowena's blessing.

Rowena was leaving at dawn, and she was keen to get to sleep so she could wake up in plenty of time to primp and preen before she vanished. Michael was a coward, so he'd never stagger down to see her off, but if any of their despicable friends reported on her exodus later on, she wanted him to be informed that she'd looked glamourous and serene, as if she didn't have a care in the world.

HESTER WAS RACING ALONG, overwhelmed by sudden chores. Mrs. Smithwaite had received an urgent message from London and she had to return to the city immediately. Her swift departure had caused an uproar.

The beautiful widow had had luggage to pack and load in the carriage. She'd required an early breakfast. She'd demanded a basket of food to take on her chilly journey.

The servants were being run ragged on her behalf and Hester was in a foul mood. She thrived on her schedules and routines. She never liked to be rushed or to have unusual incidents occur. When her orderly plans were disrupted, she was left apprehensive and disturbed.

Michael should have been the one to deal with Mrs. Smithwaite, but of course he couldn't be bothered, so the burden had fallen on Hester. She was his hostess so she had to provide the proper attention to Mrs. Smithwaite, but she yearned to flit up to her bedchamber and hide.

She was approaching the foyer, when Caleb entered from outside, and she halted. She never liked to bump into him.

It was a frigid morning, and he was bundled in a heavy coat and boots, a knitted scarf wrapped around his throat. His cheeks were rosy, his color high, and if Hester had been inclined to fairly assess him, she might have admitted that he appeared very dashing.

But she never thought about him and she wouldn't gape at his blond hair or blue eyes. He was just as handsome as Michael, having somehow missed inheriting the plainer Crawford traits.

As he dawdled, Annette Adair came down the stairs and she stopped to chat with him. Evidently, the pair presumed they were unobserved. They were too far away for Hester to eavesdrop, but Caleb leaned in and murmured a comment that had her grinning seductively. Then he furtively reached out and squeezed her hand.

The stealthy move was so shocking that Hester blanched with astonishment. What was the brash couple thinking? Were they flirting? The prospect was so outrageous that she couldn't process it.

Caleb was staring at Miss Adair so fondly that Hester worried he might kiss her. Right there in the foyer! Had he no shame? Had he no sense? Well, he'd been conceived in sin, born in sin. He'd spent a good portion of his life, studying Michael as he engaged in every vice. So, no, he had no shame or sense.

In the end, he didn't kiss her. He continued up the stairs, while Miss Adair continued on to the dining room. She was smiling like the cat that had got in the cream. Was she mad? Was she loose with her favors? Was she a tart deep down?

She was at Sutton so Michael could consider marriage to her. Had she changed her mind about being a candidate? Was she imagining she liked Caleb more than Michael? And what was Caleb's ploy by enticing her? He lived on Michael's charity. Michael had rescued him from dreadful circumstances and had raised him up to be a member of the family.

Would he betray Michael? Would he steal his brother's fiancée? Was he that diabolical?

She was so stunned that she was having trouble breathing. Miss Adair was headed in her direction, and she escaped into an empty parlor and closed the door so the foolish ninny didn't glance down the hall and realize that Hester had been watching her.

Hester lingered, wondering if she might faint, until Miss Adair passed on by. She waited, letting her pulse slow, then she slipped out and went to the foyer, arriving just as Mrs. Smithwaite was promenading down the stairs.

Her trunks had been loaded, but still, two maids and a footman were traipsing behind her, carrying a few last items. She looked gorgeous and elegant, draped in thick furs and expensive jewels. In comparison, Hester felt ancient, dowdy, and even a tad unkempt.

Hester greeted her. "Thank you for visiting us, Mrs. Smithwaite. We've enjoyed having you as a guest."

"Your hospitality was lovely," Mrs. Smithwaite told her, but there was no sincerity in her words.

"I hope your emergency in town isn't too dire. I'll pray for you."

"I'm a sinner, like your brother, so your prayers would be wasted on me."

Hester tried to be polite, even when someone was being horrid, so she didn't hurl the cutting remark she'd like to utter. She swallowed it down, but to signal her disdain for the nasty widow, she was about to march off without a goodbye.

Before she could flee though, Mrs. Smithwaite said, "Would you walk me out?"

"The temperature is freezing and I don't have my cloak."

"This will only take a minute."

Mrs. Smithwaite gestured for Hester to precede her, and it dawned on Hester that she was much too accommodating. But she'd never had the type of strong personality where she could put her foot down and mean it. She meekly obeyed, trudging out into the cold air. Mrs. Smithwaite followed her.

They stood together as the servants checked the final preparations. An outrider waved to the driver that all was ready, and a footman yanked the carriage door open, expecting Mrs. Smithwaite to waltz over and climb in.

The woman was much taller than Hester and she paused to bend down and whisper, "I'm going to tell you a secret, but I insist you keep my name out of it."

"I will if I can."

"Your brother is engaged in a dangerous and very inappropriate amour with Margaret Adair."

Hester gasped. "He's what?"

"Hush!" Mrs. Smithwaite warned. "I worked to convince him to cry off from his lunacy, but he's obsessed with her. At night, he's been observed, sneaking in and out of her bedchamber. I thought you should be apprised before it blows up into a huge scandal."

"I don't believe you," Hester said, figuring she should exhibit some loyalty to Michael.

"I don't care whether you believe me or not, but you're his sibling so you might be able to stop it. You should definitely rid yourself of Margaret Adair. Just picture the brouhaha that would erupt if Ambrosia

Adair learned about this. She's a vicious shrew and you wouldn't like to have her as an enemy."

The snooty witch sauntered off and the outrider helped her in. In a quick minute, the vehicle lumbered away. Hester didn't tarry to watch it roll off. She whirled away and went inside, her fury sparking.

It was an awful day for traveling and she envisioned Mrs. Smithwaite miserably uncomfortable the entire way. Perhaps it would snow and the roads would become muddy and clogged. Perhaps the coach would become stuck and her trip would wind up being a nightmare.

Hester could only hope.

"May I speak with you?"

Michael frowned at Hester and said, "No, sorry. I'm joining some people for breakfast at nine. If I dawdle, I'll be late."

"Who are you meeting?" she asked. "I was just in the dining room, and Margaret Adair is the only one present."

"Is she? Some of the male guests are riding with me this morning, but we're eating first. She will enliven our meal."

"Mrs. Smithwaite departed on the spur of the moment. She had an emergency in town."

"That's too bad," he said, his expression blank. "She's gone?"

"Yes, and I'm glad she left. She's very rude."

"Yes, she certainly can be."

They were in the master suite and he was eager to head down to be with Margaret. He'd promised he'd be there and he was keen to arrive on time. Hester never accosted him in his bedroom so she had to be in a dither about some issue or other. For once, he was feeling happy and spry, but she would sour his fine mood. He simply didn't have the patience to deal with her.

"I have to ask you a question," she said.

"Ask away, Hester, but please be brief. I can't bear to be scolded. How have I upset you?" Her cheeks heated bright red, and she was nervously wringing her hands, so he said, "Whatever it is, don't choke on it. Spit it out."

"Are you having an affair with Margaret Adair?"

It was the very last topic he'd anticipated, and he chuckled, as if the notion was preposterous. "Why would you suspect such a thing? I realize you like to accuse me of having low morals, but you can't suppose I'd behave that outrageously. And why would you accuse Miss Adair of having wicked character? I barely know her, but she seems to be very sweet and straightlaced to me."

"The maids were gossiping. They claim you've been flirting with her. They even claim you've been spotted sneaking into her bedchamber."

"That is a bald-faced lie! Who is spreading such a malicious rumor? Will you tell me or should I line up the maids and quiz them until the culprit confesses?"

"You deny it?"

"I vehemently deny it. Will that be all?"

She couldn't stand up for herself or continue an argument when she'd been thwarted. She mumbled, "I apologize for interrogating you, but I would be so distraught if your mischief was exposed. If Annette Adair fled in a huff, how would we persuade any other candidates to visit you?"

"On this beautiful winter morning, that is the least of my worries."

He motioned to the hall, anxious for her to leave, but she was being unusually persistent.

"You should shower Annette Adair with some extra attention today," she said.

"Why?"

"You're purportedly contemplating her for the position of countess, but so far, you've completely neglected her."

"I haven't neglected her. I've been studying her quite avidly and I'm very impressed. You did a marvelous job by inviting her to Sutton."

"You haven't been focused on her. Don't pretend. You've been preoccupied, and in your absence, your brother has been enticing her."

"Caleb has? I doubt that very much, and even if he has been, how can it hurt? If Annette marries me, or if she doesn't, it will be a decision reached between me and her mother. If Annette is fond of Caleb, it has no bearing on how her mother and I choose to proceed."

"It's wrong for him to insert himself into the situation. You should speak to him. You should warn him away."

"For being courteous to her?"

"Yes! What if he charms her? What if she begins to imagine she'd rather wed him than you?"

He scoffed. "The entire reason she's here is because she's determined to snag a nobleman. Caleb isn't one so she would never seriously consider him. Neither would her mother."

"If he interfered in your betrothal, Mrs. Adair would never forgive us and all of London would be scandalized. What would we do then?"

"It won't happen, Hester, and you shouldn't work yourself into a lather over it. Caleb and Miss Adair went on a sleighride. Her cousin was with them for the whole outing and they had an enjoyable trip. They're the same age so they probably have a lot in common. You shouldn't read more into this than there is."

"You never notice what's right in front of you," she complained. "You never concentrate on what matters."

To his consternation, she was trembling with fury, as if his responses had goaded her into a terrible temper, but in light of some of the quarrels they'd had in the past, he couldn't see that he'd said anything particularly distressing.

"I'm sorry," he told her, "but I can't debate this with you. I'm expected down in the dining room. You'll have to catch me later."

He started out, but paused at the door to glance back at her. She looked frozen and brittle, as if she might shatter into a thousand tiny pieces. He wished he knew how to help her, but she'd always been overly despondent.

Their father had never found her a husband and everyone agreed that a woman should wed, that it was unnatural to remain a spinster. Was that her problem? Would she have had a better life, a more contented life, if she'd had a home and family of her own?

If he thought it would repair her circumstances, he'd find her a husband now. He figured he could drum up a fellow who might be willing. After all, there was never a downside to marrying an earl's sister, but he wouldn't convince some poor oaf to have her. Michael would never torture any man so hideously.

The alternative was that she'd tarry at Sutton forever. As the years rolled along, she'd grow more bitter and more unhappy. Should he let that occur? Where she was concerned, he'd never been able to predict what she needed, and at the moment, he couldn't ponder his options.

He whipped away and hurried on, and he shoved her out of his mind. He was good at compartmentalizing difficult issues. And Hester was like a nagging toothache that never quite faded away. Their relationship never changed, so why fret over her? He'd proved, over and over, that he couldn't mend what plagued her.

He arrived at the stairs and dashed down them, excited to be with Margaret and hoping she'd consent to spend the day together.

"WHAT ON EARTH?"

Ambrosia Adair read the anonymous letter she'd received from Sutton House. It was unsigned, but the unidentified author was desperate to apprise Ambrosia about Annette and Margaret's conduct. Apparently, they required more supervision than Ambrosia had supplied.

The reprimand set her teeth on edge and she was aghast over the admonishment. Annette was cognizant of the fact that she was on a nuptial interview. She wouldn't disgrace herself or bring disrepute to Ambrosia. Would she?

As to Margaret, there had been that incident when she was an adolescent, but Ambrosia concurred with Annette that Margaret had been lured into folly by a group of much older scoundrels. She generally liked Margaret and felt she'd matured into a very sensible young lady.

Yet the nameless tattler claimed the Earl had developed a fascination for Margaret and she couldn't deflect his attention. Annette, supposedly, was engaged in an amour with a servant. With a servant! Her activities were so blatant that the other guests were gossiping about her.

Ambrosia hated to believe the allegation, but then, she had always socialized with Annette. She'd been available to rein in any excesses. Lord Sutton's party was the first occasion where Annette had traipsed off by herself and she was only twenty. Was she reveling in her freedom? Was she enjoying her independence a little too much?

And what about Margaret? Margaret was Annette's companion and chaperone. If Annette was involved in mischief, why hadn't Margaret noticed and stopped it?

Margaret wrote to Ambrosia every evening, but her chatty missives merely described a typical sojourn in the country. There had definitely been no mention of illicit liaisons or inappropriate suitors!

The whole sordid business sounded dodgy and her temper flared. She'd reared Annette to be a countess and she couldn't permit her daughter to wreck such a wonderful opportunity.

Her broken leg had healed to the point where she could hobble around with a cane. Her physician had furnished her with a new-fangled chair too, one with two wheels so the footmen could push her about. She was no longer completely incapacitated.

She was sitting in the front parlor by a warm fire. She rang for her personal maid who showed up before too much time had passed.

"What did you need, Mrs. Adair?"

"I guess I must travel to Sutton after all."

The woman frowned. "Are you sure you should? You're barely mobile and you'll freeze on the way. Your physician won't like you trekking about in the ice and the cold."

"It can't be helped." Ambrosia tsked with annoyance. "I knew better than to allow Margaret and Annette to waltz off by themselves. I have to be there so I can watch what's happening."

"What *is* happening?"

"Nothing of any account. I simply shouldn't have let them participate in such an important visit without me."

"When will you leave?"

"Tomorrow morning. Have the servants pack a week's worth of clothes and notify the coachmen that we're going."

"I must ask again: Are you sure?"

"Very sure. Please make the arrangements."

The woman left and Ambrosia skimmed the unsigned letter once more. She pondered whether to write to Annette and Margaret to tell the disobedient pair she was coming. In the end, she decided to surprise them. If trouble was occurring—which she didn't necessarily believe—they wouldn't be able to hide it.

# Chapter 13

Annette was sauntering down a country lane. It was a bitterly cold afternoon, the sun shining off the snow. The landscape was so bright that it hurt her eyes.

She'd been feeling housebound so she'd bundled up and had eventually gone all the way to the village. She'd snooped about and her presence as a stranger had earned her plenty of stares. Not that there had been many people to gape. Every sane person was tucked away inside by a warm fire.

She was headed back to the manor, but she was in no hurry to arrive. She'd relished having the chance to traipse off by herself. If her mother had been present, or if Margaret had been watching her as she ought, Annette would have had to bring a maid along, or not trek out at all, so she was reveling in the fact that she was totally alone.

It was the first time in her life that she could make her own choices without her mother guiding her every step, and she was wondering how she could alter her situation so she could carry on more independently in the future. She couldn't imagine returning to London and falling into the same old traps.

She'd been behaving outrageously at Sutton and she was entirely too fixated on Caleb Crawford. He was handsome and charming, was polite and interesting. He listened to her and he doted on her. He excited her as no other suitor ever had.

In her prior matrimonial forays, her mother had always been lurking, advising her as to what—and what wasn't—allowed, so Annette was trying to comprehend her fascination for him. Was she truly smitten? Or was she trifling with him because there was no one to tell her she couldn't?

What if Lord Sutton proposed? Even if she argued against a union, Ambrosia would likely insist she accept him. How would Annette deal with the pesky problem that Lord Sutton and Caleb were inordinately fond and nearly always together? Could she wed him, then ignore Caleb?

She doubted it and she was terribly afraid that her feelings for Caleb were powerful and sincere. If they were, what was she to do about them?

Behind her, a horse's hooves crunched on the snow as a rider approached. She scooted over to let him pass and she glanced over her shoulder to see who it was. When Caleb smiled down at her from his perch up on the saddle, she rippled with delight.

He was by himself, as was she, so they could converse for a few minutes without anyone gawking or eavesdropping.

"Hello, Miss Adair," he said, grinning. "Why are you wandering down this deserted road all by yourself? Where is your entourage of guards? Won't your reckless conduct cause the Earth to spin off its axis?"

"I'm being flagrantly negligent. You won't tattle on me, will you?"

"No, and I can firmly state that Sutton is a very safe spot. No miscreant would dare to accost you. They'd be too scared to incur my brother's wrath. You can stroll to your heart's content."

"I'm enjoying myself very much. I've escaped from my luxurious prison."

"Is it difficult to be so rich and magnificent?"

"No, it's very easy. I'm wealthy and spoiled and I won't apologize for it." She stuck her nose up in the air and sarcastically said, "I'm positive I deserve every splendid boon that has ever been showered on me."

"You're definitely spoiled," he told her, "and I can't abide such blatant pomposity, so it has me curious as to why I'm so eager to wallow in your captivating company."

"I've placed you under a wicked spell."

"May I walk with you?"

She pretended to ponder her reply. "Will you be courteous and cordial? Or will you harangue at me for being snooty and too set on myself?"

"I'll probably always harangue at you for your haughty tendencies. Someone should point out how conceited you are. It might as well be me."

He dismounted and came over to her. He clasped her arm and they started off. She was snuggled to his side, their bodies touching all the way down.

"I missed you today," he suddenly said. "May I admit it? Or would you rather I didn't?"

"I missed you too. I rambled through the downstairs parlors, wishing you'd find me and whisk me off on a sightseeing adventure."

"I thought about it, but I forced myself out of the house so I wouldn't be tempted. I'm trying to behave myself around you."

"Must you behave?"

He blew out a heavy breath and they stopped and turned to face one another. She'd never previously stood so close to a man and his proximity ignited sparks of exhilaration. He rested his palms on her waist and pulled her to him. They gazed into each other's eyes, cataloguing features, memorizing every detail for later reflection.

His horse was plodding along behind them and the animal watched with a wise expression. Annette was certain, if it could speak, it would tell them they were being wildly careless.

"I've been thinking about you," he said.

"I'm glad to hear it. I've been thinking about you too."

"Michael owns an apartment in London. I've been debating if I shouldn't head to town and stay there until you leave Sutton."

At the absurd suggestion, her pulse raced with alarm. "What are you talking about? No, you shouldn't leave. Why would you even contemplate it?"

"You know why. I'm so besotted, but you're about to be engaged to my brother. I can't be flirting with you like this. It's so wrong."

"My mother wants me to wed him, but I'm not sure it's what I want. I assumed I was anxious to glom onto a nobleman, but I've begun to question that notion."

"Since you met me?"

"Yes, since I met you."

He sighed with exasperation. "Listen to yourself. This is simply a petty dalliance, and if we had any sense, we'd desist immediately."

"It's not petty! Don't describe it like that."

"I've never encountered a female like you before," he said, "and I'm yearning and dreaming as I shouldn't be. I've persuaded myself that I can devise a method to make you my own, that I can keep Michael from marrying you. It's dangerous plotting, but I can't tamp down this crazed fantasy where you wind up with me instead of him."

She felt as if he'd escorted her out onto a very high cliff, and if they weren't cautious, they'd tumble over the edge. She was weighing her words, struggling to determine what her next comment should be.

Should she encourage him? Did she dare? What if she led him on, then changed her mind and decided she'd like to be a countess after all? Or what if Ambrosia put her foot down and demanded Annette consent to have Lord Sutton whether she'd like to or not?

She took the coward's route. "I can't figure out what my response should be."

"Have I overstepped? Have I misread the emotion that's surging between us?"

"You haven't misread it, but what if it's not real? It could merely be the novelty of a new acquaintance."

"It's not that," he vehemently said. "I've traveled the globe and I've crossed paths with every kind of person. I understand people and situations. I'm not confused about what's happening. If I can't have you in the end, my life might not be worth living."

"Oh, Caleb, what a vow to utter! You shouldn't be so candid."

His cheeks heated. "I'm sorry, but where you're concerned, I can't help myself."

"You needn't be sorry. I'm bewildered over how to assess your pronouncement. There would be so many obstacles to our being together. There's your brother and my mother. There's my position in Society and the fact that I'm an heiress. There's my dowry."

"I realize all of that, so are you agreeing that I should head to London? Is that what you want?"

"No! This affection that's bubbled up…" She halted and said, "Is it affection? Is that what I should call it?"

"Yes, but it's much more than that, isn't it? It seems as if I've known you forever, as if Fate has arranged for us to meet at Sutton. I'm suffering from the strongest perception that I should never let you go, but how can I inflict myself on you? It would be a hideous betrayal of my brother. It would be *me*, up-jumping to a spot where I don't belong."

"Don't denigrate yourself to me," she said. "I think you're wonderful."

"Yes, but I'm the bastard son of an earl, sired on a trollop by my randy, hypocritical father. I survive on Michael's charity. I have no money. I have no home. I have nothing of value to offer you, so by my butting in and declaring myself, I'm being selfish and even a tad cruel. But I can't be silent."

"If I could be yours," she tentatively inquired, as if testing how the prospect would sound when voiced aloud, "would you like that? If it could become a reality, would you be willing?"

"Yes, yes, absolutely! Annette, you can't wed my brother. I'm devoted to him, and I would lay down my life for him, but he doesn't deserve you. And he would never love you. I doubt he would even respect or esteem you. You've watched him. You've seen what he's like."

"He's very cold, very aloof, and he doesn't appear to be interested in me."

"It's not you specifically. He's not eager to marry anyone, but there's a trust fund he'll inherit on his birthday if he's a husband by then."

"Is that the only reason he's considering me?"

"It's the only reason he's considering matrimony at all. He's happy as a bachelor and he's not keen to stop being one. Monogamy is not a trait in his vocabulary. He revels with tarts and keeps mistresses. Mrs. Smithwaite? She's his current paramour."

Annette's temper flared, but she tamped it down. "They have a heightened relationship I didn't understand so that information doesn't surprise me."

"That's the type of depraved rogue he is deep down. He brought his concubine to Sutton, while you and my sister are here too. He's a scapegrace and liar, who knows right from wrong, but who doesn't believe any rules apply to him."

"Every aristocrat feels entitled. It's not unusual."

"When I discovered he'd invited Mrs. Smithwaite to the party, I thought about scolding him, but I didn't waste my breath. If I'd reprimanded him, he'd have laughed and told me to mind my own business. He's always carried on exactly how he pleased and he doesn't care who he hurts. As his bride, you'd constantly be shamed by his doxies and very public affairs. Could you bear to be yoked to a wastrel like that?"

"No, I couldn't."

She peered down at the ground, furiously evaluating the problems his comments had stirred. She was destined to wed into the nobility, but she couldn't imagine shackling herself to a rude, imperious fiend like Michael Crawford.

"Marry me!" he blurted out.

"What did you say? I could swear you just asked me to marry you."

"We should run away. We'll elope to Scotland, and when we return, you'll be my wife. It will mean Michael can't have you and that your mother can never fetter you to a libertine like him."

"You can't be serious," she murmured.

"I'm serious as an apoplexy! The other option is that I leave Sutton today and I stay away until you've departed. I can rush to the manor and pack a bag. Should I?"

"No! I want you at Sutton with me. I want us to flirt and play and pretend this glorious interval will never end."

"It has to end, but who can predict how abruptly? We could be socializing this evening, and suddenly, Michael might saunter up and propose. He can be hasty and fickle occasionally. He might point a finger at you and declare, *You're the one. We'll wed next week.* Then what would you do?"

She groaned with dismay. "You're making this so hard."

"How am I making it hard? If you marry me instead, I can save you from my brother. Won't you let me?"

"I'd have to convince my mother, but she'd ever agree. She'd never release my dowry to you and she'd accuse you of being a fortune-hunter. We'd be poor forever and I'd be so miserable. You'd start to hate me."

"Money isn't everything, Annette. You've been raised to suppose you can't live without it, but you could march down a different road. You could pick *me* over money and we'd be so happy."

He was so passionately sure they could break all the rules, yet somehow have a pretty future, one based on affection and mutual admiration. She could abandon her quest to be a countess, could wed for love and joy, rather than title and wealth. Would it be worth it?

When he was gazing at her so intently, as if she was the most precious thing in the world, she couldn't concentrate. She couldn't settle on the correct choice, and she was terrified to open her mouth, lest the wrong words slip out.

"I have to ponder this," she said. "I can't decide right now."

"If Michael proposes, you have to seek me out immediately. I'll whisk you away from here."

She forced a chuckle. "You talk about him as if he's a felonious criminal."

"He has no conscience and he's devoid of morals. If you wind up with him, you'll always regret it, and I will never recover from the loss of you."

With that, he dipped in and kissed her. She'd never been kissed before and she stood very still and allowed him to proceed. He didn't push his advantage, but simply touched his lips to hers. She dawdled and absorbed every detail.

He drew away and she was so overcome by emotion that tears flooded her eyes. He noticed her distress and he tugged off his glove and wiped them away with his thumb.

"My beautiful Annette," he murmured, "you can't be sad because of me."

"I'm not sad, you oaf. I'm so ecstatic I feel as if my heart is about to burst out of my chest."

"Am I wearing you down to my way of thinking?"

"I can't describe my condition, but I'm very confused."

Noises sounded around the bend, as a wagon rumbled toward them. He stepped away from her, putting plenty of space between them so, whoever was approaching, it would appear as if they were merely having a cordial chat.

As the vehicle rolled into view, he quietly said, "We're not finished discussing this. We'll make it happen. I promise."

"How positive are you? Shall we bet on it?"

"I'll win any wager."

The wagon was from the estate and he knew the driver. The man reined in and Caleb said, "Can you give Miss Adair a ride to the manor? She's been walking for ages and she's freezing."

Caleb helped her clamber up into the box, and before releasing her, he furtively squeezed her hand. The driver called to the team and they lumbered away. Annette glanced back, but one look was all she dared. She waved goodbye as if they were casual acquaintances.

He was standing in the middle of the road, his blue eyes magnetic and mesmerizing. His focus was so potent that he might have been a hero in an ancient fable. He was that splendid and it occurred to her that she might just die of despair if she couldn't have him for her very own.

Her expression had to be lovelorn and beseeching, so she whipped away and stared straight ahead. She engaged in small talk with the driver, managing to carry on a sensible conversation all the way to the front door. After thanking him, she hurried inside, but when she tried to recollect later on, she couldn't remember a word of what they'd said.

She could recollect every word Caleb had uttered though. If she lived to be a hundred, she would never forget any of them.

"Is Lord Sutton finally behaving himself and leaving you alone?"

As Annette posed the question, Margaret was glad she was turned away from her cousin. It meant Annette couldn't see how her cheeks had heated.

"Yes, he's leaving me alone."

"Are you lying?" Annette asked. "He's not the sort of fellow who would be thwarted very easily."

"Mrs. Smithwaite is gone so he'll be mourning her departure. At the moment, he's probably too bereft to bother with me."

They snickered quite nastily, then peeked about to ensure none of the other guests had heard them.

They were in an upstairs salon, where a hot fire was burning. The afternoon sun was shining in the windows and warming the temperature even more. A quartet of men, some of Michael's London chums, was playing cards on the other side of the room. They were loud and boisterous and totally ignoring Margaret and Annette who were seated on a sofa and ignoring them too.

Annette had strolled into the village and she was still chilled from it. She was wrapped in a thick woolen shawl, and she kept wandering over to the hearth and loafing next to the flames, then she'd wander back to where Margaret was reading a book.

It was the same novel she'd been slogging through in Baywick when she'd first met Michael, the one about the earl and pirate, Sebastian Bramwell. It was an exciting tale, but she was too distracted to concentrate on the story.

Annette plopped down and said, "I realize he's fixated on you, but will he eventually propose to me? What's your opinion? So far during our visit, he's acted as if I'm invisible. Except for when I stumbled on him in that deserted parlor, he and I have barely chatted."

"His deranged mind works in mysterious ways so I can't predict how he views this debacle. He could strut in this very minute and ask for your hand. I would put nothing past him."

"If I was his wife, would you be upset about it? I'm not certain you've been entirely frank about how attached you are to him."

Margaret wasn't about to be candid, for she'd be advising her cousin to spurn an earl. If Annette rejected Michael, Margaret could have no part in it. It was better to lie. "You and I won't socialize all that often in the future, so if you wed him, it wouldn't be a problem."

"Your answer is so obviously false. Are you fond of him? Just admit it."

"What good would it do? If I'm fond of him, or if I'm not, it can't have any bearing on what you choose. If you refuse him, I can't be responsible. Your mother would learn of it sooner or later and she'd murder me."

"What a tangle," Annette mused. "If I decide I'm not interested in having an aristocratic husband, would I give Ambrosia a heart seizure?"

"She's been planning on it since the day you were born. It would be a difficult goal for her to abandon."

"After my exasperating nuptial forays with Lord Grenville and Lord Sutton, it's clear I'd be insane to shackle myself to a nobleman."

"I can't fathom how you'd persuade Ambrosia that you'd like another kind of beau. I don't believe she'd oblige you."

"What if I married for love instead of title and position?"

It was a strange query and Annette voiced it in a dreamy manner that was unnerving. Margaret scowled at her and said, "Is Mr. Crawford still flirting with you? Is that why you're uttering such peculiar comments?"

"He's not flirting. I just like him very much and I'm wondering if I haven't been focused on the wrong things. Mother has always insisted I become a countess, so I convinced myself that I should be a countess. But I would be doing it to please her, rather than myself. What if I don't want it? What then?"

Margaret would be delighted to have the betrothal fall to pieces, but she was aghast to discover that Mr. Crawford was butting into the middle of the marital plotting. What was his game? He seemed so nice, but might he be a fortune-hunter after all? Annette's dowry could make even the most ethical fellow behave like a greedy fiend. Was it tempting Mr. Crawford to recklessness?

Margaret's scowl deepened. "Should I have a few words with Mr. Crawford? Should he be warned away from you?"

"Gad, no!" Annette's remark was much too vehement. "He's simply forced me to recognize that I might like to walk a different path."

"You can't walk anywhere but in the direction Ambrosia picks for you. If you're beginning to suppose you could chart a new course, I must counsel you to stop being so silly."

For some reason, Annette couldn't relax. She'd sit for a bit, then she'd stand and roam around, then she'd sit. She rose and went over to the card players, then she returned to Margaret's area of the room and gazed out the window. She was lost in thought and very forlorn.

"Margaret, come here," she said after awhile. "I have to show you something."

Margaret stood and peered out the window too. Michael was down in the driveway, chatting with an older gentleman. He was fifty or so and they looked exactly alike: same build, same height, same posture and facial features. He had Michael's blond hair and blue eyes, but his hair had faded to silver.

She might have been studying an artist's rendering of how Michael would appear when he was fifty. They were that similar.

"Who is that with Lord Sutton?" Annette asked. "Who would you guess? An uncle maybe? Has a relative arrived?"

"I don't believe he has any uncles."

"They could be father and son, don't you think?" Annette grinned impishly and said, "Might there be some skeletons in the Crawford family closet? Should I gossip with the servants to find out what they are?"

Margaret recalled Michael sharing the terrible rumor that swirled about his parentage, about his mother having an affair with a groom in order to provide her husband with an heir. Could it be true?

Even as she pondered the awful question, she shook it away and scolded Annette. "Don't be ridiculous and don't you dare gossip with the servants about him. The gentleman is probably a neighbor and you ought to leave it at that."

They continued to watch them, and eventually, the older man climbed onto his horse and trotted away. Michael stared after him until he was swallowed up by the trees. Then he spun away and started inside.

He happened to glance up and he saw her and Annette spying on him. He paused, then smiled wickedly. He was at his most dashing, his color high, his eyes a riveting blue, his lush hair curling over his shoulders.

Without reflecting, she rested a palm on the glass, as if she could reach through it and touch him. Annette immediately honed in on the outrageous gesture and she scoffed with derision. "I can't listen to you when you swear you don't fancy him. You must cease your denials. It's exhausting."

"What benefit could come from candor?"

"He's handsome, isn't he? It makes him hard to resist."

"Yes, he's very handsome," Margaret agreed.

"But looks can be deceiving," Annette said, "and he's aware of how women drool over him. I can't abide such masculine conceit. Could you imagine being fettered to such a vain oaf? His pomposity would grind me down until I was naught but grains of sand, blowing in the wind."

"It might not be so bad," Margaret felt compelled to state. "He might figure out how to be a married man. He might grow into the role."

"You are such an optimist. It really annoys me."

Michael kept on into the house so they lost sight of him. Annette glared at her and asked, "Which one of us was he smiling at?"

"I'm sure it was you," Margaret said.

Annette smirked. "He doesn't realize I exist so it couldn't have been me. Will you still pretend he's left you alone?"

"What else can I claim? If he's pestering me or not, how can it matter?"

"How can it indeed?"

Margaret whipped away and sat on the sofa. Annette nearly sat down too, but in the end, she headed off to parts unknown.

Margaret exhaled a heavy sigh. What would become of them?

If they trudged home, with no proposal tendered, Ambrosia would kill them both. Mostly, she'd blame Margaret for the opportunity slipping away. She'd accuse Margaret of being lazy and ineffective.

Or, if they raced home in celebration, because Annette had a ring on her finger, Margaret would be sent to live with another family of cousins. She'd likely never see Michael again, and in the not-too-distant future, she'd hear that Annette had wed him.

She truly thought, when that day arrived, her heart might simply quit beating. She'd be that bereft.

It was pointless to fret over the possible outcomes though. The resolution between Annette and Michael was out of her hands and she would have no say in any decision. Why obsess?

She picked up her novel to read it again, but it was slow going, and despite how she tried, she couldn't focus. She could only picture Annette walking down the church aisle, Michael waiting for her at the altar, and it was such a depressing vision that she was nauseous just from contemplating it.

# Chapter 14

Michael tiptoed down the hall toward Margaret's bedchamber. He was being very reckless, and each time he snuck in, he was risking disaster. The prior night, Rowena had caught him. Who might catch him next?

Rowena had been very brave in trying to yank him to his senses. In return, he'd sent her home without a goodbye. It was bad behavior on his part, but where Margaret was concerned, he was acting like a lunatic. He didn't need to be scolded by his paramour.

It was very late, and his friends were down in the lower parlors, gambling and generally being obnoxious. He was glad Rowena was gone, but he was tired of the motley crew of hangers-on who were still on the premises. He'd invited them to tag along because he'd wanted a barrier between himself and Annette. Now, he simply wished he'd have told them to head to London with Rowena.

He reached Margaret's door and slipped inside. Since the evening she'd locked him out, and he'd used a key to bluster in anyway, she hadn't attempted to bar his entry. She recognized that it would never work. He was vain and obstinate and he always got his way. If he decided to stagger in, he would and she couldn't stop him.

She'd been waiting for him, and she was growing so comfortable with their secret dalliance that she'd arranged the room to welcome him. She'd let down her pretty chestnut hair. A tray of wine and snacks had been delivered and a cheery fire warmed the temperature.

She'd dragged two chairs over to the hearth. She was sitting on one and already enjoying the wine. When she saw him, she toasted him with her glass.

"Your visits have become a naughty habit," she said.

"I know, but I can't stay away. You're like a magnet and I'm metal. I can't resist your steady pull."

"Should that comment delight me or terrify me?"

"It should definitely delight you. I'm wonderful, remember? And you can't resist me either."

He spun the key, then he came over to her. He dipped down and kissed her, and she kissed him back with an enormous amount of enthusiasm. He couldn't figure out why, but he liked being sequestered with her. She appeared to emit an aura that his body perceived. It soothed the beast that raged in him so he was less likely to carry on like an ass.

He drew away and sat in the other chair. She poured him his own glass and he took it from her and sipped the contents. They gazed into the flames, the moment poignant and companionable.

"This seems so normal," she said, "that we could be an old married couple."

He smirked. "I've lulled you into complacency, but you shouldn't feel safe. I can be a real monster when I'm in an awful mood."

"I realize that about you, but in the short period we've been acquainted, you've been remarkably kind to me."

"You bring out my best qualities."

"You pretend to be horrid, but you're not. Not deep down."

"You make me happy," he told her and he clasped her hand and linked their fingers.

"You make me happy too," she said, "and I can't fathom how I'll bear it after we part. Shall I stroke your ego and admit that I'll miss you forever?"

"Yes, please stroke my ego. I have so few women who ever will."

She scoffed with exasperation. "You liar. You have beautiful women falling at your feet. All they do is flatter and compliment you."

He grinned. "Maybe."

"I was spying on you today."

"Down in the driveway, yes?"

"Yes. Who was the fellow you were talking to?"

"I could tell you, but you previously ordered me to never spread rumors about my parents."

"Just this once, you can spread one rumor. He looks so much like you that I'm very curious."

"He's the man who supposedly sired me, and since you were able to thoroughly assess him, you probably grasp why the gossip won't die down."

"Does he live in the area?"

"Yes. He was a groomsman in our stables. About the time I was born, he received an inheritance from a distant cousin. He quit his job and used the money to start a horse farm a few miles down the road."

"Have you always known him?"

"No. I met him after my parents were deceased. I bought some horses from him, without having a clue of who he was. At first, I didn't notice the similarities, but Caleb pointed them out. Now, whenever I cross paths with him, I can't help but compare myself."

"Why was he here?"

"He was riding by. He heard I was hunting for a bride and he wished me luck. If the stories about him and my mother are true, he'll be a grandfather after I have some children. Not that he could ever boast about it to anyone."

"Have you ever hinted to him about your suspicions?" she asked.

"Are you joking? I view myself as a brash rogue, but that is a conversation I couldn't envision having."

"Good. What if you alluded to the situation, but he had no idea what you meant? You'd embarrass him and you'd further denigrate your poor mother."

There was a small table between them and he rested his elbow on it as he studied her. She smiled and asked, "Why are you staring?"

"You fascinate me. Are you certain you won't be my mistress? I can't imagine you leaving Sutton and my never seeing you again. Can you imagine it?"

"No, but I can't be your mistress and don't harp at me about it."

"What would you suggest for us then?"

"I suggest we furtively misbehave for the next week. We'll treat our odd friendship like a shipboard romance. Once we dock at the harbor, we'll go our separate ways."

"I don't want to go our separate ways."

"I understand, but you're very spoiled, and you can't always bend the world in your direction."

"I've always bent it so far. Why shouldn't I be able to manage it with you?"

He thought she'd utter a pithy retort, but she changed the subject. "Mrs. Smithwaite has crept back to London. Did you have a spat?"

"Yes, as a matter of fact we did."

He nearly confessed that Rowena had caught him sneaking out of her room, but he decided not to mention it. If she learned that their amour had been discovered, she might panic and kick him out. Then she'd try to prevent him from returning in the future.

She didn't press him to explain their quarrel, but said, "I didn't like her and I'm relieved that she left."

"So am I. I can spend more time with you."

"You should take this opportunity to ponder your dreadful habits. You have such odious friends, and if Mrs. Smithwaite is indicative of the women you fancy, you need to make better choices."

"I fancy *you,*" he said, "so I don't always wallow in low company."

"Yes, but your association with me will be very short and you'll swiftly revert to your vices and sloth."

He snickered with amusement. "You could be right."

She changed the subject yet again. "Could I ask you a question about your brother?"

He scowled. "That depends on what you'd like to discuss. He and I are very close and it would upset me to have you disparage him. You won't vilify him, will you?"

"No. I'm worried about his relationship with Annette. I brought this up before, but you scoffed and claimed I was being ridiculous. He and Annette have grown much too fond and they shouldn't be flirting. I'd like to put a stop to it, but Annette won't listen to me. Could you speak to him? Would that work?"

Michael might have denied her allegation, but earlier that morning, Hester had nagged about the very same topic. "He's flirting with her? You're sure?"

"Yes. You've neglected her and she's bored. He's stepped into the role of genial host and she likes him very much. I can't guess your opinion with regard to her, and I'm positive— whatever you might tell me—it would be a lie. So if you eventually propose to her, I'm afraid you may have some issues to address with your brother. Could you order him to stay away from her?"

"I couldn't envision having that conversation either, and besides, Caleb is very loyal to me. He wouldn't interfere in my marital search."

"Are you interested in Annette? If so, your courtship has to be the most lackluster ever commenced."

"Why would you think that?"

"Well, from how you've ignored her, I don't believe she's planning on a betrothal. Her mother isn't here to watch her, so she feels free to revel as she hasn't been allowed in the past. I'm terrified the debacle will blow up into a huge morass and her mother will blame me. This is a Crawford family problem and you have to resolve it. I can't resolve it for you."

Michael thought about Caleb. His brother had never obsessed over women. Oh, he'd gone to the whores, like every other sailor, when they'd dropped anchor in port towns. Michael was a member of an upscale brothel in London and Caleb visited occasionally as his guest.

But he'd never had a sweetheart. He'd never doted on a pretty girl. It was partly because he wasn't in a position to wed, due to his not having any assets of his own. Michael had offered to provide him with what would amount to a male dowry, so he'd have a house and funds to raise his circumstances, but he was very proud and very stubborn.

He'd bluntly told Michael that he'd already received plenty of Crawford charity and he wouldn't accept more of it. Yet despite Caleb's declining any fiscal aid, Michael continued to wonder if he shouldn't buy Beachhead Cottage in Baywick for him. Caleb would likely fuss over the gift, and he'd complain that Michael was being too generous, but Michael didn't imagine he'd be stupid enough to refuse it.

Caleb was still young and he'd never waxed on about finding a wife. Michael couldn't picture him being serious about Annette Adair. Especially when her mother would pick her husband and Mrs. Adair would never deem him to be an appropriate candidate.

"I don't want to talk about my brother," he said.

"What does that mean? Are you too much of a coward to confront him? You don't care if he's overly attached to your possible fiancée? You're too lazy to bother? How should I view your comment?"

"It's none of those things. I simply have limited chances to be alone with you and our time together is slipping away very fast. I won't waste a single minute stewing over topics that are irrelevant to my bond with you."

"If he elopes with my cousin, would you describe that as irrelevant?"

"He wouldn't elope so please stop fretting. At the moment, I'm not concerned about him. I'm focused on you and what I can coerce you into giving me."

She snorted with disgust. "What should I give you? If we've circled back to your request that I be your mistress, I will accuse you of badgering me."

"You're much too far away," was his reply. "Sit on my lap."

"No, thank you. I'm fine right where I am."

He never liked to be denied so he stood and stepped to her chair. He gripped her waist, lifted her, and slid onto the cushion. Then he snuggled her down, so in a quick instant, she wound up where he'd intended her to be.

"You're being a bully," she said.

"Yes. Am I wearing you down? Am I convincing you to be more amenable?"

"You're convincing me on some issues, but not on others. You're a scoundrel and I don't trust you."

"Aren't you ruined?"

"I'm *not* ruined! Shame on you for claiming I am."

"Didn't you tell me that you were seduced when you were seventeen?"

"First of all, I'm stunned you would recollect any remark I ever uttered. You're such a vain beast that I can't fathom how you listened to a word I said. And second of all, I told you I was socially ruined. Not physically ruined. I'm a maiden, so I'm not clear on the details of what's involved in intimate conduct, but there's a big difference."

"What happened? I can't recall the specifics."

"There was a regiment of soldiers stationed in my neighborhood, so it was a summer of reveling with dashing men. A group of them invited several girls—including me—to a private party and we snuck away to attend when we shouldn't have. That's it. We were caught with them, by a very angry father, and he escorted us home to our families. I've been living with the consequences ever since."

"Wasn't one of them pretending to be sweet on you?"

"Yes, he was, and I assumed his fondness was genuine. I was only seventeen so don't you dare tease me."

"What was his name?"

"It doesn't matter what it was," she said.

"It does to me."

"Why would it?"

"If I ever cross paths with him, I'll pound him into the ground for you."

"You would not."

"I would," he said. "I swear it to you."

She tsked with annoyance. "Charlie Moneypenny, and I'm certain you'll never bump into him, but if you do, and you pummel him for me, I would be delighted."

He didn't know Moneypenny, but he knew who the scapegrace was. He was a fiend who may have been complicit in Lord Grenville being captured and held for ransom by mercenaries in Spain. If Michael ever ran into him, he would definitely extract a bit of vengeance on her behalf—and on Grenville's.

"Because of Moneypenny," he said, "your Adair relatives have declared you a trollop."

"Yes. They never let me forget what occurred and they insist it proves I have no sense."

He concurred with them. "I'm betting those soldiers had nefarious plans for you."

"I'm betting they did too, but they were so charming, and they made us feel exceptional and unique. We were too gullible to understand their real motives."

"What might have transpired if you hadn't been interrupted?"

"I wouldn't try to guess," she said. "My mind doesn't wander off to lewd scenarios like yours."

"The story tells me that you might have some loose tendencies deep down. Have you ever considered that?"

She bristled with offense. "What a terrible question! What is wrong with you? Why are you so eager to insult me?"

"I'm not insulting you. I'm pointing out that you're not the person you presume yourself to be. Maybe you'd like to have a carnal experience. After all, everyone agrees that women shouldn't remain virgins. The condition is unnatural for a female."

Her cheeks heated to a fetching shade of pink. "I can't believe you spoke the word *virgin* in my presence. Isn't there a rule that you shouldn't mention such a salacious term to a lady?"

"I don't live in a world of rules and manners. I wallow in the demimonde where women carry on however they like. The doxies of my acquaintance are much happier than the debutantes I've met. You could be happier too, if you made different choices."

"I'm plenty happy," she firmly stated.

"Are you?"

The query hung in the air between them, and he figured she was about to jump into a tirade about what a rude oaf he could be, but he couldn't bear to have her castigate him. He recognized his faults and he didn't need to have her list them.

When he was with her, he liked to pretend that he was wonderful, the kind of man she deserved to have in her life. He didn't want her to focus on how he was a complete wretch. To keep her silent, he dipped in and kissed her. For a brief instant, she stiffened, as if she was angry with him and she ought to resist. But she quickly thought better of it and she relaxed into the embrace.

They continued for a lengthy interval, and during the raucous episode, the kiss varied in intensity. Occasionally, it would be poignant and dear, then it would grow passionate and wild. It was simply a fact that, when they were together, they couldn't behave.

Fate had arranged their destinies so they would collide, and despite how reckless they were being, they couldn't avoid what had been set in motion. It seemed that mysterious forces were at work, pushing them into an ardent relationship that was beyond their ability to control.

They had one week to pursue their affair and the short period was vexing him. He was a sly rogue and he could usually coax a female to participate in any sordid misadventure that tickled his fancy. He'd assumed he could coax her into mischief too, but she had a spine of steel. He doubted he'd ever persuade her to ruin herself.

They dallied for an eternity, long enough for the fire to burn out and the candle to sputter. The temperature had dropped and they were beginning to shiver. As their lips parted, she was smiling at him with such affection that his heart constricted in his chest. He would miss her very much after she left Sutton and, in the past, he'd never truly missed anyone.

He'd asked to call on her in London, and she'd refused, but why would he listen to her? What if persistent fraternization brought him what he craved? If they became lovers, she'd have to consent to be his mistress. What other option would she have?

"It's very late," she said. "You should head to your room."

"I can't leave just yet. Let me stay the night."

"And do what?"

"You know *what*."

"You really are a scoundrel, aren't you? Why nag at me to relent?"

He shrugged. "I've always been lucky. If I keep haranguing, you might change your mind."

"I won't change it so stop annoying me." She hugged him tight, her face buried at his nape. "I wish I could be the woman you need."

"I wish it too. It would be easy to give in and I promise you'd like it."

His boast had her chortling with laughter. She drew away and her gaze was kind and wise. "You are so arrogantly sure of yourself. It's what I like best about you."

"I'm an earl. I was born to be arrogant."

"Yes, but here's what you don't comprehend about me: I'll probably never have the chance to be a bride, but if some fellow is ever sufficiently insane to have me, he'll have to put a ring on my finger first in order to receive what you expect to obtain for free. I could never act so shamelessly."

Suddenly, a marriage proposal surged to the tip of his tongue. The impulse was so strong that he clenched his teeth so it couldn't slip out.

He hadn't ever wanted to be a husband, so he thought he deserved a reward for shackling himself. A rich heiress like Annette Adair would shower him with money and property. Wasn't that the whole point of marriage?

While he wasn't overly concerned about the Sutton title, he was British to the bone. A man of his station wed to improve his circumstances. He wed to raise himself up higher than where he'd started. Annette could make him even richer than he already was. She would deliver the hefty prize he believed was his due. In contrast, Margaret was poor so she couldn't supply any item of value.

He couldn't deny she was patient and compassionate, was beautiful and fascinating, and she was so fond of him. If she was his wife, he was certain he'd be happy forever, but a man didn't wed for love. He didn't wed for contentment. He wed to better himself. The reality was as simple and as complicated as that, and she didn't fit the bill in any way that counted.

Besides, if he was stupid enough to propose, he wouldn't mean it. He was a terrible cad. When he bragged about his base tendencies, he wasn't joking. He was a proficient liar and he wouldn't torment her by suggesting matrimony was a possibility. Not when he would never follow through on any vow.

He tamped down his deranged whim and grinned. "Didn't you once tell me that you'll never fall in love and you'll never marry? After we part, I'd like to presume you're so bereft at the loss of me that you'll never recover."

She chuckled. "See? You're a conceited beast."

"It's in my blood. I can't help but be awful."

"I pity the girl who winds up fettered to you. I hope it's not my cousin. If you pick her in the end, I'll worry about her every minute."

"Should I swear I won't pick her?"

"You could swear, but I'm positive you wouldn't be sincere."

It was his turn to chuckle. "You could be right about that."

They stared, cataloguing features, then she said, "There's one week left."

"Time is passing too quickly so I'm going to visit you every night."

"Should you? If we continue our nonsense, won't our separation be that much harder?"

"I suspect it will be hard, no matter how much or how little we dally."

She sighed with gladness. "You sound as if you might be smitten."

"I think I am and you've dragged me to a humiliating ledge where I'm not too proud to admit it. I'm not the sort of romantic fool who runs around being besotted. My interactions with women are quite a bit more salacious than that."

She hugged him again and murmured, "What will I do without you after I depart? You've gotten under my skin in a manner I don't like."

"You've gotten under mine too."

"I realize you can be obnoxious and detestable, but I like you anyway."

"Was that a compliment?" he asked. "I couldn't tell."

"I guess it was."

"Then I will carry it close to my heart. You're so stingy. With you, I have to take whatever I can coercing you into relinquishing."

She slid off his lap, and he clasped her wrist and tried to tug her back down, but she wouldn't let him. She yanked him to his feet instead.

"Are you kicking me out?" he asked.

"Yes. If we dawdle much longer, the scullery maids will be lighting the morning fires. I don't intend to have you caught slithering out. And would you please be more cautious when you step into the hall? You're such a pompous fiend that you never peek out first."

She opened the door and peeked out herself, then she motioned for him to hurry. He walked over to her and whispered, "I don't want to leave you."

"I don't want you to either, but one of us has to keep a level head. As usual, it has to be me."

"It's supposed to snow this evening so there will be fresh snow on the roads tomorrow. Would you take a sleighride with me? You took one with my brother, and I should have a chance to squire you about the neighborhood too. It's only fair."

"No, absolutely not. If we traipsed off together, we'd stir so much gossip."

"Could we have breakfast?"

"I might agree to that. At nine again?"

"Yes, nine would be fine."

"Don't forget we have a date, you laggard."

"I wouldn't dare forget."

Breakfast would be a poor substitute for a more private encounter. In the dining room, they would be surrounded by footmen and guests. He'd be able to sit with her, but he would have to pretend they were merely cordial, and their heightened affection would have to be concealed.

He bent down and stole a last kiss. It was a tad desperate, but then, the clock was ticking toward the minute when she'd vanish. He was chafing like a condemned felon marching to the gallows. He tried to extend the embrace, but she jerked away and shooed him out. He tiptoed off, and before he could glance back, she'd shut and locked her door.

He crept away and dashed up to his suite, which was cold and dark. He went over to the window and gazed out at the horizon. It was the dead of winter, so the nights were long, and there was no hint of dawn in the eastern sky.

He felt especially alone, especially lonely, and he missed Margaret in a frantic, almost insane fashion. How would he amuse himself when she wasn't available to entertain him? He truly suspected he would be despondent for months. Could that be right?

They had a week to flirt, then he'd have to once again fill his dreary hours with his tarts and odious acquaintances, with his gambling and vices. Yet that world was swiftly losing its appeal. What did it indicate? Was he bored? Was he changing? Was he finally growing up?

He was being particularly morbid in a manner he hated. Apparently, he liked her much more than was wise and he had to get a grip on his careening emotions. Maybe he was viewing their dalliance the wrong way. Maybe he should be glad she was departing. What good could come from continued fraternization?

Only disaster would result. If their liaison was discovered, he'd skate through the scandal with no penalty imposed, but severe consequences would rain down on her. So, yes, it was for the best that she'd be gone soon.

While she was still in residence, he would revel in her fascinating company, but he would breathe a sigh of relief after she climbed in her carriage and rolled away.

# Chapter 15

Hester rushed down the hall toward the receiving parlor. The butler had just rushed in to announce that Ambrosia Adair had shown up without warning. Hester had advised him to have the housekeeper hurriedly prepare the bedchamber recently vacated by Mrs. Smithwaite, then she'd dashed off to greet their guest.

She never liked to have her routines altered, so she was in a dither and in no mood to be cordial. She was Michael's hostess though, so she had to play the part that was expected of her. As she reached the foyer, she noticed that Mrs. Adair had many trunks and bags and they were being hauled in by footmen who grunted under the heavy weight.

Hester pasted on a smile and blustered into the parlor, saying, "Hello, Mrs. Adair. This is a lovely surprise. I'm Hester Crawford."

"Hello, Lady Hester. I hope my sudden appearance hasn't caused too much of a disruption."

"Not at all. We're having a party; the more the merrier."

Mrs. Adair was only four years older than Hester, but she was so stylishly attired and exquisitely bejeweled, that she might have been twenty-five, rather than forty. It verified the rumors that she and her daughter paraded around like sisters.

In comparison, Hester could have been her grandmother. She hadn't aged well, but she'd convinced herself that beauty and glamour were irrelevant vanities. She never left the estate, never crossed paths with anyone except the same neighbors. There wasn't a reason to flaunt her looks. Yet with her being confronted by Mrs. Adair's fabulous elegance, it occurred to her that she'd made some very bad choices in her life.

She eased onto a sofa, but she was perched on the edge, feeling as if she was in the presence of a queen.

"Your luggage is being carried up to your room," she said, "and it will be ready shortly. Have you been offered refreshments?"

"Yes, thank you."

Mrs. Adair gestured to a side table, where a glass of wine had been poured. She might have leaned over and grabbed it, but it would have been a long stretch. She was seated in a cushioned chair with wheels that would have to be pushed by servants. She'd brought two of her own footmen, and they hovered in the corner, prepared to roll her about as she demanded.

The hem of her skirt covered her leg, but Hester could see the outline of the cast on her ankle. She was hobbled by her injury, but she'd traveled to Sutton anyway. After being so adamant about missing the party, Hester was amazed that Mrs. Adair would brave the elements in order to arrive on the spur of the moment, and she assumed it was because of the anonymous letter she'd sent.

She'd been perplexed as to how else she could gain control of the situation that was festering. Annette Adair was behaving inappropriately with Caleb, and Margaret Adair was an incompetent chaperone who had to be replaced. Michael was a renowned lecher who was trifling with Margaret. He'd denied any mischief, but Hester hadn't believed him.

Hester had no ability to fix either dilemma, and Mrs. Adair seemed very capable, very stern and dignified. Hester had no doubt she would quickly mend the problems. Annette and Margaret Adair would have their conduct reined in. Annette would have to reserve her flirting for Michael, and Margaret would be shoved into the background where she should have stayed.

It would all work out splendidly and Hester breathed a sigh of relief. Since mailing the letter, she'd been aquiver with anxiety over the dangerous act. If Michael ever learned what she'd done, she couldn't imagine how he might respond. But Mrs. Adair would intervene and Michael would never realize Hester's role.

"How was the journey?" Hester asked. "Were you caught in the weather? How were the roads?"

"The trip was awful. It was freezing and it snowed most of the way."

"You're much heartier than I could ever be," Hester told her. "I wouldn't have dared to traipse about in such chilly conditions."

"I don't normally let my daughter venture out without me. I've been more spry lately and I figured I should check on her."

Mrs. Adair paused, as if waiting for Hester to admit that she was the author of the unsigned note, but Hester would take that secret to her grave.

"Did your daughter or your cousin know you were coming?" Hester asked.

"No. It's a surprise."

"Would you like me to fetch them for you?"

"I'd like to relax and tidy up first, but if you could apprise them that I am here, I would appreciate it. They can attend me at their convenience."

The butler peeked in to report that Mrs. Adair's bedchamber was ready. Her footmen jumped to lug her up the stairs, although how they'd balance the unwieldy chair was a mystery.

"We dine early in the country," Hester explained. "We'll eat at eight, with drinks and socializing in this parlor at seven. I'll have a maid appointed to assist you. If you need anything, she'll be delighted to provide it."

"I had a pair of my own maids accompany me," the snooty woman said, "so I should be fine."

Hester grasped that she'd just been insulted, with Mrs. Adair not supposing Hester's servants would be skilled enough to tend her grand self. Hester didn't indicate, not by the smallest reaction, that she noticed the rebuff.

She stood and observed the spectacle as the footmen pushed Mrs. Adair out to the foyer. They were burly boys, and without too much effort, they carried her to the upper floors. Hester would never have allowed them to lift her so precariously, but then, she wasn't the one with a broken leg.

She dawdled until Mrs. Adair had vanished from view, then she marched off and trudged up the rear stairs to the master suite. Michael had been out of the house most of the day, doing Lord knows what, but he was home and she had to inform him about Mrs. Adair.

He probably wouldn't care, but surely, Mrs. Adair's presence would remind him that he had to focus on Annette. With her mother on the premises, he would have to concentrate and make some decisions.

If Mrs. Adair witnessed how he was snubbing her daughter, she might pack their belongings and drag Annette back to London. Clearly, the wealthy, condescending shrew would brook no nonsense from Michael. He would have to propose or they'd leave. Hester felt it in her bones.

She approached his suite and the doors were open. He was talking to someone and she tiptoed over and peered around the doorframe. When she recognized who was with him, her blood boiled. Little red dots appeared on the edge of her vision, as if she was about to suffer an apoplexy.

Margaret Adair was standing in his sitting room. They were simply chatting, so they weren't necessarily engaged in a salacious antic, but a young lady never visited a gentleman in his bedchamber. What was the brazen tart thinking?

Hester studied them and their fondness was so blatant it was nearly tangible. For years, she'd watched her brother seduce and philander, had watched him lie and disgrace himself, but she'd never seen him gaze at a female as he was gazing at Miss Adair. Miss Adair was just as smitten. Had Michael bestowed a bit of flattery and she presumed his compliments were genuine?

Hester had once had an amour with an inappropriate boy. It had been her one and only spurt of recklessness and severe ramifications had quickly crushed her. They still battered her every second and she'd never recovered from her folly.

Miss Adair would swiftly learn that Michael couldn't be trusted. She'd learn that he never told the truth, that he never followed through on any promise. If he'd spewed some promises to *her*, and she expected he was sincere, then she was an idiot—and perhaps even in a great deal of trouble besides.

They hadn't realized she was lurking, and Michael wouldn't like to be interrupted, but she mustered her courage and barged in.

Miss Adair was startled and she stumbled away, as if Michael had burst into flames. Michael, however, couldn't be shamed and he turned to Hester and smiled, as if naught was wrong.

"Hello, Hester," he calmly said. "Were you looking for me?"

"Yes, I've been searching everywhere." Her tone scathing, she scowled at Miss Adair and said, "I can't imagine why you're in here with him, but I don't believe you ought to tarry. I must speak to my brother in private. Would you excuse us?"

As opposed to Michael, Miss Adair was mortified and her cheeks heated with embarrassment. "I most humbly apologize. Lord Sutton was showing me some of his medals from the navy. I shouldn't have let him."

"It had better not happen again," Hester fumed.

Michael jumped to Miss Adair's defense. "Hester, don't you dare scold Miss Adair. I invited her in, and if a transgression was committed, it was by me."

Hester ignored him and said to Miss Adair, "I'm certain that this news will astonish you, but Mrs. Adair has arrived."

Miss Adair blanched. "Ambrosia is here? In light of her injury, I'm stunned that she'd venture out in such inclement weather. Did she mention why she joined us?"

Hester wasn't usually abrupt with guests, but she was furious. "She didn't feel Annette was being properly chaperoned. She's eager to step into the role that she had relinquished to you."

"Oh."

At the admonishment, Miss Adair flinched as if Hester had struck her, and Michael leapt to defuse the situation. "I'm positive it's not that, Hester. I'm sure Mrs. Adair just hates to have missed out on our party. She always socializes with Annette and she wouldn't have liked to be left out."

Hester didn't glance at him. She simply told Miss Adair, "She's settled in her suite. I placed her in the one Mrs. Smithwaite was using. She's asked that you attend her immediately."

"I will. Thank you for apprising me."

Miss Adair rushed out and Michael, scoundrel that he was, said to her, "I'll see you at supper. Don't forget that you agreed to play a hand of cards with me."

Miss Adair didn't supply the slightest hint that she'd heard him. She hurried out and her strides vanished down the hall.

A gruesome silence descended and it was heavy and full of spite. On her end anyway, it was heavy with spite. He merely stared at her with his typical aplomb.

"You didn't have to be so rude to her," he said.

Hester was shaking so hard that she could barely stay on her feet. "How could you! You're not a dunce. You're not a fool. It's highly offensive for you to welcome her into your bedchamber."

"I was showing her some of my medals. She thinks I'm a wretch and a laggard, and she scoffed when I bragged about how often I'd been decorated for valor. It compelled me to prove I was telling the truth for once."

"She is Annette Adair's chaperone. She is not, and never will be, available for a flirtation. I have no idea what insanity you're pursuing with her, but it has to stop."

"Message received, Hester."

"I asked you about your relationship with her! I warned you that the servants are gossiping and you lied right to my face!"

"I didn't lie. I have no relationship with her—other than a casual one fostered during the party."

"You're a sinner, Michael! You're going straight to Hell!"

"Yes, I am," he concurred and he chuckled at her rage. "Will that be all? Did you need anything else?"

"I had to inform you about Mrs. Adair strutting in. So far, you've been able to ignore her daughter, but your ambivalence will have to cease. She's not the sort who will tolerate any disrespect from you."

"I will keep that in mind."

"If you actually intend to consider Annette as a nuptial candidate, you have to start exhibiting some interest in her. If you don't, Mrs. Adair will pack their bags and leave with her."

"You worry too much, Hester. The single goal in Mrs. Adair's life has been to buy a title for Annette. She will put up with me, no matter how I carry on."

Hester bristled with wrath. "I hope that you get your comeuppance someday soon. I would be so glad to have you brought low by your depravities."

He smirked, as if his bad habits were a big joke. "My depravities haven't done me in yet and I'm sorry that I constantly disappoint you."

She yearned to scream at him, to rant and rail about how he was risking his immortal soul. He assumed it would be amusing to spend eternity in Hell, and she couldn't fathom why he'd embrace that conclusion.

Why harangue at him? Why castigate and reprimand? He would never change, and his dismissive demeanor pushed her beyond the limits of what she could abide.

She fled his odious presence, and as she raced down the hall, his laughter rang out. He was greatly humored by her being so fussy and ridiculous. The sound was so maddening that she nearly whirled about and stormed back to shout at him. But why bother?

She hastened on, feeling so incensed that she wondered if the top of her head might simply blow off.

---

Ambrosia sat on her wheeled chair in a large parlor that had been opened up for dancing. She was parked in a corner, like an aging spinster, which made her gnash her teeth. She liked to be in the middle of any merriment, but her injury had ruined many facets of her situation.

Lord Sutton had numerous male friends visiting from London, and neighbors had been invited to round out the crowd. On the surface, the festivities were jolly, but she noted an odd undercurrent among the revelers, as if no one was happy. She couldn't quite clarify the reason, but she'd unravel it.

Before supper, Margaret and Annette had stopped by to welcome her. They'd pretended to be delighted to see her, but she'd perceived their perplexity over her arrival. She hadn't interrogated them, hadn't mentioned the anonymous letter or the fact that rumors were swirling.

She'd claimed she'd been lonely at home so she'd decided to join them. It was obvious they hadn't believed her, that they suspected trouble was brewing, but they couldn't identify what it might be. Well, she'd deal with them in the morning and they'd hear plenty. For the moment, she was watching, listening, and trying to deduce if the letter had any merit.

She'd been introduced to Lord Sutton, and he was a handsome devil who was very set on himself. If he proposed to Annette, he would give her very pretty children, but Ambrosia supposed he'd give her plenty of aggravation and humiliation too. She doubted the word *monogamy* had ever entered his vocabulary.

He was a rogue and libertine and any girl foolish enough to wed him would have to have a very thick skin. Should it be Annette? Ambrosia figured it probably should be. They were running out of options and Annette was twenty already. If Sutton was amenable, Ambrosia couldn't imagine she'd refuse his offer.

The Crawfords were very strange. Hester Crawford was hovered in the opposite corner. She observed the gathering, but didn't participate. She didn't chat with her guests, didn't mingle. Occasionally, she would murmur instructions to a servant, but mostly, she could have been invisible.

She was an odd duck, dressed like a nun, wearing a grey gown with no embellishment, not even a strip of lace on the collar. She was thirty-six, but she might have been sixty-six. Her hair was grey, her face lined, and she appeared beaten down by life. She was so different from her dashing brother that it was impossible for them to be related.

He hardly noticed his sister, but then, he wasn't interested in the party. He'd briefly dawdled, had danced with Annette twice and Margaret once, but other than that, he kept sneaking out so the men had to be gambling in another section of the house.

He'd been polite to Annette, but he'd been incredibly fond of Margaret. He couldn't conceal it. Margaret's affection for him was clear too, and Ambrosia had to accept that the letter writer had been correct: Margaret had formed an illicit connection with him.

With Margaret having such a disgraceful prior history, was Ambrosia surprised? No, she was not.

Ambrosia was curious about Sutton's half-brother. In the investigation she'd undertaken about the Earl, she'd been told he had no brothers. She was irked to have had the detail omitted from the reports she'd received. In her matrimonial plotting, she didn't like to be left in the dark about any issue, but her investigator wouldn't have considered a by-blow to be a *real* sibling.

She'd had her maid scooping up gossip, and she'd learned that Mr. Crawford had traveled with Lord Sutton as his cabin boy during the years the Earl had been a ship's captain in the navy.

Mr. Crawford had no money or prospects, but he was very popular. The staff adored him and the neighbors respected him. Hester Crawford loathed him though and they had no bond. They weren't even mildly cordial, which Ambrosia found very intriguing. Besides his being a bastard, why would Lady Hester detest him?

A new set was starting, and Mr. Crawford stepped into the line with Annette as his partner. It was their only dance together and Ambrosia carefully studied their every move. As with Lord Sutton and

Margaret, Mr. Crawford and Annette were outrageously besotted. They couldn't hide it.

So…Annette fancied the bastard brother, rather than a servant, as the letter had proclaimed. Ambrosia was so annoyed that she nearly had her footmen carry her up to her room, but she didn't dare leave. Not when there was so much mischief afoot.

She'd let Annette and Margaret traipse off to the country by themselves and it had morphed into a disaster. Did they deem themselves clever? Did they deem themselves on a bohemian holiday, and thus, liberated from societal restrictions?

Ambrosia would have to untangle the mess. It would be easy to rein in Margaret's nonsense. Ambrosia would send her back to London so she'd be yanked out of the Earl's dastardly clutches. He was a typical scoundrel, and after she vanished, he'd never think of her again.

Annette would be the bigger problem. She probably believed herself in love with Mr. Crawford. Their liaison was extremely embarrassing, and Ambrosia couldn't fathom why her daughter would behave so foolishly. Annette had been allowed a bit of freedom, but she'd abused it. Yet Ambrosia wouldn't panic.

Annette had always been very pragmatic, so Ambrosia would point out how ridiculous she was being, and Annette would remember her place in the world. She would quickly refocus her sights on the Earl and all would be well.

Ambrosia didn't doubt it for a second.

---

ANNETTE WAS WALKING TO her bedchamber, having just said good-night to her mother. The party down in the lower parlors was still in progress, and Annette wished she was reveling with the other guests, but Ambrosia had been weary from her chilly trip. When she'd headed for bed, she'd insisted Annette head to bed too. It had been a petty command, and Annette was bristling over it, but in the end, she'd obeyed.

Throughout her life, her mother had been her best friend. They were so similar in their opinions and routines that they never quarreled, but over the past few days, Annette felt as if she'd become a different person. She wasn't sure how or why it had occurred. She'd merely spent a brief interval away from Ambrosia and she'd decided she wasn't the woman she'd assumed herself to be.

For once, she was able to breathe without Ambrosia hovering. It was entirely possible she didn't want the future her mother had envisioned.

She couldn't deduce why Ambrosia had rushed to Sutton. Annette didn't buy her mother's story that she'd been lonely in town. If she had to guess, she supposed Ambrosia couldn't bear to picture Annette enjoying an event that didn't include her and she'd raced to Sutton because of it.

Annette had been ordered to join her mother for a private breakfast the following morning. She figured they'd review Annette's visit and how she and the Earl were getting on. Annette would never convince Ambrosia that Lord Sutton barely noticed her and didn't like her very much. Ambrosia would refuse to hear the truth.

In their marital scheming, Ambrosia was like a war general who would never surrender. She'd seen how grand the Sutton estate was. She'd seen how handsome and magnetic Lord Sutton was, and she'd be picking out baby names for Annette's first child. The whole charade was ludicrous and Annette was exhausted by it.

Suddenly, Caleb emerged from the shadows. They froze, and it was very strange, but it seemed as if Time had stopped, as if the universe was holding very still, eager to discover what would happen.

He touched a finger to his lips, warning her to silence. He was next to a bedroom door and he opened it and gestured for her to enter with him. She'd never previously received such a scandalous invitation, and she shook her head, indicating she couldn't. He smiled to apprise her it would be all right.

She glanced back toward Ambrosia's bedchamber, certain her mother would be watching, but Ambrosia's maids were tucking her in for the night so she couldn't have been standing there. Old habits died hard though and she was positive—if she went with him—Ambrosia would somehow learn of it.

She walked over to him, and they were the most difficult steps she'd ever taken, but the easiest ones too. He extended his hand to her, and she clasped it and he led her in. He closed the door and spun the key in the lock.

The room was empty, with no fire burning, so the temperature was very cold. Moonlight shone in the window, painting him in silver shades, and he was so beautiful.

He drew her into his arms, and without requesting permission, he kissed her passionately. It was the sort of kiss she'd read about in romantic novels that her classmates had smuggled into their boarding school dormitory. It was the sort of kiss she and the other girls had dreamed about experiencing someday. It thrilled and promised, it tempted and tantalized, and it stirred a desire she'd wondered about, but had never imagined she'd feel for herself.

They continued for an eternity, and eventually, he slowed and pulled away.

"Why is your mother here?" he quietly whispered.

Annette whispered just as quietly. "I don't know why. She probably wants to be sure your brother is falling in love with me. She'll recognize he hasn't, and she'll start implementing plans to push him into a betrothal."

"Would she force you into it?"

"She could try." Annette sounded very brave, when in fact, she was a coward. She'd never defied her mother on any issue.

"Don't fight with her. Pretend to agree about him. Pretend you'll marry him, but I'll save you from that fate."

"I'm not dishonest. I couldn't trick my mother—or your brother—into believing I'm amenable."

"I'm making arrangements for us to run away," he said.

The announcement was so shocking, and so exciting, that her knees buckled. He grabbed her around the waist to keep her upright.

"You're not serious," she told him.

"I'm very serious. I just need to get it organized. While I'm occupied with the details, I can't have your mother notice me or have her speculating over my relationship with you. Be your sweet, delightful self to her so she doesn't suspect any plotting."

"I'm not certain I can consent to this," she murmured. "It would be so wrong and it would hurt her so much."

He gazed steadily at her, and he appeared so fierce, as if he could smash any obstacle in his path. It had her insanely assuming she could trust him, that it would work out perfectly.

"It's not wrong," he said and he pressed a fist over his heart. "You perceive our connection; you can't deny it. We're destined to be together. It's meant to be."

It was the kind of statement a hero uttered in a fable, that a knight-of-old spoke to his beloved queen. It was the kind of declaration every girl yearned to hear from a suitor, but never did. They were stunning words, mesmerizing words, dangerous words.

"I'm having breakfast with her in the morning," she said. "I'll tell her about you. About us."

"Don't tell her. We have to be far away from Sutton before she realizes what we're about. We can't give her an opportunity to stop us."

Annette couldn't decide if it was wise advice or deranged advice. How could she hide her affection for him from her mother? She and Ambrosia had shared everything in their lives, but she understood—without a doubt—that Ambrosia would never understand about *him.*

He kissed her again and the embrace was even more passionate than the first one had been. Her pulse pounded and her veins heated. Her bones turned to rubber, as if she could melt into a puddle at his feet.

"I'll avoid you tomorrow," he said, "but you shouldn't fret about my absence. Don't look for me and don't miss me. When I have news, I'll find you."

"I will miss you. I won't be able to help it."

"Have faith, Annette. And be ready."

She was anxious to ask, *Be ready for what?*, but there was no chance. He peeked into the hall, then motioned for her to hurry out. She hesitated, too overwhelmed to dash off immediately.

He wouldn't tolerate any delay though. He laid a palm on the small of her back and pushed her out. He stared at her, his fondness clear and washing over her, furnishing the assurance that he'd take care of her forever, that she'd always be safe with him.

She dawdled briefly, wallowing in the precious moment, then she whirled away and rushed to her room.

She was brimming with exhilaration, but her thoughts were bouncing off the walls. Could she betray her mother? Could she deceive Lord Sutton? Could she run away with a man she'd only known for a few days? Could she bind herself to a bastard son, one who had nothing to offer but his loyalty and esteem?

It was the stuff of legends, of ardent tales sung by bards. Would she dare? Did she dare?

She had absolutely no idea.

# Chapter 16

"What is your opinion of Lord Sutton?"

Ambrosia stared at Annette and impatiently waited for her reply. It came quickly enough.

"He's just like Lord Grenville. He's vain, rude, and dismissive. The only difference between them is that Grenville is certifiably insane. Lord Sutton isn't deranged. He simply has no manners and he's too conceited for words."

At the description, Ambrosia snickered. "Aristocratic men are always rude and dismissive, but if we've found one who's *not* deranged, perhaps we're making progress."

"I doubt it. He's a terrible libertine too. He flaunts his lewd preferences and he's proud of his affection for slatterns."

"All men are enamored of tarts. Noblemen are particularly enchanted. I've counseled you about it. If Lord Sutton likes to philander, you shouldn't be surprised."

"He brought his mistress to the party! While I was here too! It's his sister's home, yet she was staying in this very bedchamber. Have you ever heard of such offensive conduct?"

Ambrosia was being very lazy and she was using her broken leg as an excuse to receive extra attention. She'd asked to have breakfast served in her room, so she didn't have to maneuver the stairs, and her request had been honored without complaint or delay.

A table had been set by the window and she and Annette were dining privately. The view outside was of the garden and the forest beyond. It had snowed again so the roads would be awful when she left for London. It was mad to venture out in January, and if they were muddy or blocked by drifts, it would trap her at Sutton.

Once she arranged the betrothal, she would hate to tarry, so she would pray for sunshine and dry weather to ease her escape.

"Who is his mistress?" she inquired. "Are we acquainted with her?"

"We are now," Annette snidely retorted. "Rowena Smithwaite? She's a wealthy widow, who has all the cads in the demimonde falling at her feet, but Lord Sutton sent her away a few days ago. Evidently, they quarreled."

"Did he seem overly fond of her?"

Annette scoffed. "He's overly fond of any female in a skirt. He's that debauched."

"Would he part with her if I demanded it?"

"I have no idea. He's a mystery to me and I wouldn't try to guess how his addled brain functions."

Ambrosia smirked with annoyance. Annette's first engagement, to Lord Grenville, had collapsed because he'd been in love with his governess. Ambrosia hadn't cared about his pathetic amour, but she'd expected Grenville to be unattached at the beginning of his marriage.

She wasn't a fool and she understood how prominent men behaved. They deemed it their absolute right to have affairs and consort with doxies.

But she thought, at the start, a husband should act like a husband. He should display some respect, so his wife would think she was special before he traipsed off to disgrace himself with his gambling, vice, and trollops.

Grenville had sworn he'd rid them of his governess, but he hadn't been able to oblige them. He'd been too besotted, so Ambrosia had cancelled the nuptial contracts and sued him for breach of promise. The case was still winding through the courts, with judges nervous about holding a nobleman to account, but she was positive she'd win some damages in the end.

She wasn't shocked to learn that Lord Sutton had a mistress, but if he'd invite her to Sutton, he had to be incredibly devoted. Had Ambrosia landed herself in a predicament similar to the one with Grenville?

The question would have to be answered prior to their forging ahead. It meant she'd have to corner the pompous oaf and pin him down, but he was a stranger so it wasn't a conversation she was eager to have.

"What are your feelings about him in general?" Ambrosia asked. "Aside from his lewd habits, he's handsome and dashing. Could you see yourself as his bride?"

Annette assessed matters exactly as Ambrosia assessed them so she'd been prepared for an optimistic response. When it was the complete opposite, she was stunned.

"No, I couldn't imagine it," Annette said.

Ambrosia glowered with astonishment. "Why not? He's like Grenville, but without the insanity, and he's very rich. He's the precise candidate we've been hoping to find."

"He's the candidate *you* have been hoping to find," Annette claimed.

"You've been searching for him too! Don't rewrite our matrimonial planning. We have always intended to buy you a position up in the loftiest circles. It's where you belong and where you'll be when this is over."

Annette blew out a heavy sigh. "What if we've been wrong about this? I'm not interested in being a countess. I just want to be happy."

Ambrosia spat out a cruel laugh. "Trust me, Annette. If you spend your life as a countess, you will be very, very happy. I guarantee it."

"But these fiends like Grenville and Sutton, they picture themselves as being so imperious and grand. They would never dote on me. They would never contemplate what I might need. Lord Sutton doesn't even like me. How could I wed a man who doesn't like me?"

"You're not marrying the man. You're marrying the title."

"No, I'd be marrying a living human being, whom *I* don't particularly like either. We should keep looking."

Ambrosia frowned. "Don't be ridiculous. Sutton would be perfect for you."

"In your eyes maybe, but you're not the one who would have to put up with him."

"You'd barely see him. You know how these aristocratic unions go. He would remain in town, where he could revel with his tarts and odious friends. You'd stay in the country so you wouldn't have to watch him shaming himself. He'd visit a few times a year to plant a babe in your womb, and once the deed was accomplished, he'd vanish and leave you alone. It sounds like an ideal situation to me."

Annette snorted with derision. "Listen to yourself, Mother. What you're describing is abhorrent to me. Why would you force me into such an untenable arrangement?"

Ambrosia's temper flared. She and Annette never quarreled, but it appeared they were about to bicker. Apparently, Annette's sojourn at Sutton had been more hazardous than Ambrosia had realized. It had wedged peculiar notions into her head, notions that had to be shoved out.

"What's gotten into you?" Ambrosia demanded. "We've been marching toward this moment since the day you were born."

"No, *you* have been marching toward it. I told you: I'd just like to be happy. A marriage to Lord Sutton would make me very *un*happy."

"What, in your infinite wisdom, would you suggest as an alternative? If you don't wish to use your dowry to purchase a title, what would you purchase with it? Shall we round up some poverty-stricken poets to learn if any of them would like to wed you? Shall we inquire of some snooty intellectuals or dangerous revolutionaries? Shall we troll the halls of Parliament and locate a fat, obnoxious government minister? If not an aristocrat, who shall we ask?"

Ambrosia shouldn't have been so sarcastic, but Annette was being absurd. Her radical views were preposterous and Ambrosia couldn't fathom what was stirring them. Her daughter had been raised like a spoiled princess, one who'd been given whatever she craved, but in this, Ambrosia would not indulge her.

"What do you think of Lord Sutton's brother, Mr. Crawford?" Annette suddenly said. "Have you had a chance to chat with him?"

Ambrosia vividly remembered Mr. Crawford dancing with Annette the prior evening and the pair had been blatantly fond. An improper flirtation had blossomed and it was Margaret's fault. Ambrosia would wring her neck for failing to stop it.

"Why would I have chatted with Mr. Crawford?" Ambrosia caustically replied. "Why mention the bastard by-blow of the previous earl to me?"

"He's handsome and strong, kind and generous. He's respected by everyone so he's totally different from his awful brother. He would be a wonderful husband."

"For who? For *you*?" Ambrosia sneeringly asked.

Annette's cheeks heated and she hastily said, "Not him specifically, but why can't I have a spouse like him? Why can't I have one who is kind and generous? Why must it be a vain dolt like Lord Sutton who couldn't care less about me?"

Ambrosia's initial impulse was to rail at her daughter, but she managed to bite her tongue. Annette had never had a serious beau so she hadn't ever experienced the exhilarating rush that young love could bring. She was in the throes of her first amour, but it would fade. She wouldn't like to hear it though, so Ambrosia didn't point it out.

Annette couldn't make the common choice, the dear choice. She wasn't ordinary and she couldn't follow her heart. It was a sad commentary on the state of a female's existence, but women in the upper classes were placed on the Earth to serve the men of the upper classes. They birthed their children to carry on the appropriate bloodlines and traditions.

The members of important families wed each other. They combined their massive properties and assets to grow ever richer and more powerful. They utilized their supremacy to rule the world and they never let interlopers like Mr. Crawford into their ranks. It simply wasn't tolerated.

Annette understood all of that, and she'd been reared to comprehend her role in the great scheme of the matrimonial universe. Her budding romance had caused her to temporarily forget those lessons. She was wishing a girl could wind up with the man of her dreams, but that was a fantasy that had to be quashed.

Ambrosia would have to do it gently. If she raged and issued ultimatums, it would harden Annette's resolve. Ambrosia had to lure her back onto the correct path so she recognized how far she'd wandered from what was expected of her.

She imbued her expression with as much compassion as she could muster and she patted Annette's hand. "Women like you and me, Annette, we don't wed for love. You know that."

"Yes, I know, but it shouldn't be how things work."

"Tell me the truth. Would you really be opposed to marrying Lord Sutton?"

"Yes! He's a terrible person. You've only just arrived so you haven't seen what he's like. He shouldn't be my husband."

"Then I will ponder your reservations and I will become acquainted with him. I'm certain my opinion will match yours. I'm betting I'll discover he's a corrupt wretch."

Ambrosia had no intention of deeming Lord Sutton to be unacceptable, but her remark had appeased Annette and her daughter said, "Thank you for heeding me. I was so sure you'd be angry and would call me a brat."

"I'm your biggest champion in this so I would never pick a bad candidate." Ambrosia tossed down her napkin and forced a smile. "Now then, what are your plans for today? Have you any?"

"It's too cold to go outside so I suppose I'll mingle with the other guests. Lord Sutton's London friends like to play cards for pennies in the afternoon. I'll probably join them and win all their money."

"I hope you beggar them," Ambrosia said. "Are you finished eating?"

"Yes, and I'm stuffed too. We've only been apart for a week, but it feels as if we've been separated for ages. I'm glad we had this private interval where it was just the two of us."

"I'm glad too. I'm not heading downstairs yet. Would you find Margaret and inform her that I'd like to speak with her?"

Annette scowled. "You won't scold her, will you? She's been a marvelous companion and I've been delighted to have her as my chaperone."

"Why would I scold her? It appears to me that you're having a fine visit. I have to probe her view of Lord Sutton. She's an excellent judge of character and she'll have many pithy comments to share."

"I'll fetch her for you."

Annette rose and left and Ambrosia sat very still, letting the dust settle. After it was quiet again, she muttered to the empty room, "Foolish girl!"

Annette fancied Mr. Crawford to the point where she was madly in love with the handsome bastard. The Earl was fond of him too, but Ambrosia noticed that Lord Sutton hadn't given the boy any money. Mr. Crawford was an impoverished nobody who figured he could snag Annette, then glom onto her dowry.

He was naught but a sly fortune-hunter, and in protecting Annette, Ambrosia was a veritable lioness. Mr. Crawford needed to be put in his place. Then Annette had to be hidden from him—until she was suitably married. That would be to his brother, Lord Sutton.

Was Sutton aware of the fledging amour? Ambrosia would take steps to stop it on her end, but he'd have to deal with his ridiculous sibling who was reaching far above his station.

For a bit, Annette would grieve and fuss over the severance, but she'd come to her senses, then Ambrosia would proceed with the engagement to Lord Sutton. In fact, Ambrosia would talk to him about it shortly. They'd hash out the details, and when she returned to London, she'd have her lawyers draft the contracts.

It was January, and with him being in such a hurry, she thought an April ceremony would be splendid.

"One down, one to go," she whispered.

She relaxed and listened for Margaret's approach. Since Annette would be marrying Lord Sutton, and the bloody man was obsessed with Margaret, Margaret would be an obstacle to Annette's happiness. Margaret had to leave Sutton immediately, and she couldn't be an impediment as Annette marched to her wedding.

It would be easy to be shed of Margaret, but first, she'd deliver an emphatic reprimand for how she'd failed in her duty to Ambrosia. Ambrosia never forgave a slight and never forgot a snub. Margaret would feel the brunt of Ambrosia's wrath, then she'd be tucked away in a spot where Lord Sutton could never locate her.

Ambrosia knew his kind; he was very spoiled so he wouldn't like to be thwarted in a dalliance. He wouldn't like Ambrosia to interfere, but she would interfere, and she would never regret it.

MARGARET ENTERED AMBROSIA'S BEDCHAMBER, and her cousin was seated at a table by the window and gazing out at the winter garden. Most of the breakfast detritus had been cleared away, but there was still a pot of tea and a basket of muffins in the middle. She waved Margaret to the opposite chair and Margaret walked over and slid down.

"Are you hungry?" Ambrosia asked.

"I ate down in the dining room. I'm fine." Ambrosia studied her oddly and Margaret said, "Annette told me you had to see me. What did you need?"

"How has your stay at Sutton been?"

"I'm having a wonderful time. It's a beautiful property." She leaned nearer and murmured, "Hester Crawford is a tad peculiar, but she runs a very efficient house."

"Yes, I have been skillfully tended," Ambrosia agreed, then she asked, "What is your opinion of Lord Sutton?"

Margaret had been prepared for an inquisition, and she had to tread carefully. He'd be an awful husband for Annette, and Annette would be miserable forever, but Margaret didn't dare offer a remark that might skewer the engagement. If it fell apart, it couldn't be her fault.

"He's a very typical nobleman," she said. "He's arrogant, imperious, and in awe of his own importance."

"You've watched him with Annette. How would you describe them as a couple?"

"I haven't really observed them together. Mostly, Lord Sutton has ignored her. He's so disinterested in matrimony that I don't understand why he's searching for a bride. He certainly hasn't been excited to have Annette visiting."

"Why has he ignored her? Has he been distracted? According to Annette, his mistress was on the premises for a few days. Was he busy with her instead?"

"I couldn't tell you. His sister arranged activities to keep people entertained, but he's rarely participated. His habits and motives are a mystery to me."

Ambrosia studied Margaret again and she looked aggrieved. Margaret received the distinct impression that she was in trouble. What had she done?

Finally, Ambrosia explained. "Annette was just here and she claims she doesn't wish to wed the Earl."

"I'm sorry to hear it. She mentioned the same notion to me, but she was being silly. I think she's merely suffering from pre-betrothal jitters."

Ambrosia's tone was very snide. "Will it surprise you to learn that she'd rather marry the Earl's bastard half-brother? With that being the case, I'm curious how she fraternized with him sufficiently to develop a fascination."

Margaret inhaled slowly, then she exhaled even more slowly. She'd twiddled her thumbs as the improper liaison was bubbling up, and she'd counselled Annette against it, but Annette had refused to listen. Margaret had recognized, if the flirtation was revealed, that she, Margaret, would be blamed.

She couldn't believe Annette had tattled about Mr. Crawford. Annette had to have grasped that Ambrosia would consider Margaret to be responsible for the fling occurring. Had she worried about that paltry situation even a tiny bit?

"Mr. Crawford is very charming," Margaret cautiously stated, "and I noted her heightened attention, but I didn't imagine it would blossom into a relationship of any consequence. Annette has been enjoying herself, but you've raised her appropriately. Mr. Crawford could never lure her away from her obligations to you."

"Were you chaperoning her or not?"

Ambrosia slapped a palm on the table, the sharp sound echoing off the ceiling. Margaret blanched as if Ambrosia had struck her.

"I was carrying out my duties to you and to her," Margaret said, even as she realized how desperately she'd botched matters, "but you're aware of how obstinate Annette can be. She didn't see any harm in socializing with him and I couldn't convince her otherwise."

"Annette has never been obstinate with me and you're pretending this disaster is irrelevant. It's an attempt by you to cover up your slovenly conduct."

Margaret bristled. "That's not fair, Ambrosia. I would never have let her disgrace herself. Nor would she have. She knows what's expected of her."

"Then why is she insisting she won't wed the Earl? She's eager to shackle herself to a penniless by-blow!"

"She's not serious," Margaret said, "and you're making too much of this."

"She's extremely serious and you facilitated her change of heart. She's fallen in love for the very first time and that sort of amour is difficult to abandon. It will require exhausting work on my part to yank her away from this pathetic fortune-hunter. It may ultimately prove to be an impossible task."

Margaret could have picked any reply, but the one she chose was idiotic. "Mr. Crawford isn't a fortune-hunter. Lord Sutton is very fond of him. The neighbors and tenants too. He's respected everywhere. If he's attached to her, I'm sure his feelings are genuine."

"You defend him to me?" Ambrosia rippled with indignation. "You tout his attributes? What is wrong with you?"

"I apologize. I can't seem to say the right thing."

Ambrosia abruptly announced, "You're departing for London in the morning. I'm so angry that I ought to book you a seat on the public coach, but my outriders will take you, then return for me. I want you to vanish as fast as I can manage it."

A thousand concerns pummeled Margaret. Most pressing was the fact that she was about to be separated from Michael. Their illicit dalliance was temporary, but she'd assumed she had another week to wallow in his delightful company.

She was going immediately? She was going in the morning? How could that be?

"How have I distressed you so egregiously?" she asked.

"Do you think I'm blind?"

Margaret shook her head. "No, I don't think that."

"Tell me about you and Michael Crawford."

The demand was so startling that Margaret couldn't tamp down a wince of astonishment. "You're inquiring about me and Lord Sutton?"

"We won't beat around the bush and act as if I am clueless as to how you've shamed yourself in this house."

"I have no idea what you're talking about," Margaret said.

"Don't you? Your behavior has been so outrageous that I received an anonymous letter about you and the Earl. You've been so blatant that the other guests have noticed your folly. Your nonsense is the reason I'm at Sutton. I was forced to travel in the middle of winter because you've shown—once again—that you are a tart with the lowest of morals."

"That's not true."

It would be dangerous to admit any transgression, so Margaret had to deny and deny and deny, but her mind was awhirl, wondering how her mischief had been exposed. She'd deemed herself so clever, so furtive, but someone had witnessed her foolishness. Who had it been?

The most likely candidate was Rowena Smithwaite. She was exactly the type of vindictive shrew who would create chaos as she walked out the door.

"I have a question for you," Ambrosia said, "and I won't tolerate any lies. Are you ruined?"

"No! Why would you presume that about me?"

"I've known men like Sutton all my life. You are a lonely, poverty-stricken spinster and cads like him can't resist a female in your meager situation. It's humorous for them to seduce girls like you. They do it for sport."

"He hasn't seduced me. He's been cordial; that's it."

"How dreadfully has he tricked you? Has he promised to marry you—so you'll lift your skirt for him? Is that where we are?"

Margaret gasped with affront. "He and I have barely spoken and you're being ridiculous."

"Margaret, Margaret, Margaret…" Ambrosia scoffed, as if Margaret's sins had finally been revealed. "I thought I could trust you with Annette. I thought I could send you here without worrying."

"Nothing has happened between the Earl and me," she said. "How can I convince you of it?"

Ambrosia had a pocket in her skirt and she retrieved a piece of paper and handed it to Margaret. Margaret scanned the message that had been penned. It was the anonymous letter mailed to Ambrosia, and the author had been very blunt, had been aware that Michael was visiting her room at night.

Who had seen him? Who had told? Or had *he* gossiped? Had he bragged to his friends? She refused to accept that he'd treat her so hideously. Yet he was capable of any foul perfidy. Why would she be immune from one of his petty betrayals?

Well, whoever had tattled, it didn't matter now. Margaret could only hunker down and hope she wasn't battered too badly by the rubble that was about to land on her as the walls of her world crashed down.

She finished reading the horrible screed, then she handed it back. Her cousin tucked it away out of sight.

"That should end your deceits," Ambrosia said. "When I tell you I know the truth, I *know* the truth, and I can't bear to watch you feigning innocence. Are we about to have a bastard swelling your belly?"

"No. I like him very much, but I'm not stupid. I would never participate in conduct that would destroy me."

"You're already destroyed. In my opinion anyway." Ambrosia assessed Margaret, her focus disdainful and infuriating. Then she said, "All these years, I gave you the benefit of the doubt. Other relatives snickered over your adolescent lapse. They claimed you were just like your mother, that you were possessed of her same loose morals.

Everyone has insisted your wicked blood would eventually win out, but I defended you to them. I swore your misadventure had been a youthful indiscretion."

"Please don't denigrate my mother. I don't have many memories of her and I won't allow you to tarnish the few that remain."

"She was an actress, Margaret. Didn't we ever apprise you? I don't believe we did. We wanted to protect you, but she was a renowned trollop. She lured your father away from his family, away from the ethical path he'd been on, away from all that was decent and good."

"My father loved my mother. They were happy."

"Were they?" Ambrosia smiled cunningly, as if she was privy to secrets Margaret would never learn. "She had a debauched character and you inherited it from her. Are you expecting Lord Sutton to wed you? Is that what's occurring? Are you jealous of Annette? Have you looked around at this beautiful estate and decided you could have it for your own? Is that it?"

"Why would I be jealous of Annette? She's the only one of my Adair kin who's been kind to me. Why would I steal her fiancé? You're babbling like a lunatic."

"Blood will tell, Margaret," Ambrosia intoned like an ancient scribe. "Your mother was a doxy and you are too."

"You're wrong about her *and* about me. I haven't earned your wrath."

Ambrosia tsked with offense. "How should we proceed, Margaret? What would you suggest?"

"As I have committed no crime, why should I be required to suggest a punishment?"

"You will leave in the morning," Ambrosia repeated. "Early. Pack your bags tonight and I'd like you to be on the road by seven."

Margaret gaped at her, anxious to argue, anxious to point out the reasons Ambrosia was being a shrew, but it would be futile to offer excuses. Ambrosia wouldn't listen. She'd simply twist Margaret's words and hurl more insults.

"Seven will be fine," Margaret said as steadily as she could manage. "Where am I headed? Will it be your home in London? Or will you have your servants drop me off at a rural crossroads? Will you abandon me to fend for myself?"

"I'm not an animal; I won't dump you in a ditch, as you probably deserve, but from now on, I will always be wary. You'll wait for me at my house in town. I have to wrap up Annette's negotiations with Lord Sutton, then I'll follow shortly. We'll discuss which cousins might welcome you next, although after this debacle, I'm not sure what situation I'll be able to find for you. It will be quite a bit less than you were anticipating."

Margaret couldn't resist spewing a snotty comment. "You don't need to tarry. Lord Sutton doesn't like Annette and he will never wed her. He told me so."

Ambrosia beamed with a weird sort of satisfaction. "Why would you imagine that? He and I have already agreed about her. He's proposing tomorrow and I'll have my lawyers draft the contracts once I'm back in the city. It's all arranged."

Margaret could have fainted from shock. "He's marrying her?"

"Yes. It's why I want you gone in the morning. I won't permit you to loaf and be a distraction."

If Ambrosia had pulled out a knife and stabbed her with it, Margaret couldn't have been any more wounded. Tears flooded her eyes, and there were so many of them that she couldn't prevent a few from dripping down her cheeks. She was too stunned to wipe them away and she let them fall.

"He wouldn't consent to a betrothal," she said. "He would never do it."

"Is that what he claimed to you?" Ambrosia sighed, as if Margaret was a dunce. "We both realize he's a cad so I guess we shouldn't be surprised that he lied to you. In actual fact, he was very excited about it."

"He wouldn't have hurt me this way."

Ambrosia's expression became pitying. "*He* wouldn't have? I never viewed you as a ninny or a fool. Why would he ever be concerned about hurting you?"

"When is the wedding to be? Have you picked a date?"

"April tenth. It's a Saturday, but please keep the news to yourself. Annette hasn't been informed yet and I can't have rumors spreading until it's official."

Margaret stared at Ambrosia and she seemed very far away, as if Margaret was peering at her through a narrow tunnel. Margaret was eager to ask numerous questions about the nuptial deliberations. How had Lord Sutton appeared? Had he been thrilled? Bored? Resigned?

From this moment on, he wasn't any of her business. Annette had been destined to be an aristocrat's bride and her conclusion would resolve exactly as intended. The sole glitch in the tale was that Margaret had barged into the story and tantalized the hero for awhile, but he was back on track and focused on the heroine—where he belonged.

She stood and went to the door. Ambrosia was annoyed that she'd given up so easily and she called, "Seven o'clock, Margaret. And how about if you skip supper? I'll apprise Hester Crawford that you're indisposed. I would appreciate it if you wouldn't complain to Annette about your departure. She'll be irked about it and I won't have her haranguing at me."

"I will slither off without a goodbye." Sarcastically, Margaret added, "As always, I am your most devoted servant."

"Don't speak to Lord Sutton either. You're aware that you are in the wrong and I can't have you inflicting yourself on him. I insist you leave him alone. You must sneak away without talking to him."

"Why would I talk to him? What could I possibly say that would matter in the slightest?"

Ambrosia smirked. "Precisely. You shouldn't be pestering him."

Margaret scrutinized the vicious woman, wondering why she was so cruel and horrid. She wasn't even an Adair, but had glommed onto them through matrimony, so she had such gall. Margaret didn't suppose there was a method to bring her down a peg, but she was yearning to try.

"You know, Ambrosia," she said, "you started life at a spot much lower than mine, yet you've always treated me like a scullery maid. Why is that?"

"It's your mother's fault, dear. I just explained this to you: She was an actress and doxy who seduced your father after we warned him to beware of her. No one in the family could abide her and we were so upset when they married. It was such a ludicrous farce, and unfortunately, *you* are paying the price for her sins. We've watched you to see if her bad tendencies would poke out in you, and I'm sorry to report that you've constantly disappointed us."

"Is that why you banded together and stole my father's house from me?"

For an instant, guilt crossed Ambrosia's face, but it was quickly masked. "What house, Margaret? I have no idea what you mean."

"My father used to own Beachhead Cottage outside Baywick. After he passed away, it should have been mine. I should have inherited it."

"Your father died bankrupt—because your greedy mother spent all his money. Some of our cousins bought the property at a foreclosure sale. It had naught to do with you."

Ambrosia's calm aplomb enraged Margaret to such a degree that she could barely stop herself from marching over and slapping her. Instead, she said, "I don't believe you about my lost inheritance. I don't believe you about anything."

She whirled away and left. If Ambrosia called to her again, she didn't hear.

# Chapter

# 17

Michael marched down the hall toward the master suite. For hours, he'd been trapped in the lower parlors, having to play the part of gracious host, which he hated. Hester had nagged at him for ignoring Annette Adair, so for once, he'd danced attendance on her.

With her mother in the house and watching his every move, he'd felt as if he'd been standing under a bright light.

Margaret hadn't come down to supper, or the socializing afterward, and her absence had been very distracting. He'd been anxious to ask about her, but he'd been in no position to inquire. If she ate with them, or if she didn't, it would have been out of character for him to notice or comment.

He'd intended to enjoy his regular visit to her room, and he'd just snuck in, only to find that she wasn't there either. It had momentarily panicked him, but her clothes were in the wardrobe so she was still in the manor. He had no idea where she might be though.

He suspected she was hiding from him. Ambrosia Adair was on the premises so she'd be under greater scrutiny. Perhaps she thought they should cease their misbehavior. His time with her was winding down and he wasn't even sure she'd remain at Sutton. She was Annette's chaperone, but Mrs. Adair had jumped into that role, so why would Margaret be needed?

He reached his door and went inside. He didn't have a valet, but the winter night was cold and he'd requested a fire. It was still burning so the sitting room was nice and toasty.

He shed his coat and tossed it onto a nearby chair, then he walked over to the liquor tray in the corner and poured himself a whiskey. He sipped it and pondered Annette. No doubt she'd be a fabulous bride, and what sane man wouldn't like to glom onto her dowry? But with Margaret lurking in his background, he couldn't determine whether to proceed.

He'd have to spend his married life, avoiding family gatherings, and the entire morass seemed too difficult to navigate. He didn't like dealing with complications; he'd had enough of that in the navy.

As he fumed and debated, it dawned on him that there was a strange ambiance in the air. He sniffed the area around him, being certain he could detect a hint of Margaret's perfume. Was that likely?

There was a candle burning in the bedchamber and he tiptoed over and peeked in. There she was! She was seated on a chair by the window and waiting for him. She'd made herself at home and was drinking a glass of liquor too.

They stared, not able to begin a conversation, then she said, "I didn't think you'd ever arrive."

"Margaret? What are you doing in here? I'm a tad shocked to stumble on you."

"I'm sorry I barged in, but could I speak with you? It's important."

He was rattled by her appearance, but excited by it too, and struggling to deduce what his reaction should be. If he'd been any kind of gentleman, he'd have escorted her out, but he wasn't a gentleman so he was terrified as to how the encounter might unfold.

"I stopped by your room," he said, "but you weren't there. You didn't join us for supper so I was worried. Are you all right?"

"I'm fine." She paused, then added, "Well, I'm not fine, but I'll muddle through."

"What's wrong? What happened?"

"I quarreled with Ambrosia. Annette's mother? It put me in a bad mood, and I wouldn't have been a very merry guest, so I skipped the meal."

"Why were you fighting with her?"

"She doesn't like me. She can be very petty, very arrogant, and she treats me hideously. It's exhausting."

"That doesn't explain much of anything."

She shrugged. "It's old issues. I never carry on as my relatives assume I ought, and I always live down to their low expectations."

"If they don't cherish you, then they're idiots."

"It's exactly what I've been thinking so thank you for agreeing with me."

He smiled and hurried over to her. He took her hand and linked their fingers. Affection swept over him in such a powerful wave that he was surprised it didn't knock him down.

"Tell me what's really wrong," he said. "Tell me the truth."

"Have you decided about Annette? Will you propose to her or not?"

"I don't know."

"You haven't discussed a betrothal with Ambrosia?"

"Not yet. We haven't had a chance to be alone."

She studied him meticulously, then smirked. "You're such an adept liar. How can I believe any remark you utter?"

"Let's not talk about my possible engagement to Annette. It wounds you, and I come across as a callous fiend. I'd like you to imagine I'm wonderful instead of despicable."

"You're wonderful in many, many ways, but you have a despicable streak a mile long."

"You've unraveled my secrets, but I'm supposed to be a mystery to you."

There were emotions swirling that he couldn't name. Ultimately, she stood and their bodies were crushed together from chests to toes. He kissed her as he'd been dying to do. She wrapped her arms around him and kissed him back.

She was rippling with anguish, her torment so blatant that it was tangible. He received the strongest impression that she was holding onto him for dear life, that if he released her, she might float off into the sky.

"I have to ask you a question," she said as their lips parted.

"I'll answer if I can."

Without hesitating, she stunned him by saying, "I would like to have intimate relations with you. Would you be willing?"

"*Intimate* relations," he carefully repeated. "What precisely are you contemplating? Would we strip off our clothes, climb under the quilts, and revel in some carnal activity?"

"Yes, that's what I'm imagining. Can we?"

The plea was so startling, and so unusual for the woman he deemed her to be, that he was completely floored.

A dozen replies warred in his mind. He was a scoundrel who wallowed in lewd conduct. He loved trollops and loved misbehaving with them. He'd hoped to misbehave with her too, but he'd been forced to accept that it would never transpire. But here she was, offering herself. Shouldn't he consent?

At the same juncture, agony was rocking her. Obviously, she'd had more than a casual spat with Mrs. Adair. Whatever the topic had been, it had left her reeling. She was in no condition to make such a reckless choice, and he viewed himself as her friend. Shouldn't he refuse and save her from herself?

"Are you aware of what sexual congress entails?" he asked.

"I've had it described to me. I'm not one-hundred percent clear on how it's accomplished, but I was told it's very physical."

"It can be scary and disconcerting too. Maidens find it to be very emotional, and some more timid girls are downright alarmed by it. Why would you suddenly be so eager to try it?"

"I wouldn't be scared, and if you could be my first and only, I'm sure it would be marvelous. You couldn't leave me in a jam though. I guess there's a way to keep from planting your seed in my womb. Have you heard about that?"

"Yes, there's a way," he cautiously said, "and I know what it is."

Her cheeks heated with embarrassment and he was astonished that she would mention words like *seed* and *womb*. It indicated that she was deadly serious in what she was requesting.

He wished he could open up the top of her head and peer inside so he'd have some clue as to what was driving her to such insanity. He was stalling, debating the proper course, but he couldn't deduce what it might be.

The *proper* course would be to send her away, but he was such a cad. He couldn't envision doing that.

"This is a very scandalous entreaty," he said, "and I can't figure out why you've suggested it."

"It's not all that scandalous, is it? You've begged me to be your mistress several times. If I'd agreed, we'd have regularly dallied."

"Yes, but you weren't interested in such a dubious arrangement, so what has changed? Why now? Why tonight?"

"I want something of you for my very own, something my cousins can't stop me from having. I want a piece of you that's mine and mine alone. Won't you let me have it?"

As she beseeched him, she appeared young and lost, as if she was at the end of her rope. Shouldn't he supply what she was seeking? Wouldn't she feel better?

Even as he pondered the prospect, he was kicking himself for being an idiot. Carnal deeds would not improve her mood; that was his lust talking. She'd been shoved onto a desperate ledge, but a quick romp under the blankets was not the cure she needed.

He breathed out a heavy sigh, realizing he was about to behave honorably for what was maybe the only occasion ever.

"I can't oblige you," he said. "I'm sorry. I have a horrible reputation as a libertine, so you're assuming I'll leap at this chance, but I am so fond of you. You're gravely upset, but this isn't the answer to heal what's wrong. I'd be taking advantage of you, and if you were angry with me later on, I would never forgive myself."

"I'd never be angry. I swear."

He shook his head. "We can't, Margaret. It's not a good idea."

She deflated a bit, then she swiftly regrouped.

"I understand," she said, "and I apologize for bothering you."

"It was no bother and I'm very flattered that you came to me."

"I shouldn't have. It was mad conduct."

"Not *mad* conduct. I'll call it brave and bold conduct." The paltry compliment didn't wring a smile out of her. "Would you like me to escort you to your room?"

"No. I wouldn't dare be observed out in the hall with you."

She stood very still, cataloguing his features, as if committing them to memory. Her gaze was so probing, and so thorough, that it seemed to be some sort of farewell.

Finally, she said, "I'll see you in the morning."

"I'd ask you to have breakfast with me, but I'm riding off on an excursion with the male guests."

"What time are you leaving?"

"Around ten."

"My day will be progressing very fast by then so I will definitely miss your departure. What type of adventure will you be having?"

"There's a horse auction at a nearby estate and I won't return until supper."

"I'll watch for you. Be sure to say hello once you're back."

She looked positively despondent, as if she might burst into tears, and he couldn't bear to witness her woe. He'd never exactly been a font of compassion so he couldn't guess how to cheer her.

He grinned and said, "Remember the older gentleman in the driveway the other afternoon? The one who the gossips claim to be my actual father?"

"Yes, I remember him."

"The auction is at his farm. He's an equestrian expert, and he raises horses, so I'll spend hours in his company. What do you think of that?"

She snorted. "I hope you enjoy your visit, but don't share any of those rumors with your London chums. Even if you believe they're true, it's an insult to your mother to repeat them."

"Just for you," he said, "my lips will be sealed."

"It will be chilly so please bundle up. Don't freeze."

"I will bundle up and I will ponder you every minute."

"I'm happy to hear it."

She leaned in and hugged him tight, then she slid away and hurried out. She'd reached the door to the hall, and was about to open it, when it occurred to him that he was being ridiculous.

He wasn't a gentleman. He wasn't honorable and he never chose the moral path. He most especially never refused what was freely offered by a female. She was eager to race to ruin. He hadn't dragged her to his suite. He hadn't forced her. She'd blustered in of her own accord and she was an adult.

Why not furnish what she was so desperate to have? What was his other option? Would he allow her to slink away with no mischief perpetrated? Would he mope by himself? If he let her go, wouldn't he regret it forever?

He dashed after her, saying, "Margaret! Wait! I've changed my mind."

She halted and spun around. "About what?"

"Stay the night with me. We'll dally in every wicked, debauched manner we can devise. We can make merry until dawn is breaking."

She assessed him, trying to determine if he was serious, then she said, "I'm amazed that I had to work so hard to convince you. Are you certain?"

"No, but don't listen to me. Come to bed."

He extended his hand to her and she sauntered over and grabbed hold.

MARGARET DIDN'T HESITATE. SHE wasn't having second-thoughts and she'd never be sorry.

After her conversation with Ambrosia, she'd locked herself in her bedchamber. She'd paced and fumed, had raged and wept.

She'd assumed Annette would stop by to check on her, but she hadn't. Why wasn't Annette concerned about her? Margaret's temper had started to flare, and eventually, it had burned so hotly that she'd begun to feel ill from harboring so much wrath.

It had slowly fizzled out though, and she'd been relieved Annette hadn't stopped by. Margaret wouldn't have been keen to clarify the dilemma, and she'd been left with the stunning realization that she wanted to steal something from Ambrosia. It was a petty wish, but Ambrosia would rid herself of Margaret, then rope Michael into a betrothal. She'd boasted that she already had.

Margaret had asked him about it and he'd insisted he'd had no nuptial discussion with Ambrosia. They were both liars so she had no idea which version was the truth, but it didn't matter.

Ambrosia had married lucky and she'd grown rich because of it. Her money had her presuming she was grand and superior, but she was a pompous witch who hated Margaret—for no reason Margaret could ever discern.

If Annette wed Michael, Ambrosia would revel in the conclusion, but Margaret had no doubt she'd also be gleeful over how she'd yanked him away from Margaret and had given him to Annette. Ambrosia would privately celebrate how she'd wounded Margaret.

Well, Margaret couldn't prevent Annette from becoming Michael's wife, but she could have a piece of him that she wasn't supposed to have. She could engage in the acts Annette would have to perform as his bride, but Margaret would have him first. She'd never be able to tell anyone, and no one would ever know, but *she* would know.

She would always secretly delight in the fact that he'd been hers for a few hours before he'd been Annette's. It was deranged thinking, and she wasn't evaluating the situation as clearly as she should, but she would continue anyway.

She would never wed; she understood that now. She had no assets to entice a beau, but it was more than that. With her meeting and falling in love with Michael Crawford, no other man could ever coax her toward matrimony.

Why save herself for marriage? She would surrender her virginity to him and the negligent deed would make him happy. She would depart in the morning, aware that she'd supplied the one thing he would cherish the most.

By the time they entered his bedroom, they were so excited that they were practically running. Or maybe they were terrified, if they didn't rush to folly, they wouldn't follow through. They raced up to the bed and he lifted her and tumbled them onto the mattress. They landed in a tangle of arms and legs and they giggled like schoolchildren.

They stretched out, with her nestled beneath him, then he was kissing her and kissing her and it was passionate and thrilling. She leapt into the fray, intending to shower him with all the affection and joy she could muster. Later on, after he figured out she'd fled without a goodbye, he'd realize that *this* had been her goodbye.

They carried on for an eternity and he was so proficient at it. She felt adored and special, her body relaxing into his embraces. Her anatomy recognized what was coming and couldn't wait for it to happen. He was stroking his palms across her shoulders and back, her ribs and thighs. Occasionally, he even caressed her breasts, massaging them so they throbbed and ached.

Prior to sneaking into his suite, she'd taken down her hair and had unlaced her corset so she was free and unencumbered. There was only the thin fabric of her gown to separate his hands from her bare skin. It had her yearning to be undressed, which was a bizarre notion.

She couldn't imagine removing her clothes for him, but she'd heard it was obligatory when a couple engaged in carnal acts. She was determined to behave in any way he requested. If nudity was required, then nudity he would have.

He drew away onto his haunches and asked, "Are you still sure?"

"I'm more sure than ever. Why have we stopped?"

"I have some tasks to complete. Are you cold?"

"A bit."

He climbed off the bed and stirred the fire, then he returned to her. He shifted about so he could pull off her slippers, first one, then the other, and he tossed them on the floor. Then he untied her garters and rolled down her stockings.

He sat on the mattress and dangled a foot at her, signaling she should tug off his boots.

"I'm not about to make love to you with them on," he said.

"Is that a romantic *faux pas*?"

"It's what a cad does when he's in a hurry. I am *not* in a hurry."

She worked them off and tossed them on the floor as well. They laughed about it, teasing each other, and it seemed so normal. There was no reason to fret.

He rose to his knees, straddling her, then he jerked off his shirt and it was discarded with the other items. She tried to recollect if she'd ever previously seen a man's chest. If she had, she couldn't remember when. His shoulders were wide, his waist narrow. There was a smattering of hair across the top and it ran down his belly and disappeared into his trousers.

The sight of that hair was exhilarating, and it called to her feminine instincts in an almost feral manner. She was eager to be as wild and dissolute as possible.

Much before she was finished looking her fill, he snuggled down, and he tucked the blankets around them, so they were sealed in a warm cocoon.

He began kissing her yet again, and he was seducing her, calming her, preparing her for what was approaching. She followed his lead. If he nibbled and bit, she did too. If he rubbed her intimate parts, she did the same. Every touch, every glance, every word, was absolutely perfect.

He abandoned her lips and nuzzled a trail down her neck, to her breasts. He played with them, pinching the nipples so they ached even more. Gradually, he was unbuttoning her gown, tugging it down, baring her bosom.

Her initial impulse was to hide herself from him. It was the sole moment where she'd hesitated, where panic had bubbled up, but she tamped it down. She wouldn't exhibit an ounce of fear or indecision. She would let him guide her down any path he chose and she closed her eyes and reveled in sensation.

He was toying with her nipples when suddenly—to her great amazement—he sucked one of them into his mouth. The agitation it produced was so riveting that, despite her resolution not to quail like a ninny, she nearly squirmed away to escape the onslaught.

He grinned. "Do you like that?"

"Oh, my. It feels so good. Are you certain it's allowed?"

"When you're here with me like this, everything is allowed. No matter what transpires, it's fine."

Their gazes locked, potent emotion swirling. He was seeking permission to continue, and as her answer, she simply relaxed onto the pillow.

For a lengthy interval, he focused on her breasts, each caress of his tongue sending a sort of electrical shock through her torso. It occurred to her that he was removing the rest of her clothes, and without her noticing, he'd pushed her gown down past her feet. Her chemise and drawers vanished too.

All of it happened so slowly, and with such minimal fuss, that she wasn't bothered by what they were perpetrating. She was naked and it might have been the most ordinary condition in the world.

His hand was gliding up her thigh, to the vee between her legs, and she wasn't positive what he intended. It was the spot where the male-female coupling took place, but she didn't suppose they'd arrived at that precipice yet.

Without warning, he slid a finger into her sheath. A second one was added, and he shoved them in and out, in and out, then he latched onto a nipple and sucked very hard. A wave of pleasure started to build deep inside her. It exploded out to her limbs so she might have been soaring to the heavens.

She flew up and up, and she reached a type of apex, then she tumbled down, landing safely in his arms. She was sputtering with astonishment, with joy, and he was preening, proud of himself and how adept he was at manipulating her.

"What was that?" she said when she could speak. "What's it called?"

"The French have named it *the little death*."

She smirked. "Who can argue with the French?"

"You are such a gem and I am so glad you're mine."

"Am I yours?" she inquired. "Will you always think of me that way?"

"I will consider you to be mine until I am old and grey. How does that sound?"

"That sounds wonderful."

His expression was so fond. If he'd proclaimed himself to be madly in love with her, she wouldn't have been surprised. His affection was that blatant.

The moment passed though, and he'd engaged in all the conversation he could manage. He began again and she joined in quite ardently. She was bewildered and overwhelmed, but she didn't have to concentrate. He knew what he wanted, where they were headed, and she could simply float along on the river of desire he'd stirred.

Down below, he was fumbling with his trousers, flicking at the buttons, yanking them down to his flanks. He was widening her thighs, his body dropping between them. She wasn't clear on the details of what her deflowering would entail, but she had a general idea. They were quickly approaching the epic occasion, and while she hadn't planned to react negatively, a few maidenly qualms popped up.

To her enormous consternation, she was a tad afraid.

"Are we about to…to…" she asked. She didn't have the vocabulary to discuss carnal conduct so she couldn't finish the sentence.

"We're almost there," he said. "Are you nervous?"

"I'm trying not to be, but I can't help it."

"The first time can be scary, but you needn't fret. If you're unsettled, it's merely because you've never experienced anything like this before, but your anatomy knows what to do."

"Don't forget your promise."

He snorted. "My darling Margaret, I've already forgotten it, so what was it again? If it is within my power to supply, you may have it."

"You must be careful with me. You can't plant a babe in my womb."

She'd been told that a man didn't have to spill his seed into a woman. She wasn't completely cognizant of what it involved or how it would occur, but he was a skilled roué. He ought to have learned the trick. Wouldn't he have?

She couldn't believe she'd mentioned such a risqué point, but he was unfazed by the comment. His nonchalance reminded her of what a libertine he was, and briefly, she speculated over how many other paramours had lain with him just like this.

The question was too disturbing to contemplate so she wouldn't contemplate it.

"I will be careful with you," he said. "You trust me, don't you?"

She frowned. "I absolutely don't trust you."

He chuckled. "Which is very wise, but you can trust me when we're together like this. I won't leave you in a jam."

They started in once more, kissing, caressing. He was stroking his fingers in and out of her sheath, then something else was there and it was bigger and thicker. He was pressing it into her, a little, then a little more, and her torso was resisting, as if it wasn't keen to keep on after all.

She struggled for calm, as he dabbed his thumb at the sensitive spot between her thighs. Her passion was rising, her body tensing, and as pleasure swept over her again, he gave a hard lunge with his hips, and—just that fast—he was fully impaled.

She was quite stunned, and as she took stock of her new condition, he paused and held himself very still. He was perched above her, and he looked peculiar, as if he was in pain.

"Are you all right?" he asked.

"Yes, I'm fine. Are we done?"

"No, there's more to it. Wrap your arms around me and don't let go."

"Like this?"

"Yes. Hang in there for me."

He moved in an exciting manner, pushing in all the way, then pulling out all the way. He repeated it over and over, slowly and gently, then more deliberately and rough. In the beginning, it was awkward, but she gradually figured out the rhythm and she matched him thrust for thrust.

The interval became more wicked, more wild. Their breathing was labored and they strained with exertion.

Finally, he went in very far and he groaned and hovered there for a minute, then he relaxed onto her. His weight was crushing her, but he didn't feel heavy. He felt wonderful and welcome and she couldn't bear that it had concluded so abruptly. She was frantically cataloguing details so she could review them later on.

He slid off her and rolled onto his side. She rolled too so they were nose to nose. They were grinning, whispering endearments that brought tears to her eyes. She meant the ones she was uttering, but she was sure he wasn't serious. She wouldn't fault him for it though; she'd simply gather them up and convince herself he was sincere.

"What did you think?" he asked. "Was it like you imagined it would be?"

"I had heard it was very physical, but I guess I didn't really understand. What did *you* think of it? I'm a novice at this, but it seemed very thrilling to me."

"It was remarkable and you were amazing. You have a knack for this sort of lewd conduct."

She chortled with merriment. "Are you suggesting I might be a trollop at heart?"

"Yes, and I'm lucky to have been the fellow who discovered it."

She leaned in and kissed him. "I'm so glad it was you."

"That better be your opinion in the morning. Don't you dare suffer any regrets. If you ever wish we hadn't proceeded, I will never forgive myself."

"I begged you to ruin me, remember?"

"Oh, I remember, you naughty tart, and I'm still astonished that I obliged you."

"I'm a vixen," she facetiously said, "and you can't resist me."

"That is very, very true. I've been smitten from the moment we met."

"In Baywick," she murmured, recalling their weekend in the coastal town. "Did you buy Beachhead Cottage?"

"I didn't. I considered it, and I even corresponded with the estate lawyers, but I changed my mind. I'm landlocked at Sutton and I don't need a home at the ocean. It would have been a frivolous expense."

"I was hoping you'd purchase it so I could picture it being yours. Have I told you my father owned it when I was a girl?"

"What? No! You didn't tell me."

"We used to go there on holiday when I was tiny."

"Why didn't you inherit it after he died? Shouldn't it have been yours?"

"Supposedly, there were debts to pay so creditors nearly seized it. My relatives swooped in and scooped it up at a very reduced price."

He was incensed on her behalf. "You had to work there—like a servant!—when it should have been yours. Would they have stolen it from you?"

"With how they disparage my parents, it wouldn't surprise me." She shrugged, as if it didn't matter. "It was a long time ago."

"I'm kicking myself for not buying it. I could have given it to you as a parting gift."

"It's a pretty notion and I shall pretend it happened just that way."

He shifted onto his back, and he drew her to him so she was draped over his chest. He was lost in thought, then he muttered, "I didn't pull out."

She didn't grasp the import of the confession and she asked, "What do you mean?"

"At the end? I should have spilled my seed on your tummy, but you overwhelmed me so completely that I couldn't manage it. I've never been so negligent and it's a sign of how thoroughly I desired you."

Her lungs constricted with alarm and she braced herself on an elbow and glared at him. "You promised to be careful! Why weren't you?"

She probably shouldn't have scolded him, but honestly! He was the roguish expert and she'd been a virgin. How could it have been her burden to practice caution?

"I was swept away by affection," he said, "and I was too excited. I couldn't hold back."

The excuse mollified her somewhat. "Could I be increasing? Can it occur that fast?"

He scoffed, as if the prospect was ridiculous. "No, not from just one romp. Don't worry about it."

He wasn't being truthful, was he? She plopped down so he wouldn't note how she was frowning. There were constant tales, told by ruined maidens who insisted they'd lain with a boy *just once!* People snickered skeptically and mocked their naiveté. Was she being naïve too?

She might have quarreled with him, but when their amour was winding to a close, she refused to dwell on any difficult issue. Besides, what were the odds that she'd be ensnared?

"What do we do now?" she asked.

"Now, we snuggle and chat, then we do it again after we've relaxed for a bit. Unless you're too sore?"

She stretched her legs, testing her womanly areas. They protested, but she wasn't about to admit it. "I'm rearing to go. How about you?"

"I am totally bewildered. This encounter was much more gripping than I anticipated, but then, you're a wily scamp. You've wedged yourself into my brain like an irksome gnat I can't swat away."

"Was that a compliment?" she asked. "I couldn't tell."

"It was an earnest compliment, but don't beg for more of them. You shouldn't be greedy."

"When we start in again, would you remove your trousers? I'm naked and it's only fair that you be naked too. I want to see you in the altogether—so I'll always recollect what you looked like."

"You are a tart!" he teasingly crowed. "I knew it!"

"I can't deny that you've had a deleterious effect on my character."

"I have corrupted my share of women."

"Scoundrel."

"Trollop."

Desire flared, and they marched through the entire carnal process again, with passion building, rising, and cresting. On this, her second sexual experience, she understood what would transpire so it wasn't awkward. It was very poignant and romantic and they went slowly to savor every minute.

He didn't shuck off his trousers as she'd requested, but he pulled out at the end, and she viewed it as a blessing. As their bodies separated, there was a nostalgia in the air, almost as if the universe was grieving that it was all about to conclude.

"Who was your father?" he asked, a topic that had never previously interested him. "What was his station in life?"

It was a peculiar query, and it hinted at the possibility that he was pondering whether he could marry her, that she might reveal an intriguing fact about her lineage. But she was merely Miss Margaret Adair and there was nothing remarkable about her ancestry.

He would ultimately wed a great heiress, or maybe a duke's daughter or even a princess. She was none of those.

"My father was a gentleman farmer," she said, "and no one special, just a member of the huge Adair clan. He had a small estate in the country and he died bankrupt."

"And your mother?"

"I've heard varying stories. If my relatives are feeling generous, they claim she was a fetching vicar's daughter. If they're feeling peevish, they claim she was a dissolute actress or opera dancer who lured my father to his doom."

"I'm choosing to believe she was the actress or opera dancer. You're too unique to have had an ordinary mother."

It was the sweetest comment he could have voiced and she would cherish it forever. They were quiet for awhile, and gradually, it occurred to her that he'd fallen asleep. She nestled next to him, cuddled under the blankets, and she thought this was the nicest part so far, this lazy interlude after their lust was spent.

She dawdled as long as she dared, and she figured he'd wake up, but he didn't. When she caught herself dozing too, she forced herself away. Ambrosia had ordered the carriage for seven and Margaret hadn't packed a single item. In the morning, she couldn't have the outriders waiting on her, couldn't be late in climbing into the vehicle.

If she delayed, Ambrosia would assume she was being defiant. She might write to all of Margaret's kin to ensure she never wrangled a place to live with any of them. Margaret wouldn't rock that boat. She would organize her bags, eat an early breakfast, and depart right on time.

Mustering her resolve, she tiptoed about, finding her clothes, tugging them on. She prayed he'd stir so they could have a final conversation for her to mull in the future, but when he didn't, she decided it was for the best. If he'd roused, she couldn't have dragged herself away.

For a lengthy moment, she tarried by the bed, watching him breathe. He and his chums would trot off to the horse auction at ten, and by then, she'd be many miles from Sutton. He'd return in the evening to discover she'd left. What would he think?

Would he miss her? Would he be upset that she'd snuck away? Or might he be relieved that their paltry connection had been severed so effortlessly? He was a cad who hated goodbyes, and with her stealthy exit, she'd make it easy on him. He wouldn't have to fuss with her ever again.

He could propose to Annette or not. He could invite another bridal candidate to Sutton and grow infatuated—or not. He could marry a princess and it would never be any of Margaret's business. Someday, when she least expected it, she would read about his wedding in the newspaper.

She'd briefly mourn that she hadn't been able to keep him for her own, then she'd try to be happy for him and wish him well. She would celebrate that she'd known him, that he'd been her friend.

*I love you,* she mouthed. *I will always love you and I will never stop.*

Then she spun and crept away. She peeked into the hall, found it empty, and hurried off without a backward glance.

# Chapter 18

"What are you doing?"

"What do you mean?"

Caleb glared at Michael, his temper on a slow boil, as he said, "You're dancing attendance on Annette Adair."

"She's visiting Sutton so I can decide if I'd like to marry her. Why shouldn't I spend time with her? It's obvious you're in a snit about it so I have to ask why."

"She's been here an entire week and you haven't so much as glanced in her direction. Then last night, you pretended to be her most devoted swain."

"Yes, so?"

Caleb loved his brother, but occasionally, he hated him too. On hearing his flip response, Caleb thought about punching him. He never would though. Michael was bigger, tougher, and stronger. He was a decorated warrior and hero, but he fought dirty, and if Caleb started a brawl, Michael would pound him into the ground.

"You don't care about her," Caleb fumed. "You don't even like her. Is it because her mother has barged in to watch you?"

"No. I haven't spoken ten words to her mother."

"What's driving you then? Don't tell me you're seriously considering her. I'll never believe it."

"I am considering her, Caleb," Michael said. "You know that so I ask you again: Why are you in such a snit about it?"

They'd been out in the snowy weather all day, when they shouldn't have been. Michael had been invited to a horse auction that Caleb had deemed to be ridiculous. Who sold horses in January? Michael had been determined to go, and the man who owned the animals, Mr. Pence, was an old employee of the family who'd once run the estate's stables.

If rumors were true, he was also Michael's father.

Caleb doubted the story. He couldn't imagine Michael's mother committing such a sin. She'd been a pious shrew who'd shoved her religion down everyone's throats. It was deranged to suppose she'd engage in such an immoral act.

But then, what about Caleb's father? Why had the unlikable sot grown so enamored of a doxy? Why had he sired Caleb? Both of them had been devout hypocrites.

Michael was fascinated by Mr. Pence and he could never resist calling on him. He always furtively searched for proof that he was Mr. Pence's son. As to Mr. Pence, he never provided the slightest hint that he had an unusual connection to Michael.

They looked exactly alike physically, but they shared no personal characteristics. Michael was rude and overbearing, while Mr. Pence was helpful and generous. In actual fact, he had more traits in common with Caleb than Michael, but it was ludicrous to speculate.

Michael had been born when the prior earl was wed to his wife so the Law and the Church viewed him to be Michael's father. Any improbable misconduct by Mr. Pence with Michael's mother was irrelevant.

The trip had dragged on forever. They'd left at ten and it was after five. The sun had set, the sky a deepening indigo color. They were back at Sutton and handing off their horses to the groomsmen. Caleb was frozen solid and exasperated over the jaunt. Michael hadn't purchased a single horse, so what had been the point?

The whole journey, he'd been yearning to get Michael alone so they could quarrel, but his London friends had accompanied them so there hadn't been a chance to chat privately. Now though, they were walking over to the manor and Michael was without his entourage.

Since Annette had arrived at Sutton, Michael had ignored her, yet suddenly, he appeared to be smitten as a green boy. Caleb wouldn't have it! He owed Michael for every benefit he'd received: his elevated spot in the world, his recognition as an earl's sibling, the escape from his dire childhood, their adventures sailing the globe.

Through it all, he'd never asked Michael for anything, and even though Caleb protested any largesse that was bestowed, Michael had showered Caleb with too many boons to count. Caleb had never sought any of them and he tried hard to never overstep.

Finally—finally!—he'd found something he wanted very much. It was Annette Adair and Michael couldn't have her.

"I'm in a *snit,*" Caleb said, "because you irk me beyond my limit. You don't notice her, then you dote on her. Who behaves like that?"

Michael pulled up short so Caleb had to stop too. They spun to face each other. Michael was grinning, humored by Caleb's pique.

"There's been gossip about you," Michael said. "Every time I turn around, someone complains to me that *you* are sweet on Annette. Are you?"

"What if I am?" Caleb blustered.

"Is that a *yes*?"

Caleb didn't answer directly. He had no business staking a claim, so instead, he said, "She's wonderful and you don't deserve her."

"Probably not."

"You would never love or even respect her. She'd be miserable as your wife."

"Do you think she'd be happier with you?" Michael asked.

"Yes, I do think that."

"Are you courting her? Is that what's happening?"

"I guess I am."

"Would you marry her if you could?"

Caleb should have denied it, but he couldn't. "Yes, I'd marry her immediately if I could figure out how to arrange it."

Michael was silent, debating his next remarks. He and Caleb were very close, but they often bickered. Mostly, it was because Michael was a callous idiot and Caleb ended up having to rein in his worst excesses. He was a typical aristocrat, but a typical ship's captain too. He was very spoiled and he never carried on as others were expecting.

Caleb supposed, in this situation too, Michael would be cocky and infuriating. If he uttered a stupid comment about Annette, Caleb suspected he'd punch his brother for the first time ever.

"You've put us in such an awkward position," was Michael's opening salvo.

"I don't care."

"I only mean, what if I wed her? It will create so many problems between you and me."

"You can't wed her!" Caleb vehemently insisted. "It would kill me if you did! You can't assume it's an option."

Michael's expression grew pitying. For all of his being an arrogant oaf, he really was an excellent judge of people. Despite how he could enrage Caleb with his antics, he was a *big* brother in the premier sense of the word. He understood Caleb. He knew how Caleb's mind worked. He was Caleb's dearest friend and he'd changed Caleb's life in innumerable ways, but…

Michael would choose the conclusion that was best for *him.* He would pick the most lucrative path. He gazed at the world as if he were king of it and all mortals should bow down. If he decided to propose to Annette, he would, and Caleb would never be able to prevent it.

If Michael proceeded, where would that leave them? Caleb had always been embarrassed over how he'd glommed onto his famous sibling, how he lived off Michael's charity. He'd frequently apprised Michael that he yearned to build a future for himself, one that was separate from Michael, but Michael constantly dissuaded him.

Would this be the catalyst that tore them apart?

"I'm going to tell you some hard truths," Michael said. "I'm not trying to hurt you, but some of this will sound very harsh."

"Speak your piece," Caleb stated quite bitterly. "I can already predict your opinion about Annette. You are not a mystery to me."

"Mrs. Adair intends for Annette to marry into the aristocracy and her mother will select her husband. She would never deem you to be suitable."

"You could talk to her for me."

"No, I couldn't. I recognize your stellar traits, but she isn't looking for stellar traits. She's determined that Annette be a countess. It's the sole attribute that matters to her and I couldn't convince her to consider you. She simply wouldn't."

"So you'll steal Annette away from me? Will you break my heart?"

"Is your heart engaged? You've only been acquainted with her for a few days."

Caleb couldn't explain the affection he'd developed for Annette. Michael didn't believe *love* was an emotion a man could suffer. He reveled with slatterns, and usually, he paid them for their sexual services so Caleb wouldn't waste his breath.

"What is your plan for her then?" Caleb demanded. "I've told you what I want, but you won't listen."

"I'm listening, but you're being ridiculous." Caleb bristled and Michael rushed to add, "I need you to calm down and reflect on what you're contemplating. You've let a pretty dream pop up, but that's all it can ever be: a dream."

"It could happen!" he fumed, even as he realized, deep down, that Michael was correct.

"You're too young to wed," Michael said. "You should sow some wild oats before you shackle yourself, but if you're serious about marriage, then we can search for a bride for you. It should be from an appropriate group of girls though, ones with the right backgrounds and fathers who would be amenable to an alliance with our family. It's insane for you to imagine you could persuade Mrs. Adair and you'd merely wind up more miserable than you are now."

"You could talk to her for me," Caleb repeated, "but you won't."

"I wouldn't dare approach her on your behalf and you shouldn't either. She'd be incensed about it and you'd simply get Annette in trouble."

"You think you know everything, but you don't."

It was a childish taunt, but he was just so upset and, of course, Michael was a total ass in his reply. "No, I don't know everything, but I do know that Mrs. Adair will never give you her daughter. If you conferred with her about Annette, she'd accuse you of being a fortune-hunter. You can't be eager for that to occur."

"I'm not a fortune-hunter! I've never been greedy a day in my life."

"It's how she'd view you."

"Bastard," Caleb muttered and he whipped away and stomped off to the manor.

"Would you hold on for one damn minute?" Michael called.

Caleb halted and glanced back. "Have I ever previously asked you for a single thing?"

"No, you never have."

"Well, I'll definitely never ask again in the future."

He hurried to the house and he was desperate to reach his room and sit by a warm fire. He was chilled to the bone and he was terribly distraught over his discussion with Michael. He slipped inside and started up the stairs. At the first landing, Annette and her mother were coming down. Mrs. Adair was in her wheeled chair, and two footmen were carting her down, her weight precariously balanced.

"Good evening, Mrs. Adair," he said, but the witch didn't acknowledge his greeting.

She gestured imperiously, as if she were a bloody queen, and he couldn't abide such pompous conduct. With the vicious mood he was in, she was lucky he didn't jump down her throat. He was that angry and out of sorts.

Instead, he politely asked the footmen, "Would you fellows like some help? I'm happy to pitch in."

"We're fine, Mr. Crawford," one of them said, "but thank you for offering."

He stepped over to let them pass, then he marched up toward Annette. She was quite a bit farther up, and as he neared, she leaned in and whispered, "We're going home tomorrow."

He blanched with surprise, and her remark stirred a thousand questions, but with her mother a few feet away, he couldn't pose any of them.

"I'll stop by your room at eleven," he whispered in response. "Don't lock your door."

She nodded to indicate she'd heard, then she tromped after her mother. He climbed to the next landing, and he paused to peek down for a final glimpse of her. He thought she'd peek up too, but she didn't.

He sighed and continued on.

"Mrs. Adair wishes to speak with you privately."

Michael glared at Hester and said, "I'd rather poke my eye out with a sharp stick."

"She's been wheeled into the library. I had a fire lit so you'll be comfortable."

"What does she want? Will she nag at me about a betrothal?"

"I suppose that will be the topic. Why else would you converse?"

Hester was especially furious and he was always the cause. They were surrounded by guests and he hoped she wouldn't quarrel when they had an audience.

Supper was over and they were in the family parlor. Tables had been arranged so people could play cards. Caleb hadn't appeared for the meal or the socializing afterward. Annette was seated on a sofa and reading a novel. Margaret was conspicuously absent and he figured she was hiding again.

He was agitated over their carnal incident. When she'd begged him to ruin her, he should have refused, and his participation was one of the more despicable acts he'd ever perpetrated. The event had been wonderful and reckless, and when he was so fond of her, he was trying to deduce his reasoning.

Usually, he dallied with trollops, and fornication was a physical deed with no emotion attached. Margaret had been a virgin and he'd deflowered her with hardly a thought as to the consequences. He was extremely disturbed by the poignant sentiment they'd generated and he was worried over her condition.

He was anxious to talk to her, but he didn't dare sneak away. He'd see her later; he was certain of it.

"Why are you so aggrieved, Hester?" he asked. "You're fit to be tied and I assume it's my fault. What is my most recent crime?"

"Mrs. Adair is leaving in the morning and she's taking Annette with her."

"Really? She only just arrived so that makes no sense at all. She hasn't been here long enough to decide whether she's enjoying herself or not."

"She accused me of being a negligent hostess! She claims I've allowed inappropriate relationships to blossom! Me! Allowing inappropriate behavior! Can you imagine?"

He was a tad astonished by the news, both that Margaret would likely depart with her cousins, but also that Hester had been insulted. He was incredibly irked on her behalf. She could be fussy and grumpy, but she'd organized a pleasant gathering.

He tamped down a spurt of temper, as he said, "Who has engaged in illicit conduct? Has she named a culprit?"

"You know who it is! It's you and your brother! You flirted with young ladies you should have ignored." Even though the allegation was true, he was incensed by it, and he would have defended himself, but she cut him off before he could. "Don't deny it. I warned you about your brother's fixation on Miss Adair. And I caught Margaret Adair in your bedchamber. Looking at your navy medals, wasn't it?"

Her tone was very snide and he bit down a snort of amusement. He never apologized to her and it was pointless to explain any issue. She would simply work herself into an even bigger lather.

"If Mrs. Adair is flitting off so abruptly," he said, "she must not be interested in a betrothal. Maybe she's realized I'm a very bad bet."

"If your transgressions have caused you to lose out on Miss Adair's dowry, it will serve you right!"

"Yes, I'm positive I'll regret it forever," he facetiously said and he patted her on the shoulder. "Calm down, will you? I hate that I've pushed you into such a state."

"You shouldn't have attended Mr. Pence's auction!"

"He invited me. Why shouldn't I have attended?"

"You insist on stirring lurid gossip," she hissed. "You thrive on it."

He sighed with resignation. It had been a marvelous day, riding out with Caleb and his friends, assessing a stable full of magnificent animals, but with night having fallen, it was clear his stars weren't aligned. First, he'd bickered with Caleb. Now Hester. He still had to stagger through his discussion with Ambrosia Adair.

He couldn't understand why he ever visited Sutton.

He walked away from Hester, and he took the long route to the library, sauntering slowly, sipping a whiskey on the way. When he finally reached the room, Mrs. Adair was impatiently waiting for him. He hadn't rushed to obey her summons so she was annoyed. Her dour expression was priceless.

She'd staged the space for maximum effect. She was in her wheeled chair, and it was positioned next to the hearth, as if she were a queen greeting supplicants. A blazing fire was burning so hotly, the air so thick and stuffy, that he felt claustrophobic.

The footmen had placed another chair, a smaller one, directly across from her, and she waved him to it, as if the house was hers and he was an interloper. Her pompous posturing grated on his nerves, and it seemed as if he was back in school and about to be caned for an infraction.

Merely to irritate her, he dragged the small chair away and pulled over the very grand one from behind his desk. It was larger and fancier than hers, and he scooted it off to the side so she would have to turn slightly in order to address him. He eased down and stretched out his legs, slouching casually and thus being disrespectful to her. She couldn't completely hide a sniff of offense.

"You asked to meet with me?" he said.

"Yes. Annette and I are leaving in the morning so I decided you and I should chat privately before we depart."

He should have bitten his tongue, but he couldn't. "You didn't mention your cousin, Margaret. Are you abandoning her at Sutton? Will you force her to purchase a ticket on the public coach? Or will *I* be required to send her to town at my own expense?"

"Margaret has already left for London. She went at dawn."

There were so many pitfalls opening up that he couldn't deduce what all of them were. When he and Margaret had been enjoying their delightful revel in his bed, she must have been aware of what would occur in a few hours. Why hadn't she told him?

Her behavior was very callous, very coldblooded, but why would she tell him? What could he have done about it?

He had no business speculating over her motivations and he couldn't pester Mrs. Adair as to the circumstances. At being apprised that she'd vanished, he was reeling with disappointment, but with consternation too. What could have happened? Would he really never see her again? It couldn't be possible.

He was a master at concealing his emotions and he shoved Margaret out of his mind. He'd ponder her later, after he was alone.

In the meantime, he said to Mrs. Adair, "Why have you planned such a speedy exit? And prior to you answering, I must declare that I don't appreciate how you berated my sister. She was very hurt by your rude comments."

Mrs. Adair was a tough nut and she wasn't cowed by his castigation. "Annette is here so you can consider her to be your bride. Imagine my shock when I learned she's been allowed to involve herself in an improper flirtation. I blame your sister for it, but I blame Margaret too. Both of them are at fault."

A muscle ticked in his cheek. He wasn't sure how he should respond, and he wasn't keen to participate in the conversation she was determined to have.

"What is the flirtation that festered?" he asked, when he was fully cognizant of Caleb's infatuation.

"I won't dignify that question with a reply. Everyone at this party has noticed the mischief. What I *will* state is that you haven't exactly been an angel either."

He studied the unbearably irksome woman. "Are you scolding me, Mrs. Adair? As you and I are basically strangers, you're being incredibly impertinent. What is my alleged sin?"

She'd brought a folder with her and she retrieved a letter from it. She passed it over to him, and as he scanned it, she said, "I received it in London. It was penned by an anonymous author who watched the scandalous activities unfold and felt I had to be informed. Do you recognize the handwriting?"

*Hester!*

Yes, he recognized it, but he wasn't about to admit it. What had his deranged sister been thinking? Why tattle to Mrs. Adair? It would simply get the two girls in a ton of trouble and it would stir many problems that Michael would have to mend.

"I don't recognize it," he lied. He stuck it in his coat and she was content to let him keep it.

"My leg is broken, Lord Sutton, and it pains me greatly so I am in no condition to travel. Yet after this situation was revealed to me, I raced to the country to save my daughter and my cousin. I started by rescuing Margaret from your dastardly clutches."

"Careful how you insult me, Mrs. Adair. I have a bad temper and you shouldn't ignite it."

"I am not insulting you. I am speaking the truth. How dare you seduce her!"

"I didn't; I haven't," he lied again. "I will confess to being very fond of her, but I would never cross lines with a spinster that shouldn't be crossed."

"You were observed sneaking out of her bedchamber in the middle of the night!"

He tsked with feigned aggravation. "The charge is totally false and it was obviously spread by someone who's hoping to harm Margaret. Who might it be?"

"Don't flash that innocent expression at me," she fumed. "I wouldn't believe a word you had to say about her."

"This accursed mansion has dozens of bedrooms and I've never inquired as to which one was hers. If I had wished to visit her, I would have had no idea where it was located."

She scoffed with disgust. "In my opinion, men are dogs who are ruled by lust. You saw Margaret and you had to have her. You couldn't rein in your base impulses."

"You're irritating me, Mrs. Adair, so please cease your harangue. I won't listen to much more, and if you persist, this discussion will conclude before you have a chance to utter all the grievances you're dying to share."

"Fine," she said. "How about this? Annette has been here an entire week, but you've barely socialized with her. What am I to make of such unacceptable behavior?"

"It doesn't matter to me how you view it."

"Your condescending response is typical of what I would expect from you, but are you still interested in a betrothal? If so, how can we forge ahead when Annette is convinced she's fallen in love with Mr. Crawford?"

He blew out a heavy breath. "They're not in love. They're young and they're being stupid. That's it. Once she returns to town, and you work on her, she'll forget about him."

"Are you sure about that?"

Michael wasn't sure in the least, but he firmly nodded. "Yes, I'm sure. It's merely a youthful indiscretion and we've all suffered one of those."

"What about Mr. Crawford and his feelings for *her*? How will you tamp them down?"

"I've already talked to him and I explained that you'd never consider him to be an appropriate suitor."

"Did he listen?"

"Mostly." Michael shrugged, being extremely nonchalant.

"Would he like to wed her? Has their amour progressed that far?"

"He imagines himself besotted, but as with Annette, after they're separated, their ardor will fade."

"How could you marry Annette now?" she asked, her tone scathing. "I'm told you're very close to your brother. Could you snatch her away from him and claim her for your own? There are constant stories about how selfish you can be. Could you hurt him that way?"

His shoulders slumped. "I'm dithering over what's best. The dilemma has just landed on me and I haven't had a moment to evaluate the ramifications."

"Here's another problem you've created: How could you fetter yourself to Annette when you've been so fond of Margaret? Annette and Margaret are very close too. If you were Annette's husband, how would we ever host a family event that would include you?"

"I don't know about that either," he said.

"I've never witnessed such contemptible goings-on! Due to your foul conduct, I've had to send one girl home in disgrace, and shortly, I'm dragging the other one away to prevent catastrophe. I think you owe me an apology."

"I'm sorry your trip to Sutton has been so horrid," he said. "I'm sorry your daughter's experience was less than you anticipated, but we've hurled enough venom. It's futile to continue this conversation."

"But we haven't resolved the main issue. Will you propose or not? You haven't even mentioned the prospect. Is it impossible? Are you such a fool that you'll pass up Annette's dowry?"

"You've so thoroughly antagonized me, Mrs. Adair, that I can't accurately assess the situation. With how you've berated me, I can't envision binding myself to Annette. It would mean I'd have *you* as my mother-in-law."

The snooty shrew was undeterred. She dug about in her folder again and handed over a thick document. "This is a list of the assets you'd receive if you picked her. Apparently, you need to be reminded of what's at stake."

He should have declined to take it from her, but in the end, he was too curious. "Will that be all?" he asked. "Is there any other topic you'd like to address? And if there is, may I suggest you be very brief?"

"I feel compelled to point out that you are not deranged. You've never been described as being mad. These paltry flirtations—between you and Margaret, between your brother and Annette—are minor inconveniences. How about if you spend a week pondering where we are, then call on me in town? We'll delve into this subject again, and with cooler heads prevailing, I'm certain we can reach a satisfactory agreement."

He glanced at the bottom of the page and noted the amount of money she was offering. Even though he wasn't positive he was sincere, he said, "I could probably come to London in a week."

"You have no parent to guide you in your marital decision, and it's clear your sister can't be trusted to manage it, so I will brazenly provide you with my advice: Don't be imprudent about this. Don't let your emotions rule the day. If Margaret or Mr. Crawford are upset by you becoming engaged to Annette, what is that to you or me?"

He could have furnished any retort. He could have defended Caleb or, perhaps, asked her not to punish Margaret for his idiotic affection. Instead, he said, "You are very ruthless. I've always heard that about you."

"I've heard it about you too."

He smirked, as if they were conspirators, one driven fiend to another. Then he stood and left without another word.

# Chapter 19

Caleb marched down the stairs, a satchel slung over his back, his coat buttoned against the cold winter day. He wasn't exactly being furtive, but he wasn't blustering about either. If he could scoot out to the driveway without encountering anyone, he'd be fine with that stealthy exit.

Who would he say goodbye to anyway? Hester? That was laughable. Michael? Caleb had had enough of his brother for the moment. They were bonded too tightly to part forever, but he figured a lengthy separation would be a benefit.

It was early, so there was no footman at his station by the front door. The servants were in the kitchen having breakfast, and if he'd felt like announcing his departure, they were the ones he'd have told. He'd always been more comfortable with the staff, farmers, and other laborers who worked so hard to keep Michael rich and prosperous. It was where he belonged: with the common rabble.

He reached the foyer and luck was not on his side. Hester slithered out of the shadows, almost as if she'd been watching for him. She was a bitter spinster who wasted her time dreaming about how grand her life would be after she was dead and in Heaven. She never pondered her current situation. If she'd ever been a kinder person, a less judgmental person, maybe she wouldn't be so miserable.

In his view, she'd chosen her circumstances. She was an earl's daughter and an earl's sister. She could have had them find her a husband. She could have left Sutton, could have had a family and a gaggle of children to fill the years, but she hadn't had the courage to make any changes.

In the past, he'd pitied her. He'd tried to understand her, and he'd excused her eccentric habits, but for once, he couldn't muster any sympathy.

She'd be eager to quarrel about some petty issue and he truly did not have the patience to deal with her. His initial instinct was to walk on by, as if she were invisible, but she was in a foul mood too, and she stepped to block his way.

"Are you happy now?" she asked.

He frowned and said, "Good morning to you too, Hester. Am I happy about what?"

"You had to flirt with Miss Adair. You couldn't tamp down your wicked impulses so she's been disgraced. Here in my own home! Because of you!"

"I have no idea what you're talking about and I'm busy. If you're upset, I can't help you."

It was the only discourteous comment he'd ever uttered in her presence and she was enraged by his flippant tone. "Her mother blamed me for your conduct! She accused me of being a bad hostess!"

"I hate to hear it, but Mrs. Adair is an unlikeable shrew and you shouldn't put too much stock in her opinion on any topic."

"She's a paragon of London society. People will gossip about me. They'll spread rumors about our family, how we have no morals, how we allow dissolute mischief to be perpetrated by our guests."

She was in a frantic state, her fury more pronounced than usual. She was shaking from head to toe, and there was a strange glow in her eyes, as if she was mad. If he hadn't been bigger than she was, he might have been a tad afraid of her. She appeared that deranged.

It was pointless to debate with her, and normally when she was venting, he struggled to placate her, but he was too irked to pretend that he cared.

"I escorted Miss Adair on a sleighride," he said, "and her companion went with us. Then I danced with her occasionally in a packed salon with dozens of neighbors as my audience. If that amounts to *dissolute* conduct in your mind, then I don't know what to tell you. You're being ridiculous and I'm too vexed to tarry while you rant at me."

He would have continued on, but she started shrieking with dismay. "I warned Michael about you! I warned him that your low bloodlines would come to haunt us. He wouldn't listen! He never listens to me and look what you've done!"

"Hester!" Michael called from down the hall. "What are you thinking?"

Caleb was saved by his brother rushing out of the dining room and running toward them. Apparently, he was up before noon and eating breakfast, which was exasperating. Caleb didn't want to bump into Michael as he was sneaking out.

Michael slid to a stop and rested a palm on Hester's shoulder. His touch instantly halted her caterwauling.

"Hester!" he said again, but softly. "What's wrong with you? You're in a terrible dither and there's no reason for you to be so rude. Apologize to Caleb immediately."

Hester had no ability to defend herself, especially not to Michael, and he had intriguing methods for reining her in. He never took her too seriously and he'd learned to corral her fits of temper so she didn't cause too much damage.

At being ordered to apologize, she bristled, but said, "You're correct, Michael. I'm being overly strident. I'll calm down."

She hadn't directed her remark to Caleb, and she hadn't claimed to be sorry, but he wasn't about to argue over it. He was simply anxious to escape the horrid scene.

Michael motioned to the stairs and said to Hester, "I'd like you to go to your bedchamber and remain there. Can you do that for me?"

Hester nodded. "Yes, I can do that."

"I'll be up shortly. I need to speak with you about an important issue."

She flitted by them and dashed away. They stood silently, gaping after her as she vanished. A footman had followed Michael down the hall, and Michael whispered some instructions to him, mainly to have Hester's maid sit with her until he could attend her himself.

Caleb dawdled, waiting for the dust to settle so he could keep on to the stables. But with Michael interrupting his clandestine exit, his brother would feel compelled to deliver some jabs too. Why did he visit Sutton? He wasn't welcome and he never enjoyed himself. Why extend the torment? Why assume he belonged?

Once it was quiet and they were alone, Michael said, "I can't figure out what's ailing her. She seems worse by the month."

Caleb had no opinion about Hester and he wasn't keen to chat about her. "She's always been a bit addled. I haven't noticed that she's growing worse. To me, she's always been slightly unhinged."

"You can't let her needle you. Ignore her outbursts."

Caleb shrugged. "Her caustic attitude doesn't matter to me. I'm finished putting up with her tirades and rages."

Michael didn't take the hint that Caleb wouldn't discuss her. He was determined to hash it out. "You and I didn't behave very well with Annette and Margaret Adair. Mrs. Adair was angry about how we socialized with them and she chastised Hester about it."

"Mrs. Adair is an obnoxious witch, and if she had the gall to castigate Hester, no one should be surprised."

"She and Annette left at dawn."

"I'm aware of that fact. Are you still considering an engagement to Annette?" Caleb bitterly inquired. "If she becomes your wife, Mrs. Adair will be your mother-in-law. You'd probably deserve that fate."

Michael smirked with amusement, and he finally realized that Caleb was dressed for traveling, that he had a satchel dangling over his shoulder.

"Are you leaving?" Michael asked. "You'll freeze to death and you hate to be cold."

Michael was blathering, as if they were having an ordinary conversation, but Caleb wouldn't participate or feign interest. He simply said, "I'll be staying at your London apartment for awhile—if that's all right with you."

"Of course it's all right, but then what?"

"Then…? I have no idea."

Michael grasped that there was more transpiring than a quick jaunt into the city. "What are you planning? You've been in such a snit lately. Don't you dare go off half-cocked."

"Oh, I wouldn't dream of it," Caleb sarcastically retorted.

He spun away to storm off and Michael grabbed his arm and said, "What's happening? You're furious with me, but why are you? I merely explained that Annette's mother would never permit you to wed her. You're not a dunce so my frank comments can't be the reason."

"It's not that. I'm just sick of you, your sister, and Sutton. I can't tarry here another minute."

It was about Annette, but it wasn't about her too. His pathetic flirtation had underscored what was wrong with his life. He'd never been brave enough to strike out on his own. He had no job. No home. No family.

Michael had rescued him from dire circumstances when he'd been a boy, but he wasn't a child anymore. He was twenty. Would he ever cut the apron strings that bound him to Michael? Would he ever stand on his own two feet?

"What will you do in town?" Michael asked. "Don't join the merchant marines. Don't enlist in the army. If I discover you have, I swear I'll intervene to prevent you. I'll insist they kick you out and they'll have to heed me. I'm an earl, remember?"

"Are you marrying Annette or not? What have you decided? Why don't you tell me the truth? It will give me some clue as to how far away I should travel. If you're about to be her husband, I'd rather not watch the debacle unfold. I definitely won't attend your wedding."

"I can't predict what I'll choose with regard to her. Should I lie and claim I won't pick her? I would be mad to pass up her dowry."

"Yes, and money is an aristocrat's magic elixir."

"You shouldn't denigrate money. You've enjoyed plenty of it as my sibling."

"Yes, and I'm grateful."

He was too incensed to keep spatting and he whipped away and stomped out the door. Michael shouted to his retreating back, "Caleb! Stop!"

He didn't stop though, and when Michael hurried after him, he increased his pace. Michael was undeterred and he caught up to Caleb and yanked him to a halt.

Caleb had always loved his brother, and he loved him now, but he hated him too. He hated his cocky confidence and his arrogant posturing. He hated his frivolous attitudes and abrasive demeanor. Michael skated through the world, not caring about anything.

Caleb cared about everything. He cared too much and it pained him to be confronted with all the ways they were different. Caleb worked to be decent and kind, to be helpful and useful, but as he loafed on the edge of Michael's affluent existence, those stellar traits seemed worthless.

"Write to me," Michael said. "I must be regularly apprised of where you are."

Caleb wanted to refuse, but he couldn't force out the words. "I'll write," he grumbled. "I promise."

"And calm down, would you? I know you're upset about Annette, but her mother took her to town to separate her from you. It wasn't up to me and I didn't request it."

"Quit talking about Annette!" he fumed. "I've never hit you before, but if you utter her name again, I will pound you into the ground."

"Do you imagine you could?"

As Michael asked the question, he grinned, and Caleb never could resist that grin. He tucked away his resentment and said, "I could *try* to hit you. I could try to pound you into the ground. I'd feel grand just from making the attempt."

"You better not flee the country. If I ultimately learn that you sailed to America, I will wring your bloody neck."

Caleb sighed with irritation. "I won't leave England."

"And forget about Hester and her diatribes. This is my home so it's your home. It always will be. Come back as soon as you can."

"I suppose I'm being a complete milksop, but I won't abandon you forever. If I wasn't around to keep you steady, I can't fathom how you'd manage."

"Precisely," Michael agreed.

It was a frigid morning, the temperature icy, and Michael had raced out without a coat. He was shivering and Caleb nodded to the manor.

"Go inside," he said. "I'm walking to the stables to saddle a horse. You don't have to dawdle like a fussy nanny."

To his surprise, Michael stepped in and hugged him tight. They weren't the sort of men who hugged, and they certainly weren't a demonstrative family, so it was a peculiar gesture.

"I'm sorry I hurt you," Michael said. "I'm sorry I'm never the person you wish I was."

"You're fine," Caleb muttered. "Mostly, you're a nuisance, but I've figured out how to tolerate you." They pulled apart and Caleb nodded to the manor again. "Get going. You're hounding me so I can't tear myself away."

"I'll miss you," Michael said.

"I will convince myself that you're sincere."

"It will be so quiet without you. Hurry back."

Caleb didn't reply to the comment. His presence or absence from Sutton was immaterial.

He dashed off and he reached the stables and had a horse prepared without any delay. He didn't inform the groomsmen that he was departing, didn't offer up any farewells. He trotted away as if he was off on a short trip to a destination in the neighborhood.

As he skirted the house and headed out to the main road, Michael had donned a coat and hat, and he was standing in the driveway, looking like the loneliest man in the world.

He waved and Caleb waved too, but he didn't ride over for a final goodbye. He simply continued on.

Hester was pacing in her bedchamber, while her maid was over in the corner and watching her warily, as if she were a lunatic in an asylum.

Michael arrived and shooed the girl out, then he glared at Hester and said, "Hester, sit down for me, would you?"

"No, I can't sit."

"You're overwrought and I insist you oblige me."

He clasped her arm and pushed her onto a chair. She would have jumped up, but he put a firm palm on her shoulder and held her in place until she ceased her squirming. Then he grabbed a second chair and dragged it over. He sat too, so they were toe to toe.

"I'm worried about you," he said.

"There's nothing wrong with me!" she declared, even though she wasn't very hale.

She had so much rage bubbling just below the surface and it was eager to burst out. Her mind was racing, wandering off to dangerous memories where she'd obsess over ridiculous dreams that hadn't come true. At night, she couldn't sleep and her insomnia was becoming a problem because it left her fatigued and temperamental.

"I asked you to play matchmaker for me," he said, "but it was too much of a burden. You planned and hosted this party very successfully, but it's exhausted you."

"I'm not exhausted! It would have been an excellent event, but you and your brother wrecked it. Mrs. Adair should have noticed how competent I am, but when I thanked her for visiting us, she wouldn't even talk to me!"

"Mrs. Adair is a rude harpy and we don't care about her."

"I care! I have a reputation to protect. I can't have people gossiping about me."

"There won't be any gossip," he said and he was being very kind. He was always kind to her. "I'm concerned about the other parties you've arranged and I'll have my clerk cancel them."

"But how will we find you a bride?"

"It was mad to schedule winter gatherings. We shouldn't have demanded the girls travel to Sutton so I'll meet with them in town. I'll have my clerk organize introductions for me there. You don't have to fret over it any longer. Obviously, it's been a huge drain on you."

"I have to fret over it!" she said. "I'm your sister and you have no parents to implement a nuptial search. It's all up to me! There's no one else!"

"I want you to rest."

"I don't need to rest!"

She leapt up to pace again, but he jerked her onto her seat and wouldn't release her.

"Calm down and listen to me for a minute," he said and he was gazing at her so strangely, as if she'd tipped off her rocker.

"Stop staring at me as if I'm deranged. I'm merely tired."

"Yes, I agree that you seem very weary, but I have to mention a difficult topic. It may distress you further, but I must inquire."

He drew a piece of paper from his coat and he showed it to her. It was the letter she'd sent to Mrs. Adair. It had brought the horrid woman winging to Sutton to take charge of the situation, and the sight of it was so disorienting that she felt dizzy. How had Michael wound up in possession of it?

"Do you recognize this?" he asked her.

She vehemently shook her head. "No. I've never seen it before."

At her denial, his displeasure was clear. "You can't lie about it to me and my only question is: *why*? Why would you write to Mrs. Adair? You had to comprehend that it would be devastating for Margaret and Annette. They're in a great deal of trouble now. How could you be so petty?"

"Margaret Adair was in your bedchamber! And *you* were sneaking in and out of her room at night. Everyone knows."

"No, everyone *doesn't* know. I told you nothing happened and I expect you to believe me. I am ordering you not to spread falsehoods about her." He paused, waiting for her to respond. When she didn't, he added, "Did you hear me?"

"Yes, I heard."

"What about Annette? Why tattle to her mother about Caleb? Why hurt him?"

"Your brother can't have her! It was disgraceful for him to suppose he could glom onto her, and Mrs. Adair had to be apprised."

Her strident tone was alarming and he certainly deemed it to be. He studied her oddly, as if she were a mathematical problem he had to solve.

Ultimately, he said, "I understand that I often vex you. I understand that I never behave as you'd like, but in the future, you can't be this reckless. I can't have you interfering in my private business."

"I didn't write that letter!"

He tsked with dismay. "I'm going to fetch the housekeeper. You could use a nap and she'll have some laudanum. It will settle your mind. How does that sound? Will you take a nap for me?"

"Yes, I would love to sleep. I never can anymore."

"That's what I suspected," he murmured and he stood. "Don't move. I'll return with the housekeeper very soon."

"I won't move. I will be still as a statue."

He scowled, his consternation plain, as if he thought she was ill and he couldn't deduce her ailment, but he was wrong about her vigor. She was in perfect health, her mental faculties sharp as a tack, and she would remain seated so he'd realize she'd never been better.

---

"I CAN'T BEGIN TO explain how disappointed I am with both of you."

Ambrosia glared at Margaret and Annette, her expression lethal, and she was hoping they'd cringe in fear. It didn't work though. Neither of them reacted.

Annette said, "Mother, will you cease your harangue? I had to listen to it all the way from Sutton. Isn't your throat sore from nagging?"

They were in London, in the front parlor at Ambrosia's Mayfair mansion. Margaret was on a sofa in the corner, out of the line of fire, and Ambrosia was in her wheeled chair and next to the warm hearth. Annette couldn't relax and was pacing quite aggressively.

They seemed very far away to Margaret, as if she was staring at them down a narrow lane. Ever since she'd tiptoed out of Michael's bedroom, she'd been moving like an automaton. She was staggering about on instinct, not able to propel her limbs in the proper direction. Her torso had to carry on without her guiding it. She was that bewildered by events.

She'd been wrung dry, as if maybe her veins had been emptied of blood, and ice water had been pumped into them instead. She was angry and wretchedly inconsolable, and she detested Ambrosia with such an intense loathing that she yearned to march over and slap her.

She kept recalling Ambrosia's nasty comments about her parents, which simply made her angrier. Margaret had been so fond of them and she wouldn't let Ambrosia's insults tarnish her memories.

While Ambrosia and Annette quarreled, their voices were like insects buzzing in the distance. Margaret pondered Michael, wondering where he was, what he was doing. How long had it been before he'd figured out that she'd left? Was he irked that she'd snuck off? Or was he glad to have their amour ended with no effort on his part?

He was an unrepentant scoundrel who wouldn't like a clingy female. By fleeing so quickly and quietly, Margaret had given him a priceless gift.

She hadn't grasped how deeply she'd be affected by their sexual misadventure. It had been the most negligent, most spectacular thing that had ever happened to her. When she'd begged him to ruin her, she'd assumed she could blithely participate—as a man would. She'd assumed she could enjoy a brief romp, then walk away unscathed and unperturbed.

It hadn't concluded like that though. She was dying on the inside, and she missed him so much that she truly worried her heart might stop beating. She was that distraught.

She'd heard that men considered fornication to be a purely physical deed. They proceeded for pleasure, and they could trifle with one woman, then another, without suffering any emotional complications afterward. How did they manage it? It was such a personal, intimate experience. She couldn't fathom how they could be so blasé.

The worst portion of the whole incident was that she could never tell anyone about it. It was a secret she'd take to her grave, but it was so big and so unwieldy that she was choking on it.

The room had grown silent and it dawned on her that Ambrosia had been speaking to her. She shook herself out of her stupor and said, "I'm sorry, but I was woolgathering. What was that?"

"Cousin Bertha has written from York. She's willing to provide lodging to you."

Margaret was puzzled by the remark. She didn't feel well so it was hard to focus. Her head as aching, her stomach queasy, and several seconds ticked by before she recognized the import of Ambrosia's words.

The Adair family was massive, with many relatives dangling on the fringes of the family tree. They shared numerous traits, mostly that they were fussy, pretentious, and awful. All of them, except for Annette, treated her like a leper who might infect them, or like Cinderella whom they could abuse.

If she'd been in a better condition, she might have been aghast at the announcement, but it didn't seem real. She was caught in a dreadful dream and she blandly inquired, "I'm to stay with Bertha?"

"Yes, her husband, George, agreed that you could come. Their nanny was fired so you can have her spot."

Bertha had four children who were snotty, monstrous brats and Annette bristled on Margaret's behalf. "Absolutely not, Mother! What are you thinking? Margaret is not going to York and she most especially is not going to work for Bertha and George. You have to be joking."

Ambrosia ignored Annette and said to Margaret, "You leave on Wednesday."

"You're sending her away to punish me," Annette fumed. "Why can't she reside in London with us? We have plenty of space."

Ambrosia snorted with disgust. "In case you haven't noticed, Annette, Margaret is a bad influence on you. Your trip to Sutton was the sole occasion I allowed you to traipse off by yourself. I thought I could trust you. I certainly thought I could trust Margaret to keep an eye on you, but she proved herself incompetent and unreliable. The two of you will not remain in close company. It's just not possible."

"Oh, for pity's sake," Annette grumbled. "I am twenty years old, but you're scolding me as if I'm still five. I engaged in a paltry flirtation at Sutton with a very nice young man—one who doted on me, by the way—yet you refuse to admit the liaison was at my own instigation. You'd rather blame Margaret than accept the truth."

Ambrosia glowered at Annette. "I blame both of you and I'm weary of your defiant attitude. You're my daughter, so I suppose I have to tolerate your sass, but I don't have to tolerate Margaret prancing about in my home. She's departing as fast as I can be shed of her."

A full-fledged brawl might have commenced, but Margaret was exhausted by their bickering. She presumed, someday in the distant future, she'd thaw out and be incensed that she'd been shuffled off to York and Bertha, but at the moment, she didn't care what transpired.

Even if Ambrosia had invited her to tarry, Margaret had no wish to live with the odious shrew. Her firm intention was to escape the abhorrent woman's presence forever. If she had to travel to York to accomplish it, then that is what she would do.

"It's all right, Annette," she said. "I have no desire to dawdle in London and I'd like my destination to be far from the city. It's a good idea."

Annette's temper was on a slow boil. "It's wrong, Margaret! You're guilty of no transgression and you don't deserve to be penalized for my stupidity."

"It doesn't matter."

Ambrosia's glower changed, so she appeared a tad gleeful over Margaret's easy acquiescence, and she said to Annette, "She has to vacate the premises by Wednesday. She can't be here when Lord Sutton visits."

At having Ambrosia mention him, his name jabbed at Margaret like the prick of a sharp knife, but she tamped down a blanch. Annette was very disturbed by the statement though and she asked, "Why is he coming here?"

"Why would you imagine?" Ambrosia replied. "He and I have to finalize the nuptial contracts."

Margaret had already been apprised of this terrible news, but Annette hadn't. Her jaw dropped in astonishment. "You betrothed me to him without telling me? Are you insane?"

Ambrosia responded patiently, as if she was explaining a difficult concept to a dunce. "It's your destiny to wed an aristocrat, Annette. You know that and your petty romance with Mr. Crawford has no bearing on that conclusion. Of course Lord Sutton and I entered into an agreement about you. Why wouldn't we have?"

"I won't marry him!" Annette stamped her foot like a spoiled toddler. "You can't make me!"

Ambrosia tsked with exasperation. "I view your tantrum as a result of the week you spent with Margaret. Due to her lax supervision, you were able to carry on however you liked and it has imbued you with some horrific characteristics. When you left for the country, you were my sweet, biddable child. You've returned as an unlikable, unruly brat."

"Has you broken leg addled your wits?" Annette snidely said. "Lord Sutton is an insufferable beast and any girl who's shackled to him will be a very miserable wife. I would never let you torture me by forcing me to have him as my husband."

Ambrosia shrugged, unconcerned. "As I've always pointed out, you'll be marrying his title. Not him. If you like him or if you don't, your opinion is irrelevant. Now then, I've had enough of you and I'd like to be alone."

Annette was fit to be tied. "You declare you've bound me against my will, and you assume I'll thank you, then flit off with a smile on my face. Is that what you're expecting?"

"No. It's what I'm demanding," Ambrosia told her. "We'll discuss this again when you've calmed down. I will not permit you to rage at me."

Margaret couldn't listen to them. Nor could she abide Ambrosia's bragging about the engagement. They were talking about Michael as if she had no connection to him and their disregard for her feelings had her dizzy and unsettled. She was very nauseous, as if she might vomit all over Ambrosia's expensive Persian rug.

"Would you excuse me?" she said and she stood and started for the door.

"At least one of you has the sense to obey me," Ambrosia sneeringly spat. "I appreciate it."

Margaret ignored her and marched out. She hurried to the stairs, and as she began to climb, Annette dashed out of the parlor and called up to her, "Don't fret, Margaret. I will never wed Lord Sutton. Please don't wonder if I might."

Margaret halted and said, "Whether you wed him or not, it's none of my business. I need to stay out of it and you shouldn't fight with your mother over me."

She kept on and Annette didn't chase after her, which was a relief. She went back to the parlor to continue quarreling with Ambrosia.

Once Margaret was sure Annette hadn't followed, she increased her speed. She felt as if she'd been pummeled by clubs, and as she arrived in her room, she was practically running.

She barely had time to reach her bed. She stumbled to her knees, grabbed the chamber pot, and vomited over and over. Then, shaking, wobbly, too weak to stand, she used the blankets to haul herself onto the mattress. She curled into a ball and huddled there for hours, paralyzed with grief, her mind tormented, her mood at its lowest ebb.

She prayed she would fall asleep and never wake up, but she'd never been lucky. She had no doubt that she'd doze off, then rise in the morning and nothing would have changed.

# Chapter 20

Michael was loafing in a crammed London ballroom, and as he peered about, he tried to recall why he'd come to town. His mood was low, his spirits totally depleted.

After Annette's nuptial visit had collapsed in disaster, Sutton House had emptied out quickly. She, Margaret, and Caleb had fled, then Michael had declared the party to be over and had had his friends pack their bags and head home.

It meant he'd had just Hester for company, and the manor had echoed like an empty mausoleum, forcing him to remember that he'd always hated the country. Ultimately, he'd bolted to the city too, but not before he'd hired an elderly matron, Widow Jones, from the village to tend his sister.

Hester wasn't well, and on occasion, he suspected she ought to be locked in an asylum. Those facilities were little more than torture chambers though, so he wouldn't commit her. At the same time, she couldn't be allowed to ramble about and wander in circles. Widow Jones would serve as her caretaker until Michael could deduce the best method to help her. His main problem was that he had no idea what sort of assistance she needed.

He assessed the other guests. The crowd was a mix of Society's upper crust of scoundrels and wastrels, along with a slew of notorious ladies: singers, actresses, and opera dancers. It was the precise type of fête he normally relished, but for once, he couldn't convince himself to enjoy it.

He missed Margaret and wondered where she was. He yearned to believe she was staying with Ambrosia Adair, but Mrs. Adair was such a shrew. She'd been so angry about Margaret's flirtation with Michael that he didn't imagine she'd let Margaret tarry. If Margaret had been thrown out, where would she have gone?

The answer to that question vexed him enormously and he hoped she was somewhere safe. He also hoped, if she was in a desperate situation, that she would reach out to him. He would always stand as her fiercest champion and he liked to suppose she understood that about him.

He was such a vain ass that he'd never bothered to pry out any details about her. If she wasn't residing with Ambrosia, would she be with other cousins? Or did she have friends in London? Who might have offered her refuge?

He couldn't guess and he was thinking he should write a furtive letter to Annette to inquire about Margaret's location. She would likely have information, but in light of how badly he'd treated her at Sutton, she wouldn't be keen to hear from him. She probably wouldn't even reply.

It would be highly inappropriate for him to contact her without her mother's permission. If Ambrosia discovered his antic, there'd be hell to pay, so why proceed? He'd simply fuss and stew instead. Anymore, it was the only thing he was good at.

He was missing Caleb too. When his brother had left Sutton, he'd told Michael he'd be at the London apartment, but the servants hadn't seen him. No doubt he was off pursuing secret mischief and assuming Michael wouldn't be apprised until it was too late.

If Michael eventually learned that the idiotic boy had enlisted in the army, he'd intervene to halt the foolish act. He and Caleb had been joined at the hip for an entire decade and he couldn't vanish merely because he was upset.

Michael gazed about at his many acquaintances, but he wasn't able to muster the interest to speak with any of them. He was struggling to recollect why he'd previously liked to revel with these sycophants and ingrates. Apparently, his short sojourn at Sutton had altered him in a manner he wasn't ready to acknowledge.

He'd decided to stroll to his club for a quiet drink, when he turned and Nathaniel St. James was approaching. St. James held the dubious honor of being Lord Grenville, so he was the subject of incessant gossip over his failed engagement to Annette Adair, then his subsequent and swift marriage to his governess.

Even though the scandal had occurred the prior summer, people couldn't stop tittering over the sorry episode.

Grenville had had a lengthy career in the army that had ended with him being captured by mercenaries in Spain. The poor fellow had been starved and tortured, and by the time he'd been freed, he'd been at death's door. Michael had played a small part in his release, having captained the ship that had whisked him to England.

He hadn't noticed Michael yet so Michael studied him without being observed. When Michael had brought him home, he'd been like a feral animal, half-mad, emaciated, and seeming too decrepit to survive. But to Michael's great relief, he looked stable and healthy.

During the brief voyage, Grenville had been so disoriented that Michael figured he wouldn't recall who Michael was, but when he glanced over, he grinned with recognition. He hurried over to shake Michael's hand.

"Sutton!" he said. "It's grand to see you. I've been meaning to track you down, to thank you for your assistance last year, but I haven't had the energy. Please forgive my lapse. I still suffer bouts of forgetfulness so I'm delighted to bump into you like this."

"I wasn't sure you'd remember me."

Grenville made a waffling motion with his fingers. "I remember more than you'd suppose. I'm not positive I'll ever regain a hundred-percent of my wits, but I'm not nearly as deranged as I was a few months ago."

Michael liked that Grenville could jest about his reduced condition and Michael said, "I hate to sound as if I'm gushing, but I'm amazed by how hale you appear to be."

Grenville smirked. "I wed recently. Did you hear?"

Michael was a tad startled that Grenville would mention it, but if Grenville was willing to openly discuss the incident, then he could talk about it too. "I believe the whole kingdom has heard about your marriage. The chatter has been relentless."

"Most of what you've been told is true. My bride was my governess and I couldn't resist her. She's a petite virago who is the reason I'm recuperating so rapidly."

"That's terrific news. May I meet this miracle-worker someday?"

"Of course, and don't listen to any of the awful stories about her. I'm thriving due to her dedicated efforts."

"I never listen to gossip," Michael said. "I've had plenty of it spread about me and most of it has been nonsense."

"Exactly." Grenville's grin widened. "The latest report about you is that you're considering a betrothal to my ex-fiancée, Annette Adair."

"My goodness. Are there no secrets in this city?"

"No, none." Grenville laughed. "Don't listen to the rumors about me and Annette either. I treated her abominably, and after she'd had enough of my unhinged behavior, she tossed me over, which was precisely what I deserved. It wasn't her fault."

"I was curious about it. I appreciate you verifying the details."

"She's a very sweet girl. Beautiful, educated, trained to her station. Any man would be lucky to have her as his wife, but may I shock you by delivering a bit of a caveat? I realize we're practically strangers, so it's odd for me to speak up, but I feel that I must."

Michael raised a brow. "Yes, you may shock me. I like to be forewarned. It's better than being kicked in the teeth because I'm unprepared."

Grenville leaned in and murmured, "Watch out for her mother. She runs Annette's life like a military general. I had repeated problems with her butting her nose into my personal business. It created constant friction between us."

Michael snorted his agreement. "I've already endured my own friction with her."

"If you're contemplating marriage to Annette, you should be contemplating her mother too. Would you like to have Ambrosia Adair as your mother-in-law? My advice is to ponder carefully."

"I definitely will."

"I have people waiting for me," Grenville said, "so I have to go. Are you in town for long?"

"I've retired so I'm home for good. You can contact me at my apartment or at Sutton. I'll receive any message."

"I'm here until tomorrow. London is too hectic for me, so I'm tucked away in the country, where the pace is slower. Once the weather warms, I'll invite you to Grenville Downs for a visit. You can meet my wife, Rosalie. You'll like her—even if she started out as my governess!"

"I'm sure I will like her."

Grenville walked off, and Michael loafed in the chaotic horde, replaying the hasty chat in his mind. He barely knew Grenville so the blunt information about Ambrosia Adair was intriguing. He and Grenville shared a unique position as Annette's suitors and Michael imagined they were entitled to compare notes.

Was he really interested in shackling himself to Annette? The issues with Margaret and Caleb were still sitting between them and unresolved. When he'd conferred with Mrs. Adair at Sutton, she'd tempted him with the size of Annette's dowry, but the assets produced a permanent attachment to the Adair family.

Could he bear it? No.

His accidental encounter with Grenville had confirmed Michael's opinion about an engagement. He'd pass on Annette so he had to call on Mrs. Adair and notify her of his decision. She wouldn't like it, and they'd probably quarrel, but it couldn't be helped.

His birthday was swiftly approaching, and with Annette off the table, he had to quickly pick a different candidate. The notion was exhausting and he was being confronted yet again by the recognition that matrimony didn't appeal to him at all.

He wandered through the crowd, headed for the door, when he came face to face with Rowena. After he'd kicked her out of Sutton, he'd hardly thought about her. She'd committed the cardinal sin of scolding him over his affair with Margaret, but she'd been absolutely correct to berate him.

Was he still annoyed with her? He evaluated his emotions and figured he wasn't. In fact, he was excited to see her. Maybe if he reveled with her, he'd shuck off some of his doldrums. She was very debauched, and if he took up with her again, she could lure him back into the world of gambling and vice where he thrived.

"Well, well," she said, preening, "if it isn't the grand and glorious Earl of Sutton. I heard you'd slithered to town like the snake you are."

"Hello, Rowena. Have you missed me?"

"No, not a whit. You were awful to me at Sutton and I haven't forgiven you. How did your nuptial party conclude? Are you betrothed?"

"No. Miss Adair couldn't abide me."

"Smart girl." Rowena snickered with amusement.

"I am still very much a bachelor."

She purred with satisfaction, and she sauntered over, wrapped her arms around him, and brazenly kissed him on the mouth, as guests watched and tittered.

"It's a mystery to me," she said, "why you're fussing with heiresses and debutantes. Those foolish ninnies drive you mad so it's silly to focus on them."

"That has recently occurred to me."

"You ought to wed someone like me. I know what you need to be happy."

"I'm betting you do."

"What are your plans for the rest of the evening?" she asked.

"I have none and I was just leaving."

"I'm leaving too, and while I haven't missed you, it seems you might have missed *me*. Shall we retire to my boudoir and find out how much?"

"It sounds like a marvelous idea."

He actually didn't think it would be marvelous, but he was lonely, bored, and at loose ends. She led him off to locate the butler, so they could retrieve the cloaks and hats, and he followed her like a puppet on a string.

"WHERE IS ANNETTE?"

Ambrosia glared at her housekeeper. She was seated in her wheeled chair in the front parlor. A half-hour earlier, she'd sent a housemaid to Annette's room to inform her that her presence was required downstairs, but the maid hadn't returned. Annette hadn't arrived either. The housekeeper had appeared instead, and she looked terrified, as if Ambrosia might kill the messenger.

Margaret was about to depart for York. The carriage was parked in the driveway, the outriders perched to whisk her off to the coaching inn where she would board the public coach for her long journey north. Annette hadn't come down to tell her goodbye and Ambrosia was irked by Annette's rudeness.

For days, Annette had been arguing with Ambrosia over Margaret having to work for Bertha and George. Margaret wasn't concerned in the least so Ambrosia couldn't understand why Annette was being such a pest about it. If Margaret didn't mind, why should Annette?

Every aspect of the situation had raised Annette's hackles. She was incensed that Margaret would have to earn her keep and she felt Margaret should be allowed to lollygag and reside with Bertha for free. She was incensed by Ambrosia's refusal to convey Margaret to York in their own carriage, but Ambrosia wouldn't have considered such an extravagance.

After the trouble Margaret had provoked at Sutton, she didn't deserve any favors. Ambrosia was paying Margaret's coach fare and that was more than enough courtesy.

Since Annette's misadventure at Sutton, she and her daughter had been bitterly quarreling. Ambrosia was anxious to establish some sense of normalcy, some sense of the old camaraderie she and Annette had previously enjoyed, but she wasn't sure how to manage it.

Annette had become an ungrateful shrew who bickered over every little issue, but Ambrosia had put up with all the sass she could abide. She wouldn't tolerate another minute of Annette's continued insolence.

"I have some distressing news, Mrs. Adair," the housekeeper said.

"What news? And where is the housemaid? I had her fetch Annette nearly an hour ago."

The housekeeper gulped with dismay. "She asked me to speak with you for her."

"What is it? What's wrong?"

"Miss Annette's room is empty."

Ambrosia scowled. "She already went out this morning? Is she running errands? Is that it? She didn't mention it to me."

"No, I don't believe it's errands. Her bed hasn't been slept in."

"You could be babbling in riddles. What are you trying to confide? Just spit it out."

"You should read this for yourself." The woman dashed over, handed Ambrosia a piece of paper, then she flitted off to the corner, as if an explosion might be imminent.

It was a note from Annette, and Ambrosia had to skim it over and over before the import was clear:

*I have eloped with Caleb Crawford. You'll never find us so please don't search. It would be a wasted effort. I couldn't wed Lord Sutton and you shouldn't have assumed you could force me. I'd say I'm sorry, but I'm not.*

She'd signed it with her full name, *Annette Adair,* as if Ambrosia might have forgotten who she was.

Ambrosia gaped with consternation, with astonishment, with unbridled rage.

Annette had eloped? With the illegitimate son of an earl? She could have married a genuine earl, but she'd picked a bastard half-brother? She'd chosen a poverty-stricken nobody over a rich, toplofty aristocrat? She'd been seduced by a common fortune-hunter?

After all Ambrosia had done for the girl! After all the training, education, and lessons! After all the plotting, planning, and scheming!

This—this!—was the conclusion Annette had sought?

What was the wretched pair thinking? Were they imagining they could race off to Scotland, then reappear in London as husband and wife with no penalty paid? Were they presuming Ambrosia would welcome them? That she'd give the dowry to Mr. Crawford? Annette couldn't have grown that deranged. Could she have?

Ambrosia would never relinquish a penny to a swindler like Caleb Crawford. He would expect to carry on like a wealthy nob on the money Annette should have provided, but they would be poor forever. They could camp in a ditch and choke on their paltry amour.

She would never recognize their union and they would never be accepted by the family. Ambrosia would guarantee it.

She never liked to display strident emotion in front of a servant, but for once, she couldn't maintain her usual aplomb. She wailed like a banshee, her shrieks of fury rocking the house, but she couldn't swallow them down.

She cursed, shouted, and spewed epithets that would have made a sailor blush. The housekeeper dawdled for a moment, wondering how to calm her, but there was no solace to be had. The woman sidled over to the door, then scooted out, and Ambrosia was left alone with her wrath and her scorn.

MARGARET WAS STANDING IN the foyer, tying her bonnet and adjusting her cloak to be better bundled against the frigid temperature. She was about to climb into the carriage that would deliver her to the coaching inn. From there, she would board the public coach to York. It would be a lengthy trip and she was anxious to get moving.

She'd figured Annette would show up to tell her goodbye, but she hadn't seen her cousin all morning, and she hadn't asked after her. Annette was in such a terrible mood that Margaret couldn't bear to speak with her. She merely wanted to escape Ambrosia's home and never return.

It was her explicit intent that she would never again attend an Adair family event where Ambrosia might be present too. It was time to sever their connection.

She'd thought the butler, or maybe a footman, would arrive to escort her out, but the servants were noticeably absent. A bit earlier, as she'd been preparing to depart, someone had been shouting, but she'd been too far away to hear what was being bellowed.

The commotion had gradually died down, but numerous housemaids had rushed past her room, and they'd been whispering frantically. Margaret hadn't poked her nose out to ask what was wrong. She didn't care what was wrong; she was simply eager to leave as fast as she could.

Suddenly, Ambrosia thumped down the hall. She was out of her wheeled chair and plodding along with her cane. She was walking slowly, so Margaret could have dashed out to avoid a final conversation, but she wasn't a coward. She stood her ground, feeling aggrieved and bracing for whatever insult Ambrosia might dare to hurl next.

Margaret was numb over the abrupt termination of her affair with Michael Crawford, so there was no comment Ambrosia could share that would be particularly upsetting. Any invectives would drift away unheeded.

"Did you know about this?" Ambrosia raged as she hobbled up.

"Know about what, Ambrosia? You'll have to be more specific."

"Annette has eloped!"

It was the oddest remark ever. "With Lord Sutton?"

"No, you dunce. With that bounder, Caleb Crawford!"

Margaret froze, the announcement astounding her. Then she started to laugh. She couldn't help it. Wonderful, perfect Annette wasn't quite so perfect anymore.

"Annette and Mr. Crawford?" Margaret inquired, as if testing the words to discover how they would sound. "Are you positive you're not mistaken?"

"Look at this! Read the truth for yourself!"

Ambrosia waved a piece of paper at Margaret. Margaret snatched it away, and it was a note from Annette, explaining her brazen decision. It was short, to the point, and even a tad rude, and Margaret struggled to deduce how she should view the situation.

Was she glad for Annette? Was she worried for her? An elopement was very scandalous and it nearly always ended horrendously for the involved couple. For Annette, it would mean the loss of her dowry, and thus, the loss of her elevated style of living. Was Margaret concerned for her cousin? Or had she no opinion? Why would it matter if Annette had perpetrated reckless behavior?

She loved Annette and would never like her to suffer because of her shocking choice. As far as Margaret was aware, Mr. Crawford had no money he could use to support Annette, but he was very thrifty, very handy, very clever, and his older brother adored him.

She suspected they'd be fine.

"I guess you're correct," Margaret said. "They've run off together."

"I've hired riders to chase after them. Annette will be found soon and dragged away from that swindling fortune-hunter. She'll wed Lord Sutton as planned. You shouldn't doubt it."

Margaret could have injected some sanity into the discussion. She could have mentioned Mr. Crawford's stellar attributes, how he'd be a marvelous husband, how Ambrosia shouldn't overreact, but she was too incensed to soothe Ambrosia.

"Yes, drag her home," Margaret snidely said. "I'm sure it will work out swimmingly. Good luck with that conclusion."

"When you hear from her—" Ambrosia began and Margaret cut her off.

"Why would I hear from her?"

"I'm certain, after the mischief you two stirred at Sutton, that you were fully informed of the details by Annette. You probably even provided her with suggestions as to how she could sneak away without being detected."

Margaret sighed with regret, even as she noticed that Ambrosia was showing her years. Usually, she was so magnificently attired, and she would be so prettily coifed, that she'd appear to be twenty, rather than forty. For once though, she looked her age, so obviously, this was a stunning blow. How would she survive it?

Annette had shaped Ambrosia's entire existence. Ambrosia had no spouse, no other children, and she was such a snob that most of their relatives couldn't abide her. If she didn't have Annette to fuss over and spoil, what would become of her?

Well, it wasn't Margaret's problem to solve and she didn't care how Ambrosia weathered the debacle. Margaret never liked to ill-wish anyone, but if Ambrosia endured some difficulties, Margaret wouldn't necessarily grieve for her.

"It's exhausting to have you accusing me of nefarious conduct," Margaret said, "but I'll admit that I'm not surprised by it."

"She told you about it! You helped her!"

Ambrosia was trembling, screeching, and so out of control that she might have been a stranger. Margaret had never observed her in such a frantic state and it underscored how thoroughly Ambrosia's world was being shattered.

"I never talked to her about it and I didn't help her," Margaret evenly said, "and you'll have to excuse me. I expect this to be my last glimpse of you and it's sad for me to view you when you're so angry."

Margaret opened the door and Ambrosia's tone grew pleading. "What should I do, Margaret? What if my riders can't locate her? What if she marries that confidence artist?"

Margaret could have offered a sympathetic word. She could have been her typical polite self, but she thought Annette's elopement was hilarious and she had no desire to ease Ambrosia's woe.

"If you can't stop her from marrying Mr. Crawford," Margaret said, "it seems all of your dreams will have been dashed. In light of the pitiful path I've been forced to walk by all of you, I've learned quite a lot about dreams being dashed. It's a wretched way to carry on and I doubt you'll enjoy it."

She exited the house and closed the door with a sharp click, then she raced to the carriage and climbed in. The driver and outriders had been impatiently waiting for her and they were freezing. She apologized for the delay and asked them to hurry. They leapt to their tasks and whisked her away.

Ambrosia, with her cane and broken leg, wasn't very mobile so, if she'd tried to limp out to shout a few final insults, Margaret was gone before she could haul herself outside. It was a petty victory, but meager triumphs were Margaret's specialty.

She relaxed on the seat and prayed that the roads on her journey would be dry, the conditions mild, and the temperature bearable.

Then she prayed for herself, for Annette and Mr. Crawford, for Michael Crawford whom she would always dearly love.

How was he dealing with Mr. Crawford's rash act? Was he amused by it? Was he indifferent? Was he furious? His brother had stolen his heiress. Was he irked? Or was he being lackadaisical, the man who wasn't bothered by much of anything?

He was no longer any of her business so she shut her eyes, her mind blank. There was no point in obsessing. Not about the past, present, or future. She couldn't change her circumstances. She could just stagger forward, a step at a time. Eventually, wouldn't she find some sort of a normal life?

It was a small hope, a small and private yearning, but that was the only kind she'd ever managed.

# Chapter 21

MICHAEL WAS STANDING IN Ambrosia Adair's receiving parlor. He wasn't in any mood to spar with her, and he should have delayed the meeting until he was feeling more spry, but he was anxious to get it over with.

After attaching himself to Rowena once again, he was very hungover, having instantly fallen back into his foul habits. He knew better than to wallow in such depravity, but she was just as wicked as he was so it was easy to misbehave with her.

He was disgusted with himself though. He was about to turn thirty. He was an earl and the head of a prominent family that had ruled in England for centuries. From his service in the navy, he was a decorated hero and acclaimed warrior.

Would he ever grow up? Would he ever start to act like an adult? How long would he carouse with Rowena and the other sloths and scapegraces who inhabited her world? How long could he bear it?

He had to wed and settle down. He had to proceed so the money in the trust fund would be disbursed to him. But he was also beginning to suspect—if he had a bride he cherished—he might shape up and cease being such a degenerate. He might rein in some of his more despicable impulses.

With the prospect of improved conduct at the forefront of his mind, he'd had his clerk arrange introductions to two of the girls on

Hester's list of nuptial candidates. He'd stopped by for tea with them and their mothers. The appointments had been awkward and unpleasant, the mothers fawning, the daughters insipid and silly.

He was a man of action and adventure, one who'd sailed the globe and had encountered every sort of human being. He couldn't shackle himself to a naïve, sheltered debutante. What would he do with a wife like that?

His clerk had been prepared to schedule more introductions, but Michael had told him not to bother. Each contender was pretty much the same: perfect bloodlines, toplofty family, a massive dowry. But they were barely out of the schoolroom. They had no experiences that would make them interesting to him.

He was a fellow who was nearly always bored and who couldn't abide idiots or fools. He didn't like trembling maidens and never socialized with them.

Rowena teased him about his marital search and she was openly mentioning that he should wed *her*. The idea was extremely untenable. She was a slattern, with low morals that were even worse than his own. If he glommed onto her, he'd never sober up, tamp down his gambling, or embrace his station in life. He probably wouldn't live to be thirty; he'd probably kill himself with his excessive revelry.

When he'd been escorted in, the butler had offered to pour him a whiskey. Michael had declined, but maybe he should have accepted. A dose of alcohol would have calmed his throbbing headache, but it was only two o'clock in the afternoon. He didn't suppose he should be drinking already, and he definitely didn't suppose he should have liquor on his breath when he spoke to Mrs. Adair.

He'd sauntered in unannounced so he couldn't predict how long he'd have to wait for her to attend him. She was a shrew who would like to put him in his place, but before too many minutes had ticked by, she was being pushed down the hall in her wheeled chair. A pair of footmen maneuvered her into the room, then she waved them out. They vanished like smoke, delighted to quickly escape her presence.

Michael was over by the hearth, warming himself by the fire, and she'd been parked several feet away. She glared up at him, her expression bitter and even a tad hateful. He hadn't uttered a single word yet so he couldn't imagine why she was so grumpy.

He was a bit shocked by her condition. On the few occasions he'd chatted with her previously, she'd been impeccably turned out, wearing expensive clothes and jewelry. She'd exuded youth, wealth, and vigor.

Now, she was attired in a plain wool gown, a heavy shawl over her shoulders, as if she was ill. She appeared to have aged significantly. Her face was lined, her hair showing hints of grey, as if she'd been dyeing it, but had given up. She projected a defeated air, as if she'd been fighting for scraps all her life and had finally been beaten.

What could have happened? She'd just recently visited Sutton, but she was a completely different person from the one who'd been his guest.

"Well?" she said, her tone snotty. "What is your opinion of the debacle? Are you here to explain? To apologize? To beg my pardon? Will you at least tell me you're stunned to the core of your being? If you can't admit that much, then I'll ask you to leave. I don't like you and I'm in no mood for any of your nonsense."

Michael frowned. "What are you talking about?"

"Don't pretend to be confused," she spat.

He sifted through a dozen possibilities. She was very enraged, but what had he done? He was capable of enormous transgressions, and he'd been cavorting like a madman, but he hadn't crossed paths with her or her daughter. Or Margaret. What could be driving her to such a furious state?

"I simply stopped by," he said, "to inform you that I won't be marrying Annette after all. I'm grateful that you considered me as a husband for her, but I don't think we'd suit. She's a grand girl, and I recognize that I'm being very foolish to pass up this chance, but I'm positive you'll find someone who will be perfect for her."

Before he'd arrived, he'd practiced the speech, having devised a fast, polite excuse that would sound contrite and that would indicate he realized he was being a dunce to abandon Annette's dowry. He'd expected she might argue over it, but she narrowed her gaze and scrutinized him as if he were a lunatic who'd escaped from an asylum.

"How dare you taunt me like this!" she fumed.

"I'm not taunting you. When you were at Sutton, you persuaded me to reevaluate a betrothal, to be certain of what I wanted. I obliged you. I've reviewed the situation from every angle and I've concluded it wouldn't benefit either of us."

She cackled eerily, then mumbled, "You don't know. You haven't heard."

"Heard what?" he asked like the clueless dolt he apparently was.

"Annette eloped with your brother!"

"No! When?"

"Two weeks ago. I sent riders to catch them and drag her home, but she couldn't be located."

He was so astounded that he was dizzy. "My brother and Annette? Are you sure?"

She didn't answer the question, but said, "Just so you're aware, I will never relinquish the dowry to him. He's naught but a fortune-hunter and I don't care if they starve in squalor."

Michael was struggling to determine how he felt about the astonishing development. An elopement was a brazen act that shocked the conscience of decent people. After it occurred, the negligent couple became pariahs. They were ostracized everywhere and shunned by their families and friends.

He never obsessed over issues like proper marriages and scandalous conduct. Over the years, he'd engaged in plenty of his own mischief, so what was his opinion about the dilemma?

He hadn't been interested in Annette so it wasn't as if Caleb had stolen his fiancée. Yet Caleb had proceeded prior to Michael deciding if he'd pick her or not. How was he to assess such a selfish choice? Caleb went out of his way to be ethical and honorable. He worked hard to exhibit the stellar traits Michael lacked and his bizarre scheme was so out of character.

Was he angry with Caleb? Would it change anything between them? Should it change anything?

Caleb had no money. Michael had often tried to give him some, but he'd regularly declined it. He now had a wife to support, one who was very spoiled and used to luxurious trappings, so what was his plan? Mrs. Adair wasn't about to hand over the dowry, so what would they do?

Michael supposed the shameless pair would slither to Sutton very soon to beg for shelter and assistance. Would Michael provide it?

Caleb had confessed to Michael that he was in love with Annette, but Michael had scoffed at the notion. Evidently, he should have paid more attention to what Caleb had been telling him.

"I'm sorry, Mrs. Adair," he said. "I had no idea about this."

"I don't believe you."

"Is Margaret here? She might know where they are."

At the query, Mrs. Adair was absolutely apoplectic. "You have the gall to utter Margaret's name in my presence? No, she's not here! And she will never be welcomed by me again. Because of you!"

Mrs. Adair had a bell hooked to her chair and she started irately ringing it to summon a servant. The butler rushed in and slid to a halt.

"What is it, Mrs. Adair?" he frantically inquired. "What's wrong?"

"Lord Sutton is just leaving," she said. "Show him out, and if he ever knocks in the future, don't admit him. I refuse to receive him ever again."

Michael gaped at her, wanting to protest her tyrannical attitude, wanting to hurl some insults. He even briefly considered defending Caleb to her, explaining that Caleb was a marvelous man, that he'd be a terrific husband, but it wasn't a comment she could bear to hear.

He'd been dismissed. Why tarry? He said to the butler, "I can find my own way out. You should remain with Mrs. Adair so you can tend her. Clearly, she's not well."

Mrs. Adair shrieked with offense and he whipped away and stomped off. His visit had been so short that his coat and hat were still sitting on a chair in the foyer. There hadn't been an opportunity for the butler to take them away. Michael grabbed them, yanked them on, and left.

Ambrosia Adair was a shrew and a harpy, and the only benefit to come out of the entire debacle was that he'd never have her as his mother-in-law. For that small favor, he would thank his lucky stars forever.

"You'll dine with the servants."

"That's fine."

Margaret stared at her cousin, Bertha, and she wondered what the exasperating woman would think if she could read Margaret's mind.

Bertha was a typical Adair: selfish, pretentious, condescending. She was Ambrosia's same age of forty, but she was a rundown, worn out version of their more glamorous relative. Her blond hair was mostly grey, her skin pockmarked and lined, and she was very fat. Her maids had let out the seams of her gown as far as they would go so she was about to spill out of her clothes.

Where Ambrosia had grown rich through matrimony, Bertha had wed a very ordinary solicitor. They limped along in their neighborhood society, but they were hanging on the bottom rung of it.

"You'll sleep with the servants too," Bertha said. "I wish I had an extra bedroom for you, but I don't. I realize we're kin, and you were likely expecting to be indulged, but I can't oblige any whims you might have brought with you."

"Wherever you put me, I'm simply glad to have a roof over my head."

"There's an empty bed up in the attic with my housemaids. You'll share with them."

"I'm sure I'll be very comfortable."

Margaret was answering by rote, like a lunatic who'd been drugged into a stupor. If she'd been functioning in a more normal manner, she might have been incensed by Bertha's rude treatment, but she couldn't muster any outrage.

She'd survived the frigid journey to York and she was seated in Bertha's crammed, claustrophobic parlor. Bertha was a miser so there was a paltry fire burning in a tiny stove. Margaret couldn't decide if the stove didn't emit much heat or if Bertha didn't have the money to toss more coal onto the flames.

"I serve three meals per day," Bertha said, "at seven, one, and seven. Tea at four. I don't tolerate snacking in between so I better not catch you down in the kitchen when you shouldn't be."

"I don't eat much so I won't make much of a dent in your larder."

Bertha sniffed with disdain, as if Margaret was a glutton who was hiding her ravenous proclivities.

"The children are one, two, five, and six," Bertha told her. "You understand, don't you, that you'll be completely responsible for them? I hope Ambrosia was frank with you. I would hate to have had you come all this way, only to be harboring misconceptions. You're not staying for free. You'll be required to pitch in and you won't be allowed to malinger."

"Ambrosia was very blunt in clarifying my duties."

Margaret was being incredibly sarcastic and lying like a rug, but Bertha didn't notice.

"You'll have Sundays off, but first, you'll have to attend church with the family. Every Sunday! No excuses!" Bertha spewed the edict as if Margaret were a heathen. "Your chores will resume Sunday evening, after supper is over."

Bertha paused, as if waiting for Margaret to complain, but Margaret had no complaints. She was so despondent that she couldn't stir any concern for her current situation.

She was nauseous again. In fact, she'd been sick ever since she'd departed Sutton. On the trip north, with the constant rocking of the coach, her queasiness had increased with each mile she'd traveled toward York. Usually, she was healthy as a horse, but with all that had happened, who wouldn't be physically ill?

She'd fallen in love, had ruined herself, then had snuck away from her dearest beau without a goodbye. She'd been gravely insulted by Ambrosia, with Ambrosia finally illuminating how her relatives viewed her.

Annette would still be on track to wed Michael, even though she'd sworn she wouldn't, but Ambrosia could be so adamant, so cunning and demanding. Margaret had no doubt Annette had been located and dragged home, with her elopement a failure.

Annette couldn't stand up to her mother so she might already be married to Michael. Margaret was braced for the worst, assuming Ambrosia would have rushed the ceremony in order to quash Annette's recalcitrance. She'd probably applied for a Special License so they could proceed immediately.

When Margaret learned that the wedding had been held, she seriously thought she would find a cliff and throw herself off of it.

"I'm chilled to the bone," she said, "and I'd like to unpack and rest a bit."

"You may certainly unpack, but your tasks will begin at once. I'll introduce you to the children and you'll spend the remainder of the day with them in the nursery."

She was feeling more nauseous by the minute. "May I head up to my room then? Or is there something else you need to impart?"

"There is one other issue." Bertha glared down her nose at Margaret. She was studying Margaret as if she were a bug Bertha would like to squash under her heel. "This is a Christian home and we are a Christian family."

"Of course you are," Margaret agreed.

"We exhibit the highest level of decent conduct and we insist those around us exhibit it too. Ambrosia told me that you were recently involved in another amorous misadventure."

Margaret sighed; she should have known Ambrosia would gossip. "I was not involved in a misadventure. Ambrosia was exaggerating about a totally innocent friendship."

"We're aware of your base inclinations, Margaret. You have your mother's blood flowing in your veins so you are possessed of her propensity for illicit reveling."

"I loved my mother and I would appreciate it if you wouldn't disparage her."

Bertha didn't continue her harangue on the topic. Instead, she switched to talking about morals—or Margaret's lack of them. "I will admit that, when Ambrosia contacted me on your behalf, I was dubious. She claims you've matured so I'm willing to give you a chance."

"And I'm grateful for it," Margaret facetiously gushed.

"But I will be watching you. If there is even the slightest hint of turpitude, I will toss you out. You shouldn't think I won't. I can't have a vixen living with us."

"I will demonstrate such amazing traits that you will be stunned."

"No flirting with the footmen," Bertha warned. "No chatting with the bachelors at church. I won't put up with nonsense."

"I understand."

Margaret wondered how long she'd last with Bertha. She was already sifting through the names of distant cousins, ones who hadn't yet had the unlucky honor of hosting her. How could she alter her path? How could she save herself?

It was so hard to be a female, to be a spinster, to be a poor relative. She'd always been a kind person, a good and ethical person. Why was Fate determined to crush her with constant disappointment?

"Will that be all?" Margaret asked.

"It will be *all* for now. Don't ever carry on in a manner that will make me have to address this subject in the future."

"I will be the perfect guest."

"You'd better be."

Margaret smiled a tight smile, then walked out to the foyer. Her bag was still sitting there. She occupied such a lowly spot in the house that no footman had deemed it necessary to haul it upstairs for her. She grabbed it herself and climbed to the attic.

As she entered the small room, one of her roommates was there, changing her apron. They introduced themselves and the girl gestured to a cot under the narrow window. It would be the coldest place to sleep, with drafts drifting in and causing her to shiver all night.

"That's yours," the girl said, "and those hooks on the wall are for you to use."

"Thank you."

Margaret didn't move to unpack. She was wrapped in her thin wool cloak. The glamorous furs she'd worn at Sutton had belonged to Annette. They'd been heavy and toasty, but she was back to her paltry wool. It provided little protection from the winter weather.

She sagged down onto the bed and curled into a ball, anxious to hold in some of her body's heat. The mattress was lumpy, and the straw hadn't been restuffed in ages, so she couldn't get comfortable—or warm.

"What are you doing?" the maid inquired, her consternation clear.

"I'm not feeling well and I'm exhausted from my trip. I have to rest for a few minutes."

"The Missus doesn't tolerate sloth. You've only just arrived and you're loafing. She won't like to hear you're lying down in the middle of the afternoon."

"Don't tell her then."

The girl whipped away and stomped out. Margaret figured she'd rush downstairs and tattle.

She ought to be trying to make a good impression. She should have been worried about the consequences of being viewed as lazy, but as she'd realized ever since she'd tiptoed out of Michael's bedchamber, her innards were frozen. She simply couldn't force herself to care.

"What if your brother won't let us live at Sutton?"

Annette asked the question and she'd been repeating versions of it the entire journey home from Scotland. Caleb answered with more confidence than he probably should have displayed.

"He'll let us stay," Caleb said, "and he won't be angry. I promise."

"You keep claiming he'll accept us, but your opinion of him is very different from mine. I'm afraid he'll react badly."

"Trust me. I know him better than anyone and he won't be upset. Besides, he didn't want to marry you, remember? He didn't and I did. He's in no position to complain."

She grinned. "With how you tricked him, I should start calling you *Thief*, rather than Caleb. You stole me right out from under his nose."

"Are you sorry?"

She chuckled merrily. "No, I'm not sorry, but if we've miscalculated, and he bars the door to us, what is your plan, Mr. Crawford?"

"I don't have another plan, Mrs. Crawford. Are you prepared to wallow in a ditch with me? Are you that fond? Or will you slither off to your mother?"

Annette shuddered with mock horror. "Ambrosia would kill me so I wouldn't dare. I'll remain with you, even if it means we'll have to find a very nice ditch in which to camp."

"You'll have to talk to her someday. I hate to have you fighting because of me."

"I might talk to her," Annette said, "when I'm sixty and she's eighty. Even then, I'm not sure I'll have been forgiven. In case you haven't noticed, my mother can be very difficult."

"I noticed, and I'm thinking—in many ways—you're just like her. I intend to spend my life molding your character so you're less fussy and demanding."

"Aren't I lucky?"

"No regrets?" he asked.

"None yet."

She pulled him to her and delivered a stirring kiss. It was the part of matrimony she hadn't fully considered, but now that she'd leapt in with both feet, she'd found that she liked the physical portions best of all. Her husband was so handsome, and whenever he gazed at her, her pulse raced.

It was rumored that a couple's desire eventually faded, but so far, she couldn't imagine how it would. She was delighted with her choice, pleased with her choice, and Caleb surprised her every second. He fretted that she'd been too impetuous, that she'd begin to wish she hadn't cast her lot with him, but she was happy and content. Who wouldn't want to be happy and content?

They'd been gone for six weeks so it was the end of February. They'd wed in Gretna Green, then they'd continued on to Edinburgh. They'd hidden in a ramshackle hotel where they'd basically eaten, dozed occasionally, and fornicated like rabbits.

They'd been certain Ambrosia would send men after her, and they'd needed to be so tightly bound that, if they'd been located, Ambrosia couldn't have separated them. And they'd definitely established a firm bond. She'd already missed her monthlies and she was wondering if she might be increasing.

Ambrosia had been foiled. Even if she'd stumbled on them, a baby would fetter them forever.

When they'd fled, they'd had money in their purses, but they'd frittered it away. Poverty had forced them back to England. They were parked in the driveway at Sutton House, in a rented carriage, and poor Caleb was about to head in to confront his brother.

Their grand passion would either resolve spectacularly or it would collapse into folly. Caleb had much more faith in Lord Sutton than Annette did. Which direction would the wind blow for them?

She peeked out the curtain, but even though there was smoke drifting from a few of the chimneys, the mansion appeared deserted.

"You might as well get it over with," she said. "I'm freezing and I'm anxious to be invited in so I can sit by a warm fire."

"He'll be glad to have us live with him. Why wouldn't he be? He's never here anyway. It's a big house and he won't mind if we're residing in it."

"You keep telling me that. Let's discover if it's true."

"I'll make it true," he boasted, exhibiting the cockiness she relished.

She pushed the door open. "It's time to put up or shut up, Mr. Crawford."

"I'll be back shortly and I'll be able to introduce you to him as my wife."

She kissed him again—for luck, for courage—then she practically shoved him out. He jumped to the ground and smiled up at her.

"Don't go anywhere," he said.

"Where would I go? I'm ruined and married. You're stuck with me."

He constantly worried that she'd vanish on him, and she couldn't fault him for his concern. It felt as if they were trapped in a peculiar bubble, that the real world had ceased to exist. They'd broken the rules, and they might have been swept into a strange dream, except for the fact that she had a gold band on her finger and she was queasy in the mornings.

"It will be fine, Caleb," she said. "Don't you always claim your brother is a marvelous fellow deep down? He won't judge us and he won't disappoint you. I'm sure of it."

He snickered with amusement. "I might have been lying about him being a marvelous fellow."

"Ah! Don't scare me! Just finish this—so you can bring me in too."

"I will return soon and I will have good news."

He spun toward the manor, straightened his shoulders as if bracing for battle, then he marched inside. She closed her eyes and offered up a quick prayer that Lord Sutton be granted some hasty wisdom so he'd save them from their idiocy.

Supposedly, the exalted man loved her husband so she couldn't imagine he'd toss them out. But who could predict how the insane oaf would act?

She hunkered down to wait.

"Michael."

Michael frowned, thinking he had to be hallucinating. He was standing in his bedroom suite and he could have sworn Caleb had murmured his name. He whirled around, and…?

There was his infuriating, ridiculous little brother.

"You deceitful rat!" was Michael's greeting. "I doubted you'd ever drag your sorry ass home."

His tone was scolding, but he wasn't angry. In reality, he'd been growing alarmed and had nearly taken some men and ridden to Scotland to initiate a search. He'd been terrified Mrs. Adair had captured Caleb, that she'd had him jailed for kidnapping. When an heiress ran off with a scoundrel, a wealthy parent could implement that sort of legal retaliation.

To Michael's enormous relief, Caleb appeared to have encountered no difficulties on his mad jaunt.

Caleb gulped with dismay. "I married Annette."

"I know, but I had to learn of it from her harpy-of-a-mother. In the middle of your race to disaster, it obviously didn't occur to you to inform me of your plan. I could have avoided a boatload of vexation."

"I tried to inform you, but you wouldn't listen."

"You told me you wanted her. You told me I couldn't have her for myself. You *didn't* tell me you were preparing to secretly elope."

"I'm not about to apologize," the ludicrous dolt said.

Michael scoffed with derision. "So what now? What are you expecting to have happen?"

"Would you kill me if we asked to stay at Sutton? If it will help, I don't mind begging you. Would you like that?"

Michael thought Caleb should have to squirm a bit so he didn't reply to the entreaty. Instead, he said, "Mrs. Adair ordered me to apprise you that you're a despicable fortune-hunter and she'll never give you the dowry."

Caleb winced. "I was afraid that would be her response. I hate to have Annette suffer because of my foolishness. Could you talk to her mother for me? Could you vouch for my character?"

"You're joking, right? It's my specific intent to never speak to that shrew again."

Caleb looked crestfallen, like the boy he'd been when Michael had found him living in squalor in that farmer's hovel.

"What about our residing at Sutton?" Caleb inquired. "If you kick us out, I have no idea where we'll go."

"It's fascinating to me that you didn't ponder that possibility before you absconded with her."

"I simply had to have her. I couldn't resist."

Michael stomped over so they were toe to toe. Caleb stiffened, as if Michael was about to punch him, but Michael chuckled with exasperation.

"I'm not upset," he said, "and why wouldn't you be welcome? This is your home, remember? Haven't I pointed it out to you a thousand times?"

"Yes."

"Then stop forgetting it. You're a reckless dunce for running off with her, but it proves that you're a lot more like me than you've ever liked to admit."

"I'm nothing like you," Caleb insisted.

"You're wrong. You're exactly like me."

Michael drew him into a tight hug. "You frightened me to death. Don't ever do that again."

"I won't. I'll remain here—where I belong."

They stepped apart and Michael asked, "Where is Annette? I hope you didn't leave her at the tavern in the village while you blustered over to nag at me."

"She's out in the driveway in the carriage we rented."

"Well, fetch her inside, you silly oaf, so she doesn't catch a pneumonia."

"You're fine with us moving in? You're certain?" Caleb repeated the request, as if anxious to double-check.

"No, I'm not certain, but I'm working to convince myself that I'm amenable."

"Thank you."

The utterance stirred the air, so it was too poignant for words, and Michael waved to the door. "You tend to your bride, and I'll locate the housekeeper, so she can have your room opened. I'll meet you in the front parlor in an hour. We'll have a glass of wine and you can share the details of your grand misadventure."

Caleb smirked. "It's a tremendous love story, about a damsel in distress who was rescued by a dashing hero."

"In your dreams maybe." Michael nodded him out, and as he hurried away, Michael added, "I'm delighted that you came to me for help, but I swear—if you ever pull a stunt like this again—I will beat you to a pulp for being such an idiot."

"I won't need to do anything wild in the future. With Annette as my wife, I will be happy forever."

"If you ever start to regret this insanity, I don't want to hear about it."

Caleb beamed with joy, then he rushed off. He was like an excited puppy and his elation made Michael feel old and worn out. It might be nice to have a pair of newlyweds in the manor. It might enliven the dull place, which would be a huge benefit.

He sighed, then headed out too. He had to find the housekeeper, but he also had to prepare to greet his sister-in-law. It would be awkward and strange, but he supposed they would muddle through.

# Chapter 22

"Sit down, Margaret."

Margaret sat. In the few short weeks she'd resided with Bertha, she'd learned to obey her ridiculous commands or to hide when she was in a temper.

As Margaret had suspected before she'd arrived, she had no ability to tend a group of young children. Under her indolent supervision, they were grouchy, slovenly dressed, and ill-behaved. If she'd taken any pride in her work, she'd have been aghast at her lackluster conduct, but she still couldn't convince herself to care about any issue.

Bertha had already scolded her on numerous occasions, but money was tight in the house. Late at night, Bertha and George quarreled in hushed tones about their finances. Margaret's labor was free so Bertha was being more lenient with her than she might have been with a nanny who was receiving wages. If Bertha threw up her hands and fired Margaret, she'd have to scrounge up the funds to pay someone else.

Margaret assumed she was about to endure another session where Bertha would nag about her failings, so when Bertha finally spoke, Margaret was startled.

"You were sick again this morning," Bertha said.

Margaret frowned. "Yes, I was. These past months have been very fatiguing for me. I'm tired and rundown, but I'm sure my condition will improve very soon."

"You're constantly dizzy and queasy. You dash up to your room to gag and vomit. We all hear you."

"I will admit to frequently being nauseous."

She thought about mentioning that Bertha's cook was barely competent, that the meals were atrocious, which would explain her upset tummy. But she didn't suppose she ought to complain about the food being provided.

They were sequestered in Bertha's den. She hid in it to fuss with the account ledgers or to escape the household chaos. She was seated behind the desk and Margaret was in the chair across. It was a tiny spot, a closet really, so they were very close together.

Bertha was studying her caustically and Margaret felt like a school pupil who was about to have a ruler rapped on her knuckles.

"I have to discuss an embarrassing subject with you," Bertha said. "I've been debating how to raise it and I figure it's best to just be blunt and to the point."

"Yes, please be blunt."

"I've had four children, and you haven't had any, so you don't understand why you're under the weather."

Margaret scowled. "What do you mean?"

Bertha hemmed and hawed, then said, "When Ambrosia demanded I supply you with a situation, she advised me that you'd engaged in an illicit amour and that we needed to get you out of London because of it. She was determined to separate you from the cad who had focused his attentions on you."

"I engaged in no amour and I'm weary of protesting my innocence to you. It's beginning to annoy me."

Bertha scoffed with disgust. "I expect you to be honest with me. We won't beat around the bush. Are you ruined?"

Margaret froze, her mind whirring with various replies. They were at a dangerous impasse, and she had to deny the allegation, but Bertha was glaring with such disdain that Margaret was completely flummoxed.

"Why would you ask me that?" Margaret inquired, stalling.

"You don't realize it, but I'm certain you're increasing."

It took Margaret an instant to grasp the import and she gasped with astonishment. "Increasing with a baby?"

"Yes. I'm aware of the signs, but you're not, and I would appreciate it if you wouldn't lie to me. Are you in the family way? Is that where we are?"

Margaret remained very still, tabulating the ailments that had been plaguing her: nausea, particularly in the mornings. Dizziness. Queasiness. The sense that her body was different, that there'd been a change and she couldn't define why.

She recalled the perfect evening she'd spent with Michael. They'd fornicated twice, and he'd been careful once, but negligent once. She'd asked him if a babe could catch in her womb from one reckless encounter and he'd insisted it never happened after one sexual episode.

She'd known the assertion was false, but she'd chosen to believe him anyway. It had been a minor fib, voiced in the heat of passion, and she'd blithely accepted it. Since that fateful night, she hadn't bothered to ponder the possible result, but she had to ponder it now.

She was so stupid. Of course she was increasing. Of course she was having a baby. The news clarified everything.

She braced, recognizing that her interval with Bertha had come to an abrupt end. She hoped the conclusion wouldn't be too humiliating.

She wasn't about to confess her shame so she simply said, "I should pack my bag and go. I'll be leaving you in the lurch with the children, but it probably can't be helped."

Bertha had been eager to scold and chastise, to malign and reprimand, so she was irked by Margaret's easy capitulation. "That's it?" she sputtered. "You're departing? Without an apology? Without conceding your sins? Without an expression of remorse?"

"There's nothing I'd like to tell you."

"You're a hussy, just like your mother," Bertha charged. "You're brimming with bad morals and base inclinations. Everyone in the family has watched you and waited for your downfall. When I spread word of your disgrace, no one will be surprised."

"I'm amazed it's taken me so long to prove my wickedness, but then, I have no idea how I could have satisfied you. Would you excuse me? The day is quickly passing and I should hurry."

Bertha was intent on beating the issue to death. "We all knew this would transpire eventually. Have you a defense for your transgression?"

Margaret snickered with a grim amusement. "I am just as much of a vixen as you've assumed. I've been expecting this sort of debacle to ensnare me."

"You admit to being debauched?"

"Yes, I admit it."

She stood and stepped to the door. Bertha's mouth was gaping like a fish tossed up on a riverbank and she fumed, "Well, I never! I welcomed you, even though I was skeptical about how you'd conduct yourself. I furnished you with food to eat and a bed to sleep in. And this is the thanks I get?"

"Actually, I haven't thanked you," Margaret snidely said, "and I'm not about to either."

Her ability to grovel, to placate, had flown out the window. She'd tolerated all the denigration of her mother she could abide. She'd been castigated by one of her cousins for the very last time.

Bertha was a petty, bitter wife who'd birthed four plain, unlikable children. She had a husband who could barely support her and they squabbled over trifles. Her circumstances were so meager and she was so miserable. Who was she to criticize anyone?

Margaret walked out, and though Bertha ordered her to stop, she didn't obey. She headed for the stairs, and as she reached them, George was hovering. He was thin as a rail, bald, henpecked.

"Sorry about this," he whispered. "In light of your predicament, we had so few options. Bertha was anxious to handle it like this—to punish you."

"Don't be sorry. It's my own fault."

He glanced nervously toward Bertha's den, then he slipped Margaret a pouch of coins. "I couldn't bear to have you forced out with no money. Don't tell Bertha."

"I won't and I'll pay you back—if I ever can."

He waved her away. "No need."

She nodded, then kept on. It was a terrible moment, the worst she'd ever experienced. But at the same juncture, it was the best moment of her life. She was free of her relatives, free of their vitriol and spite. None of them would ever offer her shelter again, so it meant—in the future—she wouldn't be able to lean on them and beg for assistance. She'd have to buck up and carry on without them.

From the minute she'd arrived in Bertha's stifling home, she'd felt as if she was suffocating. Suddenly, she could breathe again. She smiled with relief and rushed up to fetch her belongings.

---

Michael and Caleb were having breakfast in the dining room, but Annette hadn't joined them. Her tummy was upset and Caleb had sent up some tea and toast. He'd whispered that Annette might be increasing.

Michael was struggling to deduce what he thought of the situation. Would he enjoy having a baby in the house? Wouldn't that be a good thing? Or would it simply add to his sense of disorientation?

His world was skewed and off-balance and he couldn't find his footing. He'd presumed it would be pleasant to share the manor with a pair of newlyweds, but he'd been mistaken about that. They were madly in love and they cuddled and cooed to the point where it was embarrassing.

He'd considered an escape by returning to London. He hadn't though. He'd fled the city because he'd grown so weary of the antics he engaged in there. He couldn't stand the sycophants who pretended to be his friend and Rowena was a burgeoning menace.

Her gambling had blossomed into an addiction and she'd started to use the opium pipe too. She'd become more clingy and possessive and he was tired of her, tired of the man he was in her presence.

He had to buckle down and pick a bride, but the process was much more complicated than it sounded. He'd slunk off to Sutton, so he could have some peace and quiet as he figured out a better path, but Caleb and Annette had strolled in to distract him.

They were merely two young people, but they occupied every inch of space. No matter where he went, he couldn't avoid them.

Without any warning, Hester marched in. Her mind was very disordered and she relentlessly babbled about incidents from the past that he didn't recollect. He still employed Widow Jones to tend her, and the woman was doing an excellent job of preventing her from completely falling apart, but it was a thankless task.

In some families, when a member began to behave so oddly, they were locked in the attic, then everyone ignored the fact that there was a lunatic raging upstairs. Michael wasn't ready to implement that sort of drastic action. Nor would he put her in an asylum. There was a convent in Scotland, run by the Sisters of Mercy, and he wondered if it might not be a safe choice for her.

He'd written to the Mother Superior to inquire about costs and availability. She hadn't replied yet, and if there was a spot open, he couldn't decide whether he would reserve it or not.

Hester wasn't well. Her eyes glowed with an eerie fire and she'd gotten so skinny that she barely cast a shadow. He had to speak to Widow Jones to learn if she was eating regularly. They couldn't allow her to starve herself.

She stomped over to Caleb and pointed a shaking finger at him. "You can't live here. You just can't."

She'd never liked Caleb, but he was polite to her anyway, and he had a delicate method of dealing with her. "How are you this morning, Hester? Are you hungry? May I dish up a plate for you?"

"Didn't you hear me?" she wailed. "You have to be hidden away. No one can know."

Michael sighed and tossed down his napkin. "Hester, you're being a pest. How about if I escort you up to your bedchamber? Would you like that?"

She didn't answer him, but continued to harangue at Caleb. "It's wrong for you to be strutting about. People might realize what happened. You should be with the farmer where I placed you. He's probably worried about where you are. Shoo! Shoo!"

She motioned with her hands, as if she could make Caleb vanish, and Caleb sighed too. He and Michael shared a concerned glance, then Michael said, "I'll walk her up. I'll be back down in a bit."

Hester glared at him. "I can't loaf in my bedchamber. I have to prepare the nursery. What will I do if the room isn't prepared?"

She dashed away and Caleb asked, "What was that about? She's so bewildered and she seems to be much worse recently."

"If I put her in the convent, would you be upset with me? She might benefit from that kind of serene environment. She's been stuck at Sutton all her life and it's driving her mad. A change of scenery might help."

"I wouldn't be upset, but it's a difficult decision, and I can't advise you about it. I have no idea of what might be best for her."

"You shouldn't have to endure her repeated diatribes."

"I don't mind," Caleb claimed.

"*I* mind," Michael countered, "especially if you and Annette are about to have a child. We can't have Hester tormenting Annette when she's increasing and Hester certainly can't be rampaging after the baby is born. I don't trust how she might act."

Widow Jones watched Hester during the day, but she hadn't arrived yet, and he was thinking of suggesting she reside in the manor, rather than the village, so she could provide full-time monitoring.

She was much better at managing Hester than Michael could ever be. His solution was to lock Hester in her bedchamber until Widow Jones showed up. It was a terrible plan, but he truly thought Hester might hurt herself if she was permitted to wander about.

He followed her up to the nursery and she was sitting in the ancient rocking chair. She'd opened a box of musty baby clothes, and she was studying them, tracing a finger over the embroidery. She looked particularly unhinged, as if the sight of the clothes had unleashed the demons inside her.

"I can't tell anyone," she said to him. "It was a sin and I'm a harlot. Father told me so. I'm going to Hell and there's no way to be forgiven. No matter how much I pray, I'm damned."

He pulled up another chair and sat directly in front of her. "What are you talking about? You're not a harlot and you're not damned. I hate that you're so confused."

"No, I *am* a harlot and the baby was my punishment. You've allowed him to move in with us so he's thrown in my face every minute. It's not fair to me. Father promised I'd never have to see him again."

Michael might have been tiptoeing across a murky bog. Every family had skeletons in the closet, but it sounded as if they had secrets lurking that he'd never imagined.

Cautiously, he asked, "What baby do you mean, Hester? Was it your baby?"

"Yes, yes, and I didn't want him to be named Caleb! The farmer named him! He was supposed to be Thomas, after his father. Not Caleb. Caleb is all wrong."

Michael blew out a heavy breath of astonishment. "Are you Caleb's mother?"

"It was to be Thomas! Thomas, not Caleb! Father wouldn't let me name him, and now, he's living in my home when he shouldn't be. How can I make him depart?"

"Who was Thomas? Was he from the neighborhood? Did I know him?"

At the question, she smiled a tad dreamily, as if Michael had conjured a dear memory. "He was an actor who was here for several weeks with his traveling troupe. He was so handsome! He fell in love with me immediately and I don't care what Father thought about it. We would have been so happy! Thomas begged to marry me, but Father said, *Absolutely not!*"

For once, she appeared to be lucid so, just to be clear, Michael inquired, "Father didn't sire Caleb? Is that what you're claiming? You're his mother, and his father was your beau, Thomas."

"Father paid Thomas some money and he left Sutton forever. He never came back for me and I waited and waited! Father said I was wicked, that I deserved to be abandoned."

"Who sent Caleb to the tenant farmer? Was it you or Father?"

"It was me! I had to sail to France for the birthing. I had to hide my shame. I was anxious to leave him there, and there was an orphanage that would have accepted him, but Mother wouldn't agree. She forced me to bring him back."

"You gave him away? Not Father?"

"Me, yes! What else could I have done?"

"Did you order the man to be cruel to Caleb?"

"He was conceived in sin and born in sin. He has the Devil inside him and his immorality had to be drummed out."

She gazed at him as if she'd supplied a perfectly logical explanation for Caleb's early plight, and Michael buried his head in his hands, his misery acute.

He'd never understood his parents or his sister. He'd been so different from them and they'd exhausted him with their lectures and pious preaching.

He pictured young Hester, a rich earl's daughter obsessed with an actor from a traveling troupe. She'd been so sheltered and she would have been easy prey for a scoundrel like that. He recalled her taking a holiday journey, with their mother, to the Continent. She'd been sixteen or so, but evidently, it hadn't been a pleasure jaunt. It had been a furtive, scandalous excursion to conceal a tragedy.

How would he apprise Caleb? They'd constantly derided their Puritanical father as a disgusting hypocrite. Yet Caleb wasn't the product of his affair with a London doxy as they'd assumed. The entire story had been invented to obscure the truth.

The ground had shifted under his feet and he was so unsettled that he felt dizzy. He was trying not to blame Hester. After all, she'd been a girl, enticed by a cad, but it was her conduct later on that was appalling.

According to her, she'd instructed the farmer to torment Caleb when he was a little boy. What sort of person did that? What sort of mother behaved that way?

Deep down, a potent rage was burning and he had to get away from her for a bit. He had to calm down so he could more accurately assess what he'd discovered. He stood and said, "I have to finish my breakfast. Would you stay up here until Widow Jones arrives? She'll sit with you, but for now, I'd like you to remain in the nursery."

"Will you sneak the baby over to the farmer? I've wanted to tell you for such a long time. You must realize why he can't be in the manor. I shouldn't have to ever see him. Father promised!"

"Just stay here, Hester. Widow Jones will be up soon to check on you."

He walked out and rushed down to find his brother who, apparently, was his nephew. What a tangle! What a calamity! The whole sorry tale had him pondering whether to return to London. Maybe he should. Maybe it would be for the best.

He trudged into the dining room, but Caleb had left to help with some chores outside. Michael considered having a footman fetch him, but he was in no hurry to engage in the conversation that was required. How would Caleb react to the news that Hester was his mother? She'd always been so mean to him so it would be a huge shock.

He plopped down and cleaned his plate, even though his food was cold. As he loafed and fumed, the butler brought in the morning mail. Michael sifted through it, not overly interested, until one letter—from Baywick—caught his eye.

He thumbed it open, wishing it would be from Margaret, that she might have moved to the pretty coastal town. Mrs. Adair had dumped Margaret on some awful relatives in York. Annette had written to her, but the letter couldn't be delivered because Margaret wasn't there.

He couldn't imagine where she might be. Annette might have been able to pry out information from her kin, but her elopement had made her a pariah so it was futile to contact any of them. None of them would reply.

The note wasn't from Margaret though. It was from the estate lawyers who were arranging the sale of Beachhead Cottage. They hadn't found a buyer and they were wondering if he might still like to purchase it. To tempt him, they'd significantly reduced the price.

He stared out the window at the bleak garden. He was more landlocked than ever and Sutton House was a nightmare mansion filled with secrets. If he bought Beachhead Cottage, he could escape to the ocean once in awhile. He could stroll the rocky beaches and gaze out at the ships on the horizon.

Wouldn't he feel better? The offer was definitely an omen he ought to heed, and he tucked the letter into his coat so it could sit there all day and excite him with the prospect of his circumstances changing. He'd feel closer to Margaret too. Her father had previously owned it and she'd spent her summers there as a girl.

To his enormous surprise, the longer he was separated from her, the more he missed her. He'd been so happy when she'd been part of his life. He'd let her vanish, and he'd been *un*happy ever since.

Why not buy the property? In an odd way, it seemed that—if he purchased it—the gesture might lure her back to his side. Wouldn't it be worth a try?

ANNETTE SLIPPED INTO HER mother's London house. She hadn't written first, for she hadn't wanted Ambrosia to know she intended to visit. She'd had no doubt that her mother would have fled the city so she wouldn't have to speak to Annette.

Ambrosia was an unforgiving person, but despite her propensity for being horrid, Annette thought she should attempt to reconcile. She realized how much her elopement had hurt her mother, but Annette was delighted with her decision and there was a baby on the way.

Ambrosia had to be informed so she could join in the celebration—if she ever ceased to be so irate.

It was the middle of the afternoon, the hour when Ambrosia would be reading in the rear drawing room. Annette had entered the residence so furtively that no servant had noticed her sneaking in. She was able to flit down the various halls until she arrived at the correct spot.

Ambrosia was seated on her favorite chair, not her wheeled one. Her leg splints had been removed, but her cane was balanced close by so she could easily grab it.

Her appearance was a tad startling. For once, she looked her age. Her hair was limp and turning grey, her face lined, and she'd lost weight, as if she'd shrunk in size. It had been over two months since Annette had run away, and clearly, her escapade had wounded Ambrosia much more than she'd understood. She felt sad and guilty for distressing her mother, but she wasn't sorry.

From now on, it would always be the problem between them. Annette loved Caleb, and she was thrilled that he was her husband, but Ambrosia would never accept that reality.

"Hello, Mother," she quietly said.

Ambrosia hadn't heard Annette approaching and she blanched and glared. "Who let you in? The staff was warned about you. Tell me who it was and he or she will be fired immediately."

"Don't be so melodramatic. You're not firing anyone because of me."

Ambrosia began to ring a bell that was on a nearby table. She was summoning a footman so Annette could be escorted out. A servant would show up soon so she had to speed through the conversation.

"I've missed you," she said as she blustered in and sat down.

Ambrosia rang the bell even harder. Annette rolled her eyes and she leaned over and yanked it away. She set it aside, out of Ambrosia's reach.

They engaged in a staring match that left Annette tired, then Ambrosia fumed, "Where do you come by the gall to waltz into my home?"

"I was anxious to explain myself."

"I don't care why you eloped. I don't care why you picked a common nobody like Caleb Crawford. You're dead to me."

"Oh, Mother, must you be so angry? Can't you pardon me—just a little? My marriage to Caleb wasn't a frivolous mistake. I'm very happy."

"I hope Lord Sutton passed on my message that I'll never give you the dowry. You and your lowly husband can choke on your poverty."

"We not poor, so you can choose to be petty if you like, but it won't harm us."

"I suppose you're living at Sutton and Lord Sutton welcomed you with open arms. He's a wicked fiend who would find your nonsense to be amusing. Has he offered his bastard brother an allowance so the foolish boy can support you? Is that the trick you've managed to play? Are you staying with that scandalous idiot and wallowing in his charity?"

"Yes, as a matter of fact, we are. As opposed to you, he wasn't furious over our antic. He was very grand about it and I must admit—with my not having to wed him—I'm growing rather fond. He's proved himself to be quite wonderful, but then, Caleb always claimed he was."

"Caleb—who is a greedy fortune-hunter. Yes, I can certainly comprehend why you'd deem his assessment of the situation to be valid."

"First off, he's not a fortune-hunter, and if you'd climb down off your high-horse, you'd recognize that he's not. Second, I had to share some news with you. We've had an outrageous development arise at Sutton and I've been dying to gossip with you about it."

"Whatever it is, you needn't apprise me. I have no interest in what is occurring there."

Annette continued as if Ambrosia hadn't spoken. "Don't fall off your chair in shock, but the old earl wasn't Caleb's father."

"Let me guess," Ambrosia snidely said. "He was actually a prince in hiding."

"No, he was an actor in a traveling troupe and his mother is Hester Crawford! Her parents sent her to France to have the baby there, then they dumped him on a tenant farmer and pretended the earl had sired him."

It was a salacious story, the kind Ambrosia generally relished, but she was determined not to exhibit any fascination. Her expression didn't change.

"Hester Crawford is a flighty, nervous mouse," Ambrosia cruelly said. "What sort of dunce would be debauched enough to lie down with her? Are you sure this tale is true?"

"It's definitely true and it's been so difficult for her to swallow down the secret that it's driven her mad. Lord Sutton is thinking of locking her in a convent. She's become unhinged."

"Your husband's antecedents are even lower than I assumed."

"Yes, but I don't mind." Annette chuckled merrily. "His actor-father was a genuine fortune-hunter. The earl paid him to go away and leave Hester alone. Once his purse was full, he vanished and she's grieved the loss of him ever since."

"Like father, like son," Ambrosia muttered.

"Hester insists he's the most handsome man she ever met so it's why Caleb is so good looking. He inherited all his father's best traits and none of his bad ones."

"That's debatable. He absconded with you, didn't he?"

Annette wouldn't dither over Caleb's ancestry, character, or anything else. She kept glancing toward the door, expecting a servant to appear and knowing she had to hurry.

"Where is Margaret?" Annette asked. "Have you any idea? I wrote to her at Bertha's, to inform her that I had wed Caleb, but the letter was returned to me. What happened to her?"

"What would you suppose? Bertha fired her for moral turpitude and kicked her out."

"Margaret committed a dissolute act? You can't be serious."

"She was in the family way."

Annette gasped. "What? No!"

"Bertha is a God-fearing Christian. Margaret couldn't reside with them when she was in such a shameless condition."

"She doesn't have any money and she was a stranger in York who had no friends there. Where did she go? Did they simply toss her out on the street to fend for herself?"

"Yes, they did," Ambrosia nastily said, "and I haven't pondered her fate a single moment."

Annette tsked with offense. "On occasion, you can be so awful. Listen to yourself. Margaret was thrown out by *us*—her own family—and you're positively giddy about it."

"Her mother was a slattern, and deep down, she's a slattern too. I'm not surprised by her fall from grace."

"Well, I *am* surprised," Annette loyally stated. "Who is the father of her child? Has she identified the scoundrel?"

Annette had a sinking suspicion that she knew the answer to her question. Margaret had claimed her amour with Michael had been mostly platonic, but with some passionate kisses added in. Apparently, she hadn't been completely honest.

Ambrosia snickered spitefully. "I'm certain the culprit is Lord Sutton. You believe your brother-in-law is such a marvelous fellow, but I'm betting Margaret doesn't currently think so."

"Where is she, Mother? When she departed York, she must have provided Bertha with some clue as to her destination."

"She packed her bag and walked out and she hasn't been heard from since."

Ambrosia's expression was cold and horrid, and Annette yearned to shake her for being so derisive, but her luck had run out. Footsteps sounded out in the hall, and a footman poked his nose in and asked, "You rang, Mrs. Adair? How may I assist you?"

"Mrs. Crawford has snuck in." Ambrosia used Annette's married name in a derogatory manner. "Escort her out and watch her so she can't slither back in."

The boy was rattled by the command. After all, a few weeks earlier, Annette had lived in the house too, and had ordered him about. She would hate to get him in trouble so she stood and went over to the door.

She gazed at her mother and said, "I can't imagine when I'll see you again."

"I'll have the entrances guarded a little better so it will likely be never."

"The reason I stopped by is that I have some joyful news." Ambrosia glowered to indicate her disinterest, but Annette told her anyway. "I'm having a baby. I haven't been examined by a midwife, but the housekeeper at Sutton is convinced of it. If she's correct, you'll be a grandmother next autumn."

Ambrosia scoffed. "I've never wanted to be a grandmother."

"I hope you don't mean that. I hope you'll change your mind and be glad for me. If you'd like to join in this happy process, you're welcome at Sutton. You don't need an invitation."

"I will never call on you there. I will never welcome your bastard husband's mutt into our family."

"*Never* is a very long time, Mother."

Annette marched out and down the hall. The footman followed her to the door, as if to guarantee she left. She continued down the street, and Caleb was standing by their carriage, chatting with the outriders. He saw her approaching and he hurried toward her. He clasped her hands and kissed her on the cheek.

"How was it?" he asked.

"About as bad as you insisted it would be."

"She's a hard woman, your mother."

"You are a master of understatement. Can we go home now? Home to Sutton?"

"I will deliver you there as fast as I can."

He led her to the vehicle, lifted her in, then climbed in afterward. In a quick minute, they'd rolled away and started for the country. Caleb had brought several blankets and he tucked them around her to keep her warm. Then he draped an arm over her shoulder and pulled her close, as she reflected on her mother and how their relationship had collapsed.

If Ambrosia didn't relent, she would have a very lonely life. Annette was building a future, with a dear husband and her first child on the way. She'd love for her mother to be part of it, and she'd cross her fingers that Ambrosia would figure out how to be content over Annette's choice. But in light of how unbending Ambrosia could be, Annette wouldn't hold her breath.

"How was Mrs. Adair?"

Caleb grinned at Michael and said, "She was just as grumpy as you predicted she'd be and she was awful to Annette."

"Annette is very brave to have visited her."

"I won't argue the point. I tried to persuade her that she should delay a bit so Mrs. Adair had more of a chance to calm down. With our having a baby, Annette thought she could spur the horrid shrew to forgive us."

"Your wife is an eternal optimist."

They were in the front parlor, having a whiskey and waiting for the butler to announce that supper was ready. It would be just the three of them, without Hester or any guests, which was how Caleb liked it. Michael and Annette were his two favorite people in the world and he would have them all to himself for a few hours.

Michael hadn't locked Hester in a convent. He'd learned of a nurse who operated a small hospital for females who were ailing in their mental faculties and he'd sent her there instead. It was more of a home than a medical infirmary and her patients were from some of the best families.

The facility was quiet and modern and the staff didn't employ any of the torture regimens that were utilized in the asylums. An added benefit, it was located on the road to London so they could check on her without too much bother.

Caleb hadn't decided how he viewed Hester's ramblings about her being his mother, and he still wasn't sure he believed it. Michael had interrogated the elderly servants, who'd been with them for decades, but they swore—as far as they'd ever been told—the old earl was his father.

Hester had always been difficult, and Caleb had never shared an affinity with her, so his sentiments hadn't changed. He would be polite to her, but he would avoid her.

As Michael had prepared to cart her off to the hospital, Caleb had offered to take care of it himself. If she was truly his mother, then it had been his responsibility, but Michael had advised him to stay at Sutton and let him handle it. She'd been delirious and upset about leaving, and Caleb's presence on the journey would have created more confusion in her mind.

He felt sorry for her, but it was so peaceful with her gone.

"Annette wanted me to ask you a question," he said.

Michael raised a brow. "From your dour expression, I'm betting I won't like the topic."

"When you discover what it is, don't punch me. It would distress Annette."

"Have I ever punched you?"

"Not yet." Caleb braced for trouble, then bluntly said, "You were very fond of her cousin, Margaret. Did you ruin the poor woman?"

Michael was sipping a whiskey and his glass froze in mid-air. There was the slightest hint of an astonished reaction, but it was hastily masked.

"That's a rather risqué subject to discuss right before we eat," Michael said. "Are you trying to give me indigestion?"

"Very funny and I notice you didn't answer me. If you ruined her, just be a man and admit it."

Michael still didn't confess. "Why are you pestering me about this?"

"She was kicked out by her relatives in York because she's having someone's baby. Why am I suspecting that the cad in this debacle is probably you?"

Michael blanched. "She's increasing?"

"Yes, and I'm certain you're the culprit."

"Oh, no," he breathed. He put his glass on a nearby table and eased down onto the sofa next to it. He struggled to pull himself together so he could speak. "Where did you hear this?"

"Mrs. Adair told Annette."

"After Margaret was kicked out, have you any idea where she went?"

"No one knows. Annette has written to every cousin she can think of, but the few who have replied have no information."

Michael looked very pale, as if he might faint. "She's never had any money. Would she be wandering the streets in York and begging for alms?"

"I can't guess and you *still* haven't answered me. What if she's with child? What if it's a boy? What if it's Little Lord Sutton? If you hope to have any sort of friendship with Annette, you have to fix this situation immediately."

"How would I? Evidently, I wouldn't be able to find Margaret."

"But if we could find her, what is your plan? I liked her and you seemed to like her too. She might make you a very fine wife, and in case you've stopped paying attention, the clock is ticking toward your birthday. Why not pick her to be your bride?"

"Could I? Would it be possible?"

Michael was so bewildered that Caleb laughed. "Why would you ask such a ridiculous question? You're an aristocrat who constantly boasts that you can act however you please. You don't have to fetter yourself to an heiress. If you'd like to wed Margaret Adair instead, who is there to say you can't?"

Michael placed a hand over his heart, as if it was racing. With what emotion? Terror? Horror? Joy? Excitement?

"Could Annette locate her for me?" Michael inquired.

"She's frantically working on it, but I doubt she'll succeed. Her Adair kin have no news so Margaret could be anywhere."

Annette strolled in. Pregnancy agreed with her and she appeared to be glowing. She walked over to Caleb and he delivered a passionate kiss—with Michael glowering like a debutante's chaperone.

Michael snorted with disgust. "I didn't realize that residing with a pair of newlyweds would be so embarrassing. Aren't you required to control yourselves when you have an audience?"

"Why should we?" Caleb asked. "And I must declare that matrimony is a marvelous state for a bachelor. I highly recommend it to you. For all your complaining about having to shackle yourself, I predict you'll like it."

Michael was exasperated with them. "You two are so annoying. I've been thinking of taking a trip, a very *long* trip, and I believe I will."

MARGARET TRUDGED UP THE lane to *Mrs. Pettigrew's Private Home for Young Ladies.* It was a fancy name for the unwed mother's home outside Baywick. She'd only been away a few months so her friend, Katherine Hastings, would likely still run it. Even if she'd left, and another woman had stepped in, it was a modern facility with a female staff and Margaret would be welcome.

Katherine and her patron, Mrs. Pettigrew, were attempting to erase some of the stigma that arose from birthing a bastard. They'd both been ruined by libertines and they'd been treated unfairly during their subsequent ordeals. They were determined to assist others as they staggered through their tribulations.

When Margaret had fled Bertha's, with George's pouch of coins tucked in her reticule, she hadn't felt lost or afraid. She'd known precisely where she needed to go.

She should have skipped her idiotic jaunt to York altogether and headed directly to Baywick. She loved the pretty coastal town, and Katherine would have helped her with lodging and a job, but she'd been dazed and grieving. Without argument, she'd let Ambrosia ship her off to Bertha.

She'd grown so accustomed to living off her relatives' charity that she always presumed she had no options but to rely on them. But she was smart and thrifty, was pragmatic and loyal. She could survive on her own and she didn't have to beg from despicable snobs who detested her.

She would have her baby, give it up for adoption, then she'd start over. The people in Baywick were kind and cordial, and she would create a different future for herself among them.

She'd ridden on the public coach and she'd debarked at the coaching inn. She could have hired a carriage to drive her to her destination, but it was a short walk, and for most of the trek, she gazed out at the ocean. The scenery invigorated her and reinforced her opinion that she'd traveled to the correct place.

The building finally appeared. It was an old beach cottage, three stories, with big windows and painted shutters. It was April so spring had arrived. The grass was green and the flowers in the window boxes were blooming.

She marched up to the front door and knocked. There was no answer so she entered without waiting to be greeted. She dawdled for a minute, and she could hear plenty of activity on the upper floors, as if it was a hectic day for the servants.

Well, an escort to Katherine's office wasn't necessary. She dropped her portmanteau on the floor and she hung her cloak and bonnet on a hook on the wall. Then she went down the hall to the rear of the house. As she'd expected, Katherine was sitting at her desk.

"Margaret Adair!" Katherine said. "What are you doing in Baywick? When you departed in January, I was convinced I'd never see you again."

"Are you busy? May I come in?"

"Yes, of course."

Katherine waved to a chair, watching as Margaret lurched over and eased down.

"I wrote you numerous letters," Katherine said, "but you never wrote back."

"I'm sorry. I was overwhelmed by events and I didn't have the energy to correspond."

"My goodness. You look as if you've been sick. What happened?"

"I'm mortified to tell you what occurred."

Katherine studied Margaret and she sighed. She reached in a drawer and pulled out a kerchief. She had a whole drawer crammed full of kerchiefs. She handed it over and Margaret grabbed it and dabbed at her eyes.

"I need your help," Margaret said. "I didn't know where else to turn."

"Was it a man? Are you in trouble?"

For an eternity, Margaret was quiet, staring down at her lap, then she murmured, "Yes, I'm in trouble."

"Would you like to stay with us?"

"I was hoping you'd offer. If you'd refused me, I can't imagine where I would have gone."

"I'll ring for a maid and we'll settle you in a bedroom. Then we'll have some tea and you can fill me in on the gory details."

"I'm too wretched to confess my stupidity."

Katherine clucked her tongue. "Don't fret about it. Where charming cads are concerned, we females are always stupid. It's a problem with our gender."

"I assumed I was smarter than this," Margaret miserably stated.

"Given the right circumstances, none of us are smart enough to behave as we ought. Does the oaf in question realize what's transpired? Have you spoken to him?"

"It would be pointless for him to be apprised."

"That can't be true. I could have my lawyer track him down. Would you like that?"

"He's marrying my cousin. She's a great heiress and he'd never relinquish her dowry for me. There's no reason for a lawyer to intervene."

"I will hate him forever then," Katherine said. "And if he'd pick a fortune over you, he's an idiot, so what good is he anyway?"

Michael was standing on the verandah of Seaview Cottage in Baywick. It was a beachside property owned by Captain Jackson Pettigrew. He and Michael were casually acquainted, having served for decades as officers in the Royal Navy.

Pettigrew's wife, Mary, was a local, and when he'd wed her, he'd bought her Seaview as a wedding gift so they could spend a portion of the year in Baywick.

Michael now owned a home in Baywick too.

He'd talked to the lawyers who'd been selling Beachhead Cottage, and after a quick hour of negotiations, it had become his. He'd already hired a housekeeper and she was searching for some servants. He was enjoying the change of scenery, while trying to persuade himself it had been a viable plan.

He'd purchased a house he didn't need, one that was inconveniently located far from Sutton and London. What had he been thinking?

He was aggravated from watching Caleb and Annette coo like lovebirds, and he'd been anxious to flee the happy atmosphere they generated. Their delight in each other simply underscored how thoroughly he'd messed up his life. They had each other and he had no one. Some days, it seemed as if he was the very last man in the world. His existence was that pitiful.

His biggest regret was how he'd treated Hester. She'd always lived at Sutton and she'd been so confused when he'd taken her away. He felt guilty about it, and he worried about her constantly, but her sojourn at the hospital didn't have to be permanent. If her condition improved, he could fetch her back to Sutton.

Mrs. Pettigrew was hosting an afternoon tea and she'd invited him to stop by to meet some of the neighbors. It had been an interesting group of people, mostly wealthy Londoners who had summer homes in the area. Baywick was a popular tourist spa, but it was smaller and less glamorous than Brighton, so it hadn't adopted some of Brighton's more unpleasant characteristics.

He was gazing across the garden. The paths led to a rocky beach, and through the trees, the ocean stretched to the horizon. The waves crashed on the shore, the sound stirring his blood, reminding him that he was more content out on the water.

It was a beautiful spring day and guests were strolling, reveling in the fresh sea breeze. He studied the females in particular, their parasols twirling in the sunshine, and he thought there was no more mesmerizing sight than a pretty girl walking in a manicured garden.

A trio of guests exited the manor to join the others down in the grass. As he glanced over at them, a blond woman pulled up short and gaped as if she recognized him. She was familiar to him too.

She frowned and said, "Don't I know you? Aren't you Lord Sutton?"

"Yes, I'm Sutton, and I'm supposing I should know you too, but I can't place you."

"I am Katherine Hastings. We were introduced when you were visiting in January. You attended the public dance at The Pavilion."

"Oh, yes, I remember."

"You were hiding your identity, pretending to be a lowly ship's captain."

For some reason, she was enormously vexed with him, and he grinned and shrugged, keen to put her at ease. "I've been never lowly, but I was a ship's captain for ages. It wasn't actually a subterfuge."

Looking vastly annoyed, she strutted over to him and rudely asked, "Why are you in Baywick? To what do we owe the dubious honor?"

"Pettigrew and I were in the navy together so I've been acquainted with him since I was a boy. I bought a property nearby. Beachhead Cottage? Have you heard of it?"

"Yes, I've definitely heard of it. You've moved to Baywick?"

"Ah…yes? But probably just for part of the year. When I was here before, I liked the town very much, and I relished the notion of having a residence on the water."

"You're simply flitting about the country, are you? You're buying homes and having tea? You're free and unencumbered, weighed down by no responsibilities. Aren't you lucky?"

It was a strange and insolent remark, almost an accusation, and he said, "I guess that's an accurate assessment. I'm an adult and there are no restrictions on my schedule that would have prevented me from traveling to the coast."

Quite scathingly, she inquired, "Might you happen to recall how I earn my living, Lord Sutton?"

He scowled. "You run Mrs. Pettigrew's business for her. Is that it?"

"It's a home for *unwed* mothers, sir."

"Well, yes, so it is."

Out of the blue, she said, "I realize you enjoy your reputation as a scoundrel, *Captain* Crawford, but by any chance, might you recollect a prior paramour named Margaret Adair? You abused her shamelessly, but I'm sure in your debauched opinion, you suffered no regrets over having seduced her. Does her name ring a bell? Or is she another notch on your belt who has faded from your memory?"

At the query, he was taken aback. Margaret was the very last topic he'd expected to be mentioned. "Yes, of course, I recollect Margaret. I was very fond of her, and in fact, her cousin and I have been searching for her. She's vanished and we've been very worried about her."

"Are you married to her cousin?"

"No. She eloped with my brother." He chuckled, trying to lighten the peculiar moment. "He snatched her away, right under my nose."

"So you're still a bachelor."

"Very much so."

She glared at him, glared at the house, then she gestured to the open door. "Would you come inside with me for a few minutes? We need to find a secluded parlor and have a long, blunt chat."

He was completely bewildered by the entire conversation. "A blunt chat about what?"

"Margaret didn't disappear. I know exactly where she is."

"Where is that?"

"She's staying at my facility and *you,* Lord Sutton, are about to be a father."

# Chapter 23

MARGARET HAD JUST SPENT a long hour strolling on the rocky beach behind *Mrs. Pettigrew's* home. It was a habit she'd adopted, passing the dreary hours in quiet reflection. She was struggling to figure out what she wanted out of life, what she should do with herself, after her baby was born.

Initially, she'd decided to give it up for adoption, but she couldn't follow through. With her being ruined, she might never be able to wed so it would be her one and only chance to have a child. Plus, it was Michael's child.

Could she simply toss it away as if it were a stray puppy? Yet how could she keep it? A spinster's lot was precarious. It was hard for a female to find a job, and if she had a bastard to support, it would be impossible. No one would hire her.

Katherine operated a very modern facility and she offered various assistance to her clientele. A feasible choice was an arranged marriage. There were always men who needed a wife, but who didn't have the time or ability to hunt for one. Katherine's lawyer paired couples so the women could avoid the stigma imposed by their predicaments.

Margaret could shackle herself to a stranger, and under the terms of the contracts, the man would agree to raise her child as his own.

Her world had crumbled to such a pathetic spot that she was seriously considering the notion.

She constantly debated whether she shouldn't write to Michael. He'd been kind to her, and he'd probably help her, but she couldn't force herself to proceed. As far as she was aware, he'd either married Annette or was about to marry her, and Margaret was too depressed to insert herself into Annette's march to the altar.

It would hurt Annette for her to learn about Margaret's disgraceful dilemma. Why should they both be miserable? Margaret wasn't in control of much, but she could at least save Annette from that humiliation.

The afternoon had waned, and the sky was a pretty lavender color, the sun setting in the west. It had been a lovely spring day, but the nights were chilly. The wind off the water was brisk so she had a woolen shawl draped over her shoulders.

She'd left the beach and was walking to the house. The temperature was dropping and she had to hurry inside and wash for supper. The women dined together, as if they were students in a dormitory at boarding school. Katherine tried to foster a sense of camaraderie and normalcy, but it was difficult to feign much excitement.

Most of the current crop of guests had been shunned by their families and kicked out by them once their scandalous conditions were revealed—as she had been. All of them were in dire straits. Despite Katherine's best efforts, they were ashamed and terrified over the future.

Childbirth was a risky proposition and a huge percentage of mothers died during the ordeal. If they survived, their options were bleak.

She continually reminded herself that her situation was no worse or different from any of the other women, but she was especially tormented by what had transpired, by how stupid she'd been. She'd merrily ruined herself, with nary a thought to the consequences, and the ramifications were raining down.

Suddenly, a man exited out the rear door. He was quite a distance away so she couldn't see him clearly. There weren't any men working on the property, and generally, male visitors weren't permitted so the sight was unusual.

He scanned the garden, and as their gazes locked, her breath hitched in her chest. She appeared to be staring at Michael, but that couldn't be right. His abrupt appearance, in the exact place he shouldn't have been, was so bewildering that she was positive she was hallucinating.

She felt dizzy with confusion and she was overwhelmed by the oddest perception that she ought to dash off in the other direction.

"Margaret!" he called. "There you are!"

Yes, it was definitely him. She'd recognize that voice anywhere. Tears flooded her eyes and she started to tremble so violently that she was amazed she could remain on her feet.

He rushed toward her, and even though he was nearly running, he seemed to be approaching in slow motion. She was thrilled and disturbed in equal measure. What would happen after he reached her?

She was awhirl with questions. Why was he in Baywick? How had he found her? Why would he have been searching? What could he want?

He finally arrived and he was standing so close that her skirt tangled around his legs. They were cataloguing features, assessing what had changed, what was the same. It had only been three months since they'd parted, but they might have been separated for decades.

He broke the awkward silence. "Margaret Adair! Where have you been? We've been hunting for you everywhere!"

She frowned. "Why would you have been? And who is *we*? I don't suppose there is a person in the kingdom who would have been worried."

"Annette wrote to you in York to brag about the wedding. She was hoping you'd leave your Cousin Bertha and move to Sutton to live with us, but the letter came back as undeliverable."

"Oh, I see." Of all the discussions Margaret intended to avoid forever, Annette's wedding to him was at the top of the list.

She'd suspected it would transpire, but still, it was a crushing revelation. Ambrosia must have caught Annette and dragged her home from her elopement with Mr. Crawford. Then she'd organized a swift wedding to halt Annette's recalcitrance, but also to immediately achieve the result she sought.

Throughout Margaret's burgeoning calamity, she'd naively prayed that Michael wouldn't forge ahead with Annette. How could he hurt her so grievously? But in her interactions with him, she'd been a great fool. Apparently, nothing about that situation had changed.

"Once we realized you'd vanished," he said, "she contacted your relatives, but no one had heard from you. We were afraid you might have been dead in a ditch."

"I'm sorry you were so concerned, but I'm fine, and I wasn't keen to be located."

"Don't be ridiculous. Why didn't you travel to Sutton? Why didn't you tell me you needed my help?"

Could he really not know? Could he really be that obtuse?

He and Annette were newlyweds, yet evidently, they expected her to reside at Sutton with them. It was such a cruel idea. How could they have pondered it for a single second?

The sole explanation she could devise was that he and Annette were spoiled and entitled. They didn't waste energy considering other people or their paltry problems. They were so imperiously inclined that they'd have assumed they were being magnanimous. It wouldn't have occurred to them that it would have literally killed her to accept.

"How did you discover where I was?" she asked.

"I've stumbled on you totally by accident. I didn't have the faintest clue that you were here so I'm astonished."

"That still doesn't clarify how you found me."

"I purchased Beachhead Cottage so I can spend part of the year in Baywick."

The announcement hit her like a hard blow. Beachhead had previously belonged to her parents, but it had been stolen from her by her greedy kin. In her wildest fantasies, she'd pictured herself retrieving it someday, living there herself, but he'd be there with Annette instead. It was such a gloomy ending that she was physically ill.

She would hate to have him note how the information had distressed her so she forced a smile and said, "I'm glad you bought it. I'm certain you'll cherish it."

"I just attended an afternoon tea, hosted by Mrs. Pettigrew. I'm acquainted with her husband, from my service in the navy. She invited me so I could meet some of my neighbors."

"Good. You'll settle in quicker."

With each of his chatty remarks, she was feeling more battered and she couldn't abide much more of his casual aplomb.

"I ran into Katherine Hastings at the party," he said.

"You were introduced to her, weren't you? Back in January?"

"Yes. She remembered me much faster than I remembered her." He studied her, his expression growing exasperated. "She marched me off to a secluded parlor and she scolded me quite viciously. She can be very harsh."

"Well, in her line of work, she has to be. Why would she scold you though? The two of you are practically strangers. How could you have incurred her ire?"

He chuckled. "You don't know? You can't guess?"

"No. I can't imagine why she'd chastise you."

"Margaret! You're having a baby. *My* baby. I am the culprit in the whole sordid affair, and Miss Hastings bluntly apprised me."

Margaret was furious. "I apologize for her nagging. She shouldn't have bothered you about it. It's my secret to share—or not—and she should have spoken to me before she tattled about my private business."

"I have to admit that I'm stunned to find you in this place."

She scoffed with derision. "Babies are common when an amorous couple engages in illicit conduct. If I recall correctly, I begged you to be careful with me and you swore you would be. Afterward, when you hadn't been careful, you lied and claimed I needn't worry. I think we can agree that you might have been wrong."

"Were you ever planning to contact me?"

"Why would I have?"

At her query, he looked so shocked that she might have punched him. "How can you ask me that? How can you believe I wouldn't have fretted?"

When he'd first dashed across the garden, tears had flooded her eyes. Now, they became a tidal wave she could barely control. A few of them dripped out and she swiped them away. She was just so sad!

"I left London for York," she said, "because Ambrosia kicked me out. She insisted you were about to visit her to finish the nuptial negotiations, and she was anxious to be shed of me before you arrived."

"She told you I was about to propose to Annette?"

"No. She told me you already had and you simply had to dither over the details. How was your wedding? Was Annette a beautiful bride? Are you delighted with your choice of wife?"

The conversation was so humiliating, and she yearned to flee from it, but he was standing between her and the house. She doubted she could push by him so she whipped away and raced out to the beach.

There was no spot to hide on the rocky shore, but she had to go somewhere that was far away from him.

He was very vain though and he would never let a discussion conclude until he was done talking.

"Would you hold on for just a damned minute?" he said, the curse disturbing her. "And don't you dare cry! There's no reason to be upset."

He stomped after her and he reached her as she stepped onto the sand. He grabbed her arm and pulled her around to face him.

She yanked away and asked, "Why would I have whined to you about my predicament? It would have wounded Annette, and it would have put you in the mortifying position of having to figure out how to deal with your bastard child—at the same moment you were about to walk down the aisle with her."

He looked completely bewildered. "You think I'm married to Annette?"

"Yes. As you mentioned, Annette sent me that letter in York to tell me about the wedding, but why would I be eager to have her wax on about it? It's cruel for you to suppose I'd like to be informed."

"She wrote to you about *her* wedding. Not mine."

Margaret scowled. "What do you mean?"

"She married Caleb. Not me. They eloped. Weren't you aware of it?"

"They succeeded? How could they have? Ambrosia sent men to stop them."

"Yes, but they couldn't track down the wily pair so they're living at Sutton. With me. *They* are happily fettered and Annette is in the family way."

Margaret was so confused that she had to repeat his words back to him so she could comprehend them. "Caleb and Annette are married? They're at Sutton?"

He grinned, as if he was about to share a humorous anecdote. "I welcomed them, when I probably shouldn't have, and I can't bear to watch them cuddle and coo. I was at my wit's end when I received a note from the estate lawyers who were selling Beachhead Cottage. The property was still for sale, and at a very reduced price, so I used it as an excuse to escape."

"I was certain Ambrosia had roped you in, so I decided it would have been futile to contact you."

"I've been here for two weeks and one of the first people to cross my path was Miss Hastings. I'm an old sailor. You remember that about me, don't you?"

"Yes, Captain Crawford, I remember."

"So I never disregard portents or signs. Fate brought me to Baywick to find you."

"For what purpose?"

"I swear, Margaret, you are particularly befuddled today." He dropped to one knee and clasped her hand. With no warning, he said, "Will you marry me?"

"What? No!"

He never liked to be thwarted, and at her refusal, he glared ferociously. "No? May I remind you of where we're currently located? You've locked yourself away at a home for unwed mothers. According to Miss Hastings, you're increasing with my child. Is that true? Or will you deny it?"

"I won't deny it, but you don't want me!"

"Why would you presume that?"

"Because you've known me for several months, and you've had numerous chances to propose, but you were never interested. I even climbed into your bed and misbehaved with you, and it never occurred to you that you could choose me. You were too focused on your heiresses and debutantes."

"I was a tremendous idiot, wasn't I?"

"Yes, now get up. You shouldn't be down on your knees. You'll stain your trousers."

She tugged on his arm and he let her raise him to his feet. With him standing, perhaps his burst of temporary insanity would have passed. Once prior, she'd dreamed of being his wife. She'd been sure he'd ultimately pick her, but that fantasy had been dispelled when she'd sat in that cold, bumpy carriage on the road to York.

"You left Sutton without a goodbye," he said.

"Why would I have told you goodbye? Ambrosia had learned of our amour, and she savagely castigated me, then she ordered me to London without delay. How could I have declined to obey her? How would it have helped to apprise you? Would you have quarreled with her about it? Would you have forced me to remain at Sutton? What would have happened to me then?"

He smirked, as if her comment was hilarious. "If I'd intervened, I'm betting the end result couldn't have been any worse than what you've endured since you departed. May I confess a paltry detail to you?"

"I wish you wouldn't."

"Where you're concerned, I've made stupid choices. I cherished you beyond measure, but I persuaded myself that you were too lowly to be my bride."

"Precisely. You're a snob."

"Men of my station marry for money, and we shop for a candidate with money or perfect bloodlines—or both. I tried that route when I considered your cousin, but she was so aghast at the notion of being wed to me that she ran away with Caleb to avoid it."

"She's smarter than I gave her credit for being."

He snorted with amusement. "After she tossed me over, I interviewed several debutantes and guess what I discovered? I can't wed a young, sheltered girl. I've sailed the globe and experienced every sort of adventure. What would I do with a silly ninny like that?"

"I could have pointed that out to you, but you're so hardheaded that you wouldn't have listened."

"You're absolutely right. I told myself it had to be a debutante or no one, but I have to wed by the time I'm thirty. I previously explained to you how my father placed some of our fortune in that trust fund."

"Yes, and if you're not a husband by your birthday in June, you'll lose it. It will go to the Church."

"I was so aggravated at the prospect of glomming onto a flighty girl that I figured I should forget about the money. I like my vices and debauched habits too much, so why not simply carry on like the scapegrace I am?"

"That is exactly the type of reckless decision I would expect from you."

"I had almost convinced myself to relinquish it, then I stumbled on Miss Hastings. I found out about you and the baby. Has it occurred to you that it might be a boy?"

"Of course it's occurred to me."

"Then you have to realize he could be the next Lord Sutton."

"*If* we were married," she said, "you'd be correct, but you never wanted me to be your wife."

He scowled. "I've just incessantly complained to you about the nuptial candidates I've pondered. Was I babbling merely to hear myself talk?"

"You do like to blather on."

"I'm a wretch and a wastrel. I admit it. I drink and gamble; I revel with obnoxious companions and I'm a dreadful libertine."

"Why are you listing your faults?" she asked. "Is it to impress me or to terrify me?"

"After you snuck off, I went to London too. I tried to resume my old activities, but they held no appeal whatsoever. I hurried straight back to the country."

"Maybe you're finally growing up."

"Or maybe you changed me," he said. "Maybe for you, I'll be able to throw off the unsavory portions of my character. Maybe I'm about to start a new chapter in my life."

"If that's even remotely true, then I'm glad for you. You should shuck off your vices. You should walk a different road."

"Yes, but here's the problem I'm having. I can't travel that road alone. You have to travel it with me."

She nearly accused him of being mad, of toying with her, but common sense stopped her. What if he was serious? What if he really wanted to wed her?

From the instant they'd met, they'd stirred a potent attraction. It had blossomed into a dear affection, and on her end anyway, it had become a deep and abiding love. What if he was ready to settle down? Where would it leave them? Could she refuse the future he was offering?

She was increasing with his child and he'd shown up to propose. She wasn't in a position where she had a dozen other options. No, she was perched on the edge of a cliff and about to tumble off into a morass of shame and dishonor.

Would she remain stubborn? Would she spurn him? Would she cancel her baby's chance to have a father? To eventually be an earl? What kind of mother would behave so negligently? What kind of deranged person would make that choice?

He dropped to his knee again and he clasped her hand and kissed the center of her palm. He gazed up at her, his eyes particularly blue.

"I'm a cad and a bounder," he said.

"I won't argue the point."

"I'm an arrogant fiend who carouses with scoundrels and tarts. I wallow in iniquity and never engage in stellar conduct. But I'm weary of being so dissolute. I need to be the man *you* see when you look at me."

It was a very pretty comment and she was greatly moved by it. She could never deflect his enormous charm, and he was quickly coercing her so she'd supply whatever he was seeking. How could she ignore his entreaty? How could she resist?

"You're not that bad," she muttered, disgusted by her easy capitulation. "I will agree that you have some insufferable tendencies, but in my presence, you're fairly good at hiding them."

"Ha! You've noticed that I'm in a better condition when I'm around you."

"That's because I'm not one of your fawning sycophants and I won't tolerate any mischief."

"After you abandoned me at Sutton—"

"I didn't abandon you. Ambrosia forced me away."

He huffed with exasperation. "However it transpired, I've been so miserable ever since. Please marry me. You're beautiful and generous. You're loyal and devoted. You thrive in every situation, no matter how dire the circumstances, and you never give up. You'll be a perfect bride for me. How could I select anyone else?"

"What if I consent?" she inquired. Gad, was she considering it? How could she not? "What do you envision our life would be like?"

"I will spend each and every day, doting on you and spoiling you rotten. We'll be blissfully content forever."

"You make it sound so simple," she said.

"It would be simple." He rested a hand on her swelling tummy. "Don't forget what we've created together. Be my bride. Be my wife.

Let's build a family. I've never had one, and neither have you, so I know you want it. If you pretend you don't, I'll call you a liar."

He was prepared to furnish her with what she'd always desired: a home of her own, an ardent spouse, a gaggle of children tugging at her skirt. It was what all women craved, but it was a type of joy that had eluded her. He was eager to provide what she yearned to have. Would she be foolish and claim she wasn't interested?

"There would have to be some changes," she said, apparently having run out of excuses. She couldn't justify a rejection. Not when she was so fond of him and there was a baby on the way. Matrimony was the only appropriate solution.

He rose to his feet. "Tell me what they are and you may have them."

"No more gambling. No more doxies. No more reveling with your wicked friends."

"Is that all?" He grinned like the devil he could definitely be. "I've already implemented those alterations so that's not a difficult request. Demand something harder."

"You'd have to stay at Sutton with me. You'd have to be a husband and father. You'd have to promise me and you'd have to mean it."

"I'm almost thirty," he said. "It's time for me to renounce my juvenile antics."

"If you start to wish you hadn't wed me, if you start to miss your despicable chums in town, I won't permit you to leave."

"I won't ever leave. How could you imagine it?"

"No slatterns! I'm sorry, but I have to be most adamant about that. If your roving eye begins to wander, and fetching girls are tempting you, you have to behave yourself. If you ever strayed, it would break my heart."

"My dearest Margaret, I will never stray. I swear it to you."

"And can we travel to Baywick occasionally? Can we bring our children to Beachhead Cottage for our summer holidays? I would like to have that be my conclusion. If it can happen, I think my parents would smile down on us from Heaven."

"I bought Beachhead for you, Margaret, and we will spend our summers there."

Her pulse was pounding in her chest and she was elated, bewildered, and frightened all at once. Could she do this? Yes!

"Ask me again," she said. "Ask me to marry you."

He drew her into a bracing hug and he was gripping her so tightly that she couldn't breathe. He hovered there, as if mustering his courage, then he pulled away and said, "I love you, Margaret Adair, and I will love you until my dying day."

"I love you too, Michael Crawford, and I will never stop. Not until my dying day either."

"Will you marry me? Will you have me, flaws and all? Will you make me the happiest man in the kingdom?"

"Yes, I will marry you. I will have you flaws and all and I guarantee you'll always be glad you picked me."

"Are you sure?" he asked. "With me, there's no going back. I won't let you change your mind."

She scoffed. "As if I'd change it. I suppose we'll have some ups and downs, some hiccups and bumps in the road, but—"

He interrupted her. "No, it won't unfold that way. You'll be my bride so it will be absolutely wonderful. Every minute will be perfect. I'm certain of it."

"Absolutely wonderful," she murmured in response. "I like the sound of that."

He kissed her and she enthusiastically joined in, thinking that life was strange, Fate was strange. Numerous blessings had finally rained down on her. She would have a devoted husband, a magnificent home, a father for her child. She'd have a family of her own.

Her every dream was about to come true. She was lucky after all!

Their lips parted, and they sighed with delight, then he said, "Shall we walk inside and tell Miss Hastings that it's arranged."

"Yes, I'd like her to be the first to know."

"She's quite a virago. If you'd refused me, I would have been terrified to inform her that I had failed to persuade you."

"You didn't have to worry," Margaret told him. "Where you're concerned, I never stood a chance."

# THE END

Don't miss Book #3 of Cheryl's
*RUINED!* series

# *Absolutely Mine*

The Story of James Ralston, Lord Ralston

and

Miss Tilly Monroe

*Coming soon!*

# About the Author

**CHERYL HOLT** IS A *New York Times*, *USA Today,* and Amazon "Top 100" bestselling author who has published over sixty novels.

She's also a lawyer and mom, and at age forty, with two babies at home, she started a new career as a commercial fiction writer. She'd hoped to be a suspense novelist, but couldn't sell any of her manuscripts, so she ended up taking a detour into romance where she was stunned to discover that she has a knack for writing some of the world's greatest love stories.

Her books have been released to wide acclaim, and she has won or been nominated for many national awards. She is considered to be one of the masters of the romance genre. For many years, she was hailed as "The Queen of Erotic Romance," and she's also revered as "The International Queen of Villains." She is particularly proud to have been named "Best Storyteller of the Year" by the trade magazine Romantic Times BOOK Reviews.

She lives and writes in Hollywood, California, and she loves to hear from fans. Visit her website at www.cherylholt.com.

Printed by Amazon Italia Logistica S.r.l.
Torrazza Piemonte (TO), Italy

58476987R00227